The Sons of Heaven

BOOKS BY KAGE BAKER

The Company Series

In the Garden of Iden
Sky Coyote
Mendoza in Hollywood
The Graveyard Game
Black Projects, White Knights: The Company Dossiers
The Life of the World to Come
The Children of the Company
The Machine's Child
Gods and Pawns
The Sons of Heaven

Also by Kage Baker

The Anvil of the World
Dark Mondays
Mother Aegypt and Other Stories

The Sons of Heaven

KAGE BAKER

TOR®

A TOM DOHERTY ASSOCIATES BOOK
NEW YORK

This is a work of fiction. All of the characters, organizations, and events portrayed
in this novel are either products of the author's imagination or are used fictitiously.

THE SONS OF HEAVEN

Copyright © 2007 by Kage Baker

All rights reserved, including the right to reproduce this book,
or portions thereof, in any form.

Edited by David G. Hartwell

A Tor Book
Published by Tom Doherty Associates, LLC
175 Fifth Avenue
New York, NY 10010

www.tor.com

Tor® is a registered trademark of Tom Doherty Associates, LLC.

Library of Congress Cataloging-in-Publication Data

Baker, Kage.
    The sons of heaven / Kage Baker.—1st ed.
        p. cm.
    "A Tom Doherty Associates Book."
    ISBN-13: 978-0-7653-1746-9
    ISBN-10: 0-7653-1746-X
    1. Dr. Zeus Incorporated (Imaginary organization)—Fiction. 2. Immortalism—Fiction. 3. Time
travel—Fiction. I. Title.
    PS3552.A4313S66 2007
    813'.54—dc22

                                                                                    2007009541

First Edition: July 2007

Printed in the United States of America

0 9 8 7 6 5 4 3 2 1

To the man himself.

Desideratissime
Quia fortis est ut mors dilectio . . .

The Sons of Heaven

PROLOGUE

A Long Time Ago . . .

Before the first stone was set in Zimbabwe's wall . . .

Three boys went out one morning to fish in the river. They were too young to go by themselves, but they went anyway, taking a boat. The current pulled them away swiftly, and they traveled a long time, and soon they had no idea where they were or how to get back to their village.

They drifted close to the bank of the river, and one of the boys jumped overboard and tried to swim to shore. Crocodiles caught him, and pulled him down. The other two boys stayed in the boat, terrified, and it drifted on.

Then the river passed through a forest, where branches hung low over the boat, and as they passed under, one of the boys jumped for a branch and pulled himself up. But he screamed and, looking back, the last boy saw that there was a leopard making its way along the branch.

The last boy stayed sensibly in the boat where he was safe, all that day and all the night, and in the morning the boat drifted near to a herders' camp. He waved to them from the boat, and they came down and pulled it from the water.

Their leader was a pale fox-faced man. He heard the boy's story. After looking the boy over carefully, he took him aside. Did the boy know the story of how, after evil came into the world, God sent an ark down to help men? How it came traveling on the rainbow, filled with copies of everything that lives, and tools for all the arts?

Of course the boy knew that story. The man explained that he and his fellow herders worked for God, and they were busy collecting animals for another such ark, because another great evil was coming someday. He asked if the boy would like to help God, and the boy, who loved God, said that he would like that very much.

So the boy was taken away from the world, and woke up later in great pain in a hospital ward, with his head bandaged. There he found that what the fox-faced man had told him was not exactly true: he was indeed to work at saving things in a great ark for the future, but he would be working not for God but for someone called Dr. Zeus Incorporated. On the other hand, he would never die.

In the centuries to come, when the boy had become a man, there were times when he regretted the bargain. Dr. Zeus Incorporated took in all the man contrived to save, greedily, and stored it away, not for the good of humanity but in order to make stockholders wealthy. Dr. Zeus Incorporated manipulated nations and events in order to guarantee profits, with a complete disregard for the human suffering it might cause.

Nor was Dr. Zeus all-seeing as a god ought to be; for though it had mastered the arts of time travel and immortality, it seemed to be blind to whatever might lie beyond 9 July 2355 AD. It was whispered among immortals that Dr. Zeus might fall on that date, destroyed perhaps by an intracorporate war. Perhaps history, perhaps even time itself ended on that day.

The man learned, moreover, that many of his fellow immortals had likewise become disillusioned with their eternal work. Some had come to hate the mortal humanity they served. Some had begun manipulating nations and events on their own account, with an eye to rebellion. They had no callous disregard for human suffering; they positively delighted in it. Sometimes the man wondered whether he was the only one who remembered the reason he had been given eternal life.

He made his own plans. He raised his own armies. There were times when he was tempted to rise in rebellion himself. But, laughing ruefully, he would tell himself that he had learned one priceless law by which to live, in his childhood: *Keep your arms and legs inside the ride at all times until it has stopped moving.*

So far, it has not. But the day is coming.

PART I

The man is seated in his study. He has the gravity and silence of a pillar of black stone. There is a lot on his mind today, for the great evil about which he was warned so long ago has almost arrived. At last he rises and, putting his hands in the pockets of his modern tailored suit, advances to an inlaid cabinet in the corner.

After opening its doors, he takes out a box and returns to his chair.

He considers the game in its box.

It's an old shatrang set, non-electronic, carved sometime late in the twentieth century. The white pieces are real ivory, perhaps the last to be made before the ban on that particular animal product. The black pieces are ebony. The board is inlaid with these substances too and the workmanship is a little raw, an example of the deliberate primitivism that was in vogue during that period of history.

Contrived or not, the set summons memories. Many of them are terrible memories. The man lifts out the ebony Elephant, shatrang's nearest equivalent to the Bishop in chess. Its diagonal movement is limited to two squares in any direction, but like the Knight it can jump, most unexpectedly for those unfamiliar with the game. This piece ought to be an African elephant, but the artist has depicted it wearing an Indian elephant's howdah on its broad back, like a pavilion perched on a domed hill. Within the howdah, two tiny dark figures cling to each other.

CHAPTER 1

The Hill. Where? When?

Baby was born and, surprise! She was a little girl. There was great rejoicing in the hill about that, because girls don't happen very often. Quean Barbie was elated, enchanted: to have produced a wonderful baby girl made her feel very grand. The Uncles were all very happy, too, especially Uncle Ratlin, who was the cleverest person living in the hill.

But Baby's novelty wore off fairly soon, and it wasn't long before Quean Barbie got tired of carrying her around and irritably handed her off to the poor stupids to be cared for. If they hadn't been so stupid, they could have told Baby not to feel too badly about this: Quean Barbie loved having babies but always tired of them quickly, and always forgot about them in the excitement of making more.

Baby figured this out for herself, however. Baby wasn't stupid.

No, Baby was clever, like Uncle Ratlin; like Quean Barbie, she could make the stupids do things for her. So life wasn't so bad for a while, in the hill. The stupids brought Baby nice things to eat when she told them to, and made things to amuse her when she told them to, and every so often Uncle Ratlin would notice her when he wasn't busy, and though she couldn't make him do things very easily he was always nice, telling her stories about what fun they'd have when Baby was the new Quean.

Once Baby understood that she was going to be Quean, her life became much more complicated. All of her vague feelings of dislike for her mother had a center now, and her sense of herself was strengthened. She was more than Baby who was a girl, who was clever and gave orders. She was Baby who ought to be Quean! She had hair, as Quean Barbie had hair, though not so much. Quean Barbie had a vast bouffant of crystalline tresses, carefully woven up for her by the stupids every morning, while Baby's was cobwebby and thin, stuck up like little bushes and weeds.

Quean Barbie had clothes, too, of every color and description, brought back for her by Uncle Ratlin when he had time but most frequently by the stupider Uncles, who were easier for Quean Barbie to order around. It was hard for them to find the sort of clothes she wanted. The big people of the houses didn't seem to keep many gowns like ladies on the holoset wore, which was what Quean Barbie preferred, and the Uncles sometimes had to break into four or five houses in a night before they could get a pretty gown for the Quean.

Baby didn't need to do that. She simply sent one of the stupids to fetch her one of Quean Barbie's dresses, and as an afterthought ordered him to bring Quean Barbie's hairbrush, too. For about an hour Baby was very happy, turning this way and that in her new finery and swept-up do, admiring her reflection in the stupids' big black eyes.

But then! Quean Barbie came raving out of her chamber, flailing away at the poor cowering stupids who attended her, screaming for her hairbrush. When her wide gaze fell on Baby, what shock! What slit-eyed rage followed, what hissed nasty names like *Slut* and *Whore*! Fortunately Baby was very fast, and the stupids too stupid to get out of the Quean's way as she chased after Baby, so that Quean Barbie fell down and Baby got away.

Baby was on her own after that, hiding out in the parts of the hill where no one ever went. It was a very old hill and the kin had been there a long time, so there were tunnels and rooms long forgotten, heaped to the ceilings with trash, vacated when they'd become too full to use. Plenty of room for Baby to hide and never get caught. More: there was a forgotten tunnel to the outside, giving Baby her own private exit.

The first time she ventured up and out, she expected to see a maze of houses and streets. That was what the Memory insisted was there, a town full of brutal big people, the hairy ogres who were the hereditary enemies of Baby's race. No; only a sky sparked full of white stars and a hillside all bushes, and a long way off across fields a yellow spark from one little house, and beyond it the mounds where houses had used to be.

Baby crept out in the cold, shivering in her little rag of a dress, and ventured all the way across the fields to the house. It was much bigger once she got there, edging her way around the cattle pen and the big muddy transport parked outside. She looked through the windows and saw the big man who lived in the house, sprawled before his holoset with his big muddy boots off, just watching the holo slack-faced the way Quean Barbie did.

Baby knew what to do then, all right; the Memory served her well. With just a little coaxing the man yawned, got up and opened the door to her, and never even saw her as she walked in at knee level and followed her nose to where he kept his food. She wandered through his kitchen, poking into things, nibbling idly, helping herself to what was nice, spitting out what wasn't. She carried away a bright printed paper box of biscuits, marching back to the big man where he still stood, staring vacantly out at the night through the half-open door.

Before she left, however, Baby spotted something else she wanted: there on the back of the big man's chair was a crocheted afghan, made long ago, pink and green acrylic fiber. Baby thought it was beautiful. She took it, wrapping it about her little shoulders as she left the house.

The big man closed the door after her and returned to his chair, where he yawned again and frowned at the holo program, thinking he must have nodded off for a moment.

Baby stopped on her way back, diverted by the big beasts in the cattle pen. They were even easier to coax than the big man, and it took her only a minute to find the right ones and get a nice hot drink.

Full and warm and very pleased with herself, she started back to the hill as the eastern sky was paling. She could do everything now! Really, she ought to have a proper name, the way Uncle Ratlin and Quean Barbie had. What was the grandest possible name for such a clever little girl? The Memory helpfully served up fragments of talk, big words with a vague sense of meaning.

She decided on Princess Tiara Parakeet.

But later, huddled in her own private warren, Tiara had to admit that she didn't have it all yet. A Quean didn't curl up alone in her chamber, all by herself. A Quean had lots of kin around her, and a bright-glowing holoset to watch, and Uncles and the occasional big man to talk to. When Queans cried, they cried proudly, noisily and angrily, because they hadn't been given enough presents, and not because they were little and alone in the dark.

It was the Memory that sent Tiara poking through the trash rooms, where the panel light was dimmed because of all the piled clutter. One of these rooms had been, long ago, where the Queans' big men were thrown away when they died. Tiara knew you couldn't talk to big men anymore when they turned into bones, but she might play that they were still alive and talking to her, telling her how clever and pretty she was.

All thought of this particular game vanished, however, when Tiara finally pushed the door open and got into the bone room.

There were plenty of old bones, nasty rattly pieces of big men that Tiara didn't much like the look of, and she saw at once that they wouldn't do at all for pretend kin. But there was also a whole big man sprawled there, discarded like the rest!

No . . . not exactly a big man. Tiara stood and stared at him, and gradually the Memory told her everything: this was one of the big people's slaves, the clever immortal machines that looked just like them. *Cyborgs.* They worked for the Uncle of all the big people, who was called *Dr. Zeus Incorporated.*

The slaves were evil; the big people sent them to plunder poor little kin and steal their clever works. They had always done this, and the kin hadn't ever been able to stop them until one day, at last, a clever Uncle had devised a way to break the slaves. He'd even succeeded in catching one; though the slave had gotten away after. Such a long time, then, the Uncles had hunted for the slave, trying to catch him again, and many Uncles had been lost. It had become one of the epic stories of their race.

Though he had been finally captured, of course; kin never gave up when they wanted something. It was one of the things that made them better than the big people.

Why, it had been Tiara's own kin who had captured the slave at last, famous Uncle Zingo! Though he was dust now, poor old thing, but famous dust anyhow. And Uncle Ratlin himself had been the one to kill the slave, trying and trying with the different inventions until he'd made one that was deadly enough to do the job. Tiara didn't understand the big words and concepts that the Memory gave her, about *biomechanicals* and *electromagnetic pulses* and *disruption,* but it had been a great day indeed for Uncle Ratlin when he'd finally killed the slave.

Ever since, Uncle Ratlin had gone more and more among the big people, about his business in broad daylight even, and brought home wonderful presents for Quean Barbie. There was a great plan that was going to make them all very happy one day, that would avenge the kin and bring about the ruin of the big people and their slaves forever, and it all hinged on Uncle Ratlin's invention.

But in the meantime, the dead slave had been thrown in here and utterly forgotten. Kin never wasted thought on that for which they had no further use. That was another of the things that made them better than the big people.

Tiara picked her way into the room and stood looking down at the dead slave critically. Really, he didn't look very bad; much nicer than all those old bones. He would do, she decided, for pretend kin.

But what could you play with a thing that couldn't talk back to you? Tiara thought about it and her little face brightened. She ran off to her own hiding place and returned in a moment, carrying the pink and green acrylic afghan and a beer bottle she had filled with spring water. Sitting down beside the dead slave, she pulled his head and shoulders into her lap and awkwardly wrapped him in the afghan; then she tilted the bottle to his lips, pretending to feed him, spilling water down his waxen face.

"Pretty little baby, pretty little baby," Tiara crooned. "Drink your nice milk and go to sleep."

She had, like all the rest of her race, the power of absolute concentration on what interested her at the moment, fixation to a degree that would baffle one of the big people. So intent on her game was she, it mattered nothing to her that the dead slave trembled abruptly, that his mouth opened and fastened on the neck of the bottle, that he proceeded to gulp down the water.

"*Good* little baby," Tiara sang approvingly. "Such a good baby, he drinks it all gone. Isn't he clever! Mummy's very pleased with him."

The slave lay still, gasping for breath. She lifted the bottle away and he moved his lips as though he were speaking, but Tiara couldn't hear anything. "Oh, he's parched, he's parched and dry, he needs a whiskey to tell that story!" she sang. "Does he want a whiskey, then?"

The slave might have nodded, or it might have been a shiver. Tiara decided to play it for a nod and jumped up, running off to the spring for more water. She returned in triumph and settled back down, lifting his head and holding the bottle for him. "Drink, drink!" she chanted. "And grow up big and strong."

He finished the water and sighed, and his head sagged back on her arm. His lips moved again and this time she heard him speak, distinctly, a whisper of thanks.

"He can talk to me," she squealed in delight. "Talk to me more, slave!"

His eyes opened. She exclaimed, and leaned down to peer into them. They were a lovely shade of twilight blue, the prettiest eyes she had ever seen. All the kin had eyes like black water, except for some of the smarter Uncles; none such a nice color as this slave's eyes. They did not seem to see her, though. His lips moved again and the voice was clearer:

". . . *I have been a word in a book,*
I have been an eagle,

I have been a ship on the sea,
I have been the string of a harp,
I have been bespelled a long year in the foam of the sea . . ."

"Oh, no you haven't, silly," said Tiara. "You've been only here for years."
The slave blinked, looked confused. At last, "Little girl?" he inquired.

"You have to call me Princess Tiara," she informed him.

"Princess Tiara," he repeated. "Where are we?"

"You're in my hill, slave-baby," she said.

His face screwed up as though he were going to cry. "God Apollo, help me," he moaned, turning his face away. She took his chin in her hands and turned his face back.

"Don't cry, little baby. Mummy will take care of you. And we can play kin and you can talk to me and get me presents."

He took a deep breath, blinking his eyes. "Why, I would love to, Princess Tiara," he said at last. "But I'm hurt, you see. I can't move my arms or legs, and I'm afraid I can't see you, not in any spectrum."

"Oh!" Tiara dropped the game. "You know why? Because Uncle Ratlin killed you." She leaned back and studied him, puzzled. "How did you come alive again, slave?"

He appeared to be thinking about it. "I must have reset, or rerouted, and I've been in fugue all this time," he guessed, as though he were talking to himself. He turned his head in her direction. "Little girl? Princess Tiara. Are we in your uncle Ratlin's room?"

Tiara shook her head and then remembered he couldn't see. "Oh, no. We're in the room where the dead big people get thrown away."

"Ah," he said, shuddering. "So I've been thrown away? How long have I been in here?"

"Always," Tiara said. Her tiny brows drew together in a frown. "Uncle Ratlin will be mad. You were supposed to be dead."

"Oh, but—" How rapid the slave's breathing became. "You don't want him to be mad, do you? And if you tell him I'm still alive, he'll want to kill me again. And if he does that, I won't be able to talk to you. You see?"

Tiara saw. "It's a secret," she decided.

"Oh, yes, Princess Tiara, it's our secret. Please?" The slave's voice shook. "You won't tell anyone I'm alive in here, and I can talk to you, and play all the games you like."

"But you're broken," Tiara pointed out.

"Well, that's true, but I might get better. I'm sure I would, if I had enough time," the slave argued earnestly. "I couldn't even talk or think before, and then you gave me water to drink, and just listen to me now! I'm talking and thinking like mad."

"I'll get you more water," Tiara announced.

She got up and ran from the room, not noticing his cries of: "Wait! Little girl! Princess! Oh, please, for gods' sake, don't leave me!" When she came back after refilling the bottle, he turned his face at once as he heard her come in. "Princess Tiara?" he called desperately.

"Don't cry, little baby," she said, putting the bottle to his mouth. He gasped and drank again, so quickly some of the water spilled and ran down like his tears.

"Thank you, sweet little princess," he gasped.

"I like that." She smiled. "Tell me I'm a sweet little princess again."

"Oh, you are! You're the dearest, sweetest little princess there's ever been."

"Tell me you love me."

"I love you!"

"And I love you," she emoted, clasping her hands together and tossing her head back. "You are my perfect treasure, and I die for wanting you!"

The slave's mouth worked oddly. "My dearest love, you must never die," he cried. "Surely if you die the stars will all go out!"

"That's *nice*," she told him, her eyes shining. "You talk beautiful."

"I will always talk beautifully for you, Princess, I promise," said the slave. "I just wish I could sit up and play, too. If only I could see! Will you look for me, dear little princess, and tell me: have I still got both my legs?"

Dutifully Tiara leaned over and looked, though she knew perfectly well. "Yes," she sang. "Ten fingers and ten toes, why, he's perfect!"

"Both my feet are still there, then? And my arms and hands?"

"Yes, my treasure."

"Apollo be thanked. Am I cut, my dearest? Have I wounds anywhere?"

"My poor brave hero." Tiara pretended to weep. "They have murdered you entirely, there is blood in your beautiful golden hair."

"Is there?" The slave blinked, frowning. "Yes. I remember that. He tried to open my skull. So there's a wound in my head, my love?"

"Uh-huh."

"Ha. Well, don't trouble your heart, my darling." The slave ran his tongue over his lips. "If you'll look after me—if you'll bring me water and food—my body will have what it needs to begin repairing itself. I don't know how badly

I'm damaged, but if I can regain some function—any function—" The slave began to tremble, and calmed himself. "Why, what a grand time we'll have. And I can tell you stories—do you like stories, Princess Tiara?"

"Oh, yes," she assured him.

"Well then! Do you know, I was a Literature Preservation Specialist—" The slave's voice broke. He swallowed hard and went on, "And what that means is, I know every story in the wide world. I will be your own storyteller, princess dear, and nobody else will have such fine stories told. Only to you will I tell them. Will you like that?"

"More than anything, my prince," said Tiara and sighed. Then, in a completely sensible voice, she added, "Except you aren't really a prince. You're just my slave."

"Ah! Yes, but only *your* slave," he insisted. "I would be slave to none but the beautiful Princess Tiara. I'm afraid if you tell anybody I'm here, they'll come take me away from you."

"Nobody will do that," Tiara told him, patting his cheek. She knew how to keep secrets.

There was no time, inside the hill; except in Quean Barbie's chamber, where there was a chronometer of ingenious design to remind everyone when her favorite programs were on. With that exception there was no day or night, no sense of days or weeks passing or what that might mean.

But there were the stories, and the little rhymes the slave knew. For a long while there was Cinderella and Puss in Boots and Hickory Dickory Dock, intoned in his weary patient voice from the moment Tiara yawned and sat up until the moment she'd yawn and snuggle down beside him. She had dragged her scraps of blanket and dead-leaf nesting into the bone room and made a cozy place there against the slave's body. She left it only to find food and drink for them.

Plenty of water from the spring, and pale fish blind as the slave was blind from the dark pool under the rock. From the world outside there were berries, and hazelnuts, and bird eggs. There were snails. The slave had shuddered at these, at first, and then made a game that they were *escargot with garlic butter in white wine sauce*. Sometimes Tiara would creep down to the farm and take anything that appealed to her from the big man's kitchen, and sometimes things from his yard. Once there were towels left out to dry on the line overnight, and Tiara carried them away gleefully; for as her slave began to get better he could feel the cold, and she liked to wrap warm things about his shivering body, or wad them between him and the stony floor.

As Tiara got older and more skillful she learned to milk the big beasts into a jar, and would carry it back to her slave with scarcely a drop spilled. Then they'd feast on the cream, and with his throat refreshed the slave could go on with the astonishing stories, about Jason and the Argonauts, about Odysseus, about Rama and Sita.

Tiara loved her slave. With just a little food and care he became much nicer to look at: the wound in his head healed over and he regained use of one of his arms, dragging himself upright to lean against a wall. Nor was he loud, as the big people were, but soft-spoken, and as self-effacing as the stupids that served Quean Barbie. Tiara assumed this was because he was a slave.

The only trouble she would ever have with him was when he would cry. Sometimes he'd begin to cry and be unable to stop, and shouting at him or stamping her feet never helped; so she learned those were the times to play Mummy, and kiss the tears from his cheeks (she liked the salty flavor) and stroke his hair and sing to him. It was a strange feeling for Princess Tiara, rocking him in her arms until he'd wept himself quiet. It made her Memory come, flooding her little mind with images and words she'd never imagined. It made her heart ache.

How long does it take to tell all of the Ramayana? The Iliad? The Kalevala? All the stories of the Arabian Nights? The Cattle Raid of Cooley? Every myth and legend an immortal mind might compile in two thousand years of careful work? And telling them once would never be enough, for the devouring attention of a child. There are always stories to be told over and over, until the listener repeats them with the teller, pause for pause, breath for breath, word for ceaseless word, unappeased, unappeasable.

Quean Barbie, up in her warm chamber with her captive suitors and her silent attendants, watched game shows and soap operas and Elvis holoes. Down in the dark, Princess Tiara drank of a different brew, began to grow into another kind of Quean entirely.

Her tastes did form around romances, as she grew. Every tale of chivalry and passion the slave had ever sung when he'd been a troubadour, she loved: Tristan and Isolde, Arthur and Guinevere, Pelleas and Melisande. Every jongleur ditty about Robin and Marian. All the Shakespeare love plays, acted out in the slave's beautiful voice and with the gestures of his one good hand.

Heathcliff and Cathy, Jane Eyre and Mr. Rochester enchanted Tiara. When he recited Alfred Noyes's *The Highwayman* for her, she wanted it every night after that for years.

Princess Tiara grew small high breasts, and began to develop a certain interest in the slave's anatomy. No use; he couldn't make those parts work, damaged as he was, and he explained that it wasn't good for a little girl to start that sort of play too early anyway. Carefully, phrasing with exquisite tact, he made a request. She agreed, and the next night she went down to the farmhouse and rummaged around in the big man's bedroom as he slept. She returned in triumph with a pair of thin cotton dress trousers, and helped the slave pull them on over his nakedness. Once his man parts were covered she forgot all about them. He did look so funny, with the big baggy trousers rolled up on his thin legs!

But the clothes made him happy, and Tiara liked making her slave happy.

Now that she had breasts, now that he had trousers, the long hours of talk changed. There were still stories, but he also told her about History. He had lived a long time and knew a great deal, and he knew how to make it interesting for her. Every king or emperor or president had had a great lady who'd loved him, after all, and a story could easily be related in terms of what Theodosia had bid Justinian to do, or Eleanor bid Franklin. And he made the big world seem such a wonderful place! It was quite a shock of connection, the day Tiara realized that all the stories he'd been telling her hadn't happened inside the hill but must, of course, have happened in the big world outside.

Yes, that was a jump into another dimension. None of those people in the stories lived in cold rooms full of trash, or waded shivering through dewfall to steal food. There were elegant places where rain didn't cascade down the walls in winter, where things were fixed when they broke, where nobody had to hide in the darkness.

"I want to go out there," she informed the slave.

"I wish we could, dearest Princess," said the slave wistfully. "We could walk in the beautiful city of London, under the blossoming trees in Regent's Park. We could stay at Claridge's. We could dress splendidly and go to an elegant restaurant. I would wave my hand for the seller of roses and he'd come, just like that, and lay his wares at your feet. A waiter would bring us champagne. All the men passing by would fall in love with you."

"And would I be more beautiful than their dreams and hearts' desires?" Tiara asked.

"Oh, yes, child," the slave replied, and stretched out his hand and found her face. He traced its contours, the tiny nose and chin of exquisite delicacy, the high-domed brow and enormous eyes. "Oh, Princess, you'll break hearts in your time."

"Why can't we go right now?" Tiara pleaded.

"Time," the slave replied. "I'm not at my best, I'm afraid, and you're still so little, dearest. One fine day, though, you'll be a grand lady; and if I'm lucky, one day my legs will repair themselves. Then, if you'll lead me by the hand, we might go away together."

"What will it take to make your legs work again?"

The slave smiled wryly. "A few months in a regeneration tank would do it, but we haven't got one of those, have we, my love? I suppose if we could get room service in here we'd have a chance, and wouldn't that be nice? Regular meals, so dear Tiara could grow tall and poor old Lewis's biomechanicals had the fuel they needed to repair themselves."

"You mean we need more food," she said, focusing sharply.

"Mm-hm. Vitamins, minerals, and iron," he said airily, draping his arm around her. "We'll have them someday, I'm sure. Coquille St. Jacques, oysters creole, curried shrimp. Crème brulée, asparagus soufflé, café au lait. You'll be lovely in watered silk and pearls, and all the splendid gallants will fall on their knees to beg you for the honor of just one dance with the rare and remarkable Princess Tiara Parakeet."

She snuggled in under his arm, but her mind was still busy. "Will you be very jealous, when I have lots of lovers?" she wanted to know.

"Oh, a bit, I suppose," he said, leaning his cheek against the top of her head. "But, really, how could I be greedy? I can't keep you all to myself, a beauty like you."

He had begun to hum a little tune, a waltz composed in a place and time very far from that dark room stacked with the moldering dead, when Tiara looked up at him and asked: "Have you ever loved anybody besides me?"

The waltz trailed off into silence.

"Once upon a time," the slave said quietly.

There was a silence again, and Tiara prodded him. "Once upon a time?"

The slave drew a deep breath, and in the clear voice with which he had re-cited before kings at Tara he began: "This is a story about two lovers. It is the best love story I know, because it's true."

"Star-crossed lovers?" Tiara wanted to know.

"Oh, yes, terribly. They suffered torment, and prison, and death. Nations and powers conspired to keep them apart. But they always found each other again, you see? And at last they went away together and were never parted anymore.

"Once upon a time . . . a little girl sat in a cell like this one. It was dark and cold in there, and the little girl was frightened and all alone."

"But *I'm* not alone," said Tiara.

"No, dearest. You have me. But this little girl didn't have anybody, yet.

"Her name was Mendoza."

The man sets the Elephant back in its place, picks up an ivory Pawn. He reflects that there had been a certain political agenda in the mind of the carver; all the white figures are clearly agents of nineteenth-century imperialism. The ivory Pawn could be a controleur, a company store accountant, a missionary: high collar and hat, pointed beard and mustaches. In pose he is stiff as a wooden idol, he has none of the dynamic lines of the other pieces. Only his face is alive. His teeth are bared in a grimace of Viking ferocity, his staring eyes round with malice.

CHAPTER 2

The Benthamites had finally come for Forest Lawn.

It wasn't the first time open season had been declared on a cemetery. Centuries earlier, San Francisco had decided her civic space was at a premium and relocated her founding population (who were in no condition to protest the change of address) to a potato field some miles south of her borders. The former San Franciscans in question, however, were granted neat new plots and crypts, in fact a nice necropolis of their very own, in compensation for being evicted.

Not so the residents of Forest Lawn in Hollywood. They might reasonably have expected that politics could no longer touch them, but they'd have been in for a surprise.

The Benthamites followed the tenets of Jeremy Bentham, nineteenth-century social philosopher and reformer. Most of his ideas were fairly radical, for their era: utilitarianism, coercive law, applying calculus as a means of evaluating human happiness. His thinking on mortuary arrangements, however, was truly original.

Why, he asked, were the deceased such slackers? Instead of crumbling away in boxes and reserving to themselves two yards of land that might be put to better use for food production, they ought to be of some service to humanity! He drew the line at cannibalism, but did feel that the human corpse had a host of uses both practical and decorative, which only mere religious superstition prevented from development.

To name but one possible way in which Mortality might serve Utility: attractive persons might have their bodies preserved postmortem and presented to friends as an alternative to statuary. Mr. Bentham himself willed his body to his college in the eager expectation of becoming his own memorial shrine.

Alas, the science of taxidermy wasn't quite equal to Mr. Bentham's hopes, and the best efforts only produced a sort of macabre doll that was kept in its own handsome cabinet except when it was annually wheeled out and propped up at memorial dinners. Mr. Bentham faded from the memory of all but his unfortunate beneficiaries and readers of *Ripley's Believe It or Not!*, until the late twenty-second century when the body of his writings was rediscovered and Benthamism became the latest craze.

Altered, of course, to suit twenty-second century sensibilities. The focus then was on reclaiming the vast acres of real estate lost to public use because they were full of dead bodies. This had become a critical issue on a crowded planet, as over time funerary institutions went bankrupt and abandoned hundreds of square miles of headstone-studded earth.

Enter the Benthamites. Their benevolent organization raised funds to purchase disused memorial parks, which were then carefully excavated. After due archaeological and medical analysis, the bodies were cremated (less dental gold and any personal items with which they might have been buried), the graves were filled in, and the headstones used in the construction of public works buildings. The former cemeteries were rededicated to public use by the living. Low-cost housing, car parks, air transport stations, shopping malls . . .

And when the new plagues came and devastated that pragmatic world, and the dead outnumbered the living, still the Benthamites continued their good work to the benefit of all. Death had so terrified the moderns that they couldn't bear contemplation of his white face, mention of his name; the newly dead were whisked away to cremation and never spoken of again. In such an environment, naturally enough the last thing anyone wanted to see on a daily commute or casual drive was a graveyard! So the Benthamites grew in popularity, and therefore in power.

And therefore their ranks were densely infiltrated by the immortal operatives of Dr. Zeus Incorporated.

He usually went by the name of Victor deVere. His immortal body was neatly made and looked well in tailored clothes, so he was something of a dandy. His sharply pointed beard and mustaches were red. His eyes were green and capable of brightness, but generally focused in the flat blank stare of a hunting cat. His skin was white as paper, an unnatural pallor very unusual for an immortal, with shadows like bruises under the bored eyes.

At the crest of Lankershim his car's propellant motor stalled, and Victor keyed in an order to restart. He drummed his gloved fingers on the dash console while the car growled and thought about it.

As Victor waited, he considered the view spreading out below him: a waste of blowing sand and broken sidewalk that had been the San Fernando Valley, crossed by the unreliable trickle of the Los Angeles River and bounded at the east by the ruin of the old city itself. It was fairly attractive, as ruins went. Morning glory vines had spread rampant over dozens of square miles, hiding and softening the scars of urban war with blue flowers.

The motor started up again, but the car informed Victor that it had lost its programming and asked politely for a destination. Annoyed—for the damned thing had only to go down the hill and around the corner—Victor entered trip coordinates again. The car hummed and sped off with him, down Lankershim and along Forest Lawn Drive, in the shadow of Mount Hollywood.

At the gatehouse the security tech on duty nodded and let him through. He left the car, which was having another directional crisis, and walked on up to the modular shelter—surmounted by its holographic image of Jeremy Bentham's staring effigy—that was Labienus's office.

Labienus was sitting out on the deck, enjoying the afternoon sunlight. He was an immortal, a smooth-faced man with the gravitas of a Roman senator, though he had only been a legionary commander. He had clasped his hands about one knee and was smiling out at the old cemetery, which was certainly busier than it had been in its heyday. At the distant edges earth movers filled in looted sites, and along the fence neat rows of potted saplings awaited planting. Nearer in, a flatbed moved slowly between the opened graves, as security techs loaded up coffins to be taken away to the long work shed for evaluation.

"Look at it all, Victor," said Labienus. "The opened graves, the tombstones strewn about. What's it remind you of?"

Victor turned to regard the scene. "An old engraving of Judgment Day," he replied.

"Just what I was thinking!" said Labienus. "Too, too funny, don't you agree? Another myth brought to life by the Company. Here we are at the end of time and the earth is indeed giving up her dead. And, unless I'm mistaken, this particular spot once had an angelic visitation. Wasn't it here? It was a movie location before it became a graveyard, I remember."

Victor accessed briefly. "You're referring to D. W. Griffith's films? Angels hovering over a battlefield or some such nonsense?"

"Yes." Labienus waved a hand. "It was filmed on this very spot. Just picture them here now, blowing their trumpets, dangling above the crypt lids."

"Hilarious," Victor told him, and sat down. "You seem happy about something."

"It's been a successful day," said Labienus. "Two celebrity corpses."

"Really!" remarked Victor. "Who were they?"

"Bette Davis and Stan Laurel," Labienus informed him.

"Have we got buyers?"

"There are enough parties interested in Davis to put her up for auction. There's only been one response on Laurel, but it's the collector who owns Oliver Hardy and is trying for a complete set, so I think the Company can name its own price," said Labienus, grinning. The sale of human remains was of course strictly illegal, but there were wealthy cinephiles who were willing to pay handsomely for the ultimate in private shrines to the celebrated dead.

"A neat bit of business," agreed Victor.

"And we've located three more Company caches," Labienus continued, referring to the hermetically sealed coffins that had been filled with loot and buried to preserve them. "Mostly full of mid-to-late-twentieth-century goods. One's full of first editions of books. The others seem to be paintings and canisters of film."

"Films, eh? How appropriate." Victor looked idly at his chronometer. "Care to join me in a gin and tonic before I assail that mountain of correspondence?"

"Yes, thanks," said Labienus, and stretched luxuriously. He transmitted: *Something else, too. Quite a little St. Valentine's box turned up today.*

Victor felt a wave of nausea, but his face showed nothing as he stepped inside the office and opened the refrigeration unit. *Found something special, did you?*

Oh, yes. AIDS victim named Jason Smith, went to his eternal reward in 2007. He was in our loving hands his last six months and sealed in a biogen box immediately postmortem. The virus had mutated in him, you see, become something really wonderful. It's been percolating away all this time and ought to make quite a splash.

Victor fished out the gin and tonic and after a moment's further search found a fresh lime. Methodically he pulled on transparent sanitary gloves over his white ones. Quite calmly he mixed the drinks and replied: *I suppose you'll need me to escort him somewhere.*

China, of course. Again. Population density's jumped up unacceptably in the last three years. Can't have that, after all.

Even this close to our conquest? Stolidly Victor cut slices from the lime.

Especially this close.

I suppose I'll be working with a local operative in the area?

One of our best men: fellow named Hong Tsieh. He'll do most of the work, actually. You'll have but to deliver the merchandise.

Easy enough, Victor transmitted, and stepping back out on the deck, handed a drink to Labienus. "Here you are. Cheers, old man."

"Here's to health," said Labienus, snickering at his own joke as he lifted his drink in response. Victor smiled and drank, holding in his mind the image of Labienus's severed head rolling off the deck and down the hill, perhaps not stopping until it bounced into the river and tumbled away over stones to the sea . . .

But Labienus's head did not go down the hill until the rest of him went with it, strolling away to his car, which took him off to his comfortable quarters in the walled enclave of Old Hollywood. Victor retired to his desk in the office and set about answering Labienus's correspondence, covertly recording everything he found.

There was little of interest to the Company in his communications, nothing to directly implicate Labienus in the Plague Club conspiracy. Labienus was far too careful, and anyway there was no need for proof; the Company knew perfectly well that Labienus had been releasing viruses into the mortal population for centuries. Victor had been told to turn up the contacts, the associates, to draw in gradually the edges of the net. Hong Tsieh, whoever he might be, was the real prize this evening.

Victor forced access to Labienus's private files and began scrolling through the correspondence file headings, largely out of habit. The texts of the communications were no longer there, of course, cannily long deleted; but one never knew what might turn up. It was, at least, something to do on this miserable posting. Victor had been a mole in Labienus's organization for just over two centuries now and would gladly have exchanged places with any of the unfortunate residents of Forest Lawn, no matter how transitory their state.

"Sir?" There was a sharp double knock on the door. "Sendeb reports we've located another celebrity."

Victor sighed and pulled his attention away from the scrolling dates. "Which one?"

"Buster Keaton, sir."

Victor raised his eyebrows. Early cinema pioneers generally commanded high prices, if they were well known. "You're sure it's not Diane or Michael?"

"It says Buster on the headstone, sir. He's in great shape, too."

"Bring him up here," Victor ordered. "I'll notify Sotheby's tomorrow."

He settled back and focused on the dates again. To his annoyance, he noted that they had sped by more quickly than he had anticipated: all the way back to June 2083. He scrolled up again and then halted.

There. 15 July 2083. Message from: V. Kalugin. Subject: Concern.

Nothing else. Victor scrolled ahead with infinite care, into 2084 and beyond, but there were no other message headings from V. Kalugin. He withdrew his consciousness from the files and leaned back, folding his gloved hands in his lap, staring at the wall.

Vasilii Kalugin had disappeared long ago. He hadn't been anybody important within the Company, a Marine Salvage Specialist of low rank, but Victor had been searching for him for decades. Kalugin's wife had asked him to search, and Victor loved Kalugin's wife, and so Victor had sought Kalugin faithfully. Honorably, too.

Even so, he had never been able to find a trace of the man beyond a last communication dating from February 2083. Here now was the heading of a message dated four months later, and to Labienus, of all people.

What had been happening in July 2083? Labienus had been busy, to be sure. That was the summer the Sattes virus had swept through the prisons, and then the armed forces, of the world. Labienus had boasted, since, that that had been his finest hour: he'd managed to eliminate the criminals and the warmongers of all nations in one stroke. The virus had begun in late May in North America. By mid-July it had circumnavigated the globe, crossing Siberia to Kamchatka and then working its way down into Japan . . .

Kamchatka? That had been Kalugin's last known location. He'd been doing something classified in Kamchatka. But here was proof that at the very moment the Sattes virus had hit there, he'd communicated with Labienus—who was responsible for the virus. Had Kalugin found something out?

Could he have been such a fool as to accuse Labienus directly? Unfortunately, Kalugin *had* been a fool.

The double knock sounded again. "Sir! We've brought him."

Victor pushed back his chair. He got up and went out to inventory the corpse of Buster Keaton for the Company's sales catalogue.

Mont St. Michel, 10 August 2330

Following the devastating tsunami of 2198, Mont St. Michel had been rebuilt, almost entirely at Company expense.

Appearances had been preserved—this was France, after all—so the visitor approaching on the air ferry from Jersey might still watch as its fairy-tale spire loomed from the sea mist, as its thirteenth-century battlements and quaint village became visible. Within, however, the granite rock now housed a secure labyrinth of rooms and corridors constructed to withstand wave, wind, earthquake, or bomb blast. The causeway to the mainland had never been rebuilt, for ecological reasons (or so it had been explained at the time) and so the Mont once again enjoyed the protection of violent tides and shifting fields of quicksand.

This cut back on the tourist trade a bit, but the Company (which now owned Mont St. Michel, due to France defaulting on a debt) didn't mind. Nor did the French, really. The place was exquisitely kept up, and moreover now housed the world-class Grand Musée de Rennes, a glorious shrine to French culture, which anyone might visit if he or she had the proper academic credentials.

Victor didn't need credentials. He stepped down to the landing pier with the mortal tourists and made his way past the ticket kiosks to a private entrance. The guard posted there nodded and let him in; locked the gate behind him. Three minutes later Victor stepped from an elevator and emerged in the corridor outside the Chief Curator's private suite. The guards posted there nodded, too, but they paused to transmit news of his arrival to Aegeus before they let him in.

"Victor!" Aegeus half rose behind his desk, smiling. "Have a seat, please."

He was an immortal, solid and blond, with the look of a respectable public official. His office looked like an antique dealer's showroom. Victor, seating himself, didn't bother to stare at the massed wealth there: the paintings by Gericault and Renoir, the Cocteau lithographs, the holosculptures of Marcel Gigue, the gold and crystal and calfskin and teak that had been whisked out of the paths of armies and secured away here, for Aegeus's private appreciation.

"How was your journey?" Aegeus inquired, settling back in his late-eighteenth-century chair. On the lapel of his suit coat he wore the enamel pin representing a clock face without hands. Among the higher-ranking immortals, the pins had become cynically chic, a perverse statement of identity.

He did not offer Victor a drink from the decanter on the table at his side, though the glasses were Waterford and the ice in the silver bucket was fresh.

"Uneventful," Victor replied. He proceeded to relate the substance of his conversation with Labienus. Aegeus listened, frowning thoughtfully.

"Hong Tsieh, eh?" he said at last. "Another Facilitator. I'd never have suspected, but we'll set a trap accordingly. Good work, Victor! Our masters will be pleased with you."

"What about the other matter?" asked Victor. "The body of Jason Smith. Do you want me to divert it and deliver something harmless?"

Aegeus made a face. "Regrettably . . . you'll have to follow through on that one, Victor. Deliver as intended."

Victor blinked. His pale face went a shade paler. "Innocent mortals will die," he stated in a calm voice.

"Can't be helped, I'm afraid." Aegeus smiled sadly and shook his head. "History records the outbreak of a virulent and previously unknown autoimmune disorder in Nangjing in two months' time. It'll kill thousands and there's not a damned thing we can do about it. Pity, but there you are. Labienus will pay for it, rest assured."

Privately Victor doubted this. Aegeus had been assuring him that retribution was just around the corner for Labienus for decades now. There was always some reason to delay his arrest a moment longer, some previously unguessed-at lead that must be followed up.

"So I'm to deliver the, the body as ordered? The disease culture? Work with this Hong Tsieh?" Victor asked.

"I can't think of anybody else I'd trust with the job," Aegeus told him, nodding. "It'll be hard, I know, but you've the spine for it. Save any mortals you can, of course. And observe Hong Tsieh closely. This opens up a whole new field of investigation. We'll need to root his people out, see what they're up to. I'll expect a full report in, say, six months' time?"

"Very well," said Victor, rising to his feet.

"Good man. You're going straight back to Hollywood, I suppose?"

"I thought I'd overnight in Paris," Victor answered. "I never miss a chance to stay at Les Andelys if I can manage it."

"That place where Cazaubin was sous-chef?" Aegeus looked sincerely interested for a moment. "Excellent choice! Do enjoy yourself, please. You've certainly earned it."

He turned with an expression of dismissal and began to study something at the terminal that rose from the surface of his desk. Victor found his own way out.

But he did not go to Paris.

Fez, 11 August 2330

There was a certain quarter of the old city no longer very fashionable, close as it was to the vast power station. Here rose the white wall of a private home, high and nearly featureless, revealing nothing of what might lie beyond it. There was an old door painted blue; far up there were narrow windows, and their carved screens were also painted blue. Anyone who took the trouble to follow the wall around would discover that it enclosed five acres, and would conclude that this was the private compound of some very successful businessman or minor prince.

In a way, it was both. It was the Company HQ for Suleyman, Executive Facilitator, Regional Sector Head for North Africa. It had also become a place of sanctuary, a harem, and a family home.

Victor walked unhurriedly toward the blue door. He neared it and it opened from within, silently, and he stepped through: a white man in a white suit disappearing into a white wall. The door closed.

A mortal servant made obeisance to him, and led him down a dark cool passageway. Halfway along, another immortal stepped out from a side passage a mortal wouldn't have noticed and fell into step beside Victor. Victor had expected this. He didn't react.

"Is it another plague?" inquired Latif. He was Suleyman's son-in-immortality and he was lean and tall, with the harsh aquiline features of a black corsair.

"Yes," Victor told him. "But—is Nan here presently?"

Latif raised an eyebrow. "No," he replied. "She's back in Paris."

"Just as well, I suppose," said Victor.

"You have some news for her?"

"Possibly," said Victor. Neither of them said anything more until the mortal had led them farther into the depths of the house and up a flight of echoing tiled stairs. They came to a door and the servant bowed, made to slip away. Latif put a hand on his shoulder.

"Tea," he ordered. He looked aslant at Victor. "Two glasses, one chlorilar cup."

The mortal was mildly shocked but hastened to obey.

"Come in, Victor, please," said someone with a deep voice from beyond the door. Latif opened the door and they went in.

Suleyman was seated at a low table, upon which a shatrang board had been set up. Four mortal children knelt opposite. Three looked up to stare as Victor and Latif entered but the fourth kept her gaze fixed on the board. Her little fists were clenched. Seeing that a game was in progress, the immortals waited. As they watched, the child reached out and moved one of the pieces.

"You want to sacrifice your Vizier?" Suleyman inquired. Horrified, the child shook her head. Suleyman glanced up at the immortals. "You were distracted by my guest," he told the child. "You may withdraw the move."

"Thank you, lord," she said, and hastily put the game piece back.

"You need to learn concentration to the point where nothing, not the walls of the house collapsing where you sit, can distract you from the game," concluded Suleyman, and rising from the table he ordered the game positions to print. He collected the hard copy from the rosewood console housing his credenza and passed out the sheets to the children. "That's all for today. Take these home and study them this week. And, tell your parents, tuition is due with the next lesson! The poor old tutor has to be able to buy bread, after all."

There were some giggles at that, there were uncoordinated salaams, and the children ran from the room, waving their homework as they pattered away through the house. The game pieces retracted slowly into the tabletop and an inlaid panel slid into place above them. Suleyman turned his attention to Victor.

"It's China, this time," said Victor. "Nangjing."

"I was afraid of that," Suleyman replied. "Sit down, won't you?"

Victor sat. The servant brought the tea. The mortal knelt a respectful distance away as the immortals drank tea and chatted about weather, global politics, the investment market. He watched, fascinated, as the white man sipped from the cheap disposable cup. Had Lord Suleyman intended an insult to his guest? But they seemed on the best of terms.

Victor finished his tea and crushed the cup in an easy gesture. The mortal stared when Victor withdrew a little roll of transparent chlorilar bags from an inner pocket and tore one off. He tucked his used cup inside, sealed it with fastidious care, and set it on the tray. The mortal knit his brows in comprehension. Some biohazard? Perhaps the white man had been ill. That would explain why he was still wearing his gloves. The servant made a mental note to tip the bag down the fusion hopper without touching it.

When they had refreshed themselves, Latif gestured for the tea things to be removed and the servant departed with them. Victor leaned forward and in a low voice related the events of the previous thirty-six hours.

"Damn," said Latif, when he'd finished. "How long does Aegeus think you'll put up with this, anyway? He's got to know *you* know they're working together."

"He knows I have no choice, so my opinion doesn't matter," said Victor wearily. "And they aren't allies at all. Aegeus will let Labienus do his dirty work until the day of the Silence, and then he'll have him arrested and condemned, with sincerest outrage, no doubt. Labienus is perfectly aware the

Company is allowing him to lay waste to the mortals. He despises Aegeus for a hypocrite. And he'll make damned sure he takes out Aegeus's faction before they can arrest him."

"If we're lucky, they'll be so focused on getting each other they won't pay attention to the rest of us," said Latif.

"Oh, they have their plans for the rest of us," Suleyman told him.

"Me, at least," said Victor with a bitter laugh. "I stumbled across the memo. Probably a good idea, in my case, but it really would be a shame about the rest of you."

"We'll do what we can, Victor," Suleyman said, and reached out to thump Victor on the shoulder in sympathy. Victor flinched at his touch.

"Careful, for God's sake," he murmured. "You never know."

There was a brief awkward silence and then Latif said: "So what was that you said about finding somebody?"

Victor sighed. He explained what he'd seen in Labienus's correspondence files. The other two men listened closely. Before he had finished, Latif was groaning and putting his face in his hands.

"That would be just like poor old Kalugin," he said, leaning backward. "To be so clueless he'd go to *Labienus*, of all people, with whatever it was he'd found! It had to have been some big smoking gun about the Sattes virus, wouldn't you think? Since it was hitting where he was working right about then? And Labienus must have had him taken into custody as soon as he'd finished his job. Maybe even invited him up to MacKenzie Base to make a full report. Kalugin would have gone, too."

"But Kalugin's not in any of the storage bunkers," said Suleyman, stroking his beard. "If we knew where he'd gone after his mission—"

"Where do you go on leave that's near the Arctic Circle?" Latif wondered. "What the hell is there to do? I know Russians don't mind it up there, but still. Why'd he take his R and R in such a godforsaken—"

"Unless he didn't," Suleyman said in a dull voice. Victor looked up at him.

"But his record says—"

"Nan's been proceeding on the assumption, all these years, that that was true," said Suleyman. "He went on leave and then disappeared. But, you know, he generally used his leave time to visit Nan. Why didn't he do the same on that last occasion?"

"What was his mission?" demanded Victor, as an idea occurred to him. There followed a silence as the realization hit all three of them: Kalugin had been a Marine Salvage Specialist, which meant that his work involved securing things the Company wanted that would otherwise be lost in shipwrecks. Unfortunately for Kalugin, the most economical and effective way to accomplish this usually involved going down with the ships when they sank.

Suleyman closed his eyes. The silence resumed and deepened, as all three immortals accessed swiftly through the historical record for the year 2083. There wasn't as much as there might have been; the Sattes outbreak had caused an immense event shadow on history in that year. Mortals had been so preoccupied with the horrors of the plague they hadn't documented much else. But Suleyman found it at last, focusing on entries relating to the Russian navy.

On 21 July 2083, the navy had launched a prototype miniature submersible, the *Alyosha*, powered by an experimental fusion drive—which would have been the first successful one, if the *Alyosha* hadn't been lost that day in the Bering Sea.

The record stated that her sole crewman had been awarded honors posthumously, but his name was not recorded.

Suleyman grimaced and transmitted his findings to Latif and Victor. Latif swore and jumped to his feet. "I bet they left him down there," he yelled. "Oh, man, he's still in the damn submarine—"

Victor bit his lower lip. He bit it hard enough to draw blood, and a bright drop welled. He sighed and drew out a tissue, dabbing the blood away carefully. Then he busied himself with taking out another chlorilar bag and sealing the tissue inside it. He put the bag in his coat pocket and said, in a preternaturally calm voice, "We mustn't tell Nan."

The Aleutian Basin, 25 August 2330

"What the hell are these?" Latif demanded, scowling through the viewport. "Volcanic vents? What do they call them, *black smokers*? These aren't on the maps."

"It may have been in somebody's interest not to report them," observed Victor.

"Maybe," said Latif. "Or maybe whoever had the job of mapping this stretch just blew it off. Not a lot goes on up here anymore."

Victor nodded.

"Well, this is really peachy," continued Latif. "All these fumaroles spewing out sediment just full of metallic crap. You could hide anything down here; the sediment would bury it and the metals would keep anybody's sensors from picking it up afterward. No wonder nobody ever found the *Alyosha*."

"Do we have any chance of finding it now?" asked Victor.

"If we go to blue-sound scan for this section of the grid, we might," Latif replied. He gave the console new orders. Then he leaned back in his seat, stretching. "And we wait. You want a beer?"

"I wouldn't mind one," Victor replied. Latif got up and paced back through the cabin to the refrigeration unit. He pulled out two beers and returned to the console, as the *Met Agwe* continued its underwater search. The immortals sat drinking their Red Stripes, staring out into the gloom.

"You're not going through all that business with disposable cups and bags right now, I notice," said Latif.

"There are no mortals here I might infect," Victor replied.

"You really have no idea when it goes on or off?"

Victor shook his head. "Something in my programming of which I'm unaware, perhaps. Or a signal Labienus generates, when he requires my particular talent. As far as I know I've only been used twice—three times, perhaps. I test my blood on a weekly basis, but I've never been able to predict an episode."

"Mm." Latif shook his head. "Whatever goes down when the Silence falls, I hope Labienus gets it in the neck."

"He doesn't see himself as an evil man, you know," said Victor. "He sees the mortals as the source of all evil. His dream is for a restoration of the Golden Age: no more wars, no more pollution, no more wretched little human race. Only a few of us immortals, flitting about like fairies through the replanted forests and happy beasts."

"That'd get old real fast," growled Latif.

"Aegeus, on the other hand," said Victor, "doesn't want the mortals exterminated. They're an exploitable resource. What would we do for waiters and busboys, after all? To say nothing of other uses. We'll still need them to compose their music and paint their paintings and write their novels for us to enjoy, since we immortals are incapable of creating art."

"Well, we weren't made to create things. We were made to save them," reflected Latif. "Although . . . I don't think I'd agree that we don't create art. You remember Houbert?"

Victor rolled his eyes.

"All right, I know he was a big . . ." Words failed Latif. "But you have to admit he was a genius at design. Those pavilions he'd put up for his parties. All the special effects. I was at a New Year's Eve ball once where he . . ." His voice trailed off. Victor looked at him. "You know who else tried to create?" Latif went on at last. "Lewis. You remember him? The little Literature Preserver we've never found?"

Victor shivered. "I remember him."

"I knew him from the time I was a neophyte, at New World One. He was sort of pathetic, but a nice guy. I ran into him on a job one time in New Zealand, back in the early part of the last century," said Latif. "At a transport terminal. He was working on an adventure novel he'd spent years writing. He'd found an old picture of a mortal who used to work for the Company, some spy named Edward Bell-Fairfax. Lewis was fascinated with him. Wrote this epic about him being some kind of Victorian James Bond. Showed me some of it."

"That's rather unusual, I must admit. One of *us*, writing? Was it any good?"

Latif shrugged. "I don't know." He frowned out at the dim world beyond the viewport, turning the beer bottle in his long hand. "It was crap, actually. But he tried. He had the inspiration, for all the good it did him. At least he wasn't one of those poor amnesiac bastards we pulled out of the Bureau of Punitive Medicine—" He leaned forward abruptly and peered at the screen where the blue-sound images were playing out. "What's that?"

Victor ordered the *Met Agwe* to pause, then proceed forward slowly. "It's cylindrical."

"It's about the right size."

"It seems to be in one piece." Victor called up the single surviving photograph of the *Alyosha*. The two immortals compared it to the image on the screen.

"Mostly in one piece," amended Latif after a moment. He activated the sensors again. They listened, sifting through the gibberish that was dissolved iron, copper, zinc . . .

Latif stiffened. "There." He enhanced the image, the sensor readings. The two immortals sat there gazing at the screen a moment before Latif rose in his seat. He stalked back to the alcove where his pressure suit hung waiting, silent as the man entombed five fathoms below the *Met Agwe*'s keel.

Suleyman takes out the Viziers, ivory and ebony, and compares them.

They're more similar than other pieces in the game, for all that the artist was depicting different cultures. One is robed in a djellaba, one wears a tailcoat, but both look wise and dishonest. Both smile, fingering their beards. About the feet of both, reaching up with gestures of supplication, are carved smaller figures: the envoys of conquered tribes? Toadies? Petitioners? Lesser ministers?

CHAPTER 3

The Masters of the Universe at a Private Meeting, York, 2318:
They Deal with the Breaking Scandal

"It's not fair," said Bugleg miserably. "We didn't make that Options Research place. We didn't send anybody there."

"Well—we sort of did," said Rappacini.

"Some of us did," said Freestone. "Not me, though."

"It was one of *them* made it really awful," Rossum pointed out. "All we wanted was a place to do tests on the operatives. We never said to torture them."

"We just wanted a way for them to *not be*," agreed Bugleg.

"If only nobody had found out about Options Research," said Dippel with a sigh.

They were scientists. They were all young men, and though they had been born to different races and nations, there was something disconcertingly similar in their smooth uneasy faces. Their clothing was uniform as garments can be without actually being uniforms, plain functional garb, no complicated fastenings, no particular style. They sat around an oval table with a polished white surface that invited scribbling. In the center was a can of bright-colored doodlepens, which had been placed there to encourage creativity. Nobody was drawing anything on the table, however, creative or otherwise.

"We shouldn't have put one of the big mean ones in charge, I guess," said Dippel.

"That was probably a mistake," admitted Rappacini.

"And he didn't even find a way to terminate them," said Freestone, shaking his head. "Even though he was supposed to be superintelligent."

"They're all supposed to be superintelligent," objected Rossum.

"Maybe they can't be terminated after all," said Rappacini.

"What did we have to go make them not die for?" wondered Bugleg, staring at the table.

"Well, it seemed like a good idea when we came up with it," said Dippel.

"But now they're really mad at us," said Bugleg.

He was referring to the immortal servants created by Dr. Zeus Incorporated, and their somewhat understandable outrage at the discovery of a covert base, hidden in the deep past, where some two hundred missing immortals had been imprisoned for research purposes. Suleyman had liberated them, and gone public with the story. Some very fancy plausible denial indeed had been necessary, with blame shifted to the renegade immortal Marco, who had run the place, and who was now (fortunately) missing.

"Everything's happened so fast with this Company," complained Rossum. "One minute it was all just this really good idea and the next minute it was all this awful causality stuff that had already happened without asking us."

"Like those toy things," said Rappacini. "What are they called? You're just winding a crank playing a nice little tune in a box and then all of a sudden a lid flies open and this scary thing jumps out."

"Schrödinger's cat," said Rossum.

"No, something else," said Rappacini in frustration, and held out his arms and waggled them to suggest the thing he was trying to name. "Anyway I never liked those."

"We wrought not wisely, but too well," said Freestone.

"Don't talk like that!" cried Bugleg. "You sound like one of them!"

"No, they sound like *me*!" said Freestone with some heat. "We're the human beings here. We made them, and not the other way around. They might have forgotten that, but I certainly haven't. How are we going to stop them from taking over, that's the question we should be asking."

"Well, the only thing we can do is not make any more of them," decided Rappacini. "And keep trying to find a way to terminate them ourselves."

"Ah, but how?" said Freestone.

"We were too smart," said Bugleg, shaking his head.

The meeting broke up, as it usually did, in hand-wringing. Bugleg was still wringing his hands as he left the conference room and followed the tunnel to the parking garage.

He was a rather pale man, going bald early and attempting to hide it with a comb-over. There were a lot of medications he might have taken to regrow hair, but he distrusted them. Bugleg distrusted most things. He had big dark worried-looking eyes and weak features, and was a genius in his particular field, which happened to be chemistry. He knew very little about anything else, however.

Certainly he didn't know enough to look before he got into the agcar that pulled up at the garage mounting block. It was his habit never to look at the driver, because the drivers were cyborgs, and Bugleg was frightened of cyborgs, even though he had helped to create them. He didn't notice, therefore, that there was no head visible above the driver's seat. He just edged well away from the door once it closed for him and sat there watching his own white fingers as they knotted themselves together in his lap.

But he did notice, eventually, when the agcar failed to pull into the parking garage in his hotel. He looked up in alarm and finally realized that there was wild countryside out the windows. This was because his agcar had long since left York behind and was now merrily speeding along the A59.

Bugleg made a little terrified sound.

"Took you long enough to catch a clue, didn't it?" said a voice from where the driver ought to have been. To his horror, a face came leering around the side of the driver's seat. Bugleg screamed at it.

"Oh, come on," said the owner of the face. "Not so bad, am I? I'd have thought you'd cry hello, and isn't it Old Home Week? Perhaps you'd like a closer look, so you can see there's nothing to fear you in little me."

Bugleg shrank away as the creature scrambled nimbly into the backseat beside him, and settled itself in comfort. The agcar sped on.

"Don't mind the floatymobile," said the creature, waving its hand. "I've tinkered with the console. It's programmed to drive itself now. No nasty big cyborg slaves to hear us, you see? Just kin here. You and me." It poked him, grinning.

It was something like a wizened child—or perhaps a little man. It wore a man's clothing, a fine-cut business suit of Harris tweed. It was shod in similar elegance, wore expensive sun goggles and a shapeless hat. Somehow, though, there was something inexpressibly *dirty* about it. A sense of leaves and twigs in its thin gray hair, mud on those polished shoes, a faint hint of a moldy smell. Bugleg gasped and burst into tears.

"What're you wetting your knickers for?" scolded the creature. "Haven't the eyes to see, have you? But they're our eyes, I can tell. Stop that weepiness now!" It reached out and slapped him, quite hard. Bugleg gulped and cowered, but he stopped crying.

"You haven't caught a clue yet, alas." It sighed, pulling off its sun goggles and hat, and leaned forward to stare very hard at Bugleg. "Look, you dim booby. Don't you see it?"

Anyone else looking on would have already realized—as Bugleg was only now beginning to realize—that there was a certain similarity between the two of them. Big head on a spindly neck, dead-pale skin, sparse hair, same weak features and pursed mouth. Only, the creature had a meager gray beard and mustaches like bits of gray string hanging down, and its big green eyes were sharp, malevolently intelligent.

"You—you—how come you look like me?" said Bugleg at last.

"Like I said," the creature told him, "we're kin."

"I don't have any family," said Bugleg.

"Don't you, though? Adopted by somebody, I'm sure. Raised among them, like all the others. You've had brothers and brothers your Dr. Zeus Incorporated has bred and raised, generation on generation down, cousins by the dozens, too. Mixing their big blood with ours to get themselves brainy little hybrids, since their tribe's too stupid to come up with their grand inventions by their own selves." The creature bared its teeth, tiny teeth like a baby's. Bugleg himself had never lost his baby teeth. He blinked now, trying to comprehend what he was being told.

"You're lying to me," he said. "You're some kind of monster."

"Not I," snapped the creature. "I'm a man! I'm the disinherited right human heir to all their grand places, the original white man, and so are you. Have they bred the Memory out of you, stupid? You don't know the story we all know, how we were smarter than the big tribe from the get-go of time, flying in our ships when *they* was still smacking chips off flint to make themselves tools for their clumsy hands? But they chased us, stole our inventions from us, so we had to hide ourselves. How could you not remember? We've *all* got the Memory."

"I don't know what you mean," said Bugleg. The horrible little man glared at him a long moment, and then looked around the inside of the car. On the seat between them was a small box of disposable chlorilar gloves, kept there by Mr. Bugleg in case he had to touch anything dirty. His visitor pulled on one of the gloves and, before Mr. Bugleg had time to protest, thrust his hand into Mr. Bugleg's open mouth.

"Wowf—aughf—ack! You scratched me!" cried Mr. Bugleg, when the hand had been withdrawn. The creature ignored him, neatly pulling the glove inside out as he removed it from his hand. He tied the wrist shut and tucked it away inside his coat.

"I'll do a bloody DNA test, then, and prove it to you. They've been enjoying themselves in the sun whilst we've hid under rocks in the damp, all these centuries of the world. They stole our children to breed, so we stole theirs. You and me both came from that game! But they cheated, see. They made themselves slaves who could go back through time, and do their thievery for them. They created the *cyborgs*."

"No," said Bugleg. "I did that. I mean, I was on the design team."

"They was using you to do it," the creature jeered. "Think they'd ever have come up with Pineal Tribrantine Three by themselves? Not likely! And you did your kin proud anyhow, because their clever weapon's turned in their hands now, hasn't it? Fine Dr. Zeus is scared to death of his cyborgs. Wishes he'd never made them."

"Yes!" cried Bugleg, suddenly comprehending. "They're mean, and now they're mad at us, and we can't make them go away. They'll take over!"

"That's right. So Dr. Zeus came crawling to us of all people, sent his big men in their gray coats to ask ever so nicely whether we couldn't help them. *Oh, please, nothing will make our cyborgs die, would you ever give it a try?*" whined the creature mockingly.

"What?" said Bugleg. "Dr. Zeus is just a logo. Nobody came crawling to you."

"That's what you think, ducky," the creature replied. "It was before you were born, but it was your Company, don't think it wasn't. Old Uncle Zingo was there and he told me the whole of it, how it was sweet to see them go down on their big knees, pretty please! Well, he graciously said yes, and they made sure we got what we needed to experiment. And what I'm here to tell you, my big stupid hybrid cousin, is: we've kept our part of the deal. We've done it at last. Come up with a way to solve your problems."

Bugleg's pulse raced. "You can make the cyborgs—be not immortal?"

"Can and have, I say!" the creature assured him. "I've come up with a stuff that'll kill them dead as doorknobs."

But Bugleg had turned his face away, was cringing again. "Not *kill* them," he said. "Killing is wrong. We just want—"

"Say no more," purred the creature, holding up a hand. "You want a nicer word? Say my stuff will terminate them. Better still, say it'll switch them off. Because they're not really people, are they, now? Just things you made."

"Yes," said Bugleg, brightening. "Yes! Just things. And they're mean."

"And you need to switch them off."

"Yes. Because they do bad stuff."

"So they do! But we'll stop them, you and me. I've got something that'll switch them off forever and aye, melt their machine hearts inside them." The creature pulled a fine enameled case out of his breast pocket. He extracted something and held it up with a flourish. "Allow me to present my card."

The beautifully embossed letters said S. RATLIN in large type, and underneath in smaller type the word *chymist,* followed by a commcode and an office address in a Celtic Federation country. Bugleg being unable to read, however, stared at the card in painful incomprehension. "You have to tell me what it says," he said petulantly.

"Aw, Christ, you're no fun at all," said Ratlin, and gave the card a little shake. In a clear voice it recited its text aloud.

"Chemist?" Bugleg sounded it out wonderingly. "But that's what I do, too."

"Big surprise," Ratlin said. "No, silly, you take the card; it's for you, so you can contact me when you need to. See? Just slide it in the READ port on your console and it'll give me a knockknock. Now. How do you want to administer the nastiness?"

"What?"

"The stuff I've made, to shut down your cyborgs. It has to go inside them," Ratlin explained. "Can you call 'em all in and tell 'em it's vitaminery they're supposed to get? Have 'em all drop their britches for a nice injection?"

Bugleg was astonished at such cleverness. But, as he thought about it, certain objections presented themselves. "They're too smart," he said at last. "We made them so they get all their vitamins out of their food themselves. They never need injections. So if we were all, 'We're going to stick you with needles now' they'd know something was funny."

"Hm, hm. And if you gave 'em pills to swallow they'd suspect that, too, wouldn't they?" growled Ratlin, knocking his knuckles against his forehead. "Too obvious, pills."

"They're programmed to scan everything they eat and drink." Bugleg sighed. "That makes it hard. They don't eat or drink anything bad for them."

"Hmm."

"Except—" Bugleg's eyes widened as realization hit him with unaccustomed force. "They *do* eat and drink bad things! Like, uh, meat. And those drinks people used to drink. Coffee. Wine. You know."

"Vices?" Ratlin grinned at him. "Your precious slaves have vices, have they? Well, now we've got 'em by the short and curlies. Think, boy. What's their most favorite vice of all?"

Bugleg wrinkled his nose. "They call it *Theobromos,*" he said with distaste. "It's, like, chocolate. It's full of nasty things like hormones and it makes them . . . drunk. They eat it whenever they can."

"Well then," Ratlin said, rubbing his spidery hands in glee. "We'll hide the stuff in chocolate. They'll bolt the nice chockeys down and bang! That'll be the end of your problem."

"That's so smart," cried Bugleg in admiration. "And . . . and right, too. Because if they were nice, they wouldn't eat that stuff."

"No, of course they wouldn't. Use their own sinful appetites to bring 'em down, why, it's only justice."

"Yes. Only . . . we can't do it yet," said Bugleg, the excitement fading from his eyes. "There's the Temporal Concordance. It says they don't get terminated during recorded history. So the only time we could, uh, switch them off would be after the Temporal Concordance runs out. When the Silence falls."

"The Silence . . ." Ratlin tugged at his beard. "Hm. That's in the year 2355, right? Thirty-seven years away. Hellholes, I'll never live so long. I'm terrible old, as kin goes, all of thirty. Even you may not live so long. We go quick through the world."

"We can live that long if we take Pineal Tribrantine Three," said Bugleg.

Ratlin peered at him in amazement, and then grinned like a saw blade. "So we might. Your clever medicine keeps the years away from your cyborgs, don't it? Oh, yes, you're kin and no mistake. How do we get us some Pineal Tribrantine Three?"

"I can make it in my sink," said Bugleg proudly.

"That's a boy," yelled Ratlin, bouncing in his seat. "Devious and deep. Oh, we'll do great things together, we two. And how do we get us some Theobromos to tamper with? Lots and lots of it?"

Bugleg's face fell. "It's hard to get," he admitted, knitting his brows. "All the nice countries stopped making it. It's against the law. You can only get it in the countries where they still do bad things like, um, selling meat and alcohol."

"Like the Celtic Federation?" Ratlin inquired craftily.

"Well—yes."

"Where I keep a business office, where I strut around unbeknownst to the big tribes, because I'm High Hybrid and can pass for one of them? What if I was to go into the business of making chocolates, eh? Lovely dainties to tempt your cyborgs? And the cleverest part is, we've got thirty-seven years to set the trap! By the time we spring it, your slaves'll fall for the trick, because they'll have been happily stuffing themselves with Ratlin's Harmless Chocolates for thirty years and more. They'll be so used to 'em they won't even think to scan." Ratlin's voice rose to a happy scream.

Bugleg drew back a little nervously, but his heart was racing. "Then—we'd have all we needed," he said. "The only hard part would be making sure the cyborgs all ate it at the same time. There are a lot of them."

"Right. Timing's everything. Logistics! Got to work that out. Well, you leave all that to me." Ratlin put his sun goggles back on. "They'll never suspect a thing."

Paris, at That Very Moment

"How stupid do they think we are?" said Aegeus, looking disdainful. Ereshkigal—dark, slinky as an immortal Siamese cat—shrugged and set the surveillance device on automatic record again.

"You don't think it's true, do you?" she asked. "It's impossible. Nobody's ever manufactured a poison we couldn't detect."

"And I'm quite sure they haven't now," Aegeus replied. "Though all the same . . . if there were such a substance, we'd want to be certain it didn't fall into the wrong hands. In fact—"

"In fact, if *we* had it—" Ereshkigal anticipated.

"It might come in damned useful against any eleventh-hour purges by the other cabals," said Aegeus. "Yes! Well, well, see what's to be gained by an adequate budget for intelligence?"

"What should I do now?" inquired Ereshkigal. "Let them go ahead with their plans and monitor their communications?"

"Exactly," said Aegeus. "Give them all the rope they'll need. At the last possible moment we'll step in and confiscate their work. We'll see who gets terminated then."

"You're so clever," she told him, settling back on the divan.

"Aren't I?" He settled back beside her, smiling. He made a gesture, an exceedingly ancient one, of sexual invitation.

"Now, now." She shook a finger at him. "You didn't call me all the way from San Francisco for this, did you?"

"No," he admitted, looking annoyed. "You need to know something."

"I see," she replied, and her body at once lost its pose of languid sensuality. "What exactly is it I need to know?"

"There's a . . . client, of the Company's, a rather special case," Aegeus said. "He's been living in Europe the last few centuries. He's decided to come home to California."

"Centuries?" Ereshkigal's eyes widened.

"Yes. You're to coordinate his relocation with his handler. See to it that everything goes smoothly. There are a few specific lies that must be told, and you're the woman to tell them."

"*Centuries?*" Ereshkigal repeated. "What do you mean? Is he one of us?"

"Not exactly," said Aegeus.

"He's either one of us or he's a mortal, Aegeus," said Ereshkigal.

"I said he was a special case," Aegeus reminded her. "You worked in New York at the end of the nineteenth century, as I recall. Do you remember the millionaire, William Randolph Hearst?"

"Of course I do," said Ereshkigal. "But he was mortal."

Aegeus snickered. "Only temporarily, it seems," he replied. "It's a long story."

Montreal, Simultaneously

"It took them long enough," said Labienus, setting his surveillance device on automatic record again. He looked nothing like Aegeus, yet somehow they shared the same indefinable look of public probity, dignity, and authority.

"How likely is it they've actually managed to find a toxin that works?" wondered Nennius, who might be brother to either the aforementioned immortals. He scowled as he sipped from a glass of sherry.

"Oh, very likely," Labienus assured him. "They've had that little drone you gave them to experiment on for, how long now? Five decades?"

"Thereabouts," said Nennius. "There wasn't that much to Lewis; you'd think they'd have finished him long ago."

"Perhaps they've been perfecting it, whatever it is." Labienus poured himself a glass. "Here's to the waters of Lethe! There really are too many of us anyway. I wouldn't be surprised if some of our immortal brethren actually jump at the chance to die, when the time comes."

"And leave the world for us to bustle in? Bravo," agreed Nennius. "You'll monitor the tiny cretins closely, I suppose? Be prepared to step in at the last possible moment and grab the goods?"

"What else?" Labienus smiled. Nennius raised his glass in salute.

"I'll set my best people on it. Now! The reason I came out here in such a tearing hurry is, I've got a private collector who's willing to pay anything for the corpse of Harry Houdini. The only catch is, he wants the monument bust as well. Can you arrange it?"

Labienus made a face. "The bust's available. The corpse, unfortunately . . ."

"Ah. It's in bad shape?"

"Not exactly. It's not there, that's the problem. When we got his coffin open, it was empty."

"Damn," said Nennius, mildly outraged.

Fez, 9 July 2355

Suleyman sets back the Viziers and draws out the ivory Rukh, turning it in his hand. It's a heavy piece, depicted as a crusader-era stone tower in the Norman style. On the battlements stand two scowling warriors in generic European army uniforms. They are disproportionately large. At their feet crouches a dog, his ears and muzzle sharp points, and his head is lifted as though he is baying at the moon.

CHAPTER 4

The Castle in the Clouds, 2333

Time for the news!

The big boy set down his little dog and stood up. He sighted along the row of tiny holoprojectors mounted through the room at eye level (his eye level, anyway) and focused sharply on the first one to send its picture flaring into light and color, about halfway down the wall. He began to snap out a staccato rhythm with his fingers.

As the opening fanfare sounded he was abruptly *there* in front of the floating image, watching as the first snippets of program teaser played. Just as the commercial interlude was beginning, a projector on the wall opposite put forth its lit image, commencing a news broadcast from another region. He whirled and absorbed its lead-in; whirled back as another image appeared, and darted to another apparition as it came, and so to another and another, as the whole of his long study glowed with a babel of voices and bright forms.

By this time the big boy was moving rather too fast for a mortal eye to follow, and it was just as well. Any mortal would be profoundly unsettled watching his movements, which resembled a bizarre dance, sort of a cross between the rushing assault of a grizzly bear and the effortless glide of a hummingbird between the vivid ghosts. Image to image to image, he was actually managing to watch all thirty news programs simultaneously.

His speed wasn't the only unsettling thing about him. It was impossible to tell his age: twenty? Twenty-two? There was a blank innocence to his face that recalled childhood. His eyes were blue-gray, set close together above a long straight nose; his features were even and smooth, his mouth a little pursed. And yet there was a certain grimness to the young man impossible to explain, the gravity and isolation of a granite mountain range.

His little dog had prudently found herself a place under a chair, well out of range. The big boy was a kind master, but to be stepped on by William Randolph Hearst—even by accident—was very, very bad.

Anyway, she hadn't long to wait; within three minutes the phantoms had begun to fall silent, wink out. News programs weren't very long in the year 2333.

The big boy slowed in his dance, turning before the last of the images went dark, frowning thoughtfully. Then he paced back along the length of his study to the work console at the far end, by the windows. *Click, click, click,* his snapping fingers punctuated his progress. He seated himself before the console, took up its buttonball and settled down to work.

His buttonball, by the way, was of the old-fashioned variety with alphabet option as well as all modern commands. The big boy could read and write. It was only one of the many things that set him apart from the mortal public he guided, and only one of the reasons he took it upon himself to guide them.

RED PLANET MARS SEQUENCE TOO LONG, he wrote. GIVE THE AMERICAN VIEWER A BREAK! DON'T MAKE THEM SIT THROUGH A LECTURE CLASS ON THE HISTORY OF SOCIALISM. FIND SOME MORE SUCCINCT WAY TO MAKE IT REAL TO THEM.

CELTIC FEDERATION CLIP GOOD. MAKE THIS A CONTINUING FEATURE. POSITIVE CLIPS, DANCE, WEAVING (BUT AVOID MENTION OF WOOL), CALLIGRAPHY, AND ABOUT THREE EPISODES INTO IT AN OVERVIEW OF HISTORY. SUGGEST: SIR WALTER RALEIGH INVENTED GENOCIDE, RESPONSIBLE FOR LUNG CANCER? BUT NOT SO BLATANT WE GIVE THE BRITISH CONSUL AN EXCUSE TO SQUAWK AGAIN.

WHAT HAPPENED TO TEXAS-MEXICO TREATY SEQUENCE???? PUNCH UP IMAGES! IF YOU CAN'T GET GOOD FOOTAGE THERE USE STOCK SHOTS AND DOCTOR THEM.

He sent this message and began another. His little dog, having ventured out from under her refuge, trotted across the room and curled up at his feet. She settled her head on her forepaws, ready to nap. Then she lifted her head and stared around suspiciously.

The big boy noticed at once. He looked down at her. "What is it, Helen?" he said. His voice was unnerving too, high and soft. During his mortal lifetime, it had been described as the fragrance of violets made audible.

She whuffed and jumped to her feet. He turned his cold gaze out into the room, following the direction of her attention.

Everything as it ought to be: his room much the same as it had looked for the last four centuries, his Gothic pieces neatly ranged above the surveillance equipment, his fabulously ancient books in their sealed cases, the portrait of his mortal self—somewhat older than he appeared now—staring back at him from its accustomed place above the long polished conference table. A mortal man would have been fooled.

And how likely, was it, after all, that anybody could get past his surveillance system up here on La Cuesta Encantada? Even if they made it over the perimeter boundaries and into his high gardens, La Casa Grande itself was well protected from any but invited guests.

But the big boy got to his feet, picking up the little dog and tucking her into the corner of his arm. She snarled at the unseen presence, uttering terrible threats in little-dog language. He touched her muzzle and smiled at her, briefly, before his face resumed its dead implacable expression.

"You may as well take a breath," he said quietly. There was a gasp from beyond the far doorway as someone followed his advice.

"Damn," said someone, "I forgot about the dog."

He dropped into the doorway—apparently from somewhere near the ceiling—a short, dark man in a slightly rumpled business suit. Nervously he shot his cuffs, smoothed his hair, stroked his close black beard and mustaches to neatness. With a final tug at his lapels, he turned and regarded the big boy with a dazzling smile. "Hey, Mr. Hearst, how's it going? Long time no see, huh?"

Hearst raised an eyebrow. "Joseph Denham," he said.

"Gosh, it's been a while since I used that name. But, yeah, it's me." Joseph adjusted the knot of his tie. "You're looking great these days! And I mean that sincerely. So you got your castle back again, after all these years. It must have felt swell to come home."

"Mr. Denham," said Hearst, "can you give me a good reason why I shouldn't call my security team and advise the Company of your presence here?"

"Yeah," said Joseph. "I've got some information you need, Mr. Hearst. Trust me—you really should hear me out."

Hearst looked at him in silence a long moment. "I can do that," he said at last. He turned and indicated a chair with his gaze. "Come in and sit down, Mr. Denham. And I'd like to ask you a couple of questions first, if I may."

"Sure! No problem," said Joseph. He crossed the threshold and went straight to the offered chair, where he made himself comfortable. Hearst picked up the hand unit of a household communications device—rendered in best Retro style to resemble a candlestick telephone—and waited a moment.

"Mary? Send up a tray with a couple of glasses of ginger ale, please. Thank you."

"Gee, thanks," said Joseph.

"You're welcome." Hearst sat down across from him and leaned forward to put the little dog on the floor. She went straight to Joseph's shoes and became very interested in sniffing them, now and then reminding him she was on duty with a stern *whuff*. Joseph did his best to ignore her, saying only: "She looks just like the one you had the last time we met."

"She's a descendant, actually," said Hearst, watching the little dog. "I call them all Helen; makes it easier, in the long run. Of course, everything's in the long run now." He raised his eyes to Joseph. "At least, I think it is. Maybe you'll be able to tell me about that, Mr. Denham."

"Okay," said Joseph. "What do you want to know?"

"Quite a few things," said Hearst, looking at him steadily. "First: were you involved in that Bureau of Punitive Medicine place? Were you partners with Marco, that immortal who went crazy?"

"No," said Joseph. "Absolutely not. I was searching for somebody myself when I found the Bureau. I couldn't tell anyone directly, but I tipped off Suleyman, the North African Section Head. I figured he'd rescue those poor bastards if anybody would. But no, I am not now, nor have I ever been partners with Marco. What else did you want to ask me, Mr. Hearst?"

Hearst watched the little dog for a moment. "What's going to happen in the year 2355, Mr. Denham?" he said at last.

At that moment the elevator clanked and began to descend behind its brass grille. Hearst held up his hand in a gesture indicating they should wait, and Joseph nodded. The elevator rose again and a mortal woman emerged, bearing the tray of drinks Hearst had ordered. Hearst thanked her and she departed. Joseph cleared his throat as the elevator descended once more.

"So you've figured out about 2355, huh?" he said.

Hearst nodded. "Dr. Zeus Incorporated gives us all manner of tidbits of information about the future world, but I've noticed that I'm never told about anything occurring later than the year 2355. No investment information beyond that year at all. Why? And that absurd magazine they send me, *Immortal Lifestyles Monthly*—well, if you read it carefully you notice that there are no references to anything written or created after that date. No books after the year 2355, no pictures, no inventions, nothing!"

"Yeah," said Joseph, reaching for his glass and taking a sip of ginger ale. "We call it the Silence. Have you asked the Company about it, straight out?"

"I've made certain inquiries," said Hearst. "I have yet to receive a plain answer from anyone."

"No surprise there. The official answer is that 2355 is when Dr. Zeus finally goes public, when immortals will finally be able to live openly." Joseph swirled ice in his glass and looked sidelong at Hearst. "They say they don't give us any movies or whatever from after that time because we'll be able to discover them for ourselves. I don't think anybody has ever believed that."

"So you're saying that you don't know, either." Hearst looked down at his little dog. Joseph shook his head.

"There're theories. Global cataclysm in that year, for example. Or that there's an intracorporate war, and the winners maintain transmission silence after 2355 so nobody in the past knows who wins or how. You want to know what I think?"

"Yes, I do."

"I think that's the year when the Company doublecrosses its immortals. We've worked for them from the beginning of time—immortals like me, anyway; you're a special case—with the promise that one day we'd finally get to the wonderful Future and share the great stuff we've spent all our lives obtaining for Dr. Zeus. I think it's a crock. I think they'll come up with some way to finally kill us, or disable us, and cancel out their debt. You want to know why I think that, Mr. Hearst?"

"Please tell me," said Hearst.

Joseph stood up and looked Hearst in the eye. "Because they're doing it already. That's why I'm on the run, pal, that's why you got that request to let the Company know immediately if you ever saw me again. You want to know the truth about the Bureau of Punitive Medicine? The Company ran it themselves! Marco was just the guy they had standing guard there. It was a research facility they had, to find a way to reverse the immortality process."

Hearst nodded. "I was afraid it was something like that."

"And it was just the tip of the iceberg," Joseph said, beginning to pace. "The Bureau was only one of the places the Company locks away operatives it doesn't want anymore. There are at least seven others, not as bad as the Bureau but holding more people. I've seen 'em, Mr. Hearst. And there's worse.

"You remember Lewis? The guy who worked with me in 1933?"

"The fellow Garbo was so taken with, yes." Hearst smiled at the memory, but Joseph's eyes were like flint.

"You should have seen what the Company did to *him*," he said. "They handed him over to—to an outside agency, let's say. So he could be experimented on, like a lab rat. Nice, huh? I know, because I was there. I nearly got caught, too. If you followed their orders right now and called the Company, they'd do something worse to me."

"I'm not given orders," said Hearst, with a momentary flash of human emotion in his eyes.

"You don't think so?" said Joseph. "You've done everything the Company wanted you to do for them. They've given you stuff in return—hell, they made you immortal, you own Company stock—but you aren't calling the shots, friend."

Hearst sat silent a moment. At last he reached down and snapped his fingers for Helen. She came at once. He stroked her, scratched between her ears. "I assume," he said, "that you're not taking this lying down? You immortals, I mean." He smiled for a second. "*We* immortals."

"You got it," Joseph said. "We're immortal, we're indestructible, and we can outthink them. The only advantage they've got is, they know everything that's going to happen up to 2355 and we don't. Kind of levels the playing field, huh? But it also gives us hope, Mr. Hearst. See—what if *we're* what happens after 2355?"

"A war in Heaven?" said Hearst. "The Titans rising in rebellion against Zeus? It seems a chancy business, don't you think?"

Joseph shrugged. "We've already had the eternal punishment thing, at the Bureau. So what have we got to lose?"

"I don't know that I haven't got a great deal to lose," said Hearst. "You haven't shown me any proof yet."

"Hey, you want proof, and I don't blame you one bit, friend. My group has managed to get hold of some of the Temporal Concordance. You know what that is, right?"

"It's the logbook of the Future," said Hearst, "the Company's record of everything that's going to happen."

"Yeah. The one we're never allowed to see, except a little at a time, so we can be where they want, when they want us to do their work for them. We found a section." Joseph reached out with his index finger. "May I?"

Helen snarled. Hearst closed his hands around her and blinked as Joseph set his fingertip between Hearst's eyes. "Downloading—" said Joseph, and Hearst felt a shock wave, a sudden expansion of his memory. It was a sensation not unlike being hit in the head with a bundle of newspapers hot off the presses. Dates, events, names filled the place behind his eyes.

"Oh—"

"There you go," said Joseph. "You feel a little dizzy, right? Don't worry, that'll pass. I only gave you a tiny bit but boy, have you got a scoop! You can beat all the other news services to the draw for the next three years. But you'll also find private communications in there, between officers in the Company, stuff we weren't meant to see. You can draw your own conclusions about it. I'll be back in touch in a few years to see how you feel then, and whether or not you want to do business, okay?"

He rose to his feet. Hearst put up a hand. "If you please," he said. "I'd like to know how you got past my surveillance."

Joseph grinned. "Hell, Mr. Hearst, I'm over twenty thousand years old. Remember? I can get past a few cameras and motion sensors. Though I'd appreciate it if you'd take me off the record." He gestured at the holocams that had been steadily observing him. "I'll bet you can do that, huh, a clever film editor like you?"

"Unnecessary. You have my word I won't tell the Company you were here."

"I believe you, Mr. Hearst, honest, but you know what? They go through all your surveillance records routinely anyway," said Joseph.

"No, they don't!" said Hearst.

"Yeah, they do. You know Quintilius, your Company liaison? That's part of his job. The Company doesn't trust anybody, least of all its own people. The only reason some Company security officer isn't hearing everything we say right now is because my datalink implant was disabled a long time ago." Joseph tapped the bridge of his nose. "And they never installed one in you, I guess because you're a special case. Or maybe they figured you have so much surveillance on yourself already, there was no point in spending more to duplicate it."

He stepped back and looked Hearst up and down in an admiring kind of way. "I have to tell you, I'm impressed with the job they did. You're really unique, you know?"

"You keep saying that I'm a *special case*," said Hearst, rising to loom over Joseph. "What are you implying, exactly?"

Joseph retreated another couple of paces, but smiled disarmingly. "Hey! You've been a stockholder for four centuries now, you know the Company product. You know they never, ever make adults immortal. They always start with little children. Except for you! You were the only exception there's ever been to the rule. You're smart enough to figure out there's something fishy about the year 2355; you must have wondered about yourself, too, huh?"

"I did ask about it," said Hearst. "I was told I have an unusual genetic makeup."

Joseph's smile got wider still. "Oh, yes, you could say that. They didn't lie to you, Mr. Hearst, not about that."

"Why don't you explain, then?" Hearst scowled down at him.

"Next time," said Joseph. "I promise. Really."

He winked out.

Hearst was only momentarily surprised. Turning his head and scanning for the trajectory of Joseph's departure, he exhaled in annoyance. "Stay," he told Helen, setting her down in his chair, and then he winked out, too.

Down through La Casa Grande he sped, faster than mortal eyes could have followed, over his high fences, pursuing the fading blip that was Joseph in hyperfunction; but the head start was too great. On a knoll of rock he halted and stood peering out across the miles of his domain (for everything within mortal sight, and immortal sight too, for that matter, was his). He could just make out Joseph's signature, fading into the coastal mountains to the north.

"Darn," he said. After a moment he put his hands in his pockets and walked slowly back up his hill, thinking very hard as he went.

Just as he came to the wide staircase below the Neptune Pool, a tour vehicle pulled up and he heard the docent say excitedly: "Ah-yah! This is very special, everybody. See that man? That's Mr. William Randolph Hearst the Tenth! His ancestor was the one who originally built this wonderful place. He came here from Europe and saved it all when there wasn't any more money to keep it open to the public! Wasn't that nice of him? We don't get a chance to see him much, because he's very busy—"

Hearst ducked his head in embarrassment and considered hurrying away, but reflected that it wouldn't really be polite to do so; there were a dozen mortal faces pressed to the windows of the tour vehicle, staring at him eagerly. He gave them a shy smile and stood there on display while the tour group disembarked and came rushing over. It was largely a party of reenactors, wearing passable early-twentieth-century costumes. One carried a SoundBox blaring out early jazz music. Hearst winced. He preferred modern music, on the whole.

He shook hands, answered a few questions, and hoped they'd all enjoy their visit to his house before he departed with the excuse that he had work to do.

As he stepped across the threshold of La Casa Grande, he wondered plaintively why contact with mortals made him so uncomfortable. It was easy to love them in the abstract, delightful to plan for their welfare; even now his heart warmed at the thought of their enjoyment of the splendors of his great house. He loved listening to the tourists' reactions, as the docents pointed out this particularly fine Flemish Madonna, or that marvel of Persian figured tile.

He was a little lonely when there weren't guests downstairs, trooping through his echoing halls. He liked watching their progress on the surveillance cameras.

But he never liked looking into their mortal faces, clasping their mortal hands, talking to them. He never had, honestly, even when he'd been a mortal man himself. Only the endless building plans, only the work made him truly happy.

Nothing really mattered, except the work.

PART II

CHAPTER 5

Back in the Hill

Still no way to measure the hours or the years, in the darkness, but they went by. There were times when icy sweat beaded the walls and ran down to pool on the floor, and the slave's teeth chattered in his head as he told Tiara the love story. In those nights Tiara struggled through frozen weeds to the farmhouse, and had to use every ounce of her will to make the big man rise from his bed and open the back door, gazing asleep into the darkness while she slid past him and rifled his shelves.

There were times when the air was heavy and stale, hard to draw into the lungs. A living reek came floating down into the places of the dead, nasty smells from Quean Barbie's domain. But then the wind would shift, and a faint sweet breath from outside would find its way down, telling them about stars and grasses and blossoming thorn. Those were brief nights, but Tiara found she could range farther, run more swiftly then. She brought back wild plums for her slave, and hazelnuts, and with her hands she caught trout in a starry pool.

She carried them back in great haste, always, because the sooner she and the slave could eat, the sooner it would be time to cuddle close again and listen to the story. Tiara liked the heroine, Mendoza, well enough, identified with her in fact, the little girl who had been lost and alone in the dark and yet survived to become a fine lady; but Tiara's favorite was the Englishman who died and came back again, just like her slave, who described him with such vividness Tiara felt sure she would recognize him in a second, should she ever meet him.

And how brave he was, and how clever in all his incarnations! But especially as Commander Edward Alton Bell-Fairfax, who was in the story the longest. Tiara could well appreciate a ruthless hero, and listened spellbound as the slave described the sea battles Edward fought, the adventures in mangrove swamps, and the duels with villainous slavemasters, the secret missions for his government, the beautiful ladies so grateful to be rescued or so eager to betray state secrets to him. Actually Tiara wasn't sure she exactly approved of the other ladies, but the slave explained that Edward only romanced them because he hadn't found Mendoza in that lifetime yet, and as soon as he had he would be faithful unto death.

But how awful the story of his death, when it came! Tiara wept and stormed and struck her slave, begging him to make the story come out some other way. He reminded her that this story was true, that he had to tell what really happened to Edward. And to Mendoza, arrested by evil Dr. Zeus, only because she helped Edward, condemned to be confined to a vat like one of the glass jars Uncle Ratlin kept big people parts in, floating and dreaming, neither dead nor alive.

What a relief to hear how the Englishman was going to be reborn and come back to rescue her! Tiara hugged the slave then. The slave wiped tears from his blind eyes and asked if she'd liked the story. She assured him it was the very best story in all the world, and ordered that he begin it all over again. How could he refuse? He was her slave, after all.

The long, long hours in the darkness dragged on, as the story was told and told again, and then one night somewhere during the years the slave broke off in mid-telling with the strangest expression on his face. "What is it, my treasure?" Tiara wanted to know, sitting up.

"I—Great Caesar's ghost! My lower right quadrant diagnostic just came online," the slave cried. He groped forward with his hand and felt his legs. "Yes! Yes! And there's a signal getting through!" He began to laugh, a high-pitched shuddery laugh, and tears ran down his face. As Tiara watched, astonished, he flexed his right foot.

"Your leg moved," she announced.

"Did it? Is it moving now? I can't make sense of what I'm reading—oh, Princess dear, do you know what this means?" the slave gasped.

"It is moving! What does it mean, lover mine?"

"It means there really is some hope, after all," the slave told her, reaching out again to touch his leg and reassure himself. "If I can get my legs back, if I can walk, we can get away from here, Princess."

"And see the big world? And go to London? And have adventures?" Tiara leaped up in excitement.

"Absolutely!" The slave collapsed back against the wall, his thin chest heaving. "It must be all that food you've been bringing in, now that you're becoming so clever at foraging. All those trout, and the hen eggs. I'm finally getting enough fuel to run the rest of my self-repair program."

"Can we go away right now?" Tiara began to dance.

"Not yet," the slave told her. "Yikes! What pins and needles. Oh, but it feels wonderful. Listen to me, sweetheart, I'll need both legs working to walk. And we'll need a plan. Silly me, all these years I never made one, but then I never really thought—"

"If you eat more, will your other leg work, too?" demanded Tiara.

"It ought to—but it's not just a question of eating, you see?" The dreamy vagueness had gone from the slave's voice; he sounded more sharp and alert than she could ever recall. "There are specific chemical compounds I need. My body must convert them into fuel. Potassium, magnesium, and iron. Selenium. Calcium."

"They sound delicious, my heart's darling," said Tiara, but uncertainly, because she had never heard of such things.

"Ah, but where to find them?" The slave frowned, thinking very hard. "Can't exactly jog down to the corner shop for orange juice and bananas, can we? No indeed. And liver's not easy to come by either, unless you were able to steal one from some unsuspecting cow." He turned his blind face in her direction. "Sweetheart, my adored one, what does he farm, that mortal you visit? Cattle alone? Or would he have rows of green stuff?"

"Nasty green stuff," she told him, frowning and shaking her head. "I tasted it. Berries are nicer, and plums."

"To be sure they're sweeter, dearest, but will you bring a leaf or two of the nasty for your poor old slave to try? Raw kale would suit very nicely, I think." The slave hugged himself, shivering with happiness. "Roots of any kind, if you can find them. Oh, Princess, think of being free. Think of walking in the sunlight. I'll take you to the gardens, the museums, the theaters, the shops! What a time we'll have . . ."

Tiara could barely wait. She ventured far afield, farther than she'd ever gone, and did what Quean Barbie would have indignantly refused to do: dug roots with her own slender hands for an old slave, and filled her arms with nasty cabbagey stuff. It made her very cold and cross, to labor across the muddy night fields, and she was tired when she came back to the bone room; but her heart beat all strangely when she saw the slave sitting up, listening for her, his lined face anxious.

He ate so gladly of the kale, and coaxed her to try it, though she still spat it out and shuddered. Ah, but potatoes and carrots! Tiara couldn't believe how delicious they were. She went back to the farmer's field the next night and dug all she could carry away with her. The next night she did the same.

The next night, as she was working her way through the heather to the edge of the terraced field, a figure rose suddenly, looming against the starlight, and a gnarled hand caught her by the wrist. She screamed, so high and shrill no human ear could have heard her, and bit frantically at the hand.

"Hello hello," hissed her captor. "I'd keep my voice down if I were you, stranger in the night, sweetmeat. Sweeney sits in the dark with a sling well loaded, ready to bash out the little pretty brains of you, if you make free with his truck patch again."

"Uncle Ratlin?" she said in surprise, and somewhat muffled around his withered knob-knuckles. She lifted her face to stare at him, and he at her, in mutual astonishment.

Uncle Ratlin was terribly big for kin, nearly as tall as her slave might be if he could stand. And whiskery! The stupids' gray skins were smooth and hairless, but Uncle Ratlin had a straggling beard and wispy elflocks trailing from under his hat. He was wearing big people clothes. But of course, he had to; for Tiara recollected now that he went out among the big people, did Uncle Ratlin, fooling them into thinking he was one too, so that he could further his grand scheme to ruin them all.

He peered at her now, his wide green eyes puzzled. "How should you know me?" he wondered, pursing his thin mouth. He thrust his face close and sniffled at her. "Was it you Sweeney was grousing about down at the Rising Moon, *you* stripping his fields? Pretty ripe girl, what hill are you from? There's no kin in this county but mine."

She drew back haughtily. "Unhand me, sir," she ordered. "I am the Princess Tiara Parakeet."

He bared his tiny sharp teeth in a smile. "No you're not! Hellholes, I know you. You're Barbie's Baby!"

She bared her teeth right back at him, but he snatched off his hat with his free hand and danced round and round in the starlight, dragging her with him. Down in the shadow of his cowshed, the farmer Sweeney heard their scuffle and loaded a rock into his sling, straining his eyes to see through the darkness. Uncle Ratlin heard him and stopped abruptly. He crouched and ran through the heather, and Tiara had no choice but to run with him, until they made the shelter of a hazel thicket and vanished into its rustly shadow.

"Now then," whispered Uncle Ratlin, "now then, my treasure, my love, and haven't you grown up sweet! But where've you been, darling, all these long years?"

"I have been in London," she informed him. "S-staying at Claridge's and sipping champagne."

He gaped at her, and then his eyes narrowed. "Not too likely, lovey. But you've been around big people, haven't you, and learned things? *London,* she says. Where were you really, I'd like to know? Silly bitch Barbie killed you, broke your baby neck and left you outside for a dog to find, or so I always reckoned. She does that now and then, in her little fits of temper. But she didn't, did she? You must have run off."

"Yes," said Tiara, realizing she had to tell him something. "I ran off."

"I was ready to break her neck myself when I came back home and found no Baby," he told her, his eyes shining. "Well! No more presents for her. Only for you, sweet thing. Who needs blowzy Barbie anymore, with you grown up and cherry-ripe? You'll come back with me, now, and spit in her old eye."

"I will not," said Tiara, summoning every ounce of dignity. "I decline, thou baseborn churl."

"Listen to her, listen to her, what fine words," Uncle Ratlin cackled. "Oh, dearie dear, I know what it is with you. You're High Hybrid like me, you've got a brain! And you must have been living under a library all these years, too. Well, you'll have no trouble putting old Barbie in her place. She's got the weight and the fingernails, but you'll be quick and smart. Don't be afraid of her." He groped under her dress in a friendly sort of way.

"Never," Tiara replied, reeling a little at what the Memory was telling her: she might kill Quean Barbie now, if she wanted! And take her place in that warm chamber, and watch whatever she wanted on that holoset herself, and have all the fine clothes and presents.

. . . And the game would begin, the endless game of romance, waiting for the keen pleasure of the vacant-eyed big men the Uncles would catch for her. Sometimes they'd be sampled, hairy massive darlings, and returned sleepwalking to wherever the Uncles had caught them, but sometimes they could be kept. Between times she could amuse herself with the Uncles and have little stupid babies, popping them out in litters for the other stupids to care for; but by the big men she'd have fine clever boys, Uncles like Ratlin and his brothers, and perhaps one day after years of Uncles a little girl, clever and lovely, a reflection of her own glory!

Though one day the girl would grow up and turn nasty . . . and of course the big men never lasted forever, even if they were as beautiful as an Elvis, even so they'd clutch their hearts and groan one day and the stupids would drag them away to the bone room . . . where her fair-haired darling slave had been thrown when Ratlin killed him. *Thought* he'd killed him. Careful, careful now.

"I am not interested in your kind offer, sir," she told Uncle Ratlin, though the Memory was telling her this was the life she was meant for, this was the life that offered everything she could possibly desire for herself, lovers and status and presents!

"Ah, now." Uncle Ratlin looked at her anxiously. "You don't really mean that. I know what it is. You're scared of the old bitch. Sweetie, precious babe, she's *old*. And think of the kin. If you don't come back, honey love, what'll we all do? No new stupids to make things, no new Uncles to plot for us! And there's such plotting to be done, now that we've almost got the delivery system perfected. Don't you want to see our ancient enemies ruined entirely?"

Tiara shivered, searching the Memory for the right thing to say. "I wouldn't go back for all the tea in China," she said, though she had only the vaguest idea what that meant. "Live in that bitch's house? Wear her clothes? Sleep in her sheets? You reek of her, you faithless bastard." And she gave Uncle Ratlin what she hoped was an imperious stare.

To her great delight he cringed and whined. Then he looked crafty. "Clever little thing, good baby girl, she's holding out for a better price," he crowed. "That's my darling, what a Quean you'll make! What do you want, sugar, do you want a SoundBox? You want lipsticks? You want cider from the Rising Moon? Or is it nicer things and more refined you want, my jewel? Of course! You're an educated young lady, and I wonder how? But it's holonovels you want, *Love's Purple Passion* and *Her Scarlet Amours,* isn't it? I can bring you all your sweet heart could possibly require, baby love."

"No," said Tiara, lighting up inside because she'd had the most wonderful idea. "I spit on such things. If you are to win my hand, base varlet, you must be worthy. I shall set you a task, and if it is fulfilled to the letter, I shall be yours; but only then."

What a thrill, to see Uncle Ratlin stand speechless with amazement, and annoyance, and *respect*! And he was caving to her, he was going to obey. She could even make Uncle Ratlin obey her now, Uncle Ratlin who was the cleverest uncle who'd ever lived. She threw back her head and laughed at him.

He gnashed his teeth, tugged at his skimpy beard. "Yes, dear," he muttered. "What is it my little Quean would have her servant do?"

"I won't live in that hill," Tiara told him. "It's old and it stinks. I want you to make a new place. Set all your stupids to work on it. A fresh green hill with a clean heart, no trash, no leaks in the tunnels. It must be painted and papered, with windows on the world and curtains of whitest lace. It must be heated and full of fresh air. I want furnishings of the finest, the best you can steal from the big people, and I want—I want a holoset bigger than Barbie's. Do you hear me? These things must I have, or you'll never touch my white skin."

"That'll take years, honey of my heart," groaned Uncle Ratlin. "And I've the plot against the big people going forward, you know. It's almost sprung."

"What do I care?" Tiara said, tossing her head. "Do as I say!"

He growled up high in his throat, but knelt before her and kissed the raggy hem of her gown. "It shall be done, my blossom," he promised, though he showed his teeth. "And where will you be staying in the meantime, might I inquire?"

"I haven't decided yet," she told him. "At a fine hotel, perhaps."

"More likely in the cellar at Wicklow House," Uncle Ratlin guessed. "Am I right? Is that where you've been hiding all these long years? Must be! They've got a grand old library and I never thought to search there, never thought a little thistledown thing like you could float so far."

"A lady never tells her secrets." Tiara put her nose in the air. "And now, if you have no further business, I shall betake myself home."

"And might I escort you?" inquired Uncle Ratlin craftily, bowing and sweeping off his hat to wave it in the direction of the road.

"I thank you, no," she told him, and set off herself, following the stream-bank down to where the water trickled through three big culvert pipes. She crawled in and waited there, under the road, willing Uncle Ratlin to leave with all her heart. After a while she could hear him sighing and padding away through the darkness, away to the front entrance to the hill.

When she was certain he had gone she crawled out and there, as in a dream, a little trout was gliding silently along in the sandy pool. Fast as thought she had it out and flapping on the bank; hooking a finger in its gill she carried it back, in through the old back door and down into the darkness.

Her mind was whirling full of bright images, she could barely think for the claim the Memory had on her just then. What if a new hill *was* made for her, what would it be like to live in such a place? To have her own bright room . . . and lovers, and the likes of Uncle Ratlin waiting on her . . .

But she came through the door of the bone room and there was her slave, huddled up against the cold, turning his blind face to the sound of her. Her heart contracted painfully. The other memory mustered itself, all the places he'd taken her with his voice, all the promise of adventure in the outside world, and love that had nothing to do with sampling men like bonbons, and everything to do with passion and sacrifice and glory . . .

"What is it, child?" The slave stretched out his hand to her. Weeping, she came and laid the trout in it, and threw herself down beside him. "Ah! Fish. Why, Princess, what's the matter? What's happened, my dearest?"

"I met Uncle Ratlin outside," she said, gasping. She felt him draw breath sharply, she heard his heart begin to pound.

"I-Is he coming here? Has he found us out?"

Oh, he was all coming to pieces, her poor darling, he was beginning to tremble. She sat up and put her arms around him. "He has not, nor ever shall," she vowed. "He will never hurt you again, my treasure."

"He'll try to kill me again, and I can't die," the slave gasped. "I wanted to, I tried, I'd have done anything to make him stop, but I couldn't die! No matter how I screamed—and screamed—"

"Hush! Hush, lover mine," Tiara said. "Talk like Commander Edward. Courage, man! We're not beaten yet."

The slave bit his lips to try to control himself. "Yes," he mumbled, "Edward, what would Edward do? Edward would do something clever. Edward would analyze the situation, yes, with perfect sangfroid. Tell me, beloved, what happened out there? Why were you crying when you came in? What did Uncle Ratlin say?"

So Tiara told him how she'd set Uncle Ratlin a task to delay him, just like Odysseus's wife postponing the suitors with her weaving.

"Oh, that was clever, my lovely girl," the slave told her. "You see the benefits of a classical education? I wonder how long it would take him to dig such a hill?" His voice began to go rattly and too fast, like a broken machine. "I expect if he concentrated on it he'd go very quickly indeed, he never gives up, never gives up when he's after something, I prayed he'd get tired and sleep but he never seemed—no, no good there, Edward, calm down, courage, man! Uncle Ratlin's doing something else, isn't he? His grand plot?"

"He's almost got the delivery system perfected, that was what he said," affirmed Tiara.

"Delivery system," repeated the slave. "Delivery? As in, weapons? God Apollo, he must mean—"

"He thought he killed you," realized Tiara, "and so he thinks he can kill all the slaves, that's what the grand plot is. So the big people can't send them to plunder us anymore." She stared into the darkness, marveling at the bigness of the plan, about which she had never thought except in a general taking-for-granted sort of way. It was the history of her race, after all. It was the struggle that had always been going on, to hide from the wicked big people forever. But . . .

"It doesn't matter that he hasn't really killed me," said the slave, clinging to Tiara. "I'm disabled enough as it is . . . listen to me, Tiara, this is very important. You understand that I'm a cyborg? Do you know what that means?"

"Yes," said Tiara slowly, though the Memory was conflicting with the reality she knew. The Memory was insisting on big stalking figures, wielding guns that sprayed death, and poor little kin falling and gasping in the tunnels. Those were the *cyborgs*, surely, and not her own dear slave with his fair hair, with his beautiful blind eyes? Nor Mendoza, who had fallen so passionately in love? And yet—

"You know that I'm more than a machine," said her slave. "And I would never hurt you, dearest Princess. But I and my kind are slaves to the big people, to Dr. Zeus Incorporated. It was Dr. Zeus who sent us in to raid your tunnels and steal your inventions, do you see? And the Company did worse, my darling. They carried off little children of your race and bred them, to see if they could make them invent things in captivity. I know; I saw the proof.

"And because I knew about it, I was betrayed. Dr. Zeus let your people know where to find me, and let me be taken and brought here, where your Uncles did such things—" The slave's voice choked off.

"But why?" Tiara said.

"Because Dr. Zeus is afraid of its slaves, Princess," replied the slave, shuddering. "We are stronger and more clever than the big people, and we never die. If we decided to disobey—if the others knew what has been done to fools like me, or to Mendoza—we might make an end of Dr. Zeus. They don't know how to get rid of us, do you see?

"Dr. Zeus struck a bargain with your kin, my darling. Ratlin told me so himself. Come up with a way to kill us, and in return Dr. Zeus would leave them alone. That's the great plot. Kill two birds with one stone, you see? Steal your people's technology to make themselves powerful, and then let your people do the work of disposing of the thieves."

"Oh, betrayers, oh varlets vile," cried Tiara.

"Yes. And you know, dearest Princess—Dr. Zeus cannot be trusted." The slave turned his face to her. "My people were promised freedom and reward when we had completed our work for the Company. Look what they've planned for us instead! And I very much fear they'll doublecross your uncle Ratlin as well. For, once he's presented them with the weapon they ordered, what need will they have to treat your people fairly? What will prevent them from killing you all, or taking *you* as slaves? Do you want that?"

"Never, never!" Tiara was horrified. This was a great deal too much immediate reality for her liking.

"We immortals might prevent it," said the slave, lowering his head. "But not if we were all crippled as I've been crippled, stacked like so much cordwood in some Company bunker. What will we do, my Princess? How can we save your people and mine?"

"We must be brave," Tiara decided. "We must be heroes." Her eyes grew wide, as all the heroines of all the stories beckoned to her from the shadows, inviting her to become one of their number.

"If only I knew how much time had passed," fretted the slave, "if only I knew where to find the others! I might crawl out of here, even blind, and if I could somehow get word to one of them—Victor or Suleyman—"

"No," said Tiara, rising slowly to her feet. "I will be the beautiful spy. I will pry secrets from Uncle Ratlin."

CHAPTER 6

500,000 BCE: Mr. and Mrs. Checkerfield Are Not Receiving

The Botanist Mendoza can't keep track of time very well nowadays.

She sits at her credenza in the ship's botany cabin, utterly absorbed in an analysis of lysine content for her latest attempt at *Mays mendozaii*. The sun has dropped blazing into the sea, and she hasn't noticed. She wouldn't notice if her hair were on fire. As a matter of fact it is on fire, with a cold blue flame that plays over her features, but she neither sees nor cares.

Certainly she has no idea that she figures as the heroine in a tragically bad adventure novel written by an old friend. She doesn't remember Lewis. Just now, she doesn't remember much of anything.

It's entirely likely that she'd still be staring at the credenza screen by the time the sun climbed up out of the sea again, were it not for the fact that she has someone to look after her.

The door to the botany cabin opens and an extraordinary thing enters, a skeletal creature of gleaming steel, moving scorpionlike on a number of legs. Its skull face and glowing eyes could frighten an unprepared observer into coronary arrest, but Mendoza is oblivious to its approach.

The steel thing stops beside her and proffers the dinner tray it carries. She glances up briefly.

"Thank you, Flint," she says. She becomes fascinated by something on the screen and her hands, which had begun to rise to accept the tray, halt. She remains frozen like that as the minutes pass by. The thing she has addressed as Flint waits patiently.

But the cameras mounted in the upper corners of the room swivel and focus on her, and a moment later the image of a man materializes beside Flint.

Mendoza doesn't notice him either, though he too is extraordinary. Large, powerfully built, attired in a three-piece suit. His wild hair and wild beard are black. He wears a gold earring and looks capable of frightening the Devil himself, though his voice is only mildly reproachful as he says, in a gravelly baritone: "Now then, Mrs. Checkerfield, you stop that and eat yer dinner afore it gets cold."

"Oh." Mendoza looks up from the screen, startled, and notices the tray again. "I beg your pardon, Sir Henry." The fire in her hair dims, dies down a little.

As she takes the tray and lifts the cover from the dish, he saves her work and shuts down the credenza. She notices that no more than she'd noticed the sunset. She turns her whole attention to her meal. Only once or twice does she stall, blank-eyed suddenly, fork halfway to her mouth; and both times the Captain reminds her, and she starts and obediently resumes her meal.

She is not, in fact, a person of diminished capacity. Her problem is exactly the opposite: she is a cyborg, a botanist Preserver drone, formerly the property of Dr. Zeus Incorporated. Mendoza was the inadvertent recipient of a massive transfer of data that overloaded even her fantastically augmented brain.

The Captain has been able to restore function, but only very slowly has he been able to guide her toward any data integration. In the meanwhile her only defense, emotionally and mentally, is a concentration on particular details so intense it resembles autism.

The blue fire is a different matter. It's called Crome's radiation. It's generally only produced by mortals who have been diagnosed as *psychic,* and it's generally invisible. Cyborgs aren't supposed to be able to generate Crome's radiation, visible or otherwise. That Mendoza does, however, is the least of her problems right now.

When she finishes at last, Flint collects the tray and scuttles away to the galley. She turns back to the credenza, but the Captain (Captain Sir Henry Morgan, to use his full name, only indirectly any relation to the legendary pirate) steps close and holds her attention with his sea-colored gaze.

"No, dearie. Exercises come next, remember? And then it'll be time to go see our Alec."

He pauses slightly before he pronounces the name, though she misses it.

"Alec!" Mendoza's face brightens wonderfully. And literally; the cold fire leaps up, dancing. "Okay."

He leads her away, up through the decks of the vast ship to its infirmary.

It should perhaps be further explained here that Captain Morgan is neither a ghost nor a man. He is an Artificial Intelligence, housed for the most part within the ship that bears his name. He is arguably the most powerful AI in existence, which is remarkable, considering that he started out life as a Pembroke Playfriend designed to monitor and amuse children aged four to eleven. He has long since ditched the cocked hat and scarlet coat his little master originally conferred on him, but he is still a pirate, to the deepest core of his consciousness.

In the infirmary, he guides Mendoza to a diagnostic table, where she reclines. A device swings up from the edge of the table and a metal plate touches her left temple. She closes her eyes, sighing.

"Running program seventeen–fifty-two ten," the Captain announces. "Tell me when the little lights turn green, now."

After a moment she says faintly, "Green."

"Good. Five equations this time. Ready? Begin."

A moment passes and she gives no signal, but he nods.

"That's it. That's my girl. Only a little more now: temporospatial calculation from this here grid, aye. You see it? Give me the answer."

"Five hours in thirty-five point two kilometers," says Mendoza without hesitation.

"Beautiful, ma'am," he assures her. "Red light now. Watch for it! Let me know when."

Seconds pass. Mendoza begins to frown. "Let me know when," the Captain repeats. More time goes by and Mendoza clenches her fists, saying nothing. The blue flame flickers high and wild.

"Well, that still weren't bad," the Captain tells her soothingly. "Time. Coda and Exit Three." The device swings back under the table and she sits up, blinking, looking dazed.

"Yer doing grand, dearie. I'll wager none of them Company cyborgs could survive a upgrade like you got and still have anything left to think with! But my girl's smart as paint, ain't she? Now, bedtime. Alec's waiting for you."

Mendoza smiles and lets him lead her into the adjoining room.

This formerly housed the ship's decompression chamber. That area has been transformed into a regeneration tank by filling it with the blue oxygenated medium used for intensive life support. Through its windows can be glimpsed a man, floating motionless in the azure light.

His body is long and lanky but powerfully made, with a slightly odd articulation in the arms and shoulders, and his head and face look a little odd, too: very high wide cheekbones, wide mouth, long nose with a certain irregularity in its bridge suggesting it has been broken.

He is, at least as far as birth certificates and fingerprints go, Alec William St. James Thorne Checkerfield, seventh earl of Finsbury. Appearances can be deceiving, however. The mind occupying Alec's corporeal premises, so to speak, belongs to another gentleman, long disembodied but arguably still alive, who answers to the name of Edward Alton Bell-Fairfax.

Or would do so, were he not deeply unconscious. This is because he is recovering from a near-fatal accident and being rendered immortal in the process. His severed leg has been reattached, his shattered bones mended and converted, atom by atom, to indestructible ferroceramic. Tiny biomechanicals are working through his body, modifying or replacing organs, transforming, transmuting, perfecting, and the sea change has been under way for some weeks now.

Mendoza walks to the window of the tank and presses her hands against it, peering in. The flame about her burns steady, a clear jet. Minutes pass. She appears to have forgotten anything but the man in the tank, and the Captain knows if he doesn't do something she'll stand there all night.

"Bedtime, dearie," he reminds her.

"What?"

"Bedtime. Look! There's yer bed and nightie. And, see? Coxinga's bringing cocoa. You get undressed now like a good lass."

"Okay," she says, and takes off her clothes. The Captain watches her intently, not because he is a lecherous old Artificial Intelligence, but because in this, as in all things nowadays, she tends to focus on one action so closely she forgets anything else.

But she manages to put on her nightgown and climb into the white infirmary bed without further prompting tonight; accepts the proffered cup of cocoa from another of the skeletal creatures and drinks it down. The creature reaches out to take back the empty cup and busies itself picking up her clothes from the places she dropped them. She has focused on the man in the tank again, staring at him with wide black eyes.

The Captain sighs.

"Go to sleep now, darlin'," he tells her. Her eyes close and she relaxes completely, sinking back into the pillows. Coxinga pulls up her blankets for him.

The Captain stands regarding Mendoza thoughtfully. After a moment he extends a yearning hand and places it on her brow, as flames leap up through his illusory fingers.

His gesture of affection is not meant for her, though he's quite fond of Mendoza, in his way; Artificial Intelligences are just as capable of devotion as human beings are. She's a well-behaved and obedient cyborg, but what really matters is that she loves *his boy.* Somewhere behind her brow, in a locked file, his boy's consciousness is trapped. So is that of a similarly disembodied gentleman named Nicholas Harpole. Edward Alton Bell-Fairfax shut them both in there, and only Edward knows the code to release them.

The Captain has taken care of Alec since Alec was five years old. He's not quite sure what the other two entities are. They were once living men, earlier versions of Alec produced by the same Company responsible for creating him from recombinant DNA. When they had served the Company's purpose and been killed, an electromagnetic recording of their personalities—memories, emotions, skills—had gone into storage in their files and remained there, inactive, until Alec accidentally downloaded them into his own brain while fleeing from the Company into the deep past.

The result was a remarkable case of multiple-personality disorder for Alec and a continuing logistical nightmare for the Captain. The only thing on which the three gentlemen wholeheartedly agreed was the fact that they loved Mendoza, who had known each of them in their successive incarnations.

Nicholas Harpole, who lived in the sixteenth century and was a scholar and heretic, managed to adjust somehow to massive culture shock and loss of the foundation on which his religious beliefs stood; but then he was an extraordinary man.

So was Edward Alton Bell-Fairfax.

Edward lived in the nineteenth century and was a political agent for the British Empire. He absorbed all the virtues and most of the vices of that massive institution, along with the cold-blooded practicality that enabled him to do his very unpleasant job. He died heroically in the service of the Gentlemen's Speculative Society, an earlier version of Dr. Zeus Incorporated. His subsequent discovery that they lied to him most of his brief life has not been received well and, unfortunately for his creators, Edward has read *Frankenstein.*

He doesn't think much of his other selves, either.

He dismisses Nicholas as a medieval zealot, limited by ignorance and religious superstition. Cybergenius Alec is in his opinion a dunce, the inevitable product of a soft and degenerate age, and worse: for Alec had been naïve enough to smuggle weapons to a particularly foolhardy group of rebels, and the result had been the destruction of an entire colony on Mars. Hence Alec's flight, with technology he'd stolen from Dr. Zeus, into the past.

Edward's perception of these other selves has decided him that *he* alone is fit to inhabit Alec's body. His effort to achieve this state of independence has been partly responsible for the accident that brought him, maimed and broken, to the regeneration tank, and Mendoza to her present state of impairment, and Alec and Nicholas to . . . well, to the place they now inhabit.

But even if the accident had not occurred, Edward's efforts to kill Alec should have been in vain. Edward is, after all, only a recording, nothing more than a program Alec himself is running, in disassociation response to the psychic trauma of having two additional lifetimes thrust into his memory. Or is he? Why can't Edward be shut off?

And what exactly has happened to Alec and Nicholas?

In the Library

The room has no windows and no doors.

No amount of cozy décor can make up for that fact, not the paneled walls, not the leather-upholstered chairs, not the antique lamp with its pool of yellow light, not the rows and rows of beautifully bound books. Not even the endlessly resupplied decanter of fine old brandy.

The two men in the room are identical in every respect to the man floating in the regeneration tank, except that they wear clothing: black subsuits, the last garments they donned before being trapped in this place. There is no clue to tell them how long they've been here. Neither hair nor nails have grown, and neither of them needs a shave. Despite the fact that they have emptied the decanter more times than they have bothered to count, no bodily functions have demanded their attention.

One of the men is sprawled on the floor, holding a glass of brandy on his chest. The other man sits in one of the chairs, holding a book from which he reads aloud. He has a beautiful voice, a smooth tenor like a well-tuned violin.

". . . 'The bar silver and the arms still lie, for all that I know, where Flint buried them; and certainly they shall lie there for me. Oxen and wain-ropes would not bring me back again to that accursed island; and the worst dreams that ever I have are when I hear the surf booming about its coasts, or start upright in bed, with the sharp voice of Captain Flint still ringing in my ears: "Pieces of eight! Pieces of eight!"' "

He falls silent. Without a word Alec passes him the glass of brandy. He takes it and drinks; refills it from the decanter, and watches gloomily as the level in the decanter rises back as if by magic.

After a moment, Alec sits up and looks at him. "Is that it? That's the end of the book?"

"Ay," says Nicholas, taking a sip of brandy.

"But . . . but Jim doesn't sound happy," says Alec. "What's he mean, he wouldn't go back to Treasure Island? It's the defining event of his whole life. He'd rather go back and serve drinks at the Admiral Benbow?"

"Belike he was wise enough to know when he was well off," Nicholas replies. "Thou went'st adventuring, and see to what dismal end thou art brought."

Alec shivers.

"It's not the end," he says quickly. "Edward'll let us out. The Captain will make him let us out. We won't be in here forever! It hasn't even been nine months yet. Has it?"

In fact it has been longer than nine months, and both of them know that perfectly well. Nicholas sighs.

"No, surely not," he lies. He is more resigned than Alec to the idea of being trapped here. He has been dead longer, after all.

"And when we get out, man . . ." Alec smacks his fist into the upholstery of the chair. "Edward'll be sorry."

Nicholas just nods, though he wonders uneasily whether Edward is not already sorry. For the—hundredth?—time, he looks over at the shelf where the broken brandy glass sits. Edward had provided them with a matched set when he trapped them here, but there had been something like an earthquake within a few minutes of their arrival. One of the glasses had been shattered, the very fabric of the room had flexed and seemed on the verge of tearing apart before sudden quiet had returned. It had taken them hours to pick up all the books from the floor.

They haven't discussed the earthquake much since, because there is a real possibility that its occurrence meant something went terribly wrong with Edward's plan and they are locked in here for eternity. Nicholas watches now as Alec leaps to his feet and punches the chair again.

"I wish that was him," says Alec hoarsely. "I'd like to knock that superior smile off his face, like *this*—" He punches the chair once more, harder, and harder again, until it slams backward into the wall. He seizes it, ready to break the thing into kindling.

"Peace, thou!" Nicholas rises to his feet. Alec turns as if to fight, but Nicholas catches his fists.

"I want to kill him," gasps Alec, shaking. "I never wanted to kill anybody in my life, but I'd like to kill *him*. One stupid mistake on Mars and I snuffed out three thousand people, but nothing, *nothing* ever gets rid of Edward Alton

Bell-Fairfax. Hey, do you suppose we're in Hell?" He pulls free, grinning bitterly at Nicholas. "Mr. Puritan Christian?"

"We might be," says Nicholas, in a low voice.

"At least I'd finally be where I belonged, yeah?" says Alec. "Not quite what
I'd expected, though. I should have got here in a fiery crash or, or a special
state execution, and there ought to be demons queued up to eat my liver for
all eternity or something, under flaming brass letters ten feet high spelling out
'The Hangar Twelve Man Gets What He Deserves!' Instead, I got this shracking library. And you. I don't know how you fit into the picture at all."

"No more do I," says Nicholas. He stares over Alec's shoulder at the dark
wall, and attempts to summon faith. He can't. His time in this room has not
reconciled him with his God.

"I used to think if I died, it'd make up for everything I'd done wrong," says
Alec, slumping into his chair. "But things just got worse, didn't they? Because
I failed Mendoza. Edward's got her all to himself now, and he'll do whatever
he wants with her."

"I have failed her twice," says Nicholas. Alec looks up at his bleak face and
regrets his words.

"Though he'd never actually hurt her," he says. "Really. He's a bastard, but
Edward wouldn't do that. He'd take care of her. Look, this isn't helping either
of us. Why don't you read again?"

He hands Nicholas the brandy glass. Nicholas sighs, goes to the shelves
and peers at the ranged titles a moment before selecting one. He returns to his
chair and opens the book. Clearing his throat, he begins:

"The Origin of Species by Means of Natural Selection, or, The Preservation
of Favored Races in the Struggle for Life, by Charles Darwin . . ."

Outside the Library

The Captain lifts his hand from Mendoza's brow and sighs. Where, in that
wrecked storehouse of memories, is his boy? He extinguishes the lamps in the
room. Its sole illumination now is the glowing blue tank and Mendoza's blue
fire, like the most outré of nursery lights, and he scans his systems to determine that all is well on board the *Captain Morgan*. Yes, everything's shipshape;
but satellite data is coming in to warn him of a storm approaching this part of
what will one day be the Atlantic Ocean. He lets his visual image dissolve, and
turns his attention to setting a course for safe anchorage.

The great ship claps on sail, tacks and glides away through the night.

Edward Triumphant

Night again. No storm now, in fact the *Captain Morgan*'s becalmed on a mirror of burning stars that move only slightly more than the stars overhead.

Encouraged by this extreme stability, the Captain has chosen this night for the ultimate step in Edward's immortality process.

He has prepared the modified 4/15 support package to insert in the brain. It will be a complicated surgery, requiring removal of preexisting hardware through the nasal fossa and installation of the support package the same way.

Once it's in place, two things will happen: the process of augmentation of Edward's mental powers will begin, and a small pulsing time transcendence field will be generated within the cavity of his skull. Blood will flow in and out; nothing else ever can, from that moment, and if the blood supply should be contaminated or cut off, the support package will substitute its own analogous fluid, which will, endlessly recycled, keep the brain alive in a fugue state until repair becomes possible.

As soon as tonight's work is completed, the biomechanicals within Edward's body will finish the process of transforming his mortal skull to ferroceramic and he will be, to all intents and purposes, as immortal as Mendoza. Indeed, he'll be superior; she was made from an ordinary human child. Edward, like Alec and Nicholas, is not human. His brain has greater capacity, better connections, and a host of other engineered improvements. His body, likewise, surpasses the human model in a dozen subtle ways.

Mendoza is fast asleep in her bed in the infirmary, mildly sedated with a theobromine derivative. The Captain would prefer she sleep through the operation, for a variety of reasons.

This is the night on which the Captain would have fulfilled his program to the greatest extent possible, and perhaps only a machine could appreciate the sense of frustration he is experiencing. But for Edward's treachery his boy would have been, finally and forever, *safe*.

He still has one shot left in his locker, one hope to restore Alec's consciousness to its own body. He materializes, now, before the blue-glowing tank in the infirmary, but his form is shifting and indistinct, a screen of woven fire with a vague man-shape. What will intimidate Edward? After a moment's thought he solidifies into his usual appearance, but wearing the uniform of the mid-nineteenth-century Royal Navy, an admiral's rig, with the added touch that his beard and hair are wilder, blacker, coiling like poisonous snakes.

Wake up, you bastard.

Edward's eyes open, so pale a blue that through the cerulean bioregenerant they look colorless as glass. They attempt to focus; squeeze shut as disorientation overwhelms, open again. He bares his formidable teeth.

Mendoza! Edward sees through the glass the sleeping figure in the white bed, and flails an arm in an attempt to reach her.

I salvaged Mendoza. She's a strong little girl; she'll mend even after what you done to her. You'd best save yer worries for yer own damned hide.

Edward turns his face, sees the Captain, and the image has its intended effect: for a split second he looks terrified. He moves defensively and the motion sets him turning gently through the blue fluid. As he turns he stares about him, realizing where he must be. By the time he completes his revolution and faces the Captain, he is smiling, narrow-eyed.

Why, Captain, whatever could you mean? transmits Edward.

I mean you got exactly five minutes to bring my Alec back from that site you got him stowed in, or I'll make it so damned hot for you you'll wish you was still dead.

Hmm. You can't mean that literally; you won't damage this body you've taken such pains to keep alive. And what a job you've done! I feel quite fit. Is that my missing leg, reattached? My compliments, Captain. You've worked wonders for me. I must be very nearly immortal by now.

That's Alec's leg, damn you! And you ain't immortal yet, laddie. I ain't going ahead with the last step until I get what I'm after. Give me the code to access that site. Let me rescue my boy, and you'll get yer bloody immortality.

But brother Alec's quite safe where he is, Captain. Likewise brother Nicholas. Edward's smile widens as he looks out at Mendoza. *What file location could be safer? My own true love bears them, as it were, in the womb of her memory. However, even she doesn't know how to set them free. My safety precaution, of course.*

Give me that code, you lying son of a whore, or you'll be sorry.

I doubt that very much. Checkmate, Captain, old man! Now, why don't you get on with the business at hand?

The Captain has hoped to avoid this moment, but is driven to a last, untested resort. He glares at Edward, who is shaken by a sudden spasm. Edward's right hand clenches, rises to his face, strikes his chin lightly.

What—

You been in that tank months, my lad. Don't you think I might have had the chance to install a little extra subroutine, whilst I was a-mending you,

in all that time? Something to control yer motor reflexes, like? Just as a bargaining point?

Edward's eyes blaze at him. Slowly, with tremendous effort, the hand unclenches, the arm lowers.

Oh, bugger. Well, it was worth a shot.

Don't think you can trifle with me! I want life again, Captain, and I'll have it, Edward transmits sharply. *I've work to do in this weary world. You have my word as a gentleman I'll release Alec and Nicholas . . . as soon as we've made flesh to house them.*

Mendoza turns and murmurs uneasily in her sleep.

Come now, Captain. We don't want to wake my dear wife. Get on with it!

The Captain indulges in some language that would blister the paint off a warship's hull. He growls assent, an ominous noise that seems to come from everywhere within the ship. A pair of padded clamps emerge from the wall of the tank and seize Edward's head in a secure grip, and cables snake out through the fluid and secure his limbs.

The specialized servounit descends into the tank and moves straight toward his face, extending its sharp-edged probe. Edward struggles, but is held fast.

So it's a checkmate, is it? Sure you don't want to give me that code, Commander Bell-Fairfax, sir?

Edward closes his eyes tight. The Captain urges the probe nearer. It whirrs and Edward's eyes open to regard the little razor edges turning, each in its own clever pivot.

It's a bluff, damn you. You don't dare injure me.

Did I say I was going to injure you, Commander? Not I; though if I took it into my head to do that, I could repair any damage I done good as new, so I reckon you'd better not tempt me.

But it might come to just that, mightn't it, Captain? Be certain you know exactly when to pull back. Perhaps you can repair anything you do to my body, but what if you damage my mind? Suppose I go mad and forget how to retrieve Alec? It might happen that way, you know.

Bloody hell, boy. If I was a kindly old pirate like Long John Silver, I'd admire the nerve of you. But I'm a machine, Edward, ain't you forgetting? I got programming tells me what to do, not feelings. I'm supposed to protect my boy. I want that code! And if I have to hurt you to get it, there ain't nothing will stop me once I start. You see?

Edward controls his panic. *Why, Captain. The minute I gave it up you'd lock me away somewhere unpleasant and give this body back to Alec. Consider my choices: eternal life at the cost of a little discomfort versus whatever you'd do to me once I'd lost my tactical advantage.* He masters himself enough to widen his eyes and, in a fair approximation of Alec's voice, transmits: *Please, Captain sir, I'm still your boy! Even if you did let Edward kill me. You wouldn't really let him lose me forever, would you?*

It is a moment before the Captain responds.

You little bastard. You won't give an inch, will you? Yer going to force my hand. Well, I'll just follow orders, like the honest seaman I am. I'll get on with the immortality process, by thunder. But unless you want to go through it fully conscious, you'll give me that code now.

Do your worst; it won't be enough.

I reckon we've struck, then, says the Captain grimly. **Here's yer immortality, damn you.**

He activates the probe. Edward stiffens in horror as it seeks tentatively and then cuts deftly into its target. After a moment he is unable to keep silent, and altogether it is a good thing that Mendoza is sedated and can't hear him.

Three times, the Captain pauses in the procedure to inquire whether Edward will give him the code. Edward is unable to reply coherently, but he will not yield.

By the third time his voice, which has lost its dignity and its control, so much resembles young Alec's that the Captain would be weeping if he were not a machine. Still, not until the probe has traveled halfway to the brain does the Captain concede, grant Edward victory and merciful unconsciousness.

CHAPTER 7

Extract from the Journal of the Botanist Mendoza:
Furiously, in the Bedroom

I just broke a table in half.

Clearly I am not quite myself yet.

There are, for example, surgically tidy holes in my memory. I know certain unspeakable things happened to me, at a place called—no, can't remember it. Can't remember anything about that. It might have happened to someone else, as far as my memory is concerned.

Yet other memories have returned with disgusting clarity: I know that I'm a Crome generator, burdened with freakish precognition. Look at me, blazing like a damned dish of cherries jubilee. Or the Ghost of Christmas Past.

What happened?

I remember staring, fascinated, at the Indian maize analysis. The eternal quest, for fields stretching to far horizons, kernels bright-striped in all possible colors, gritstone meal feeding multitudes that thrive . . .

Unbidden before my sight came an image: the figure of a man woven together out of grain stalks, bound with bright ribbon, his featureless face an enigma.

I rubbed my eyes. The image meant nothing to me.

Abruptly, Sir Henry was standing at my side. He looked somber. "I've work for you, dearie," he said. "Come with me."

"Okay," I said, and started to obey, but the figures drew me in again as soon as I turned my face to the screen. Sir Henry had to order the credenza to save and shut itself down. I sat blinking at it until he waved his hand in front of my face—how humiliating!—and then allowed myself to be led away through the ship.

We went to the infirmary and there was my darling's body, floating in the blue light. I went at once to the window. Who did I think I saw?

Why, the one constant in my patchwork memory. We'd always been together. I could dimly remember when we walked in the garden of a Tudor manor house, though that had been a long time ago, and there was something sad about the memory. I had vague impressions, too, that we'd worn the clothing of many other eras. That was all I knew for certain. I had an uneasy feeling that bad things had happened to us, and that *Alec* was only one of his names . . .

Sir Henry had followed me. He put his mouth close to my ear, as though I were deaf. "Would you like him to come out of there now?"

No lapse in my attention then. "Oh," I cried. "Yes, please! How do we get him out?"

"I'll drain the tank, and you get undressed," he replied. "Then you go in and help him. You'll know what to do."

I hurried out of my clothing as the bioregenerant medium gurgled away, and Alec's body sank down through the tank until it lay in a fetal curve on the tile floor. It looked blue and drowned, but the red scars from the augmentation surgery had already vanished, healed without trace. The spiraling tattoo pattern across his shoulders was pulsing like blue neon. To my joy I saw he was already trembling, one shaky hand was groping across the tiles.

"Alec!" I splashed in, fell to my knees beside him. "Up, up, come on, my love!"

Such joy. I got my arms around his chest and hauled him into a sitting position. He was turning his head blindly, as the thick blue fluid streamed down from his face, and his lank hair was dark with it. Even in such a moment, he was beautiful to me. Deftly I slipped behind him and performed a Heimlich maneuver.

His head reared up and he spat out a tremendous gob of the bioregenerant. Lurching forward onto his hands and knees he began to cough, violently expelling the stuff from his lungs; I pounded helpfully on his back, yelling, "That's it, darling!"

He pushed himself upright, threw his head back, drew in a first whooping breath as I clung to him, laughing and crying. He began to laugh, too, wild gurgling laughter, gasping as his lungs continued to clear. Raising his fists at the ceiling of the chamber he howled: "LIIIIIIIFE!"

Lowering his arms he wrapped them around me and held me tight, swaying back and forth, gulping for breath a moment; then he bent to kiss me. I was so happy.

"I've missed you terribly, Alec, you have no idea, but you're all right now and we'll never lose each other again—" I babbled between kisses. He rose with me into a crouch and stood slowly, and all mortal clumsiness had gone forever from the motion of his body. I didn't know, yet, addled as I was, what was different about him.

But he must have been acutely aware of the change. He stood still a moment, his eyes wide. "Great God," he said, his voice hoarse and hushed with awe. "So this is—"

"This is how you're supposed to be, Alec," I told him in my charmingly vacant way. "Good as new!"

He looked down at me, such speculation in his eyes.

I led him out to the shower, chattering away like a blissful idiot. He started at the first touch of spray on his changed skin; then opened his mouth and drank, seemingly fascinated by the taste of water. I cupped my hands and washed him, sluicing away the last of the bioregenerant from his body. He seemed greedy for sensation, opened each of the bottles of shampoo and soap to inhale their fragrances, gleeful.

When we stepped out, he seized the nearest towel and buried his face in it, became so involved in some mysterious worship of terry cloth that I had to take another towel and rub him dry. Oh, he liked that; liked it even better when I brought his silk robe and wrestled him into it. He noticed the infirmary cabin beyond, and barely let me tie the robe closed before he went bolting out there to run his hands over the blanket on the bed, seize up the glass vials and bottles to admire their sparkle. When I brought him his torque, he actually put out his tongue and *tasted it* before letting me slip it around his neck; exclaimed over the bright gleam of his wedding ring when I put it back on his finger.

He was beginning to laugh again, and I laughed with him, so giddy I had forgotten to dry myself or put on a stitch. Sir Henry, who had discreetly disappeared, was making polite throat-clearing noises to give me a clue, but I was oblivious.

"Ah," yelled my darling, noticing the door. Only a split second he fumbled with the lock before he ran out on deck. There he stopped, transfixed with amazement. The twilit sea still gleaming, evening star and new moon bright, a million stars, yes, I'd have stared too if I were seeing them for the first time with an immortal's senses.

He caught his breath. He was trembling. At last he spoke.

"'. . . *Look how the floor of heaven*
  Is thick inlaid with patines of bright gold:

There's not the smallest orb that thou behold'st
But in his motion like an angel sings,
Still choiring to the young-ey'd cherubins;
Such harmony is in immortal souls;
But, whilst the muddy vesture of decay
Doth grossly close it in, we cannot hear it.' "

By the end of the Shakespeare quote he was shouting, his glorious voice without strain echoing from the masts and spars cathedral-high above us.

I could have stood there forever, just smiling at my monster through happy tears; but he turned to me as if for confirmation and *then* he noticed I was still naked. He advanced on me, caught me up in his arms with a whoop of triumph and bore me inside to the bed. "Now," he yelled gleefully, "my love, we'll change the world!"

And there, above me, poised, he halted: frowned. "You're hurt," he said, perhaps as it occurred to him that I was on fire with Crome's radiation.

"No, no, Alec, I'm fine," I told him, stroking back his wet hair. As though I could have concealed the shame of my impairment! "See? And you're fine, too."

But he placed a tentative hand on my forehead. "Just—there—"

I suppose he didn't know then the words for what was wrong, but he must have been able to see it clearly enough. He got that determined look on his face, the one that means he *knows* he's right regardless of reason or reality. He took my face in his hands and pushed into the wrecked place in my mind, which did hurt. I cried out once; then surrendered, as I always have, and he was inside me in an entirely new way.

Was it like roaring through darkness, across a landscape lit here and there by the fires of war? Everything burnt, blocked, misaligned? Rows of lights blinked out of sequence: he changed their pattern. Tumbled and scattered structures sprawled before those all-seeing eyes of his: he righted them, arranged them into order. Meaningless dark unkeyed strings of numbers flamed into reason and purpose for him. What had taken Sir Henry months to even begin by therapy, proceeding painfully and with infinite effort, my lover accomplished in a moment. Only that one secret file he left hidden from me, Alec and Nicholas encrypted, such loving treachery.

What was it like for me, being healed of the ruin of my wits? It was exquisite pleasure, indescribable but certainly better than sex. I had lost all fear and was yielding everything up to his probing mind, even those blocked and obliterated files, although I think he hadn't quite got to them when . . .

Well, there were no longer walls between us, in his new state, and he didn't know how to shield his mind from me. The darkness was lit, and in that illumination we beheld each other with utter clarity, absolute intimacy. Communion at last.

I screamed, did my best to pull away from him. He was holding me far too close for that and I went limp in his arms, staring up at him in horror. "You're not Alec!" I said.

Distantly we heard Sir Henry's bitter laughter.

"No, my dear," the man who held me admitted, and his poor face was white as though I'd just driven a knife into his heart. "My name is Edward Alton Bell-Fairfax. I believe you loved me, once."

I wish I hadn't taken so long to understand. He looked as though he had begun to grasp what Eternity means while I lay there silent, as though it had at last occurred to him that he is now unable to die, even if he might want to.

But I groped in my newly-restored memory and there it was, 1863, the deck of the *J. M. Chapman* where my Victorian gentleman lay dying in my arms, gunned down by American Pinkerton agents who were, understandably, attempting to foil a British plot to seize California from the embattled Union.

". . . Edward? But they killed you—"

"Not quite," he told me. I threw my arms around his neck and burst into tears. For a moment, it was 1863 and some wonderful, improbable thing had happened, to be greedily accepted without question. "I came back for you," he said. "I set you free."

But since when did my tragedies miraculously reverse themselves? Where was Alec, to whom I'd been married before the accident? The man I'd supposed was some kind of reincarnation of Edward himself, whom I had in turn taken for a reincarnation of my lost love, Nicholas Harpole? . . .

I reckon you'd better come clean and tell her the whole truth, Commander Bell-Fairfax, sir, suggested Sir Henry from the ship's speakers. There was a certain grim triumph in his voice.

It was a little late for that, however. The moment I wondered, my repaired cyborg brain instantly filled me in on what I'd been missing the last couple of years, during which Edward and Alec *and* Nicholas (!) were all crammed together in one body, struggling in an ever-escalating war for dominance. I had all the data gleaned from my perfect communion with Edward's cyborg brain, too. I knew everything now, including how he'd come to lie here beside me.

It hit me like an anvil dropped out a window. I writhed from his arms, sat up.

"Edward," I gasped, "what have you done?"

At least now I understood the abrupt changes in his (their) moods all those months we adventured together on this ship, those inexplicable moments when his (their) speech would switch from twenty-fourth-century Transatlantic slang to Tudor English to that smooth, suave, and ever-so-well-bred Victorian voice . . . stammering a bit now as he told me how he'd reluctantly come to the conclusion that the others weren't worthy of me, how therefore he'd found a way to take sole possession of Alec's body, imprisoning Alec and Nicholas somewhere while he planned to *perhaps* grow them new bodies, using the only available womb . . . mine. But by the time he paused to catch his immortal breath, I wasn't listening anymore.

Nicholas Harpole. My beloved, not dead after all though his body was ashes, not even reincarnated, the man himself as I last knew him in a cell in Rochester in 1555. He had not rested. He had found me again, and Edward—

"You betrayed him." I covered my face with my hands. "Oh, Edward, you betrayed them both."

"No! All I wanted was to have my own life back," Edward said. "I had work to do! And if they hadn't been squeamish, there'd have been no need for any deception."

"But you tricked them anyway," I said. I was too furious to look at him. "Oh, Nicholas! He could barely speak to me—" I closed my eyes as the tears started again. "And poor Alec—"

Which was when I remembered the reason I had gone *willingly* into that unspeakable place of unspeakable things. Alec, playing at being a hero, had stolen a Company shuttle and smuggled a bomb to Mars. With my help.

"Oh, dear God, he was the Hangar Twelve Man!" I said in horror.

"I'm afraid so," said Edward, reaching out to turn my face to his. "Scarcely the mate you deserved, you see? The boy was a fatal blunderer—"

"He was a fool, but he wasn't an evil man," I said. I struck his hand away. "Nothing like the opportunist you are. You were just going to take everything from him, weren't you? His ship, his life, and . . . me."

Edward drew himself up, unflinching. "You, at least, my dear," he said. "Can you blame me?"

"Yes," I said. "Damn you! You'll always find a way to destroy yourself. Split you into three, and you just turn on each other! My God, you've done it again, only this time you're able to sit here and argue the point with me."

"I am not arguing with you," said Edward coolly, though he was still very pale. "And I point out that no one has been destroyed."

"No, just consigned to some—some void in my memory!"

"And what better place for him? What would Alec have done with eternal life, but wasted it? I at least have a purpose in this world!" said Edward, with heat. "And if Alec hadn't been *betrayed,* as you put it, if he were sitting here now and all had gone according to the Captain's plan, Nicholas should have been consigned to a much less congenial void. And so should I. Doubtless that would have displeased you less, however."

"*NO,*" I screamed, beating my fists against the mattress. "No, you big— Why am I even trying? I have spent years, innumerable years, unbearable *years* of my life mourning for you! All the lost chances, all the false starts—" I was still fighting furious tears as I raised my head to glare at him. "You liar. Oh, you smooth liar. All that business about wanting to have a baby of our own was a lie, too, wasn't it?"

"Not as such," he hastened to say. "It truly was my intention to provide for Nicholas and Alec, and what better way? Only think, my love, what transcendent intimacy this miracle would confer. You will become our fount of life! Poor Alec will know a mother's love at last, and Nicholas—"

"What're they supposed to do when they grow up?" I cried in horror. "Can you imagine the conflicts for them? Did it ever occur to you to wonder how *I* might feel about this?"

"My love, your happiness has been my greatest concern," he assured me, sliding an arm around my shoulders. "All your life, you have been deprived of any shred of domestic felicity. No hearth. No home. No children. Your maternal instincts, so long denied, can be expressed at last in our union. Consider, my dearest love, that I now have the power to grant you fulfillment as a woman!"

"Who the hell are you to decide how I ought to be fulfilled as a woman?" I said, throwing off his arm. He caught both my hands in his, and I couldn't pull them away.

"The missing half of your soul," he said, looking earnestly into my eyes. "And I stand beside you on the threshold of a destiny of which you have never dreamed."

Nice words. He had me soothed for a moment, before it occurred to me they were familiar somehow. He was paraphrasing something I'd said. He was quoting from . . .

"You read my journal?" I demanded. He winced, and I knew he had read it.

Haar, Edward, yer on a reef now, chortled Sir Henry.

And with that I jumped up and went marching out on deck, still shooting sparks, ignoring his conciliatory noises as he chased after me all the way to

Alec's stateroom, and into Alec's vast bed with its dreadful pirate motifs and crimson counterpane.

I flung myself down in it and pulled the coverlet up, rolling as far from Edward as I could get and still remain in the bed. And I thought that would be that, and lay there shaking with anger and remorse. But he advanced across the bed like a big cat and reached out to put his hand on my shoulder.

"My dear," he said, "this is no way to begin a marriage."

Furious, I rolled over and swung at him, intending to knock him across the room. Long ago I'd belted Nicholas once, poor darling must have seen stars, but he forbore to hit me back and dear God I'd wished I could cut off my hand the second after, I was so sorry.

But Edward is no longer a mortal man. No mortal eye could have seen his hand closing on my wrist, so quick he caught me. He held me immobile a long moment and space/time creaked with the strain, I'd swear, irresistible force pitted against immovable object, until at last I began to tremble and he forced my wrist slowly backward. I tried to spit in his face, but my mouth was too dry.

"No," he said in a patient voice, staring down into my eyes. "I will not lose you like this."

I writhed in an attempt to throw him off. I might as well have struggled against the weight of a planet. He held my gaze with those pale eyes, the black pupils dilated wide, and the fight just left my body. I wondered, briefly, if he used to do this to the people the Company sent him to kill, if they dropped their defenses and waited meekly for his knife, his garrote, his big clever hands . . .

He wouldn't let me look away from him. Lowering his face to mine, he inhaled the scent of my skin, and kissed my cheek. He kissed my throat slowly, to the pulse under my ear.

I can't honestly say he raped me. He was so careful, took such infinite pains with me, was as gentle as Nicholas had ever been, and not even the knowledge of what he'd done to Nicholas was enough to keep my body from doublecrossing me. It just surrendered. I grit my teeth to think how little time it took before I was weeping, pleading with him softly, and not to be let go.

Such a persuasive hand, with its gold wedding band gleaming. I wear the ring's mate. Nicholas married me, with those rings made from one gold doubloon, in the pirate city Alec wanted so much to explore. But Edward will be my husband.

Damn him.

He didn't even gloat afterward. I wasn't allowed that much high ground over the man. He was tender, he was courteous, tucked the sheet about me decorously before turning away after I made it clear I was in no mood for postcoital chat. Was confident enough of his victory to go to sleep with me lying there beside him, though I might have done anything.

What *do* I do about this man, this superior product of a self-righteous age, who has had the monumental arrogance to decide Nicholas and Alec are unnecessary to my happiness?

Though he says they never loved me enough. He points out that Nicholas left me, when he discovered what I really was; and Alec was just as horrified to learn the truth. Only he, Edward, was able to absorb the idea of cyborged immortality without revulsion, and love me anyway.

No. That's his version of the story, told to show himself to the greatest possible advantage over the others. My lying darling bastard . . .

He looks stupid when he's asleep. Big mule-face is relaxed, what outlandish features he has anyway, how can I stand to have those immense teeth near me? And all the color drains out of him. But the second he wakes, everything changes utterly. The hot blood rises to his skin and the sharp soul looks out of those eyes, the features become animated, fantastically charming and clever. A blazing angel housed in his base clay. Bloody golem.

Or maybe the more correct term would be *nephilim.* No Sons of God getting mighty men on mortal women; only Facilitators in charge of the Company's breeding program to produce his ghastly predecessors, the old Enforcers. Giants in the earth indeed. Pale-eyed slaughterers, utterly self-righteous, unstoppable. Like my lover.

Listen to him snoring. How many nights have I fallen asleep to that sound? That one imperfection is left from his mortal days, that irregularity in the bridge of his nose. Some damned inept Company operative rammed a black box up it, moments after his birth. Poor tiny beloved, almost his first sensation in life must have been suffocating pain . . .

Well. Having got up and wandered the ship, smashed a little furniture, gotten a grip on myself, and ordered writing materials from Sir Henry, here I sit at two-hundred hours attempting to work this out, as that man sprawls in our bed.

Edward Alton Bell-Fairfax.

The distinguished gentleman homicide. Brave, resourceful, clever, ruthless, sentimentally fond of Shakespeare, serviceable villain, capable of subduing any moral qualms he might feel in the service of whatever great lie he currently believes. Now he's set on rebellion against Dr. Zeus. Does he even understand that, of the three men, he is the closest to being the perfect superslave the Company was seeking when it designed them? That he has the greatest capacity for real evil?

He's learned nothing from his life and death that I can see, he still has all the presumption of the empire-building age in which he drew his last mortal breath. Now he's immortal, and has plans for the world. My lover. My *husband*.

I lost my human soul when I lost Nicholas. Mars Two damned me with Alec, poor fool as he was, and all the improbable hope he represented. Now what have I left to lose? And how well we always understood each other, Edward and I. We were equals. Matched blades. Professionals.

God help me. I have no moral center at all, have I?

None at all. I look across at that beautiful insolent profile, even idiot-slack with sleep, and I know I would do anything he asked. Edward braved Hell for my sake. He fought an unthinkable monster for me. His resolve and his courage have enabled us to flee the Company successfully, and his cunning may yet bring it down.

I love that man lying there with my whole heart and my whole soul. Whatever he is, monster or angel of light, I belong to Edward Alton Bell-Fairfax.

But I don't trust him.

Do I have the strength to leave him?

Edward Imperator

By the time Coxinga creeps in cautiously with the breakfast tray, Mendoza is leaning up on one elbow to watch Edward as he sleeps. Her eyes are tired, her mouth a thin line. The blue flames are barely visible now, a faint corona around her.

Good morning, ma'am, the Captain greets her quietly from the speakers, preferring not to risk a visual projection. **Wind's out of the northeast, two-foot swells, temperature is—**

"Were you really going to shut him off, Sir Henry?" she asks him.

Ah—well now, dearie, I didn't have much choice, you see. You was perfectly happy with my Alec, you'd never have missed what you didn't remember . . . and it wouldn't have worked, the three of 'em fighting it out in one body for all time.

"Maybe not." She looks up at the nearest camera. "But what's done is done. I won't have Edward shut down, or whatever it was you were going to do to him. Ever."

And my boy, ma'am? What about Alec?

"What about Alec," Mendoza says, in an exhausted voice. "What about the Hangar Twelve Man? He can't have known what he was doing when he took that bomb to Mars. Can he?"

No, by thunder! He never meant to hurt nobody! Please, ma'am, he's with you already; you can give him flesh again. Give me back my little Alec, what set me free.

"But is it right?" says Mendoza. "I know what he is now. What they all are. What will he do to the world this time, if I give you your boy?"

Why, what harm should he do, with you there to see he don't get a lot of damn fool ideas in his little head? And no bastard of a Dr. Zeus leading him astray no more.

"A fine moral example I am." Mendoza does not smile. "I can't even say no to *you*, can I? But I want Nicholas, too, do you understand? I want my soul back."

Bless you, dearie, that's talking!

"Twins. I must be out of my mind. I assume you can disable my contraceptive symbiote?"

Already have done, ma'am.

"Have you now? That's interesting. I wonder what else you did, while I was too damaged to understand?"

Aw, now, ma'am, it weren't like that at all . . .

"Wasn't it? I didn't notice Flint or Billy Bones coming to my rescue, when Edward had his wicked way with me. Afraid to damage the body, even if Alec isn't in it anymore?"

Er—erm—well, now, I'm sorry about that, but there's that there Asimov's Law of Robotics, you know, and . . . and anyhow I'm programmed to look the other way when events of a personal and private nature is going on. So I gave you yer privacy and beat to windward, ma'am.

"Yes, I'll just bet you did." She reaches out to stroke back Edward's hair from his brow. "What a strange little family we're going to make, eh?"

Edward opens his eyes and smiles at her.

"And I'll bet you've been listening to every word we've said, haven't you, you evil man?" she says, leaning down to kiss him.

"Why, no, my dear, I haven't," he lies.

Breakfast and a seduction make relations much more cordial.

"*This* is what I've wanted," says Edward at last, sprawling back amid the pillows. He pulls her in close and kisses her. "The charming Botanist Mendoza, and a body with which to do hers justice."

"Oh, you want a great deal more than that," says Mendoza sadly, snuggling against him. "World domination at least, I'm sure. The ignorant masses forcibly taught the earth-shaking benefits of your big ideas. You never stay in my bed for long."

"You haven't forgiven me yet, have you?" Edward looks down at her.

"Not at all, señor."

He smiles and leans his head back again. "You needn't worry, my love. No more doomed crusades. At last, I have the power to fulfill my purpose in life! Breaking the Company will be only the first step. Human society can be re-organized along rational lines at last, and they *will* benefit from my rule, depend upon it."

Mendoza sighs. "And you have the right to rule the mortals because . . . ?"

"The mortals themselves created me to do so," says Edward, quite seriously. "And it is not only my right, but my sacred duty. Struggling humanity must be assisted, and who better than I to destroy darkness and bring enlightenment? I am, after all, superior mentally and physically in every respect, and now as a cyberorganism—"

"Let me give you a download, Ubermensch, and show you where that line of thinking got mortals," says Mendoza sharply. She sets her index finger between his eyes. He smiles indulgently at first. Before she has finished transmitting data he is frowning.

"What a ghastly mess. But you're missing the point entirely! I *am* a superior life form, whereas Nietzsche and his ilk were no better than immoral savages, and in any case I won't need armies—here, let me counter your argument with a Shavian interpretation of the—" He downloads to her.

She blinks, accessing the material, and scowls at him. "That's all very well, señor, but look closely at what the Church of God-A did with that idea—" More history is downloaded, and Edward shakes his head impatiently.

"The clear fallacy here is that—"

"You're still thinking like a mortal—"

"If you'll just consider these figures—"

Data hums and zips between them, until the air about their bodies crackles with static charge. Mendoza leans away at last.

"I don't know why I'm bothering to argue," she says bitterly. "But don't expect *me* to go along with your plans, señor. As soon as I've got Alec and Nicholas back, you can go off and be God Almighty on your own."

Edward pulls her close again at once. "Oh, no. My own love, you're wise enough to make the best of things," he says, ever so smoothly. "You are, after all, my partner, my equal, my predestined mate. You'll stay with me."

"I won't."

"Stay with me." His arms close a little more tightly. His voice is so tender, so winning, it could persuade an angel to leap into the fiery gulf. "Only think what a glorious adventure lies before us! Domestic happiness, ours at last. Freed from our shackles to live as a true man and true woman, we will explore together the limitless horizon of this new world. No masters to whom we must answer, no missions hanging in the balance. We have at last the time we lacked . . . my *wife*."

Mendoza winces, remembering lost chances and false starts. She glares up at him, and grasps at the only straw she can. "If I stay, I want something from you, señor."

"You will have anything it is in my power to give you," he assures her.

"All right: I want twenty years, before you descend on the mortals and conquer them. Postpone your divine purpose for humanity, at least until after you've grown bored with our domestic idyll."

She looks him in the eye. He smiles, unaware that this moment will decide the fate of the world.

"A mere twenty? Of course! Given our present position half a million years in the past, give or take a millennium—I think we needn't be in too great a hurry to send Victor Frankenstein chasing across the ice floes. You'll bear our children first, my dear, and who knows? It may prove instructive to raise a pair of young cyborgs after all," says Edward grandly. Mendoza arches an eyebrow at him.

"Why, señor, can you possibly have anything left to learn?"

"I do assure you, I am by no means omniscient yet." Edward looks down at her, sincere. "I'm only just beginning to grasp things. What a fog mortals live in, what limits are imposed on a man's vision by human pain and weariness! I myself was blinkered, for all I thought I saw. And our masters were as blind as the rest of the mortals. To give but one example—why have you submitted to their tedious *mechanical* time transcendence all this while, when the better way was so obvious?"

"What?"

What? What better way?

"Ah! Of course. They must have deliberately obscured the truth when they programmed you, or you'd all have escaped them by this time," Edward concludes to himself. He turns puzzled eyes to Mendoza. "Still, even an elementary knowledge of temporal physics should have enabled *some* of you to work out the equation for yourselves—"

What equation?

"This one," says Edward, and transmits it to the Captain.

"Am I missing something here?" says Mendoza, just as power fluctuates all over the ship. She gasps and clings to Edward. He is ignoring the wavering growl coming over the ship's speakers, that now resolves into a stream of astonishing profanity; he is peering down at her instead, looking concerned.

"You don't know," he says. "Why don't you know?"

"What are you talking about?" demands Mendoza, and draws back a little at the look in his eyes as he takes her face in his hands. "Please! What—"

"Ah! To be sure. It must be the Crome's radiation. We won't need that, now; simple enough to correct the flaw. Don't be frightened," he says, but she gives a brief scream as he is suddenly in all places at once, present in every memory she has, seeing through her eyes, pumping through her heart, inhaled and exhaled and utterly inescapable, "I'm simply reading you—"

When her vision clears at last she thinks for a moment Alec is with her again, because he is staring down at her in such wide-eyed surprise. Then the expression changes and she thinks he must be Nicholas, such compassion is in his face. But it's Edward's voice saying: "Oh, my poor little girl. It isn't the Crome's after all. You could never have known, could you?"

"Known what?" she says feebly.

Of course she bloody couldn't, she's only got a human brain, roars the Captain. **Yer the only one what's ever worked out that equation! Damn me for a Twonky, boy, do you know what you've just discovered?**

"Hush," Edward tells him, and gathers Mendoza into his arms. "Don't be afraid, dearest. I'll teach you—you'll learn—I'm certain you can learn. You're a bright, good girl, and you've a perfectly good little brain—well, as soon as the Crome's is dispensed with, but then—"

"What do you mean, I've got a little brain?" she says in outrage.

"Hush," Edward repeats. His eyes grow wide and earnest again as he looks into hers. "It's really quite simple. To put it in terms you might understand—*lato sensu*—when one has eternal life, and the potential to be in any place in any time, one is *de facto* in all places in all times, and therefore—no, that won't do, you won't—you do understand what actually occurs when a wave collapses into a particle, I assume? Oh, this is futile. Here. Much simpler to give it to you directly." He lowers his face, presses his brow against hers.

"But—!" says Mendoza, beginning to struggle.

Are you certain she can take a download that size, sir?

"Don't be ridiculous, of course she can," says Edward distractedly. "Can't you, my girl? You *will* be my equal in all things."

"Edward! I don't—"

But his grip on her is unbreakable. The bed erupts in blue fire. It shoots upward, touching the carved beams of the ceiling. Then, as Edward makes a minor adjustment—easy as tightening a loose screw, for him—it vanishes without trace. Mendoza goes limp. The wave of Edward's will rises, engulfs her, informs her.

Hours later they are still in bed, motionless, unchanged. Mendoza sighs suddenly and shivers, lifting her head, blinking up at Edward. "Oh," she says at last. "But that can't be right. Can it? That's too obvious."

With a smile, Edward pulls her in again. Two hours later:

"But that would mean—" she says abruptly.

"Yes, yes, she's got it," Edward crows. "You see, Captain?"

"But this means—"

"Yes!" says Edward, kissing her. "Yes! *Denique caelum.*"

"It means—we're free," says Mendoza. Tears form in her eyes. "No wonder you've been smirking in that impossible way! Dear God, you really have broken my chains."

And in a street in Paris in the year 1645—

And in the midst of a herder's camp in Mongolia in the year 848—

And in Times Square on New Year's Eve, 2014—

And in front of the Papal throne in the Vatican in the year 1856—

And in a plaza in Madrid in the year 2213—

And in a jungle in Venezuela in the year 5001 BCE—

And in the garden of William Blake, in England, in the year 1782—

In that simultaneous moment and place, mortal witnesses are startled by the abrupt materialization of a naked man and woman embracing passionately. Then the man looks up in annoyance, and adjusts perception. The lovers vanish.

Only William Blake is unsurprised.

CHAPTER 8

*London, 2333: Meeting of the Board of Directors:
They Divide the Spoils*

"We can't start until all the board members are here, sir," explained Lopez.

"They ought to be on time," Rappacini fretted.

"Most of us *are* on time," said Roche in annoyance. She sat, with the other investors, at one end of the table. The scientists—Rappacini, Bugleg, and the rest—sat at the other end. This was not the only way to tell them apart; for the investors, being all of them very wealthy men and women, were dressed in highly individual and (for the twenty-fourth century) flamboyant clothes. One of them even wore a bright blue waistcoat, a gesture of personal adornment so extreme he'd be branded an Eccentric, if he hadn't so much money.

Lopez, who stood at his place mid-table, wore a plain gray business suit, elegant but understated. On its lapel was a small cloisonné pin depicting a clock face without hands. On Company property he was required to wear it in the presence of mortals, that they might distinguish him from a human being.

"It's only the new member who's late," Hapsburg (the investor with the blue waistcoat) explained. "He might have gotten lost on the way from his hotel. I don't think he's ever been in England before."

"This is the American?" said Bugleg with obvious disdain. Rossum nodded, making a what-can-you-expect gesture just below table level, where the people at the other end couldn't see.

The door to the conference room flew open and the missing board member walked in. He wore a smartly cut business suit and carried a large paper bag that bore the logo of the Southwark Museum. It rustled loudly as he set it down beside his chair.

"Sorry I'm late," he said, leaning forward at his place and looking them over. "Stopped for souvenirs and then my driver got lost. Why didn't you people mention there was more than one bridge over your river? London *Bridge,* that's how the song goes, doesn't it? Not brid*ges.* Mike Telepop, hi, I'm coordinating executive of Paramount Adventures. What have I missed?"

"Not a thing, sir, we waited for you," Lopez assured him.

"Thanks," said Telepop, surveying him. "You're the cyborg, huh? Christ! You people really don't look any different. Great job, guys," he added, directing his last remark to the scientists at the other end of the table.

"Very good, sir." Lopez cleared his throat. "Ladies, gentlemen: it's been a banner quarter for Dr. Zeus Incorporated. Response on our Day Six Resort project has far exceeded our original estimates. I'm pleased to report that the first three seasons are fully booked, and preorder reservations topped twenty-five billion pounds, well above projections.

"Revenues from historical artifacts alone brought in seventeen point five billion pounds. You've probably heard of the Michelangelo portraits we auctioned at Sotheby's, but some of our less publicized finds were also notable: the lost early stories by Ernest Hemingway, three Stradivarius violins, a set of previously unknown poems by Jalal ad-Din Rumi, the original score for Gilbert and Sullivan's *The Gods Grown Old.*" The smooth voice went on and on, cataloguing wonders unimaginable, unbelievably rescued from the devouring maw of Time. The investors sat there, occasionally looking impressed. The scientists looked bored and impatient.

". . . for which we can thank our hardworking team on the Pompeii project. Another item expected to do well at auction is the holograph script for *A Midsummer Night's Dream,* with Shakespeare's own notations—"

"Hey." Telepop put up his hand. "Don't we get first crack at stuff like that?"

"Certainly, sir," Lopez said, looking up from his list. "If you outbid the revenue estimates."

"I thought we got a Company discount," objected Telepop. Lopez did not reply, turning to look at the other board members, and at last Roche shifted in her seat and sighed.

"Well, yes, we do," she admitted. "Some of us have private collections."

"That's what I heard," said Telepop. "Like some of you have whole museums full of stuff just for yourselves?"

There was a lot of blushing and avoided gazes at that. Rossum shrugged.

"It's only a lot of old things that *I* wouldn't look at twice," he said. "No use to anybody except by making money for us. If you want to keep something back so you can buy it, go ahead. Hapsburg has all those ugly statues out of the World Trade Center by—who was it? Rodent?"

"Rodin," snapped Hapsburg. "They aren't either ugly."

"And Morrison has a complete set of the first drafts of the novels of Sky-walker Lucas the Third," Rossum continued maliciously, but Telepop looked impressed.

"Wow, you know how to read?"

"No," said Morrison, glaring at Rossum. "I just like knowing they're mine. But it's nobody's business I have them."

"Well, I don't care, okay? I just want to buy some Shakespeare souvenirs," announced Telepop. "Because there was, like, almost nothing but T-shirts at the museum gift shop. What is it with you people anyway?"

"I'll just earmark that Shakespeare script for you, then, sir, shall I?" Lopez said, unobtrusively making a tick against the list.

"Yeah, do it. Thanks. Hey!" Telepop's eyes lit up. "We've got the Ben-thamites working for us, too, don't we? How much would I have to spend to get *Shakespeare*?"

"I'm afraid he's not for sale, sir," Lopez replied. "He's buried on private property and was only disinterred temporarily, when the holo for the museum was being made."

"Really? I thought there was supposed to be a curse or something," said Telepop.

"Yes, apparently there was," Lopez told him, chuckling.

"So there's no way, with a little quiet payoff, we couldn't just . . . permanently borrow him?" said Telepop hopefully.

"That is *so* Yank," cried Morrison in indignation. "He's *our* painter, after all."

"Playwright, sir," Lopez corrected him.

"Hey! You people won't even show Shakespeare's movies over here," yelled Telepop. "At least we're not ashamed of our big moneymakers."

British lips were pursed. "Perhaps we ought to move on," suggested Lopez.

"Are you sure he wasn't a painter?" inquired Morrison sotto voce.

"Quite, sir. Now, for a brief preview of our third quarter investment strate-gies: Dr. Zeus will concentrate its energies on acquiring a number of small in-dustries in Senegal, which stands poised for an economic boom after a meta-flu epidemic devastates its neighboring nations late next year. Opera-tives are already in place in the following firms: Katanga Specialty Systems, Qwel-Juice Consolidated—"

"This is what the prospectus was talking about, right?" Telepop exclaimed. "The Temporal Concordance thing? Our big database that knows everything that's going to happen, so we can always invest in stuff that'll boom?"

"Yes, sir, exactly," Lopez told him, and the others nodded.

"Boy, this is great. How can we lose?" said Telepop, gleeful. The other board members regarded him pityingly. Being a new associate, he didn't know the truth about 2355 yet. Strictly speaking, neither did they. That was the problem.

Now Telepop's grin faded as an idea occurred to him. "There's no chance this database thing can . . . like . . . pull a Hal and take over the Company, is there?" he inquired of Lopez. "Like in *Cyborg Conquest*? No offense, you know, Lopez, I'm sure none of you people would do anything like that, but—some big inhuman machine thing might—"

"Not to worry, sir," Lopez waved away the questions. "The Temporal Concordance isn't an artificial intelligence. It has no personality or individual consciousness of its own, any more than an antique computer had." He smiled tolerantly. "Hollywood has no equal when it comes to providing top-notch entertainment, but as one of its movers and shakers, you certainly know that ordinary reality won't entertain people for long! And so, instead of making a holo about dull old civil servants like me, you wisely chose to make a holo about eight-foot killer androids. Smash hit! And may I say, sir, that I found myself on the edge of my seat, rooting for the plucky human heroes?"

"Really?" Telepop beamed. "That's great."

Lopez smiled and stood back, pleased to have fended off another bout of servophobia.

As soon as the door opened for him, Bugleg emerged from his car and hurried away without a word to the driver. This was his usual practice, so the driver wasn't particularly offended.

Bugleg made his way to the aglift and rode up to his floor, peering nervously around; entered the admission code and slipped inside his apartment. Comforting dimness, soothing silence. Or—no—wait . . .

There were noises coming from his bedroom. He stood still a moment, heart hammering, ready to turn and run into the hall again. Gradually he recognized the sounds as coming from one of his more private games, and something like a sense of outrage strengthened him enough to creep forward and see who was there.

Ratlin was sprawled on his bed, comfortably propped up on the pillows and staring in absorption at the hologame projecting from the entertainment console. He didn't look a day older than he had on the occasion of their first meeting, fourteen years previous; in fact he looked a good deal less withered, which made his resemblance to Bugleg more striking.

On the coverlet beside him were his sun goggles and hat, and something else: a pair of flat rectangles, one oddly bumpy and one glossy with embossed art and writing. A box, full of little brown things, and its lid.

Then Bugleg realized just exactly which game Ratlin was playing. Even as he reeled with the shock, he was hit by another jolt; for as he watched in horror, Ratlin reached into the box for one of the brown things and *put it in his mouth*!

"Stop it!" he screamed. Ratlin glanced at him in annoyance, chewing.

"What for?" he asked. "You took long enough at your bigwig meeting. I was getting ever so bored waiting for you to grace this place with your presence."

"You can't—you're not supposed to—DON'T LOOK AT MY GAMES," cried Bugleg, grabbing the control from Ratlin's hand and switching it off. The forbidden images vanished into darkness. He heard Ratlin snickering.

"Oh, dear, doesn't want anybody to know he's into naughtiness, eh? Well, well. What a pity we're on the same side, isn't it? I could blackmail you six ways from Sabbat."

"You weren't supposed to come in here," Bugleg protested, nearly weeping. "This is my private room. These are *my* things. Nobody's supposed to see."

"Then it's lucky for you we're partners, you big stupid lout," said Ratlin, and slid off the bed. "Want a chockie?" he added, offering the box.

Bugleg drew back as though he had been offered a nest of coiled snakes. "No! Those are poison!"

"No, silly, think I'd be sampling 'em myself if they were?" Ratlin scowled at him. "They're the wholesomest treat on the market. You ask your cyborgs! Mine's the kind they buy, and why? Because Ratlin's Finest really is better made, see, and richer, and's got more expensive ingredients than anybody else's. Not to mention it's easier to get, since I had the competition arsoned."

"No, no." Bugleg had closed his eyes and was shaking his head obstinately. "Chocolate is poison. Refined sugar is poison. Butterfat is poi—" He broke off because Ratlin, impatient, had crammed a chocolate in his mouth. He chewed twice, involuntarily. His eyes popped open, round with horror.

"See? They're nice," gloated Ratlin.

Bugleg's eyes were tracking frantically around the room for a place to spit out his mouthful. On the rug? But the cleaner would notice. On the bed-spread? Same problem. On the table? It might splatter his control box and mess the circuits. In the lavatory? Yes, and wash it down the sink—

All the while, however, his jaws were moving quite without his permission. By the time he finally ran to the bathroom and spit into the sink, there wasn't much left of the chocolate. Weeping in self-loathing, he rinsed away the nastiness.

"You liked it," said Ratlin, right there beside him. He elbowed Bugleg convivially. "You did so. I could tell. A little bit of pure pleasure for you, eh, cousin?"

"I wasn't supposed to," gasped Bugleg. "It's wrong!"

"Bugger wrong," Ratlin scoffed. "Who's ever going to know about it? A sweet silent thrill in the safe dark, and it won't show, no, not at all. Long as you wipe that dribbly bit off your chin," he advised.

Bugleg turned to the mirror and busied himself with wiping the last trace of the chocolate away. "I don't want to talk about that anymore," he said.

"No, of course not," agreed Ratlin. "You want to talk about our little wonder drug. Got it all ready for me?"

"Yes," Bugleg replied, drawing a deep breath and flicking lint from his shoulder. In control again, he turned and led Ratlin to a closet, where he drew out a broad wide band of black material, in design something like an old-fashioned money belt. The inner flap held twenty-one little ampoules of a strange-looking substance: bright teal sediment at the bottom and red-purple clear stuff at the top.

Ratlin grinned in satisfaction and fastened the belt about his middle. "That's fine," he said. "Keep me young and limber another year. Good boy."

"When should we tell the others about our plan?" asked Bugleg.

"Oh, not for a while, yet," Ratlin told him, rebuttoning his coat. "Don't want 'em getting qualmish, or dropping an unintended word to the slaves. Anyway I've bought a place of my own to make the wicked stuff. When we strike, it'll be like lightning; all we'll need your friends for is getting the air transports for delivery everywhere at once."

"All right," said Bugleg, nodding. "So we just wait."

"That's what we do. Twenty-two years to go!" said Ratlin. He donned his hat and goggles. "I'll be on my way, now, cousin mine." He strolled to the door, pausing to glance back into the bedroom. "You can keep the sweets," he said slyly, and by the time Bugleg had managed to stammer out an indignant refusal he was gone.

Bugleg stood, listening to the faint sound of Ratlin's departing footfall. After a long moment of indecision, he reached up and switched off all the lights.

Nobody could see him now. He couldn't see himself. Trembling, in pitch blackness, he groped his way to the bedroom.

Meanwhile, in San Francisco

"But not a word about where his laboratory is," complained Ereshkigal.

"Oh, it'll be easy enough to trace," Aegeus assured her. "We'll get a couple of our mortal people in as plant workers, to keep us abreast of developments. Wouldn't you think? It's not as though we want to stop the little fools."

"No, of course not," said Ereshkigal. "In fact, we might want to seriously consider helping them. The sooner we have the substance in our possession, the greater our advantage."

"Precisely," said Aegeus, idly unwrapping a bar of Ratlin's Crunch.

While at the Same Moment in St. Petersburg

"We'll need to set somebody on that laboratory location," mused Ashoreth, leaning back in her chair. "It's got to be somewhere in the Celtic Federation, just like the confectioners'. Wouldn't you think?"

"Very likely," said Labienus. "Easy enough to trace what real estate he's purchased lately."

"We really might want to consider a preemptive strike—" Ashoreth suggested, just as a muffled groan was transmitted through the surveillance audio. She bit her lip, but Labienus laughed outright.

"That's it," he cried. "Enjoy yourself, you poor little hypocrite! Can you imagine what he'd be experiencing right now, if Theobromine affected his nervous system the way it affected ours?"

"I'm not so sure it doesn't," giggled Ashoreth, as a raucous panting came through loud and clear.

"No," said Labienus, increasing the volume. "He's got a hologame on now. Listen."

" 'Totter Dan in Microbe Land,' " concluded Ashoreth after a moment. "Why, Mr. Bugleg, you shameless libertine."

"Oh, why shouldn't he indulge?" said Labienus. "Eat, drink, and be merry, mortal. After all, you've only—" He paused to consult his internal chronometer. "Twenty-one years, nine months, two weeks, six days, five hours, thirty-six minutes, and ten seconds in which to do so."

CHAPTER 9

The Pirate's Lair, 2337

Until the last big earthquake, Point Reyes had been merely a peninsula north of San Francisco; now it had the distinction of being an actual island, though only a modest and brackish stretch of seawater connected Tomales and Bolinas Bays. Still, it was now necessary to cross the San Andreas Fault by bridge to get out to Inverness and the other little communities on the eastern shore. It was a cold windswept place, a high tableland in the sea, forested on its leeward side but all bare rolling hills to windward.

A road ran out along the high hills, now and then veering close to the leaning fenceposts of abandoned farms, beyond which collapsed mounds of silvered planks and skeletal wind-bent cypresses kept their ghosts to themselves. Isolation, desolation, driving wind and fog. Cold waves broke with a sound like cannon shot on the long windward beach.

Hearst piloted the agcar westward, fighting the wind. The road was weedy, obscured with drifting sand. He had passed no other vehicle since he had crossed the bridge at Olema.

He'd have spotted any other vehicle, too, because it would be hard to find a more exposed stretch of road than this that trailed out its length between the two inclement shores. If anyone were watching him, whether by satellite or field glasses, they might have tracked his progress for miles without so much as a tree branch blocking the view.

But then, Hearst told himself, Joseph had probably counted on that when he'd specified Drake's Bay as the place of their rendezvous.

A mortal waiter had stepped up to the table in Alioto's and presented Hearst with a slip of paper, explaining that he'd been asked to deliver it.

Having fun shopping for antiques? So, you've probably had plenty of time to think about my little present. Want to talk about it now? I promise I'll pick up where I left off. Drive out to Drake's Bay any time in the next three days and I'll see you there. Come alone, please.

"Is it a threat, mister? You want a Public Health Officer?" the waiter had said, wringing his hands. He had been unable to read the note. In fact, it was the first written communication he had ever seen, strange enough to alarm him.

Hearst grinned at him, tucking the note away. "No, no, don't worry. It's a joke. From a friend."

The waiter had blinked, uncomprehending. Hearst felt a momentary flash of irritation at the general obtuseness and timidity of the present generation of mortals. He ordered another glass of fruit tea and sat looking out on the bay, pondering whether there wasn't a way to inspire mortals to a little more bravery, a little more zest for life . . .

He crested a hilltop now, and before him the road went steeply down to the little museum at Drake's Beach. No other cars and not a living soul in sight.

Hearst was smiling to himself as he put his hands in his coat pockets and strolled across the parking lot. This was sort of fun! Like being in a spy novel. And here he was, where Sir Francis Drake was said to have paused in his career of looting Spanish galleons long enough to repair his ship . . . well, in one of the places that claimed that distinction. The precise site of Drake's landing remained a question over which Californians argued with astonishingly uncharacteristic viciousness, even in the present meek age . . .

The museum was closed. Hearst wandered around on its outer deck, peering through the windows. Nothing to see but the painted backdrops for the natural history dioramas, and they didn't amount to much with the holoes shut off. Nothing about Drake in evidence at all; not even a plaque. But then, pirates hadn't been politically correct for years now. Hearst sighed to himself as he walked down to the beach, remembering his boyhood fascination with Captain Kidd.

What was wrong with mortals nowadays? Surely a little bloody-mindedness was natural for children. He'd delighted in toy cannons and wooden swords, himself. Maybe a bit late into life, but he'd learned better eventually, enough so that he could point with pride to the laws he'd had enacted for the improvement of humanity. Mortals had become such spiritless creatures . . .

Having activated his record function, he began to murmur to himself: "Memo: possible series of adventure holoes for children. Revise history where necessary to make my point but present red-blooded, two-fisted fellows who weren't afraid to take action. Ladies, too. Joan of Arc, Susan B. Anthony, Edith Clavell, Sally Ride, Araminta Gonzales, Miriam Meyer . . . High production values, plenty of costumes, color. All that is necessary for evil to triumph is for good men to do nothing. Let's be less passive, kids! Of course, we need a cause for this, something to galvanize them all, some common enemy . . ."

So absorbed was he in his idea that he very nearly forgot why he had come to that place, and strode down the beach like a juggernaut until he found himself in the middle of a boggy tidal spit, looking across the waters of Drake's Estero. As he was turning and retracing his steps to dry sand, he heard a throat-clearing noise and looked up.

He couldn't spot anyone. Scanning, he encountered some kind of scrambler field.

"Well, I'm here," he announced, and walked in the direction from which he supposed the noise had come. Rocks, sand, seaweed, driftwood, and the dun-colored featureless hills rising beyond. He found a redwood log easily four feet in diameter and leaned against it, sighing.

"Yeah, it's a little dreary, isn't it?" said Joseph, popping up from behind the log. "Great place for a private meeting, though, huh?"

Hearst turned to him. Joseph was dressed in complete camping gear: plaid flannel shirt, bellows trousers, hiking boots, and an outdoorsman's hat with ear flaps.

"I came alone, as you can see," said Hearst.

"Hey, I knew you would. You're that kind of guy," said Joseph cheerily. "So. Hearst News Services had a great three years, huh? Beat the competition to quite a few breaking stories! That must have felt good. Of course, the other stuff I gave you might have got you a little sore at the Company. Those private memos between members of the Board of Directors, for example. Not very nice things they say about us immortals, are they?"

"No," said Hearst. He'd been outraged when he'd accessed the information, even keeping in mind that it might have been faked to win his support, but he'd managed to bite his tongue and greet Quint as though nothing unusual had happened when Quint returned from his European acquisitions trip. Subsequent quiet investigation strongly suggested that Joseph had faked nothing. "It *is* mostly the mortals, too, isn't it? They don't care for you Old Ones at all."

"Nope," said Joseph. "And they aren't crazy about you, either."

"Oh?" Hearst frowned.

"Nope. Want to see more proof?"

"Darned right! I understand why they're afraid of the likes of you, even if they created you. But I'm a stockholder, for heaven's sake," said Hearst. "And a special case, remember. And, by the way, you were going to explain about that—?"

"Yes, sir, Mr. Hearst, and I'll be glad to do that, just as soon as I've convinced you. I'll show you what Dr. Zeus *plans* for 2355, regardless of what may actually happen. Okay? Excuse me a second, here—" Joseph reached up and set the tip of his finger between Hearst's eyes. "Download."

Straight into his consciousness the data flowed, for immediate access, not much information content, really; but after scanning through it Hearst stiffened and turned pale. Joseph stood back, looking sympathetic. "It's a shock, I know," he said.

"What does that mean, *Designated: Removal*?" stammered Hearst.

"About what you think it means," said Joseph. "These are the people who built the Bureau of Punitive Medicine, remember?"

"But why *me*?" Hearst said. "Why am I on that list?"

"It's a long story, Mr. Hearst," said Joseph. "Let's walk." They set off along the shore of the estero, picking their way through the dune grass, back into the hills.

"The Company would have gotten rid of you sooner, but you've been really useful to them," explained Joseph. "Your money, that big house of yours where they could stash stuff, your ability to manipulate the public's perception of reality especially!

"And they knew they were going to need you long before you were even born, see? So your parents were watched closely. Dr. Zeus likes to have iron-clad guarantees that history will happen the way it's supposed to.

"An operative was sent to look after your mother when she was expecting you. The operative—guy named Jabesh—thought he'd have a nice easy job. He was wrong. Your mother miscarried in her first trimester."

Hearst stopped on the path. "What are you saying?"

"You couldn't have been born the way you were, Mr. Hearst," said Joseph quietly. "There were genetic problems. Did your father ever talk about his brother who died young? Anyway, Jabesh panicked. It was his job to see that you lived. So . . . he broke a few rules."

"What did he do?" Hearst demanded. Joseph started forward again but Hearst did not follow, so Joseph turned back.

"He . . . uh . . . remade you. Out of a field repair kit he had. You know what a DNA chain looks like, right, all those little linky things connecting the spiral, each piece containing part of a person's genetic code? Apparently you were missing a bunch of stuff, and he ... patched the missing places with this other, special material from his field repair kit. And it worked! Your mother never knew what had happened. You were born right on schedule."

"You're not talking about recombinant DNA!" Hearst looked aghast.

"No! No genetic *engineering,*" Joseph assured him. "Don't worry. Just a repair, see? But with this other special stuff added, you were sort of naturally augmented. It affected your appearance, and your, uh, personality, and a few other things.

"Samples of Jabesh's work went into the Company vaults, and that's why you could be the exception to the no-adults rule when they made you immortal. They didn't have to work from your worn-out eighty-eight-year-old DNA with its replication errors. They did a perfect restoration from the new-minted stuff Jabesh created," Joseph said.

Hearst was silent. Joseph edged back a few paces, peering up at him worriedly. "I'm sorry, pal. I know it's got to be an awful shock—"

"Shock?" said Hearst, and Joseph saw in amazement that he had begun to smile. "Why, this is wonderful! This accounts for a lot. I always knew I was different."

"Yeah?"

"I've always had this sense of destiny looming over me." Hearst began to pace forward again in his excitement, and Joseph scrambled ahead of him, walking backward to stare up into his face. "I never really felt as though I fitted in anywhere but places I made for myself, and now I know why!"

"So you really don't mind?" said Joseph doubtfully.

"Gosh, how could anyone mind something like this?" cried Hearst. His eyes were shining. "I owe this Jabesh fellow my life! I'd like to shake his hand and thank him." He paused and looked at Joseph. "Say, do you think I could? Where's he stationed these days? I could look him up—"

"I'm afraid you couldn't, Mr. Hearst," said Joseph. "He's one of the ones who's disappeared."

"What?" Hearst's grin faded.

"He's lost." Joseph held out his hands in an apologetic gesture. "Unaccounted for. The last entry in his personnel file has him being transferred to a numbered site, which probably means the Company doublecrossed him."

"But why?"

"Because he knew the truth about you, I guess. Only two operatives ever knew—Jabesh and me—and he's disappeared and the Company would disappear me, too, if it could catch me. I'll bet even Quintilius wasn't told everything."

"But why go to such trouble to hide the truth?" said Hearst.

"Because what Jabesh did was illegal as hell," said Joseph. "The Company does things to obtain its objectives that contravene all kinds of laws. Jeez, even making cyborgs like me is prohibited!

"Can you imagine how mortals would react to learning that somebody like *you* existed, especially when you've built up a communications empire that controls what they see and hear? For crying out loud, a lot of people said you were a monster when you were mortal! What would they think now?"

Hearst scowled. Joseph gulped for breath and continued: "But if you disappear too, eventually—it's all taken care of. The Company won't get into trouble."

"No," said Hearst. "The Company *is* in trouble."

"Hey, that's the spirit," said Joseph, grinning, but his voice was just a little uneasy. "We knew you wouldn't take this lying down. That's why we approached you in the first place, Mr. Hearst."

Hearst leaned down to look him in the eye. "You said that when this fellow repaired me, he used special material. What was special about it, Mr. Denham?"

"That's a good question, and I'm glad you asked," said Joseph.

"I look nothing like you or any other immortal I've ever met," said Hearst. "You all blend in, you don't stand out. Unlike me."

"Yeah. You've hit the nail on the head, as usual, Mr. Hearst. See—the Company conducted some breeding experiments a long time ago," said Joseph.

"How long ago?"

"Oh, before I was even born." Joseph looked uncomfortable.

"But you're over twenty thousand years old!"

"Yeah," said Joseph, bending down to pick up a piece of driftwood. "Wow, look at this, it's shaped exactly like a duck. Neat, huh? Yeah. This was way back when Neanderthals and Cro-Magnons were running around. The human gene pool had a lot more options in those days. The Company was just getting its field operations up and running. But it had a little problem.

"There was this nutty religious movement that got started among the mortals. It was really fanatic and violent, okay? And anti-technological, too, I might add. They didn't think much of the invention of fire, and something like a Clovis point would have really outraged them. They wanted to keep the universe simple.

"Anyway—here the Company was, waiting for human civilization to get started, and it didn't look like it was ever going to do that, thanks to these tattooed murdering loonies, who called themselves the Great Goat Cult. So . . . Dr. Zeus decided to fight fire with fire."

"What do you mean?"

"They needed soldiers," said Joseph wearily. "We Preservers were no good for the job. We're programmed to avoid dangers at all costs. So the Company set up this huge breeding program. They crossed Neanderthal and Cro-Magnon, and a couple of other races who didn't make it into the fossil record. When they got the results they wanted they took the children away—they only took males—and made them immortal warriors. They called them Enforcers."

"Are you saying that's what I was made from?"

"Yeah." Joseph looked up at Hearst, turning the bit of driftwood in his hands. "And it shows. You believe absolutely in everything you do. You're big, you're powerful, and . . ." Joseph cast about for a better word than *frightening.* "Something about your appearance impresses people. You must have noticed."

"All my life," said Hearst. "Do I look like an Enforcer?"

Joseph shook his head. "You still look like a human being, Mr. Hearst. There's some resemblance around the eyes, maybe. And your voice! They were all tenors and countertenors, because of the way their larynxes were positioned. You inherited that."

"I notice you're using past tense," said Hearst.

Joseph nodded. "The Company doublecrossed them, same as it's doing to its Preservers now. Out of three thousand men, only two officers escaped the purge, one of 'em because the Company put him to work in a secret place, doing stuff they thought nobody'd ever see."

Hearst's eyes widened. "Do you mean the Bureau of Punitive Medicine? Marco was an Enforcer?"

"Yeah."

"But he's evil!"

Joseph tossed the piece of driftwood away. "Mr. Hearst . . . the devil's in Hell, punishing sinners God sent there because God wants them punished. That's the devil's job, inflicting fire and the worm on all those screaming souls. He's obeying God's will, right? So would you say the devil is evil?"

". . . Yes! Because he disobeyed God in the first place," said Hearst a little desperately.

"Marco disobeyed, too," said Joseph. "That's why he got stuck with that job at the Bureau. Mind you, he really did like to hurt people, but there was no doubt in his mind he was working in a righteous cause. He escaped just before Suleyman liberated the Bureau. Christ only knows where he found to hide, but I hope I never run into him in a dark alley."

"I don't want to have any part of those creatures in my blood," said Hearst. "Not if they were capable of such things!"

"Oh, they weren't all like Marco," said Joseph. "The best of them were heroes. They had a moral code. They served humanity by executing its criminals. As long as the Enforcers were around, there were never going to be wars. Any mortal who tried, died.

"You know how I became immortal? The Great Goat Cult massacred my family. I saw my mother killed, just before an Enforcer patrol came along and caught the Goats in the act. Wiped 'em out. I looked up and saw my salvation in this big ugly guy, reaching down his bloody hand to me."

Joseph's voice was resonant with emotion. For a moment Hearst saw past his absurd costume, and caught a glimpse of the creature centuries had cast up on this strange shore. He cleared his throat. "You said two Enforcers escaped. What became of the other one?"

Joseph smiled. "Oh, he's still around. The Company couldn't break him."

"Was he one of the good Enforcers?" Hearst asked.

"He was the best. The biggest, the smartest, and in fact the very guy who saved my life, which makes him my father, as we'd say, since recruiting new operatives is the only way we reproduce. In a way, he's your grandfather. You want to meet him?"

"Yes," said Hearst. But he was not prepared for what happened next.

Ten meters away from where they stood, the hillside moved. Hearst whirled around to stare. He cried out in horror. A massive figure was detaching itself from the landscape, a thing the color of the dun grasses and dead wood and stones; yet it wasn't transparent, was not wearing camouflage but merely faded dull clothing. He realized it had been sitting there, perfectly motionless, from the beginning of the conversation.

And now it was pacing forward with the steady inexorability of a rolling wave, and Hearst drew back at its approach.

The body looked human enough, though immense; still, there was something wrong in the articulation of the powerful arms. And from the neck up—

Not human at all, no, impossible, the wide head had a flattened shape like a helmet, the wide brow sloped straight back, and the clean-shaven face below was far too big. Huge broad cheekbones and an enormous domed nose. The mouth had an equine quality, wide and forward-projecting, suggesting immense teeth. The jaw was heavy, powerful, somewhat underslung. The hair, which was the same dun color as the hillside, began far back on the brow and was worn long, bound behind, flowing down the back like a horse's tail. But there was a human intelligence looking calmly out from under the heavy brow ridges. The eyes were the palest blue Hearst had ever seen, almost colorless.

It walked up and stopped, looking down at Hearst. Hearst fell to his knees, unable to speak, staring transfixed.

"Get up," said the creature, chuckling. "I wasn't made to be worshipped. Only feared and obeyed." It had a soft high voice, the sort of voice you might expect an angel to have, but oddly flat and toneless.

Hearst struggled to his feet at once, his long coat flapping. "My God," he said shrilly. "What are you?"

"Weren't you listening to him?" The creature put a hand on Joseph's shoulder. "You know what I am. And now, you know what you are."

"Father, allow me to introduce William Randolph Hearst," said Joseph. "Mr. Hearst, allow me to introduce my father, Budu."

"H-hello," said Hearst. Budu smiled at him. Hearst's eyes widened. He had never seen teeth that big in his life and the dentition was certainly not human. Joseph laughed.

"Boy, this is really something. Look at the two of you! It isn't exactly what you'd call a family resemblance and yet, you know, there's just this indefinable *je ne sais quoi*, a certain titanic quality—"

"Shut up, son," said Budu.

"Okay."

"Well, Hearst," said Budu, "you've heard what my son had to tell you. You've seen his proof. What do you think of Dr. Zeus Incorporated now?"

Hearst gulped and composed himself in haste. "I—I think they're treacherous. Evil. Absolute power has corrupted them absolutely. That's what I think of them. Sir!" he added.

Budu nodded, considering him. "I'm going to punish them," he said. "They have betrayed the mortal race they created me to serve. The mortals among them will die in blood and flame. They'll be luckier than the immortals in their number. You have resources I need for this judgment. What will you say if I tell you I require your service?"

Hearst fought the urge to kneel again. "I'd say yes! I mean—yes, yes, I'll help. What do you need me to do?" he said, and to his dismay felt tears forming in his eyes. He couldn't ever remember when he'd been so frightened, and yet so irrationally exhilarated. "Please, sir. Anything."

"You can solve some of my logistical problems," said Budu. "I need a troop carrier big enough for three thousand men."

"Why, I've got a superyacht that'll carry that many," Hearst said. "The *Oneida Six*. She's at your disposal, sir, whenever you want her!"

"Thank you," said Budu.

"And we have to lay our hands on three thousand pairs of pants," said Joseph. "All triple-X sizes. You own any Mr. Tall or Big clothing outlets?"

"I can arrange clothes. My gosh," said Hearst, wiping away a tear. He looked from Joseph to Budu. "What are we going to do?"

"Wake the sleepers," said Budu. "Revive my men, that the Company betrayed. They're hidden in underground bunkers all over the world. We'll collect them and mass them to attack, at a certain place on a certain day in 2355. There will be no mercy." He smiled again. "Afterward, there will be no Company.

"If we survive, we'll free the ones who've disappeared and care for the mortal race again, as we were made to do. The mortals will have safety. They'll have law. They won't have free will; but you've lived long enough now to know that mortals have no free will anyway."

He reached out his big hand and set it on Hearst's shoulder. Hearst trembled, but his voice was joyful as he said: "Yes! You're right, they don't really. And the ones who have even a little free will hate it, they hate making choices for themselves. I tried for the longest time to help them, you know, but in the end I just gave up and started ruling them. I think that's what they've wanted all along."

Budu nodded. "I've watched these children of this last age. They've grown tame and quiet. We won't have to kill many of them, I think."

"Why would we have to kill any?" Hearst said, faltering slightly.

"Because there will always be those mortals who will lure children into bushes to murder them, no matter how enlightened men become," said Budu patiently. "There will always be cannibals in the midst of plenty. You know this. They must die, so the innocents can live in peace."

"Oh. Well, yes, of course," said Hearst. "I see what you're saying. Like shooting rabid dogs. Unfortunate, but necessary."

Joseph looked from Hearst to Budu. He cleared his throat. "So, okay," he said. "We've got a lot to do and only eighteen years to do it in. Let's get organized! We need to figure out a way to work around Quintilius, we need some secure meeting places, and we really do have to start stockpiling those triple-Xs, okay?"

"Okay," said Hearst, hugging his coat around himself. Budu glanced upward.

"We need to move first," he said. "The surveillance satellite will come into range in fifteen minutes."

"I know where we can go," said Hearst. "The museum. There's a porch where we can get under cover. Come on!"

He led the way back to Drake's Beach, barely able to keep from skipping as he went. Here he was, becoming embroiled in a plot that would, to all intents and purposes, bring about the end of the world as he had known it; and yet he hadn't felt this light-hearted and giddy since before his mortal father had died. For the first time since attaining eternal youth, he actually felt *young*.

This was going to be fun!

Death Valley, 3 June 2342

"What possesses mortals," Victor wondered aloud, "to build castles in the midst of desolation?"

"You don't like the climate?" Labienus looked surprised. "What a shame."

Victor looked at him askance. It was true that the air was dry and clean, that the hot wind moved against the skin like an angel on the make; it was true there was an eerie grandeur to the old house lifting its turrets above the drifting sand. But it was nowhere, and even its ghosts had fled the 122-degree heat in terror. "A little extreme for me, I'm afraid," Victor replied.

"I suppose." Labienus stepped out on the balcony beside him, surveying the desert with satisfaction. "As for your question, well, isn't it obvious? They build out of the pernicious mortal desire to vandalize Nature. Marking one's territory in the most grandiose way possible. Look at this place! A monument to the ego of a cheap little confidence trickster. Only its remoteness has presented it from being vandalized in its turn. One has to say that much for the monkeys: they generally destroy their own eyesores, saving Nature a good deal of work. She'll have to take this place, though," he concluded thoughtfully, looking down at the ground floor, where the desert was already coming in through the doors and windows.

Victor thought it was a shame the mansion hadn't been kept up. It was a beautiful house. The rooms were dim and cool and pleasant.

"In the meanwhile, however, it does make an ideal retreat," said Labienus, stepping back inside. Victor followed him.

Three of the echoing rooms had been secured and fitted up with communications equipment, as well as some furniture and other conveniences. Labienus paused to consider certain figures moving on a screen before turning back to Victor.

"Well! I know this was a long way for you to come, but I've got another job for you," he said. "I've had the most delightful idea."

Victor did his best to look intrigued. "Pray enlighten me."

"For the Silence," Labienus told him. "You know that the others have long since agreed that we'll need to make a preemptive strike. The last official communication will be sent at eleven hundred hours Pacific time on the morning of 9 July, 2355. Obviously we want to be already in full control by then. We'll send that last message ourselves, as a smokescreen."

"Yes, obviously," said Victor. "We'll move the night before, I imagine?"

"Of course," Labienus said. "We'll hold a dinner party. A Last-Night-of-the-World-As-We-Know-It feast! Full formal dress, and only the cream of the cream invited. An epicurean menu and wine list, something out of the old days."

"Like the banquet you held at Cliff House," said Victor quietly.

"Eh?"

"The night before the 1906 earthquake, in San Francisco."

"Yes! Just so. And, this is the really original part, a grand musical menu! All the selections to accompany our meal will partake of Doomsday. We'll want a good recording of the *Dies Irae,* and the climactic scenes from *Damnation of Faust* and *Don Giovanni*—and of course that piece by Libbens with the clever name."

"Die Liebestod von Adolf und Eva," said Victor.

"Exactly. I'll leave the rest of it up to your discretion. You're generally clever at arranging these things." Labienus waved a hand. "And as for the guest list— all the chief leaders of the Disloyal Opposition, naturally. Dear old Aegeus himself at the head of the table. No mortals, I need hardly mention; the Board of Directors can be taken out later, at our leisure. The servants will all be our own. Armed security techs, every one of them."

"Armed, sir?" Victor raised an eyebrow. "Surely you don't mean armed with disrupters."

"Don't be obtuse! Even stuffed full of dinner, Aegeus could dodge a disrupter beam. I've seen him do it." Labienus smiled at the memory. "No; simply with carving knives. Close-quarters grappling, a few slashed throats, a few expert beheadings before they regain function. A mere matter of numbers carrying the day. We might do anything with them then. Might even revive some of them, after we've taken over and completed the extermination! They'll have to admit they were given an imaginative evening's entertainment and a damned fine meal. Once they've got over their pique at losing, they'll agree it was all for the best."

"Brilliantly clever, sir," said Victor. "What a sense of style you have. Had you contemplated a suitable location? Here, perhaps, or Transylvania? Or the Paris Opera House?"

"No, it'll have to be Catalina Island," said Labienus with a sigh. "Shame, really, but timing will count for a good deal; we'll need to go straight to the command center after we dispose of the opposition. We'll still have the final stages of the plan to oversee, after all. All the same, I think you'll manage to dress up the banquet facility there. Won't you? Use your imagination."

"Of course, sir."

"But start now," Labienus admonished him. "I shouldn't think it'll be easy finding the ingredients for an old-fashioned feast in this day and age, let alone a mortal who can prepare one. At least it'll divert you from dwelling on the Silence. Don't disappoint me, Victor! I want that night to become a legend in itself."

"It will, sir," Victor replied. "You may rely on me."

Mont St. Michel, 5 June 2342

"He wants a banquet, does he?" speculated Aegeus. "Well, points on style, I must say. Though I do think this proves what I've always said: he's mad as a hatter."

He pivoted sharply in his chair to look as a sudden gust sent rain cascading down the leaded windows behind him. Rain, and then hail, so much the tiny knobs and balls of ice rattled like a firing squad. The faceted crystals of the chandelier winked in the gray light, reflecting the tumult beyond the glass.

"Regrettably, some of us do go mad," said Victor.

"The defectives do," Aegeus told him. "Those of us with any strength of character seem to keep perfect hold of our wits. Very well! We'll give him his dinner party. We'll even help with the catering. If I'm to endure an attempt on my life I'd just as soon enjoy a hearty meal first, wouldn't you? But we'll turn the tables on him in that little matter of throat-cutting. He's appointed you to manage everything; you'll just see to it that the techs on duty are loyal to *us*, and target his people instead."

"With carving knives?" said Victor.

"Why not?" Aegeus watched the storm. "Brutal, but undeniably effective. Labienus wouldn't have got as far as he has if he didn't have flashes of genius now and then. It won't serve him this time, however. I'll see his head on a pike before the night's out, Zeus Kosmetas be my witness!"

"No inquiry before a tribunal?" Victor inquired, shifting in his chair. It was gilt, seventeenth-century, exquisite, and quite uncomfortable.

"Come, come, Victor, when would we find the time for a trial?" said Aegeus, smiling in disbelief. "No. It'll be quick and dirty, and so much the better, if you ask me. With the blood on his hands, he deserves a worse fate. All those poor little mortals! How many millions would you say he's murdered, he and his people? You ought to have a pretty good idea, poor fellow. You've been obliged to watch most of his crimes."

"I'd have no difficulty cutting his throat myself," said Victor, folding his gloved hands. "Will I be permitted?"

"I'd say you've earned it," Aegeus told him, smiling. There was a blinding flash and then a long roll of thunder that set the chandelier pendants tinkling. "Ha! There you are. Divine Zeus sounds his approval."

"How nice for us all," said Victor. The thunder grumbled away into nothing; the hail was stopping now, leaving an unnatural quiet in its place. Aegeus leaned back in his chair, studying Victor.

"I know this has all been hard on you, of course," he said carefully. "You've been outrageously used. When all this is over—perhaps there'll be something we can do for you."

Victor lifted his head and stared. *"Perhaps?"*

"I'm sure it's possible to rewrite your programming," said Aegeus. "I can't promise anything, of course, but I do think the chances are good we can reverse what was done to you." Victor nodded, not taking his eyes from Aegeus. Aegeus looked away. "How's that poor fellow at Suleyman's, the one they found buried in the submarine?" he inquired. "He was a friend of yours, wasn't he?"

"An acquaintance," said Victor. "He's in a repair facility. May be there for years. He was in appalling shape, unfortunately; quite unable to tell us what happened. His wife is with him now."

"Wife?" Aegeus lifted an eyebrow. "An immortal marrying another immortal? I've heard of that happening, but it seems so ill-advised. You know, *till death us do part*? We'd have no chance of escape at all!"

He laughed heartily, and Victor smiled. Another torrent of ice water swept against the windows, so that they fogged and clouded, dimmed the light on all the silk and gilt and silver. It might have been the ballroom of some doomed luxury liner; briefly Victor saw it tilting, tilting in its last moment before slipping down into eternal darkness.

London, 2345: Another Board Meeting:
They Welcome the Next Generation

"I'd like to introduce one of our best and brightest," said Freestone with pride. "Francis Chatterji!"

Chatterji, resplendent in an early twentieth-century tuxedo and cape any vampire would covet, stood in his place and smiled. The investors nodded at him gravely, but Bugleg stared and cried: "You're dressed weird."

Freestone glared at him—Chatterji was *his* protégé—and some of the investors snickered, but Chatterji smiled again and nodded.

"Yes, sir, that's correct. I'm an Eccentric, but I've compensated."

"And compensated very well!" added Freestone. "It might interest you to know, Bugleg, that many of our most productive idea persons are Eccentrics."

"You have to put up with that in creative types," growled Telepop. A lot of worries had descended on his head in the last twelve years, not least of which was wondering what was going to happen in 2355. "Well, Chatterji, what do you do?"

"I work with the stuff of history, sir," Chatterji replied. "The actual events. Our committee solves problems relating to the Company's day-to-day activities in the past and provides our operatives with the means to accomplish their objectives. It, er, helps to have a detailed knowledge of things like—well, people's clothes, and their inventions, and what they ate and drank and everything."

"Is that why you wear those clothes?" demanded Rappacini. Chatterji looked apologetic.

"Actually I find it really does help me fix on the past. I can focus on it more easily if I'm not all surrounded by modern artifacts. Things," he added for the benefit of those present who didn't know what an artifact was.

"And he's come up with a brilliant new *conceptualization* of the past," crowed Freestone, throwing an arch glance at Bugleg. "Tell them, Chatterji."

"Well—it wasn't me alone, really—" Chatterji demurred. "We found that things worked much more smoothly if, instead of trying to relate to the past as though it were this, er, long straight ribbon stretching back into darkness, that we had to smooth the wrinkles out of—well, think of it instead as a sort of picture puzzle. You see? All the pieces are already there and we know what it's supposed to look like. What we have to do is figure out the best and most efficient way to put them all together."

"Fabulous," cried Hapsburg, who had no idea what he was talking about. "You see? It pays to recruit geniuses." The other investors nodded in agreement.

"And then, you see, it's also a little bit like chess, because you've also got your operatives that you can move around to do things for you in the past, which is their environment," Chatterji explained.

"So this is . . . a new invention?" Telepop wanted to know.

"No," replied Chatterji, "it's a new way of looking at temporal physics, which provides a better means of dealing with the temporal paradox of sequential/simultaneous eventuality." He lost them completely with that, he could tell. He held out his hands and added brightly, "And it cuts overhead costs by sixty percent!"

"Oh," said Roche. "Wonderful. We're lucky to have people like you, Chatterton."

"What are you working on right now?" Rossum wanted to know.

"We're sort of . . . to use the idea of a puzzle again, you could say what we're doing is sorting through the box and, er, picking out all the pieces with straight edges," said Chatterji. "Trying to establish a frame within which we can work, you see? And then we feel we'll be in a good position to tackle the prehistory problem. That's seeing if we can work out a way to deal with that Great Goat Cult thing."

"Will that be hard?" Roche looked concerned.

"We don't think so. I mean obviously we've already solved the problem, temporally speaking; we just need to figure out when and how, and then do it."

"Okay," said Rossum dubiously.

"We've made up a five-year timetable, and we've got our best people working on it," Chatterji told him, a little defensive. "All projections indicate we'll bring it in under budget, too."

"Of course you will," said Freestone. "We have the greatest confidence in our young people, Chatterji. Please, sit down."

Chatterji sank into his chair and half rose for a moment, adjusting his cape.

Lopez, smooth and unobtrusive, set a glass of water at his elbow and he grabbed the glass and drank gratefully. "New business?" Hapsburg asked.

"Yes, new business. What do you have for us, Lopez?" inquired Freestone.

"The report concerning our holdings on Mars," said Lopez. "As you're no doubt all aware, Areco has just filed suit against the Martian Agricultural Collective, claiming they have failed to meet the terms of the original settlement contract which will expire at midnight on 31 Christmas, 2351 . . ."

Everyone present made a face. What was going to happen in Mars Two in six years' time was, sadly, well known to the board members, and the topic caused stress levels to rise in all those present except Telepop, who was already stressed out and preoccupied with a paradox of his own: how *The Revenge of the Cyborg Virgins*, despite being one of the highest-grossing releases in history, had still failed to turn a profit.

When Bugleg left the meeting he followed his usual procedure: he let the cyborg driver take him to his apartment warren, where he climbed out and hastened to the aglift. When he got in, however, he rode it *down* to the garage floor below and emerged again. Blinking around fearfully he went out to the mounting block, where a big sleek car waited. The door swung open and Ratlin grinned at him. "Get in."

Bugleg looked around, pulling a pair of sun goggles from his coat pocket and slipping them on before stepping into the car. The door slammed shut and the agcar zoomed away from the block with a lurch, almost hitting a fusion conduit as it went around the corner. Bugleg gasped; Ratlin waved an impatient hand.

"What's to be afraid of? I never hit anything head-on."

"You should be more careful," Bugleg told him.

"I'm careful about what counts," Ratlin snapped. "Do you want to see this place or not, cousin? 'Cause I can pop the door and leave you crying in the unkind light by the side of the road, and don't think I wouldn't do it, too!"

"You're mean," Bugleg told him resentfully.

"Damn right I am," Ratlin retorted. "Takes a mean fellow to get anywhere in this life."

"But that's wrong," Bugleg insisted. "Being mean is wrong."

Ratlin snarled at him and reached over to the door controls. "I'll do it," he threatened. "I'll pitch you out! Out, crash, on your big stupid sanctimonial head."

They bickered along like this for the next while, as the agcar sped on in the general direction of Wanstead, veering unsteadily through the sparse traffic, and they barely noticed when it turned in at last under an arch that bore the legend: MANOR PARK PUBLIC STORAGE.

"Here we are," observed Ratlin. The car swerved into a parking space and, shutting itself off, settled to the ground. He ordered the door open and managed to restrain his urge to boot Bugleg as he climbed out. Emerging himself, he set off briskly down the long corridor into the depths of the storage complex.

It was dimly lit and funereal, as all such places are, and made more so by the décor: here and there in niches along the walls, following the Benthamite creed of utility in all things, were mounted the more attractive of the headstones and other memorials that had graced the old Manor Park Cemetery. Neither Bugleg nor Ratlin had much appreciation for art, however. They hurried along in silence and at last stopped in the gloom before a door numbered 666.

"Here." Ratlin keyed in a code and the door opened with a sad little chime, the first few notes of a well-known funeral march. Bugleg didn't get the joke, however, and followed him unsmiling into the chamber beyond.

It was one of the bigger units the storage facility had to offer, but there was barely room to walk its length for the hundreds of green chlorilar drums stacked deep and high. Bugleg had to turn sideways and squeeze after Ratlin, who ran chuckling along the access way. "You see?" he cried. "All you could ever need. The stuff your dreams are made of, the answer to your prayers!"

"I don't pray," said Bugleg crossly, looking up at the towering drums. "That's *sick*. Anyway, this says it's food," he added, pointing to the universal symbol on each drum showing a spoon and fork.

"Well, of course it *says* it's food," answered Ratlin, baring his teeth. "Stupid, think it'd have a label on it says Sweet Poison, Cyborgs Only Please? You mooncalf. Says it's treacle! But if you look at it magnified you'll see dear little monsters sludging about in the stuff, ready to rip and rend any cyborg's innards they can get their hooks into."

Bugleg winced. "But—but not hurt them. Just shut them off. It won't hurt anybody."

Ratlin just stared at him, too amazed to be annoyed. "Oh, no, of course it won't hurt anybody," he said at last. "Your slaves ain't anybody, after all, are they? They'll just swallow it down and fly off into the sky on pink wings, see if they don't."

When they emerged, neither of them noticed the agvan parked near the entrance, though it had not been there when they went in. Ratlin's car sped away
down the street, clipping a light standard near the corner but not enough to
slow it appreciably as it set its course back to Neasden.

No sooner had it gone than the van's door opened and Labienus emerged,
followed by another immortal. They hurried into the storage facility, replaying
the audio surveillance transcript and counting the footsteps they heard. When
they stood opposite the door of unit 666, Labienus halted and tilted his head.

"Here," he said, inhaling deeply. "What's that, Kiu? Would you say that's
treacle?"

"No," she replied, closing her eyes as she analyzed it. "But it's something
we're meant to think is treacle."

"Ha." Labienus considered the keypad and scanned for thermolumines-
cence. He struck the lit keys in order of faintness, the brightest last. The tiny
dirge played for them and the lock disengaged. With smiles of self-
congratulation they went in.

Ten minutes later they came out with a sampler tube full of a dark brown
substance, carefully sealed in a biohazard pouch. "Analysis is all very well,"
Kiu was saying, "but the proof will be a test, of course."

"Of course," Labienus agreed. "I have a number of deserving brethren in
mind. It's been long enough since the Options Research scandal that we can
risk a quiet disappearance or two."

Kiu just nodded. There was no other vehicle parked on the street when
they returned to the van, because they would have noticed if there had been
one. Not until after they had climbed into the back and the van had driven off
did another surveillance van, nearly identical, come slowly around the corner
and park.

A pair of immortals emerged and, looking around cautiously, made their
way into the storage facility and straight to unit 666. When they came out they
too had a biohazard pouch containing a sampler tube full of . . . treacle?

"Maybe we should tie it to the roof of the van," joked one of the immortals.
The other one looked at him in disdain.

"I've worked for Aegeus a lot longer than you have," he said. "When he
says there's a hazard, you can be damned sure there's a hazard."

"I'm not reading one," his companion scoffed, tucking the pouch into his
coat pocket as they walked out to their van.

"What would be more dangerous than a hazard *we* couldn't perceive, you fool?" snapped the other immortal. His friend considered that and abruptly looked terrified. He took the pouch from his pocket and held it at arm's length until they got to the van, where he dropped it in a biogen box and closed the lid firmly.

PART III

CHAPTER 10

In the Hill and Out of It

It was the scariest thing Tiara had ever done, but all the great heroines walked with her, advised her, so that on a star-dizzy night she went out to the distant front of the hill. There she found the concealed trail up to the front door, and paraded there until the wind took the scent of her down into the tunnels.

Not long to wait then. She retreated into the barbed darkness of a bramble hedge until Uncle Ratlin came peering out, casting to and fro uncertainly.

"Is it you, Baby doll?" he hissed. "Come to pay us a visit for lovely old time's sake? Getting a little randified? Oh, please let it be you."

"It is I, and no other," Tiara told him. "But I've not come to give, not at all. I've come only to see how you're working on my new hill. Where's my holoset of a thousand channels? Where's my lace curtains and fine things?" Uncle Ratlin trembled at the sight of Tiara and reached out as though he'd dearly like to squeeze her, but controlled himself with effort.

"Why, my dear—my dearest—a fine hill like what I'm making for you takes time, you see? Takes near as forever. I've got your Uncles Glot and Spondip, you remember them, well, I've had them out searching all night every night for just the right spot, clean sweet stone with water running through, and the air just wobbly enough so the big people can't see it too easily. And haven't they found the prettiest site in all the world!"

"Have they now? And is it near to here, Uncle dear?" Tiara inquired, edging a little closer and then retreating.

"Eeeee! Oh, the turn of your little ankle, sweetmeat—well, it's not so near as Barbie knows about it, but not so far we mightn't run there in a short hot night," Uncle Ratlin told her, rubbing his hands over himself nervously. "And we'll run there when it's done, shall we, darling, just you and me and the

Uncles? And a host of stupids to wait on you? Leave old Barbie here to stew in her own grease? No killing, if you like. Just walk out the door, whore. Eh?"

"Perhaps." Tiara circled around a gorse bush, peering through its flowers at Ratlin. "Though of course there's the big people to worry about. I want none of them tracking up my nice stain-resistant carpets with their muddy boots! Especially the cyborg ones, the slaves."

"Well, but there's my famous plan, you see!" Uncle Ratlin grinned and ventured forward to the bush. "There won't *be* any of the slaves by then, darling. We'll have killed them entirely! Not so long now neither. Delivery system perfected, don't you know?"

"And how should I know?" Tiara found a shaft of starlight and began to dance in it, pretending to watch her gray shadow but keeping an eye on Uncle Ratlin. "I am young and beautiful, and you killed the slave dusty long years ago, before ever I was born or thought of. How'd you kill him, anyway? Was it waves of death from a gun?"

"O, no, my love," Ratlin told her, coming around the bush into the starlight. "That wasn't enough. We tried and tried with the disrupter fields, but he was proof against that now; shoot him however many times we might, though he turned purple and red like brambleberries, he always went pink again in the end. His nasty little inside things were taking care of him, had learned to reprogram themselves, you see? I'd get so tired, staying up so late, blasting him, and I'd think he'd die, he'd go all stiff and blue and we'd be so happy—but or ever the day broke, he'd shiver and draw breath and start that damned crying again. I cried, too."

"Poor dearie," cooed Tiara. "Poor Uncle. How it must have vexed your heart! But however did you really and finally kill the wicked slave, then?"

"Well—" Uncle Ratlin scuttled forward and made a grab for her, but Tiara was too swift for him. She leaped into the branches of a tree, so that all he had in his hand was a scrap of her cobwebby gown, and he whined and tore at his beard in frustration as she laughed down at him from against the stars.

"Tell me," she demanded. "If I'm to be your own Quean I must know all."

"It was his biomechanicals, darling girl!" He yelled the secret aloud and then froze, with only his darting eyes moving, casting suspicious glances side to side.

"Biomechanicals?" Tiara flexed and sprang, higher into the tree.

"No use to blast him, you see?" Uncle Ratlin told her in a lower voice, following her along the ground. "Except that it made him hold still awhile. And in that little while we could cut him, take samples of his nasty cyborg blood and look at it up close. Got a good look at the tiny dreadfuls that crawl about in his body and make him live. And, darling, it was me—not Spondip nor Glot nor Moonifan, but onliest me—that thought, well, we could make those, too, couldn't we? Our very own biomechanicals to make war on his?

"And that's what we did, sugar. The stupids made them for us all according to plan. So tiny you couldn't see them but through a glass, our very own bitsy black crabs in a vial of death for the slave."

"How wonderful," said Tiara, hating him. "How marvelous. And did you give him them to drink, and blind his blue eyes that way, poisoning his sore body?"

"Drink? No." Uncle Ratlin scrabbled experimentally at the tree bark, peering up through the branches at her. "We shot him so he lay still, and then we put them in a needle and stuck them into his heart. He'd have puked up anything we gave him to drink, you see? Because he knew we had him. But the others won't know!

"And you should have seen, my lovey, seen how he clawed and scratched and cried for breath. How his face went black, as our things moved under his skin! This time when he choked his last it really finally and forever was his very last. We took turns watching, Spondip and I and Stilcheese, hours we waited, but he never went pink again. Never breathed. Dead, at last!"

"Oh, at last," echoed Tiara.

"And that was when we knew we had the Ruin in our own hands, my adorable Quean," said Uncle Ratlin, attempting a short leap up the tree and not quite making it. "The perfected Ruin to avenge the kin. Such cleverness! You hark now. The slaves are frightful greedy for chocolates."

"Chocolates," repeated Tiara uncertainly, pushing at the Memory for a definition. It supplied her with a mental image of bright-wrapped bars and boxes on shop shelves, a nice smell, sweet and luring.

"Creams and kisses and syrups and mousses," gloated Uncle Ratlin. "They can't resist them. Your uncle Ratlin owns a chocolate fabricatory and has big people working in it."

"Oh, you never," Tiara scoffed, but she leaned down a little more closely to hear.

"I do!" Ratlin insisted. He jumped and caught a low branch. He hung there a moment, panting with effort, before he went on: "How proud you'd be of your big fine uncle if you could only see! Big people laboring to make their own Ruin for your uncle Ratlin, and them never knowing. Big people nodding and scraping and doing my will. I'm as important as anybody on holo, I can tell you."

"Can I believe this?" wondered Tiara, retreating upward again. Ratlin looked up despairingly and hoisted himself astraddle the branch.

"Believe it, for it's all true," he implored. "And oh, my rows of silver vats mixing the creams, my dearie, and oh my vacuum-sealed Packaged Assortments! With a lovely picture of rosebuds on the box, just think, and curly writing saying RATLIN'S FINEST."

"I am amazed, and know not what to say," Tiara told him. She dangled her legs just out of his reach. He whimpered and reached for her, but she drew back and ordered: "Tell us more!"

"It's all to trick the slaves! Haven't they indulged themselves with my Raspberry Truffles and Marzipan Fudge Delights this many a year, with no harm to themselves at all? *They'll never suspect a thing!*" Uncle Ratlin began to hump the branch in his neediness.

"But what ought they to suspect, you strong clever studling uncle?" Tiara coaxed.

"That the terrible day will come when the big people gift them with special-ordered assortments, a box for each slave, here, 'thank you for faithful years of service!'"

"But that's wrong," cried Tiara. "That's stupid, to kill their own creatures they made. How like the murdering big people."

"Ain't it, though?" Uncle Ratlin grinned up at her. "Stupider than they know, because with their slaves gone, they'll have nobody to protect them when we pay them out, and bloody hell how we *will* pay them out for all they've done to us! Ages since forever hiding in the hills, afraid of their bullies and thieves, but never again, not once their slaves are all dead. They're not so big or so holy-holy when they're afraid. Oh, I've vials of poisons to hiss into their air, leak into their water. I've pulses to shut down their machines. We'll see who's so high and mighty, this time three months have come and gone!"

"You are just so clever," Tiara exclaimed. "Three months, you say?"

"I do," Ratlin told her, clambering up to stand on his branch. "And once it's all over and done there'll be all the time in the world to dig you your beautiful hill. All the pieces are in place, my pretty thing."

"Well, you've won my heart entirely. Nothing must be allowed to stand in the way of such a triumph! I graciously grant you delay in the delivery of my own hill. If you can do all this, sweet Uncle, you shall surely enjoy my favor when the world's won."

"Not a little favor *now*?" Uncle Ratlin leered slyly, peering up her skirt. "To console your poor old uncle and send him back to the workshop with a spring in his step?"

"Oh, you've no time for such things," Tiara told him airily. "Now that I know what work you have in hand, I really must insist you get on with it. Avenge the kin, Uncle, and become the hero I dream of, and then, oh, then, I'll come to thee in a sheer negligée to passionate and provocate thy heart!"

So saying, she launched herself out into the air and caught the branch of a neighboring tree, and swung away through the night. Ratlin vaulted after her with a shriek, but he was not so young as he had been. He fell from the bough and landed in the long grass like a windfall apple. He lay there weeping and listening to her laughter fading away, little silver-bell laughter like the stars themselves laughing.

The slave suffered a collapse when Tiara explained the whole plot to him. For close to an hour he lay curled in a heap, and forgot where he was and who she was, and it took all her patience to talk to him gently. At last she lay down beside him and put her face next to his, and stroked back his hair, and sang to him until his terrors subsided a little. "And, you know," she told him, "my treasure, my own, it'll never happen at all."

"It won't?" He groped with his working hand to knuckle away tears.

"No indeed, because we'll thwart his black designs." Tiara sat up, and pulled him up with her. "We'll be like brave clever Commander Bell-Fairfax. We'll make up the finest plan in the world. We'll warn the slaves, just as Bess the landlord's daughter warned her lover with her death, only we will not die. Now, how will we warn them, my dearest?"

"I don't know." The slave began to shake again. "I don't know where any of them are—don't know how to get word—Joseph would have known, but Joseph, poor Joseph, they shot him and he lay there crippled and it was my fault—"

"Stop it right now," Tiara ordered, and wound her arms around him tight. "You must think of what's to be done, not sad things. You'll be as clever as Odysseus. Just think, poor Aladdin lay in the dark, just like you here now, despairing of all hope forever, and didn't he have a happy ending? Yes, with a genie in the lamp?"

"Arabian Nights," the slave gasped. "Suleyman! Joseph had a friend—and he was powerful, he had influence—he was a Section Head—and he told Joseph a way—Oh, think, Lewis, think!" He smacked his forehead with his fist as though to beat the memory back in, once, twice, again, until she caught his hand and held it still.

"No more hurting yourself," she commanded. "You will surely remember."

"But what was it Joseph told me, that time?" the slave wailed. "You could get messages to Suleyman if there was anything you'd discovered, you could send him word and the Company would never know. You could go to a place—you could leave a message—oh, I didn't use to be like this, you know, I could remember anything, but it's all scrambled up inside—Allah, Allah is merciful, Allah is compassionate, yes, *yes*! Compassionates. The Compassionates of Allah." The slave began to giggle helplessly, and she let him laugh until he had run out of breath.

"The Compassionates of Allah?" she prompted, as he began to murmur the words to an old song. He nodded. "What is that, my golden beloved?"

"A religious order," he replied. "Black brothers who help the poor. They had houses in every big city. And Joseph told me—he said you could leave a message for Suleyman with them, and they'd see he got it. Oh, but that was years ago. I wasn't always here, you know. I was a good operative."

"The very best, my darling," Tiara assured him, but she was getting impatient. "So all we have to do is go to Compassionates of Allah and say, 'Here is a message for Uncle Suleyman'?"

The slave was silent a moment. "I suppose we could do that," he said in a clearer voice. "I suppose so. But . . . warning him wouldn't be enough. If there were only a way to send him some of the biomechanicals themselves . . ."

"Why, my heart's darling?"

"Because if he could analyze them, he could devise an upgrade that would protect the rest of my kind," said the slave, thinking very hard. "Latif is a genius. Little Latif, he was only a baby then, neophyte in his school uniform and he sat right there at the table with us, with Joseph and Mendoza and I . . . and he's the only one left now." He drew a deep breath. "She held me. She stroked my hair. But she never saw me, me or anyone, she just looked straight through us all with those black, black eyes because she was seeing *him*. Only him, ever, like a nun meditating on the names of God. I used to wonder what it would be like to love someone that much, and then I . . . What could I have said to her? She was going away in the morning and I was going to England, and I never thought, my God I never thought—"

"But you're thinking now, my darling," Tiara crooned. "And Mendoza has gone away happy with the brave commander. So no more crying. How do we get Uncle Suleyman some of the biomechanicals?"

The slave calmed at her touch, gradually. His face worked with the effort of thought. "A blood sample from me," he said at last. "I'm still rotten with the damned things. There's a war going on inside me all the time, I can hear them fighting. My nanobots versus the ones your uncle designed. We could ship it off to Suleyman parcel post, I suppose . . . except how? Let leeches suck on me and send them in a biopouch? Ah, but they'd die." He began to shiver. "Don't cut me."

"Nobody will cut you." Tiara pulled his face down and kissed him. "Come now, my warrior of the sun. Lie down and I will soothe your heart." He obeyed her, shaking as though he had a fever, and she stretched out next to him again.

"*'I have been a prisoner on the rack,'*" he murmured, "*'I have been a slave pierced with hot irons. I have been a supplicant for my own murder. I have been consigned to the house of the dead . . .'*"

"No, my adored, of course you haven't."

"What story am I in?" he asked faintly.

"My story," Tiara replied, and sang to him until he fell asleep.

It was only a stupid. It had no visible gender and no life of its own, not that it would have known what to do with an independent life if it had one. When one of the Uncles or Quean Barbie gave it an order, then it felt alive; then there was work to be done, a sense of purpose! And that was all it knew of pleasure or pain.

It could think, but not in the same ways or for the same reasons you or I think. Indeed, some of its thoughts were deep and profound, even brilliant, impossibly detailed and splendid constructions of a logic we would find incomprehensible. But it never thought unless it was ordered to.

It hadn't been ordered to think in a while, because it had gotten lost in a less frequented section of the hill, wandering in the wrong direction down tunnels that were darker and colder and more choked with trash the farther it went. Quean Barbie was unlikely to notice it was missing and send others to look for it. She never knew from one moment to the next how many stupids she had.

Sooner or later it would stumble and fall, and forget to get up, and it would die. A complex enzymatic reaction would then take place, reducing its body to a powdery shell. If the other stupids were with it at the time, they would carefully break and scatter the shell, so as not to leave anything lying around in the way; but if it died alone, its husk might lie there forever, ashes and chalk, perfect image of a living thing. As much of a living thing as it had been, that is.

But then!

She was there in the darkness like a white flame, and Her glorious hair streamed upward like white fire, and Her eyes blazed with meaning. Its little lipless mouth gaped in wonder. It tottered to be closer to Her, even as She struck out at it, a glancing blow to make stars dance in its eyes. *Trespasser!* she screamed at it. *I will kill thee!*

I will die, it agreed, and knelt to oblige Her.

But before it could shut down its heart, She had seized it by its fragile arm and was staring intently into its eyes. *No,* She told it, *thou shalt not die. I have work for thee.*

Work. Now it knew pleasure, now it was alive, and its breath came quickly in its shallow chest and it blinked its moist eyes. It waited, trembling, for the impetus of Her will. She told it what She needed it to make. She described what the made thing must do, and its qualities. *Yes,* it agreed. *Yes, yes.*

So intent on the work was it that it did not even notice when She withdrew. It crouched on the floor, sorting quickly through the piled debris there, adding this bit of wire or that oddment of glass to a small but steadily growing heap, discarding some as new concepts suggested themselves, grabbing up others as solutions to certain problems occurred to it.

It didn't need light. It didn't need food or rest. Nothing mattered except its work.

When She returned it had completed its task, and held up proudly what She had required of it. She took the work from its hands, and it felt its arms grow suddenly heavy, its heart falter. She had retreated from it and now its life was retreating, too. It felt neither grief nor resentment nor weariness nor peace. There was nothing there to feel. Between one moment and the next it was gone, like a soap bubble vanishing.

Tiara knelt beside her slave, examining the device the stupid had made for her. It looked for all the world like a perfume atomizer, a little globe of colorless glass with a nozzle and a bulb. Gingerly she held the nozzle to the slave's left arm, the useless one, and squeezed the bulb.

There was a hiss; the nozzle suckered into the dead arm and a red fog began to roil inside the globe, spinning and condensing. The slave woke, opened his blind eyes and drew breath to scream. She clapped her free hand over his mouth. The hissing stopped; she looked down and saw that the globe now seemed to be made of ruby-colored glass, and was heavy and suddenly very cold. She pulled it away and set it down. Droplets of chill began to frost it. On the slave's arm, there was a tiny red wound where the nozzle had been, but it crusted black almost at once.

"Poor dear, it's only me," she told the slave, and lifted her hand. His head rolled to one side and he gasped for breath. She pursed her little mouth. "You have to tell me how clever I am, now, because I've just done a splendid thing, my lover," she informed him.

"You're very clever," he whispered. "Please let me out of here."

"Sweet brave darling, it's *me*," she reminded him. "Your own Princess. I'm trying to help us, remember?"

His lips moved as he repeated what she'd said, but silently, and then his face was a study in confusion. His eyebrows drew together. "Princess," he said. "All right."

"You have got to stop this," she told him, sternly but graciously. "We'll never get anything done if you're crazy all the time."

"No, we won't," he agreed feebly.

"Now, listen to me. I took the blood sample we need. Here it is, see?" She lifted his good hand and put the blood-globe in it. His face twitched in surprise at the coldness. "It's going to stay nice and fresh and cold and not die, so Uncle Suleyman can look at it and make an upgrade. Remember?"

"I remember," the slave replied, but he said it too fast; she could tell he was just saying it. She took the globe away lest he drop it and gathered him in her arms with a resigned sigh.

"Poor baby," she said, as much to herself as to him. "This is all too much stress and nervous tension for you. You need to relax and have a lovely vacation. We'll go to London to look at the Queen, frighten the little mouse under her chair. And we'll stay at Claridge's . . . and we'll drink champagne . . . and we'll buy beautiful clothes in all the shops . . . and we'll go to the British Museum . . . and all the men will dance with me. Remember how we're going to do that, my own?"

"Claridge's," said the slave wonderingly. "Oh, my . . ."

"But you must tell me, my truest love," she went on, and her voice sharpened a bit, "you must tell me what I'm to do next. How do I get the blood sample to Uncle Suleyman? Think for me, now."

The slave thought until sweat beaded on his brow. At last the pieces of broken chain connected, and he was able to tell her.

Tiara fed him well before she left, trout and snails and young greens from the field, as much as she could find in haste. Then she covered him up in the towels and her afghan, telling him to go to sleep. As an afterthought she took pieces of dead men and arranged them around him to obscure the view of anyone unwelcome looking into the room. Then she made her way swiftly to the old tunnel, and ventured out into the night.

It was a bigger night than it had ever been. The horizon was much wider, and there were greater wonders and worse dangers than there had used to be. She looked past the familiar little light of Sweeney's farm and considered the pale curve of the road that ran beyond it, out of sight beyond the black hill that had been the limit of the known world for as long as she could remember.

Anything was out there. Everything was out there. London was out there, and all the people in the stories. And she was Bess the landlord's daughter, and she was all the other heroines, about to go into the unknown, and bravely, too.

Tiara drew herself up and sprang forward with a salmon's leap, and ran down across the heather like a breeze passing through the night, so light was her footfall. She reached the road sooner than she had expected to, and sped off along its dark length.

Knockdoul was no place at all. Three houses and two shops? And one of them doubling as parcel office and public house? But Tiara had never seen any place so huge, and she cringed in its shadows with her heart pounding.

She did not know which were the shops, but one had a big bowfront window, and peering into its darkness she saw shiny things arranged on shelves, all neat, and the Memory insisted this must be what she wanted. There was no one within. She had to climb up to a high window and glare in at a lumpen big lady who stirred at last from beneath her quilt and came slowly downstairs to the back door.

The shopkeeper opened the door and stood gazing thoughtfully out into the night, drinking in the cold air and listening to the distant lowing of cattle, all of which got into a dream she was having . . . She moved aside absently to let Tiara pass, never seeing her.

Tiara ran to the front of the shop and paused, staring, breathing deep. So many smells! None that she knew at all. Fighting her panic, she made herself pace carefully along the shelves, looking for the things the slave had described.

There, by the rows and rows of printed picture cards, were the shiny boxes and silly spangles of ribbon, all flat and ready to be assembled into a pleasing gift for a loved one. She jostled the rack slightly as she poked among them and the pretty cards began to call out their recorded greetings in tinny voices, faint in the night, *To my loving wife! Happy birthday to a dear nephew! Congratulations on the occasion of your civil union! Deepest sympathy!* She bared her little teeth at them until they stammered into silence. And there were bright carry-bags, too, and that was useful. She took what she needed and thrust it into a rustly bag, and dragged it after her as she continued her search.

In a high case Tiara found the brown bottles arrayed, and had to spring up on the counter to reach them. She peered at each one, searching for the long writing that the slave had told her about, writing that began with a mark like a bird's foot or a cleft stick; and that was how she found the vitamin supplements. She loaded them into the bag and sprang down. What else, now, was lacking?

Easy to find the polarized dark goggles she needed, though they were dusty and flyspecked on their display rack. Who needed such things in that gray rainy country, except holidaymakers hoping to ski? And easy to find the writing things, the thin cylinders. Her eye was drawn to a lovely one, thicker and bigger than the others, its case and cap all decorated with swirly patterns. As she pulled it from the display there was a click, and a ghostly voice told her: *You'll be glad you've selected the Little Book of Kells Calligraphy Master! Price is One Punt Eightpence. For information on entering the all-parish schools penmanship competition for 2355, kindly apply to the keeper of this shop.*

One punt eightpence? Yes, that was the other thing she needed. She found the cashbox and puzzled over it only a moment before she got it to disgorge the greasy leaves of paper marked with pictures of bearded men and harps. They smelled fearfully of big people, but she crammed a good wad of them into her bag.

Nothing left, then, but to sprint up the stairs to the big lady's bed-sitter and rifle her closet. These weren't Princess clothes at all! Bulky cable-knit things and floppy frumpy stuff. No gauzy moonbeams or cobwebs. Tiara wrinkled her nose at the sight of them, but selected what she needed without lingering, reflecting that this was a disguise after all.

Her bag was quite heavy, tearing now. Tiara helped herself to one of the pillow slips off the big lady's bed: much better. She rearranged her goods and, hefting the bag over her shoulder, ran lightly down the stairs and out into the night.

The big lady woke with a start and drew back from the doorway, realizing that she'd been sleepwalking again. Muttering to herself, she shut and locked the door and creaked back up to bed.

Tiara made for the garden wall, but found she was unable to vault it again with her bag. She turned to find another way out, and stopped, staring.

She'd scarcely glanced at the place on her way in; now it took her attention fiercely. A square of green walled by stone, with roses tidy all along the wall, white roses echoing starlight, and how the stars were glittering down! And such perfume, and the bright shimmer of water in a stone basin. And a man.

He did not move. After a moment Tiara understood that he wasn't a real man but a stone figure, no taller than she was, really; only the distance and the starlight had made him seem big. She ventured close.

The man was smiling so kindly, with such a gentle face, but staring past her with blind stone eyes, just as her slave stared. He was holding out his cupped hands before him. Clear water welled from his palms, and trickled down over his fingertips to drop into the stone basin. He seemed to be offering Tiara a drink.

She came forward, enchanted, leaning close to look into his hands. There were rippling stars reflected in the water. She bent her head and drank thirstily. It was good water. She could taste the stars.

"You have our royal thanks," she told him grandly, but he said nothing. Suddenly Tiara wanted her slave very much.

There was an arched gate in the wall just beyond, and she slipped out through it and ran away. So light her footfall was that even with the bag, she made no sound as she left Knockdoul behind her.

It was quick, the journey back. Was this all it took to cross the boundaries of her old life? Tiara looked out in astonishment at the wide world she'd explored, beginning to go pale in the creeping dawn, and saw it was only a little place.

And yet her old world was smaller still. She pushed her way down through the crawlhole to the bone room, and her heart pounded against her ribs to see her slave still there, huddled where she'd left him. She swept the old brown bones aside and knelt to kiss his cheek. He jumped and shivered, opening his eyes.

"It's me, darling one, jewel of my heart," she told him. "Such presents I've brought you!" Tiara upended the pillow slip and spilled out her loot, the bright stuff and the clothes and the brown bottles. The slave heard them rattling out and his eyebrows drew together in confusion, then arched wide with amazement. He levered himself upright.

"Great Caesar's ghost," he cried hoarsely. "You did it? You've gone and come back? Oh, where's my time sense? My Princess, my beautiful brave one!" His nostrils flared as he caught the scent of what was in the brown bottles. "And you've brought me vitamins—" He groped frantically for them.

"To be sure I have, sweet lord," she crowed, and pressed a bottle into his hand. He turned it between his fingers, unable to get it open, until she saw what was the matter and took it back. " 'Having said this, Calypso laid her table, setting out in abundance Ambrosia and pouring the red nectar; and so the way-opener, the Swift-Arriving, drank and ate,' " she quoted teasingly. She twisted the neck from the bottle and gave it back to her slave, who gulped the contents down as though they were nectar and ambrosia indeed.

"Oh," he cried, when he had swallowed them, "oh, well done, Princess. That was a high-mineral supplement. God Apollo, I'll be walking down Brook Street in no time! Is there any more?"

"Long-vexed royal Odysseus, there is so," Tiara chanted. "Bottles and jars, jars and bottles, and all for the darling one. Will you have more, my hero?"

The slave laughed wildly. "Ah, I could fill myself so full I'd rattle! No, no, best to be temperate. Drink down some water, yes, metabolize a little at a time. And you're the hero, the heroine, my little goddess, you're rosy-fingered Dawn herself."

" 'And the goddess gave him a skin of dark wine, and another of water,' " Tiara recited, fetching him the beer bottle they kept water in. He drank it down as she watched gleefully. "But wait! There's more."

"You found paper to make a parcel?"

"How much would you expect to pay," she sang, fetching out the present kit, "for this beautiful parcel-post-wrappy thing? Thirty punts? Forty? Fifty? Well, you can have it all today for our low, low price of only free!"

"Oooo," chortled the slave, and felt about for it until she set it in his hands. His thin fingers turned it and turned it, as his face grew thoughtful. "Yes," he said. "I know what this is. It folds into a box, doesn't it? Here are the seals and tabs. Well done, well done. We'll need only to pack the sample with something so it doesn't rattle about." He set it by. "Did you find a pen, my love?"

"The very beautiful Little Book of Kells Calligraphy Master," Tiara replied, putting it into his hand with a flourish.

"Really?" The slave ran his thumb over its shaft until he found the activator button, which he pressed. The pen came on with a little beep, and its red light winked to show it was readying the laserjet. "How exciting! We must have a scriptorium."

Tiara had no idea what that might mean, but it turned out to be a broken lighting panel laid across the slave's lap and underpropped by four skulls of roughly matching sizes. The torn paper sack was torn further, into a sheet of serviceable size and flatness, and Tiara arranged it before the slave and held it for him as he lifted pen to paper.

Here he paused a moment, sucking in his lower lip as he thought very hard. At last he began to write, slowly and carefully shaping the letters he could not see. In straggling but beautiful Latin, he wrote:

HAIL SULEYMAN,

I, LEWIS, OUT OF THE DEPTHS GREET YOU. WE HAVE FRIENDS IN COM-
MON. JOSEPH WAS WITH ME WHEN I WAS SO UNFORTUNATE AS TO BE
BETRAYED BY OUR MASTERS, WHOSE DEEDS YOU HAVE SUSPECTED. THEIR
DEVICES YOU MAY KNOW BY EXAMINING CAREFULLY THE ENCLOSED,
WHICH IS MY OWN BLOOD HORRIBLY INVADED. I IMPLORE YOU, DEVISE
REMEDY FOR THIS INVASION, BEFORE IT IS SET LOOSE ON OUR KIND. BE-
WARE GIFTS OF THEOBROMOS, FOR THEY WILL BEAR THE INVADERS AS
THE TROJAN HORSE BORE GREEKS. PLEASE EXCUSE ERRORS IN PENMAN-
SHIP AS I HAVE NEITHER LIGHT NOR EYES. BE WARNED BY MY MOST MIS-
ERABLE EXAMPLE.

"If only there was a way to render 'biomechanicals' in Latin," the slave fussed, laying down the pen.

"What is Latin, my treasure?" Tiara looked admiringly at the flowing uncials.

"A secret language," the slave told her, laying a finger beside his nose. "No one's spoken it in centuries, but Suleyman will be able to read it. You see? We're terribly clever, darling. Where's that box got to, now?"

The parcelmistress turned, frowning, and looked about her tiny office. Where had the voice come from? She started involuntarily as it sounded on the air again. "If you please," it insisted, "I want to send a parcel to Compassionates of Allah. It's a present for Uncle Suleyman."

A bright-wrapped package came over the edge of the counter. The parcelmistress leaned forward and stared down at the little girl who had spoken to her. There was a moment when her brain raced wildly to make sense of what she was seeing.

The child was white as ashes, wore polarized goggles, a lot of bulky clothing and a stocking cap, though her tiny dirty feet were bare. Was she a Traveler's child from one of the caravans? Was she an albino? The Compassionates of Allah were all black men, so perhaps—

"A nice birthday present for your uncle?" the parcelmistress inquired, pulling the little box onto the mailer. It was weighed, enclosed in a mold, and the mold was injected with foam that expanded into a protective shell and dried instantly. The mold withdrew, leaving the parcel ready for its label.

"Yes indeed," the child replied, in such a piercingly sweet voice the parcelmistress very nearly forgot what she was doing. She shook her head in confusion and turned to the microphone.

"And where would he live, your uncle Suleyman?" she asked. The child simply stared at her, expressionless behind the great black optics of her goggles. "Er—nearest charterhouse of the Compassionates of Allah, would it be?"

"Yes indeed," the child repeated.

"That'll be in Dublin," the parcelmistress told her, and asked the printer for a label with the correct address. It came whirring out on an avery, and she tore it off and affixed it to the parcel. "Two and seven, dear."

A grubby ball of money bounced up on the counter. The parcelmistress decided the child was certainly from the caravans; nobody but tinkers and road trash used cash anymore, even here. She took the old bills gingerly and turned to make change, but when she turned back she was alone in the room. She stood there, blinking a moment, as her memory of the visitor faded, shifted, altered. Without thinking she dropped the change in her pocket and set the package with the others, where the van boy would pick them up that afternoon.

And he did so, and the little parcel began its long journey. The first stop was the tall house full of robed black men, where a Communications Brother peered at the address and frowned in puzzlement. He took it to the office of the most reverend of the gentlemen there, and after a brief discussion they lasered open the foam case and beheld the package. They opened it cautiously and found the letter.

Within three hours the parcel had been sealed up again and locked in a case, which the reverend Brother carried with him as he boarded the transport to take him out of that rainy green purgatory, away to a blessed land of light and warmth . . .

CHAPTER 11

Extract from the Journal of the Botanist Mendoza:
In the Infirmary

So I suppose we're omnipresent now. Omnitemporal? But not truly omnipotent, as Edward hastens to correct me: "Only to the limits of my observational ability, my dear."

It appears that the truth about Time is rather more complex than we were told in school. Dr. Zeus explained to its little cyborgs that mortals perceive time in a linear way, because they have no other frame of reference; but in reality (they said) it is more of a spiral than a line, and when you learn to step across from one part of the spiral to another, you can travel through time. It would seem, however, that the Company wasn't telling the truth. As usual.

Whoever first learned how to travel in time, whether it was the Company or those little pale people from whom it stole its technology—it appears they took one look at the awful incoherent vastness of it all, screamed, and hastily projected conduits of artificial linear time with which to travel through the mess in a more or less orderly way. The restriction against being able to travel forward in time was a result of the conduit system. Real time is nonlinear, chaos, all-simultaneous, extending through every direction and dimension at once, and Edward alone knows what this does to causality. Entropy is an artifact of mortal perception.

We, of course, are beyond all that now, ascended beings that we are.

Here outside of time, it doesn't seem to make that much difference. I must admit it's pleasant, terrifically liberating. We can stop the sun in the sky if we choose, we can prolong the nights indefinitely, we need never eat nor drink again if we aren't so inclined; but avoiding linear existence grows unsettling after a while. There is that suspicion that if we simply blissed out and meshed with Eternity and each other permanently, we might . . . oh, I don't know, be transformed into beings of pure energy or some other cliché, and of course that would never do. Not with the plans Edward has for Ruling the World.

I do feel better knowing that the Crome's radiation is gone, I must say, even if Edward did shut it off without my permission. He does a lot of things without my permission.

Though even if I had ever been able to use the Crome's for psychic powers, I wouldn't need it now.

Edward's still stalking about Byronically exulting in his newfound immortal senses. (Ha-*ha!*) His mortal senses were pretty hot, so I can only imagine what he's experiencing.

No, that's not true . . . because I can do much more than imagine. I have only to poke around a little and I can summon up every one of Edward's memories, some of which are pretty ghastly. But I see with equal clarity how he hated the work he was set to do, so I forbear to judge. After all, I have killed mortals in my time.

I am equally an open book, wherein he reads at his pleasure. This makes our sex life exquisite and truly interesting, but we're learning to be careful about doing it out of bed. Honesty can be painful.

He knows, for example, that I was more than a little peeved at his appalled pronouncement on the tininess of my mental faculties compared to his own. He has repeatedly apologized. In this new world, where he strides like a self-assured god, his only remaining worry is how I feel about him.

Sir Henry has already offered to maroon Edward somewhere, if I'll say the word, and take off with me himself, once little Alec's with us again. Very sweet of the old dear, but I don't think he could do it. I think Edward would part the seas and come stalking after us, or something equally impressive. He's a demon when he wants his way.

And to whom would I flee? I have only connected emotionally with three other people in my entire immortal life, and one of them (Joseph) I would gladly shoot on sight. Nan has a happy and nearly normal marriage; what would she make of mine? Lewis, perfect gallant that he has always been, would cope with the Captain somehow, and we'd undoubtedly find a way to hide from the Company, but we couldn't hide from Edward. And . . . I have hurt Lewis enough.

No, I remain with Commander Bell-Fairfax.

He's been courting me. Charming little picnics for two on idyllic deserted shores, with delicacies he's stepped sidelong through time to procure. Moonlit suppers and dancing on deck, the waltz of course because that's what he remembers best from mortal life, with Sir Henry grumpily providing accompaniment on a cyber-concertina. Treats and pretty things he imagines I'll like, and I have to admit I do, though I'm afraid to ask where he got them.

He serenades me, primarily nineteenth-century airs and bits of opera, rendered in best nineteenth-century bel canto style. He has full access to the entire repertoire of music from all eras of history, mind you; but he happens to think that civilization reached its full flowering in the nineteenth century, so I get a lot of Donizetti and Hubert Parry. Especially *Jerusalem,* which he adores, with its William Blake lyrics. And how delighted he was to discover that the Black Dyke Mills Band will still be recording in 2355! Four and a half centuries' worth of stirring brass marches, God help me.

And he'll draw me a hot bath, with perfumed crystals and fragrant soap, and usher me in with great ceremony, and attend on me in his shirtsleeves, and pour champagne . . . and scrub my back . . . and lavish care on me, to the point where I'm moaning and half-drowning in the tub, until he swathes me in a towel and carries me off to bed, the smug bastard . . . and all the while, deep down inside in a place he won't even admit exists, he's terrified I'll stop loving him.

If I were a nastier woman than I am, I'd feel this was sweet revenge, after all the centuries I've mooned hopelessly after him in all his incarnations. But . . .

I have seen, now, into that secret place in his heart. I've seen the pathetic idyll he'd never admit to himself he wanted. It shone in his imagination like a beacon, through all those years he walked down dark alleys in his masters' service: quite an ordinary little terrace house, with a respectable back garden, respectable polished furniture, respectable afternoon tea properly served by . . . a respectable little wife?

Ah, not quite. Rather, a black-eyed Lady Death haunted his dreams, a phantom in crinolines. The consummation he never feared and came in fact to long for, as the list of his crimes grew, the only bride he felt he deserved.

How miserably lonely my bad darling has been, so much of his life.

And they planned for that, didn't they, those three odd little men who created him? Cut him off from all human affection, so his immense capacity for love had no focus but the abstract ideals with which he was programmed.

I think about this and I can forgive him anything, anything, all the little irritations of his pompous and patronizing speech, all his ingrained habits of deviousness and subtle bullying, his propensity for mental rape . . . I can even, almost, forgive what he did to Alec and Nicholas, especially as their return to life is now definitely scheduled.

For Edward has decided it would be a great experiment to produce a pair of Extreme Superbeings, the latest thing in evolution and all that. Infants *born* to immortality, as opposed to poor dull mortal children pithed and filled with hardware, as I was. Of course, they will need central memory files, for which Nicholas and Alec will do nicely. "It's bound to be an improving experience for both of them!" he said.

And I'm to bear their bodies in my womb, as I bear their memories in mine.

I can feel around the location in my data files, a sort of cleverly masked information bulge. I wonder if this is what it will feel like in the flesh, in another month or so? This the logical outcome of Edward's idyll, of course: a pair of Baby Deaths in one cradle, in a respectably appointed nursery.

I walk such a tightrope, over such a yawning gulf, between love and horror.

Sir Henry has attended to the matter with his customary stealthy efficiency, of course. New custom biomechanicals were designed, and more material was extracted out of the vial we stole from Alpha-Omega. A pair of blastocysts divided themselves from a common ball of cells.

They were implanted in my body. I wasn't aware, at the time; Edward decided it would be too traumatic an experience for me, so he just took it on himself to render me unconscious, gently, and did it without asking. I would be angry about this, if I hadn't had the uneasy realization that he was quite correct.

When I try to imagine the procedure or in fact any medical procedure, my heart pounds, my mouth dries. Just the words *cold steel* terrify me. Edward, at least, understands my unnamable horror.

He says children should arise from an act of love.

I would not do this for any reason but love.

My own biomechanicals have been responding to a subroutine Sir Henry installed, and are manufacturing so many hormones I'd probably be hysterical and pimply, were I not already off-balance in this strange new life Edward and I share, where the sun rises and sets when we remember to notice it doing so.

The clock has lost its hands. Time has no meaning for us, we have stepped outside it now and into eternity; but for love's sake I will take nine months' worth of its weight on myself again.

Edward Progenitor

The Captain is gleeful.

Two identical embryos, perfectly formed. I'd show you in obstetric holo

but they ain't no bigger than beans, bless their weensy hearts! Which is
beating, now. Yer a right congenial berth for 'em, dearie. They got little
arm buds, little leg buds, and little bitsy buttons what'll be fine big
belaying-pins one of these days, begging yer pardon, ma'am. Nice knots of
neural tissue, more brain than a mortal brat would have at this point.

"But can they live in such things?" demands Mendoza. "Is it enough
brain?" She is nervous, pacing.

Aye, ma'am, it's enough. Remember what they are.

"I know. I just—" She unties, reties her robe, and still doesn't seem to be
able to get it right, as Edward takes her elbow and leads her to the bed.

"Come, my dear. It's more than time." He helps her in, orders the lights to
dim. All is cozy intimacy. "The good Captain will keelhaul me, I'm sure, if I
delay another hour."

Damn right I would, too.

"You see?" Edward smiles wryly. "And he's a machine of his word, so we
mustn't cross him. Let's free the prisoners from durance vile. This part will be
easy, I do assure you. Even pleasant."

"Does Sir Henry have to be here?"

Ah! Rest easy, dearie, I'll just go chart a course somewhere.

"And I'm cold . . ." she says, shivering.

"I'll warm you," Edward replies, climbing in beside her.

Mendoza clutches the lapels of his robe. "Should I be unconscious? Would
that work better?"

"Ssssh." Edward kisses her. "Don't be frightened." He clears his throat.
Hesitantly at first, he begins to sing.

"Where the bee sucks, there suck I; In a cowslip's bell I lie;
 There I couch when owls do cry. On the bat's back I do fly
 After summer merrily. Merrily, merrily shall I live now
 Under the blossom that hangs on the bough."

His is a surprisingly pleasant tenor.

"Oh, that's nice," she says. "Shakespeare, isn't it?"

"Yes, it is." He strokes back her hair.

"A fairy song," she says. Her arms go around his neck timidly. "They're like
tiny little fairies right now, aren't they?"

"Lying in the heart of the blossom," he tells her, looking into her eyes.
"Warm and safe."

He grants her time, now, gradually she relaxes in his arms, and slow pleasures melt her defenses. With her guard down, access to the most defended of sites becomes possible, and he unlocks the file . . .

In the Library

". . . My, gen-tle, p-Puck. Puck? Come . . . hit—hi there." Alec frowns at the words.

"Hither," Nicholas corrects him.

"Hither. Thou, re—remember? Remember. Est. Ssssince, once, I sat, up, on a, pro . . . pro . . ."

"That is an M. Sound it out."

"Promm—onn—torry. And. Heared a, m-merm-aid? Yeah. Mermaid on a d-duh—dolp? . . ." Alec knits his brows.

"PH sounded as F, Alec." Nicholas yawns.

"Dolf—in. Dolphin? Dolphin's, back—"

The floor begins to tremble.

"Oh!" Alec looks up, sees the books vibrating on the shelves.

"God's holy wounds," mutters Nicholas, leaping to his feet.

Alec stands too and drops the volume of Shakespeare's comedies, but it dematerializes before it hits the floor. Alec's eyes widen and he clutches at Nicholas as more features of the room start vanishing, breaking up. "What's happening?" he demands.

"Hush—" Nicholas looks up sharply. "What's that?"

Alec shuts his eyes. "That's . . . voices?"

They are silent a moment, listening. Nicholas's eyes light with a desperate hope. "I would know that voice in my grave," he says. The chairs vanish.

"That's *her*," yells Alec. "Mendoza!"

And the world rips apart, becomes blinding light and inexplicable noise as they are hurled together, Alec and Nicholas, into the maelstrom, shot madly from their sphere. Only for a second: then they are lying stunned in a new place, but they no longer have the senses to determine anything about it. Adult consciousness tries to nest in a tiny and barely-formed brain, retains its memory and sense of self but loses all other function.

Blind panic terror! . . . And then the gradual consolation. Warmth. Music coming from somewhere, an unceasing double drumbeat, a voice.

———

"File opened; download completed," says Edward. "What a brave girl you were."

"Oh, that was lovely." Mendoza stretches, kisses him. "Merrily indeed."

"I'm working on my technique, my love. And so, Nicholas and Alec are liberated! We're all friends again now, I trust?" Edward cocks an eye at the camera. Then his grin fades, his eyes grow suddenly wide. Abruptly he leans up on his elbow. "Good God."

He throws back the covers, rolls on his side, stares.

"You're sure they're in there," Mendoza says, looking uneasily down at her body.

"They are," Edward tells her, his face pale. "But I—I can feel them!"

"You didn't do something like download them into you instead of me?"

"No. You've got them. Just—there." He gingerly touches the approximate spot. "But how on earth can *I* feel that?"

Why, yer the amazing all-powerful Edward, ain't you? Yer just picking up their little life signs, is all.

"There are no words for this," Edward says, looking rather as though he's going to be sick.

"They're all right, aren't they?" Mendoza demands. He nods.

"All life begins this way, doesn't it?" he says, in a tone of dread.

Recombinant DNA clones implanted in a cyborg? Hell no.

"No! Like—that." Edward sits up, looks down at Mendoza's body. "The little person. That exquisite detail. The arteries like threads, the budding limbs, the *potential*."

"Well, yes," Mendoza replies. She looks into his anguished face. "Darling, what is it?"

"Mortals have no idea what they do," he says at last. "I had no idea! And now we're trapped in linear time with them for the next score of years—ye gods, what have we done?" He leaps out of bed in his horror and begins to pace, tying his robe closed, tangling the knot.

"They'll be so small," he says, "And anything could take them while they're still vulnerable, anything! Good God, a wave over the bows. A tumble through a hatchway. The responsibility—we'll have to prepare. Safety devices installed on everything. Suitably warm clothing. Properly digestible meals. Do you realize we haven't even planned a nursery yet? WHAT THE HELL ARE YOU LAUGHING ABOUT?" Edward turns raging to the nearest speaker, though the Captain's amusement has been rolling throughout the entire ship.

Haar! Divine retribution be a fine thing, to be sure, that's all. I'll just go draft plans for converting one of the guest staterooms into a nursery, shall I?

"Do it," snaps Edward. "And let me see the blueprints the moment you've finished."

CHAPTER 12

Three Months:
Extract from the Journal of the Botanist Mendoza:
Monsters and Ice Cream

This is driving me mad.

I don't know what to wear.

You would think, wouldn't you, that with a closet full of clothing from all the historical eras through which we've traveled, I could find garments that weren't uncomfortably tight or hideous? I can't. I feel like screaming. All I want to wear are Alec's Hawaiian shirts, hanging forlorn in the wardrobe. They smell like him and are comforting, recalling happy amnesiac days. But then my horrible swollen legs show.

Edward assures me they are not swollen. Edward is lying. Edward is flawlessly dressed himself, has had Smee the servounit cut him perfectly tailored proper Victorian attire. Edward may be jumpy as a cobra on speed, but there is nothing wrong with Edward's body. I'm the one who's distorted, bloated, disgusting . . .

I am being irrational. I am experiencing a panic reaction because my immortal body has always been the one unchanging, inalterable constant in my life. I have gained *five pounds*. I had never gained a pound in all the years since 1554. It's not right, not natural, *I'm not programmed for this.*

How the hell do mortals do it? And they do it all the time!

I feel like a battleground. Sir Henry must continually monitor and reprogram my biomechanicals to be certain they don't sense the babies as intruders and abort them. The babies, of course, have their own biomechanicals who would fight back. I have nightmares of the little things building a fortress of steel inside me, firing cannons, assembling siege machinery . . . Let's not even go into the absurdity of immortal cyborgs adjusting to midnight feedings, baby clothes, toys, teething; nor the question of what sexual feelings I may or may not eventually have for someone who's been in my womb, no matter how unrelated we are.

Edward is trying to help. He is trying very hard to be helpful, even with the strain he's under, which is only that of an omnitemporal being who's just been jolted out of his smugness by the discovery that there are some things in the universe beyond his control, ha ha, and I can't even enjoy gloating about it.

"My dear, you are ravishing in my eyes," he told me.

"No, I'm not," I said. "Oh, God, don't touch me."

"Now, then," he said coaxingly, parting the clothes to peer in at me where I crouched weeping in the back of the armoire, "if you'll come out like a good girl, you'll have a treat. Wouldn't you like that?"

"Don't you speak to me in that condescending manner!" I screamed. "How dare you?"

"My dear, this is simply a hormonal tide making you miserable," he assured me. "You're not yourself. It's perfectly natural."

"No, it isn't!"

"Yes, dearest, it is. I've just been accessing Molesworth's *The Encyclopedia of Maternity*, volumes one through twelve, which, in addition to containing numerous helpful suggestions for improving the state of mind of the mother-to-be, all too plainly delineates your present symptoms." Edward dodged as I threw a shoe at him.

"You *enjoy* being a cyborg, don't you?" I muttered.

"I will overlook that remark. My love, you know you can't stay in the wardrobe." Edward reached in, groping for me.

"I may as well," I said, starting to cry again. "I can't work. I can't find anything to wear."

"I've had something made up for you. Won't you come out and see?" He got my wrist and tugged gently. "In addition to which, I've found something in the refrigerated pantry that the good Doctor Molesworth specifically lists as appealing to the appetites of prospective mothers. Remember our provisioning expedition to twentieth-century San Francisco?" He held up something above the shirt rack where I could see it, and waved it back and forth enticingly: a half-gallon carton of Double Fudge Death Wish ice cream.

"Oh, that's so sweet of you," I cried, overcome with remorse at the way I'd been yelling at him. "But, darling, I can't possibly have any."

"Content analysis reveals it to be rich in calcium," he informed me. "Moreover it contains walnuts, which are an abundant source of fatty acids vital to the development of brain cells—" He lunged while I was distracted and lifted me out into the room. I leaned my head on his shoulder and sobbed.

"I know," I said, "but it's full of Theobromos. I can't have that while I'm pregnant, it wouldn't be good for the babies."

"Ah." He looked chagrined. "Well, perhaps this will console you." He set me down on the bed, and hopefully held up an amazing negligée: flame pink silk, cut more daringly than anything the heroine of the most pornographic romance novel might wear. I burst into fresh tears and didn't even try to explain, just let him think I was crying in gratitude as he helped me into it.

"There we are," he said soothingly. "We needn't get up today, after all. We'll put up our little feet, there's a girl, and here are fresh handkerchiefs to wipe away our tears and—and would we like to watch a holo?"

"Yes," I said, blotting my face. "I want to watch *Dracula*."

Which version, dearie? inquired Sir Henry.

"I don't know!"

Not to fret, now. Here, darlin', we'll just put on Evans Spielberg's from 2105. Got good reviews at the time, aye.

"Okay . . ."

Edward propped pillows solicitously and settled himself beside me, as Sir Henry lowered the holoprojector into the room and dimmed the lights. I could see the lines of strain around Edward's eyes.

"That ice cream's still sitting there," I complained. "And we're in linear time, so it'll melt."

"I'll get it, my dear."

"Here we are, omnipotent omnipresent immortals with fantastically augmented intelligence, and the minute we're stuck back in linear time we forget a simple thing like ice cream melting." I fell over into the pillows in my misery. "How are we going to *do* this, Edward?"

"Now, now," said Edward, and looked down at the ice cream with sudden interest. "H'm! What an ambrosial fragrance. I'll have a little of this, if you don't mind."

"Okay," I said, distracted by the bloodred film credits coming up in midair and the overture to *Swan Lake*. Edward sat down again and, prizing the lid off the carton, dipped in the spoon he'd brought for me. He tasted cautiously. His pupils dilated.

"H'm!"

"Hush," I told him crossly, snuggling against his shoulder as I watched the prologue describing the horrific circumstances of Vlad Tepes's youth as a hostage among the Turks. Edward ate Double Fudge Death Wish and watched, too.

His remarks for the next forty-five minutes were confined to statements like "You'd never get your victim to hold still for *that* unless you broke his back first," and "That was an artery, for heaven's sake! Where's the blood?" When the action of the film moved to England, he began to giggle at the accents used by the American actors. At Dracula's courtship of Mina, a tender scene I particularly liked, he all but fell over snorting with suppressed laughter.

"Do you mind?" I said, turning to glare.

"Sorry. Sorry, my love," he said, scraping tentatively at the bottom of the carton with his spoon. I followed his gaze.

"Oh my God, have you eaten the whole half-gallon?"

"It would appear so," he said musingly. "Wonderful stuff, this."

"Fine! Now you're intoxicated," I said in indignation. "Didn't your brilliant genius Recombinant brain tell you about what Theobromine does to us?"

"Yes," he said. His pupils were enormous, black as Dracula's cape. "But I rather enjoy new sensations. It's not quite like being drunk. Far more pleasurable."

"How nice for you," I said, and turned my attention to the holo again. Edward set the empty carton and spoon aside and put his arm around me, pulling me close. He began to nuzzle my ear and I shivered and melted against him, even though we'd come to the scene where Dr. Van Helsing was shooting up heroin. "Mmmmwatch the movie . . ." I said.

"Now, *this* is intoxicating," Edward murmured, letting his hands roam. He pressed his face against my skin and inhaled.

"Uh-huh," I said. He buried his face in my hair.

"How I love your hair on the pillow, all disarrayed as you sleep," he said indistinctly. "You draw your fists under your chin and scowl so, like a bad-tempered child. When you open your eyes to me, there's a bloom on them, after deep dreams, as though you were blind. Oh, little girl, I'd buy all your matches. I'd carry you home with me, and warm you, and you wouldn't die after all . . ."

"No, of course not," I said, and then: "What?" When had *he* ever lain awake staring at *me*?

"And I love your accent," he said.

"I don't speak with an accent."

"Yes, you do. Cinema Standard and, when you're sleepy or tired, you do just the faintest violence to your aitches." He wrapped me in his arms and lifted me abruptly, turning me to him, and leaned down until we were nose to nose. "Two and a half days. The fifteenth to the seventeenth of March, 1863. That was all we had . . . and yet, after the first hour, I could have drawn your little body in chalk, sculpted it in ivory, so perfectly I knew you. What horror I felt, to discover I loved you . . ."

I blinked at him. This was not, I need hardly mention, anything like his usual style.

"Because you thought you might have to kill me," I said.

"Mm." He nodded. "But also because . . . one must avoid entanglements of that kind in the service, lest it impair one's efficiency . . . damn them. I knew what you were from the moment I saw you. I ought to have caught you up and ridden away to safety, and Whitehall be damned. All those wasted years . . . running about with a sword trying to end the slave trade by myself, like a boy out of Marryat's books. And then the Society's tool, filling graves for them. Why did I never understand . . ."

"That it was vanity?" I said.

"Mm, but so much worse—" His gaze sharpened, tried to focus, and he pulled himself together and made an extra effort to speak distinctly. "Delusion. Because, the thing is—human progress begins, not with one lone man with a weapon, however heroic. Nor with subtle governments, be they never so altruistic. It begins with a man and his wife in bed . . . and . . . how could I ever hope to govern humanity, without having been even that human?

"I will serve *life*," he cried, and kissed me forcefully. "I will love my wife and my children, and—and do everything I couldn't do when I was a mortal man, and—all the sentimental commonplaces will have a glorious new meaning, and—"

Oh, my God, he's finally got a clue, I thought, so overwhelmed with tenderness for him I forgot about the movie. But the lash of his introspection swung around and caught me a good one. For after all . . .

How human was *I*? Haughty cyborg brat. Bad-tempered child, prize to be carried off. Tragic adolescent perpetually mourning her lost love. Reactive victim. That's all I've been, for millennia. Now the long drama is over, do I have the faintest idea what to do with a happy ending? How can I? Incomplete immature thing that I am, am I even capable of changing? And yet I must, now. I found myself trembling in panic.

"I think I'd like to learn how to garden," said Edward thoughtfully. He looked down, surprised, as I clung to him. Nicholas, in his genuine concern for my soul, had comforted me. Alec, with thoughtless kindness, had offered me rescue from my eternal slavery. But what was *this*, flowing out of Edward like light, as he lifted my chin and gazed into my eyes? Was it strength?

Horrible violence on the holoscreen, the air was drenched with gore, and we were so oblivious it might have been a pastoral scene with butterflies. Edward flooded his consciousness into mine, and what with all the Theobromos and hormones it was a wonder our brains didn't melt.

Dracula went about his awful business and was liberated at last. He floated in a golden apotheosis to heaven, redeemed by love, but we didn't notice a thing until the inhuman comedy fell silent and the end credits rolled.

Six Months:
Edward Hortulanus

The botany cabin has undergone a change in the past few months. It had previously a wild, overgrown sort of look; now it has the lush appearance of a Victorian hothouse. Potted ferns, sago palms, and bromeliads rise in green luxuriance, many-hued begonias droop from hanging baskets, little citrus trees proudly display green and red and golden fruit. Boxwood obelisks and topiary are arranged in careful patterns. The air is rich with the heavy perfume of gardenias.

Mendoza is reclining in a cushioned deck chair in the midst of it all, draped with shawls, and she, too, has undergone a change. The second trimester is nearly concluded.

"I'm not sure I can relax in here, darling," remarks Mendoza. Edward, who has been busily clipping a rosemary bush into what he feels is pleasing symmetry, lowers his shears and looks at her in concern.

"But this is the closest we can manage to supplying the calmative effects of Nature," says Edward, "as recommended by Dr. Molesworth. Short of putting in to some island, which may very well be a primeval Eden but may also be infested with tropical diseases, wild animals, and hominid savages."

"They couldn't hurt us," says Mendoza. "You know that perfectly well."

"But I should prefer to avoid drawing attention to ourselves," Edward replies.

"Couldn't I just get up and water the maize cultivars?" asks Mendoza.

"Dearest, your little projects must wait—" Edward tells her, commanding the misting system to activate. Mendoza looks black daggers at him.

"It's not a *little project*," she says. "It's an attempt to produce a perfect grain to feed the starving masses of mortals, and I've been working on it for centuries. Don't you refer to it in that dismissive tone of voice, as though it were a—a needlework sampler!"

Edward orders the soothing music flowing from the ship's speakers to drop down a decibel level or two. "My love, I never meant to imply anything of the sort. Of course it's a laudable quest! Though I do feel I ought to point out that if a cultivar with adequate lysine levels has eluded your grasp thus far—to say nothing of the fact that there is no appearance in the historical record, prior to the year 2355, of any such marvelous gift to mankind—"

"Oh, shut up!" she snaps, blinking back tears.

"Very well," says Edward stiffly, and, noticing a Duke of Wellington fuchsia that doesn't quite meet his standards of harmonious proportion, advances on it with the shears.

"All right, I'm sorry. But don't prune it back like that, you impossible—ai!" She grips the arm of her chair until the wood cracks.

"My love?" Edward is with her instantly.

"What the hell are they doing in there, playing hockey?" Mendoza gasps.

#χλεσ*κγ*Scared!

Edward stiffens as though electrified.

"Did you hear—?"

"What?" she looks at him, alarmed.

≅%8ωιλια**Where??

"That's Alec!" Edward whispers. "Can't you hear?"

"No!"

***νιχηολ**Ow!

"That was Nicholas!"

"You mean they're transmitting?" Mendoza looks incredulous.

***ασμηαρ**Stop kick!

Damnation, the boys are online, yells the Captain. Mendoza jumps at his sudden voice and Edward distinctly hears twin screams of alarm from within her body, has a sense of wildly flailing limbs.

"Ay! God and bloody Saint James," says Mendoza through gritted teeth.

Might I suggest you transmit back, Commander Bell-Fairfax, sir?

Edward reaches over and places his hand on Mendoza's belly. *Hush,* he transmits, and perceives a sudden silence, an alert attention. *Hush, gentlemen. You're perfectly safe. You'll—er—arrive shortly.*

"Well, that seems to be working," Mendoza says hopefully. "They've stopped dancing on my bladder."

Bad man, transmits an accusatory little voice, sharp and clear now.

That's my boy! That's Alec!

SINFUL man, transmits an even more accusatory little voice.

Edward! transmits the first voice, and a dizzying wave of anger surges toward Edward out of the ether.

Bastard! transmits the second voice, no less vehement.

Yes, yes, all right! I admit you've been inconvenienced, Edward transmits back.

INCONVENIENCED?

I'll make amends, in loco parentis, on my word of honor. You'll have the best of everything. The years will speed by like so many days! The happiest of second childhoods and then, I promise you—

Piss off, bad man!/Smite thee!

Edward exhales in annoyance. *I see. Well, perhaps if your brains weren't the size of marbles just now, you'd be capable of listening to reason. Can you understand this much? If you thrash about, you'll hurt Mendoza.*

Mendoza!/Rose! And then, heartbreaking, a mournful crying, such a little lost sound.

Lost her again!/Again!

No! No, listen for her heartbeat, do you hear it? Just as I promised you. She's with you. You'll be all right. Be good little fellows and go back to sleep now.

Want her . . . /Want her . . .

But the transmissions fade out into silence. Mendoza, who has been watching Edward closely, demands: "What did they say?"

"Rather what you'd expect, under the circumstances," says Edward shakenly, collapsing into the chair next to hers.

"So the biomechanicals are working," she muses, "because they're already able to transmit. What a thought, eh? No years of surgery to endure, like I had."

Begging yer pardon, ma'am, but I've still got the support packages to install. That'll happen in their teens.

"Poor little bastards," says Edward.

Ah, now, sir, the bitsy darlings'll never feel a thing, the Captain assures him with black good humor. **They'll be completely anesthetized.**

"How nice for them," retorts Edward.

"They must be pretty crowded in there by now, eh?" Mendoza speculates, in a bright voice with only the barest edge of suppressed panic. "And it'll get worse. How much longer?"

"Ninety-two days, seven hours, and three minutes precisely," says Edward. Mendoza winces.

"I had this dream," she says. "They were born and they were a couple of little robot children. Little brushed steel baby heads, you know?"

Aw, now, dearie, never you fear; there ain't no way they'll take after me.

"And I put them on the bed, but they fell off and broke. I was appalled," says Mendoza. A tear rolls down her cheek.

"Think nothing of it. A fairly common nightmare for the mother-to-be, according to Molesworth," Edward says, reaching over to hold her hand. "Something every mortal woman learns to bear with."

"How do mortal women manage this?" says Mendoza, despairing. "The discomfort isn't so bad, but . . . This is just too *inevitable*. What if the dream was the Crome's, coming back? I mean, if their little skulls will be vulnerable . . . if they aren't made fully immortal until they're in their teens . . . something really could happen to them."

Edward feels his mouth go dry at the thought. He squeezes her hand, but says firmly: "Nothing of the kind will occur. I have every confidence."

"Confidence in whom?" Mendoza says. "Fate? Destiny? God? We never had any of them on our side before."

"That was before," says Edward. He lifts Mendoza's hand to his lips. Her scent comforts him. She leans back with a sigh. Kissing her hand but not relinquishing it, he leans back, too. *The Lark Ascending* continues its melodic flight on the ship's intercom. Flint bustles clanking across the threshold, bearing a laden tray.

"Ah! Teatime," remarks Edward.

Nine Months:
Edward Paenitens

"No," says Mendoza, "I'm only eight centimeters dilated. Calm down, babies, calm down. Poor little things, they're scared."

She herself is tranquil and self-possessed, concentrating thoroughly on her task. Edward, by contrast, is sweating where he sits beside her, holding her hand. He focuses in on the children and can only get a sense of wild turmoil, panic, terror.

"I'm quite proud of your composure, my love," stammers Edward.

"I am finally," says Mendoza, "in control of something. Sometimes it's *good* to be a cyborg. Nine centimeters. He's crowning." She levers herself up on her elbows. "Get ready, Edward."

Edward scrambles around to the front of the bed and his jaw drops in dismay.

What he has always fondly euphemized as an orchid, an iris, splits wide, and a gush of bright blood precedes the domed crown emerging.

The sight and scent of the blood disturb him deeply. Edward remembers:

Raiding an Ivory Coast barracoon, and a warrior with glistening black skin charges him. Edward cuts him down, in a fountain of blood, but another comes at him, and another, until the last has dropped and Edward stands weeping, splashed with blood in the stinking sunlight, among dead men he had wanted to liberate. When he finds the Portuguese slave trader at last, cowering in a hut, Edward hacks him to pieces.

He remembers—

Watching as Able-Bodied Seaman Price takes the twelfth lash, and then another dozen. Captain Southbey orders another dozen then, and the midshipmen are pale as paper, the other officers looking on nervously but saying nothing. The surgeon's assistant wrings his hands but says nothing, as the count goes on: four dozen. Six. Eight. The blood is a mist in the air. "Sir, this exceeds your authority," says Edward, putting his hand on Southbey's shoulder. Southbey turns on him in white rage. Then Southbey is down on the deck, his broken teeth scattering, blood spurting from his nose and lips and eyes as Edward methodically beats him with both fists, unable to stop, knowing it will mean court-martial and a death sentence—

"Ten centimeters." Edward remembers—

He has stalked the little thief half the night. His quarry is a wretched nonentity who broke into a Society stronghold, and there stole something of unimaginable value, saw something he ought not to have seen. The sentence is death, of course. Patiently Edward closes the distance, until the thief in his panic enters a blind alley. He realizes his error and turns, but Edward is there. The thief staggers backward, gabbling out a frantic plea in a language Edward does not know. "Hush," says Edward sternly, and cuts his throat, and the blood jets forth—

—And Edward now, with his augmented mind, hears the translation at last: *"Please! Take the thing! They made me do it, they're holding my wife and the baby—"*

"Oh—" He raises shaking hands as the head is thrust forth, its purple features flattened and apelike, a tiny subhuman monster! He very nearly shouts with horror but controls himself and catches the head, wondering heartsick what he can possibly tell Mendoza. The body emerges and the head sags back, such a little vulnerable chin and throat, little hands waving in terrified blind protest. Abruptly the whole thing is writhing there in his hands, trailing its blue pulsing cord, turning its head from side to side, opening its mouth to draw in breath and scream—

And Edward watches unbelieving as its body turns pink, as its head decompresses and assumes a fairly human shape, as its squashed features resolve into something familiar. Trembling, shivering, squalling, Nicholas has returned to the world and the flesh. He is still inexpressibly hideous, in Edward's eyes.

But Mendoza is holding out her hands, and so Edward gingerly places the baby in them. Her composure is gone, she seems uncertain, at a loss, peering into the tiny face; but her hands move as though without her knowledge, drawing the struggling little thing close, cradling him on her breast, stroking him.

How shall I ever console her?

"Oh," she says, beginning to smile. "Oh, it's *Nicholas.*"

"I'm so sorry," says Edward brokenly.

"Look at his beautiful hands . . . what?"

Never mind that! Where's my boy?

For still, on the ether, one faint voice shrieks in terror and disorientation. *Alone! Scared! Where?* Steadied by the necessity of calming someone else's panic, Edward seats himself again and observes the crown of the other twin's head just appearing.

Don't be afraid. Come through. We're here.

"Second birth initiated," says Mendoza, transcendently serene once again. Alec slips back into the world with ease, trailing the afterbirth behind him, shrieking his dismay.

There's my boy! That's my Alec!

"Little Alec. Oh, what a sweet face!" Mendoza stretches out her free hand.

HAAR! Bless him, what a sight for sore eyes!

Edward thinks he looks like a greasy yelling goblin, but is thankful the child is alive and undeformed.

He has rolled up his shirtsleeves and is bathing Nicholas, clutching the bloody sponge in one hand, when he looks down at the baby's birth-compressed head. The sight brings before his eyes the grim vision of the old Enforcers: helmskulled giants on a battlefield, warriors righteous and unstoppable, gleefully smashing sinners into red pulp with flint axes. Death and death and death, whatever the argument, the answer always death. Joyous death. And did their son, in a newer and more elegant edition, succeed to his fathers?

Didn't he just. A hundred dark doorways, quick kills, sprawled bodies. So sorry, nothing personal: for the Good of the Realm. For the Greater Good of Mankind. Pieces on a game board, pawns removed, cast aside. Every one of them beginning like this tiny new thing before him in its bloody bathwater. So much effort to create such perfection, such limitless potential to be—pushed from a hurtling railway carriage, garroted, poisoned, shot, stabbed, sabered, or blown to pieces by cannon fire, Rule Britannia!

And this new thing, and it is a new thing for all the freight of ancient passions it bears in its memory, its design of twisted spirals that gives it its fathers' hands and voice and brain with all their demonic sense of purpose, called out of the void by alchemical science. What else has it inherited? What will it do?

What have we done?

Nicholas begins to shiver and cry again. Edward hurriedly swathes him in a towel and picks him up to comfort him, and the little thing is so helpless and weighs nothing, nothing at all.

We have done so much worse than sin, little brother, Edward tells him, shuddering. *One hardly knows what to call it. We had damned well better save the world. How on earth else can we ever atone?*

Unsteadily, Edward swaddles Nicholas in the blankets that have been prepared. He fits on Nicholas's head the striped stocking cap: there. Little pirate on a big ship. He trades off with Mendoza and bathes Alec, and soon there are two little pirates mewling in her arms. "Aren't they wonderful?" says Mendoza, smiling down at them.

"They look like a brace of skinned grouse," says Edward morosely. Gazing down, he looks for slacker Alec, benighted Nicholas, his two despised rivals, failed images of himself. The old contempt will not come, somehow. He remembers, he remembers for all three of them:

Little Alec looking hopefully into the faces of strangers, hoping one of them would be Roger Checkerfield, come home from sea at last, but he never came. Nicket made to kneel and pray beside the green grave mound, that they told him was his mother's, when he wondered for the first time: where is my father, then? . . . And, buried deep, a little Edward who followed the butler like a hopeful puppy. "Will you tell me about the war, Richardson?" . . .

What were their faults but his own? And now they must start the pitiless journey all over again. They are so small, and their feeble wails tear his heart.

"Are you *crying*?" Mendoza looks up into Edward's face, startled. "Oh, darling!"

"Well, who wouldn't be, says I?" remarks the Captain, assuming a visual image. "I call that a right nice morning's work, now. Look at 'em there, like a couple of little angels! Of course I'll have thirty years of work to do all over again with my Alec, but does old Captain Morgan mind? Hell *no*, he's just a machine—"

"Oh, shut up," says Edward, wiping away tears. "I should think this calls for a photograph to commemorate the occasion."

"You mean a holo, don't you, Commander sir?" offers the Captain helpfully.

"Whatever," says Mendoza.

So, an image in the family album: the woman all respectably gowned, tucked up in the vast gold-and-crimson pirate bed, looking tired but pleased with herself. In her arms, the swaddled babies, comical in their little caps. Standing to either side, the two male figures: what might be a slightly crazed but very proud grandfather, with his black beard and evil grin, and here the other man, cold and dignified as he stares down the maker of the image.

He has the weight of a thousand generations on his shoulders. There is new purpose in his pale and haunted eyes. He will be a father.

CHAPTER 13

Extract from the Journal of the Botanist Mendoza (transcript):
In the Bedroom

I can't get over what beautiful hands they have.

And the pattern in the hair on the back of their little heads, the perfect clockwise spiral. Not so much as a birthmark on either of their perfectly identical bodies. Mostly identical. Alec gets much redder in the face, in fact all over, when he screams. And he screams a lot more loudly. Neither one of them seem to need much sleep, so this is quite an occasion, both of them down at once, gives me a moment to update this . . . I'll have to dictate these entries from here on in, because I can't hold a baby and manage a pen or plaquette. Flint, I want the striped blanket. Yes. Thank you.

How neatly he fits in the angle of my arm. As though it had been designed for his rest. I suppose in the larger scheme of things it was, wasn't it? Ohh, look: rapid eye movements. When he's awake they focus sharply, as a mortal child's could not at this age; and they were from the moment he opened them that same pale blue, the color of Spanish glass . . . shh, shhh, Nicholas . . . little Nicket.

Do mortal women maunder on in this inane way, about the children they bring into daylight? How do they bear it, holding this tiny little thing in their arms, knowing all the perils it has to go through once it stands alone? This is terrifying.

In fact—I can't imagine why I'm not crouching in a corner with my hands over my head, whimpering in fright. You know, you go along for three thousand years of immortal life and one day is pretty much like another, even with catastrophic tragedies now and again, and you just assume nothing will ever change. Then, one fine day, everything changes forever. I am the first of my kind to do this reproduction thing, and I haven't the faintest idea how to proceed.

Mortal women have mothers, aunts, sisters, and grandmothers to consult and advise and Greek-chorus for them generally, and I have . . . a pirate.

No offense, Sir Henry. The modifications on Flint are impressive, the bottle holder and the padded waldoes or whatever those are, and the concertina-playing apparatus and the, ah, dangly mobile thing. I'm sure Alec likes it. He gurgles and stops crying whenever you make the pirate doll dance for him.

And the cradle is lovely. How clever of you to build it to match the rest of the bedroom décor. I'm sure any little boy would love a cradle built to look like a pirate ship. All that gilded carving, and the blanket and hangings in red velvet, with those gold-embroidered skull and crossbone motifs . . . It's just so *huge* . . . Yes, I know Edward had that Whiteley's one with the bunnies picked out, and I was thinking maybe something in powder blue and pink, but—no, no, I don't mind at all. Edward doesn't, either. Really.

And I understand about the health benefits and all that, and I know you'd love to feed Alec by yourself, and I was quite impressed with the way you gave him the vitamins. But I'm not certain I can hook myself up to that thing. In fact, I'm certain I can't. I'm sorry . . . yes, of course, later he can have juice and I don't know what. You'll do a wonderful job then, to be sure. Mm-hm. It's an adorable dimple, you're right . . .

. . . And there goes Flint, wet nurse of the Spanish Main . . .

No, darling, I was just talking to Sir Henry. Everything's all—what? No, I think it's just drool. Go back to sleep. There . . . Poor thing, sprawled flat on his back and so he's snoring most amazingly; but it doesn't seem to disturb Alec. It's sweet of him to cuddle Alec like that, considering Alec pees on him whenever he gets the chance. There have been several unfortunate incidents on the changing table already.

Oh, no, no, no, Nicket, are you having a bad dream? You open your eyes and you look so bewildered. What other place to you go off to when you're asleep, Nicket, to be so surprised to wake in my arms again? Shh, shh. *Ay la le lo . . . dum de dum . . .* If you were a mortal baby I'd wonder what could possibly be in your little memory, to give you bad dreams. As it is . . . Nicholas Harpole is in there somewhere. Once you were a man, and I loved you in a green garden. What are we to do now, my dearest? . . .

He's like a tiny stroke victim, nearly as helpless as a mortal baby. Presumably all his adult mind is there, but its powers of expression are limited. Same with Alec, apparently.

We were alarmed by the impairment at first, but Sir Henry assured us their brains aren't damaged; they simply haven't been programmed yet, haven't the software to make their new bodies work. They haven't even been augmented, though they have all the potential of neophyte cyborgs. And, since there is no immense Company educational system to feed data into their tiny heads, Edward and I must do it.

Edward was in favor of one immense download to each of them, but Sir Henry reminded him, with a remarkable minimum of four-letter words I must say, about what such a mass transfer of information did to *me*. Edward was instantly horrified and contrite. So Sir Henry showed us, patiently, how to make up careful infant-sized data packets, and supervised the first installation session.

We sat together here on the bed, and I took Alec in my arms and Edward took Nicholas, because at that point Alec was still screaming every time Edward even looked at him, though Nicholas began to shriek too the minute Edward picked him up, and Edward looked so nervous . . . Sir Henry told him where to set his index finger between Nicket's eyes. Remembering the sessions from my own childhood, I followed suit.

We downloaded the packets. It was so strange; from screaming in outrage, suddenly the boys grew still, and Alec got such a *listening* look. I could feel the data running out of me. It made me catch my breath; and I glanced across at Edward and saw his eyes wide, his pupils dilated. I leaned against him, partly for strength and partly to comfort him.

Afterward the little boys fell instantly asleep, as their greedy brains processed what we'd given them. We just continued to sit there, watching them in a stunned kind of way. Posthuman parents. Sir Henry assures us we're doing fine.

When they woke up again, we could see at once that the downloads had had an effect—Nicholas seemed to have gained control of his hands, and Alec wasn't going cross-eyed when he tried to focus at all—so I suppose Sir Henry's right.

Now we coordinate programming with feeding. It's easy for me when I nurse them, a little more complicated for Edward as he holds a bottle of mineral supplements in emulsion, but he manages anyway. He's very brave.

Even after we've finished installing all their augmentation, they'll have to be trained in physical skills like hyperfunction, and taught how to assimilate all that fantastic knowledge with which they've been gifted. Edward was right: nobody's ever done this before.

And so of course no cultural frame exists for this peculiar relationship of ours, Nicholas. The man I loved, to passionate madness, is now this tiny little boy in my arms. We will never dance that particular dance again. I don't think.

Doesn't matter. Nicholas Harpole, here you are, a refutation of pain. Your mortal agony, your martyrdom in greasy ashes by the Medway River: all undone. You're warm and whole and full of milk and Death has finally died, the bony bastard. His scythe lies broken at my feet.

Oh, Alec, no, no . . . don't wake up poor exhausted Daddy.

I can't tell yet whether Alec's forgotten his old life. I wonder if he's forgotten what he did on Mars? Please, God, let it be so. Even damaged as I was, all those months we traveled together, I was generally able to identify which of the three of them was in control of Alec's old body. And Alec, at the times we should have been happiest, used to get the most wretched look in his eyes . . .

On the first day I ever met him, I was struck by what a knot of self-loathing was caught about Alec's heart. That was the Company's plan, wasn't it? To so motivate him with guilt and shame he'd do anything to try to redeem himself? Even something as profoundly, quixotically stupid as smuggling weapons to the Martian Agricultural Collective . . . And then he was supposed to conveniently die, as Edward and Nicholas died.

That he didn't do so has left us with the problem of a broken hero on a downward spiral. What are we going to do about that, Alec darling? Can we heal you? Has providing you with a new body changed anything?

But for now Alec crams his fist in his mouth, and sucks on it contentedly as he falls more deeply asleep. There is a round spreading patch of milky Alec-drool on Edward's starched shirtfront. It will stain.

Once it was blood . . . I'm not quite sure what to make of the change in Edward.

What, oh what has come over the all-powerful master of temporal equations? What has shaken his confidence in his ability to fulfill his divine purpose? (And isn't it remarkable how a confirmed atheist like Commander Bell-Fairfax was able to entertain such a delusion in the first place?)

If I didn't know better, I'd say he was going through postpartum depression. I've certainly no trace of it, myself; I seem to lack that possessive, desperately unhappy love I have observed in mortal mothers. Edward, on the other hand, has become fanatically protective of the children. He gets up five times in a night to check the cradle to see if they're still there, still breathing. He turns white if one of them rolls too near the edge of the bed.

I thought it might be fun to have Smee make up tiny jammies for Alec, in loud Hawaiian shirt print, but Edward won't hear of it; he feels the material's unsuitable, *might give the infant a rash!* Or perhaps it just offends his slightly rigid sensibilities. So, as our lives continue to be remade in his Victorian image, the little boys are decked out in white lace and smocking. There are going to be some awe-inspiring conflicts when they get older, I can see that already.

Quite apart from the fact that he was lying to get his own way when he told me we should start a family, Edward really did believe all that business about the maternal instinct being the foundation of a woman's soul. He actually thought I wouldn't be psychologically fulfilled as a woman until I managed to reproduce. Well, surprise! He seems to be the one going through the transformation. For an omnitemporal immortal, he's a nervous wreck. Nine months ago, he thought he was almost a god. But now . . . no one knows what helplessness is, until they have children.

He dutifully set up a feeding/installation schedule, and managed to control his temper when the boys' tummies refused to go along with it. He will lie quietly beside me when we have them both on the bed like this, simply watching them, for hours. Can it be that *Edward* always wanted children, on some buried level of his psyche? Do men really want to be fathers?

He has kissed the babies once or twice, furtively, when they're asleep, though I know he despised the men that Alec and Nicholas were. If he has forgiven them their imperfection, has he forgiven himself? He broke my chains; can he break his own?

The Ephesians would have us believe that men can't nurture, that they're mere sex-and-violence machines, useful for producing Y chromosomes and best banished from the home once their reproductive task is finished. Men themselves buy into this lie, often, I think. I know Edward was bullied into believing it, by the Company agents who trained him. So the deep protective instincts he really did have were twisted, and what a sad accommodation he made with the life's work they set him to do: killing to make a better world for the children he'd never be allowed to have.

Wise programming, I suppose. How could he ever have been induced to sacrifice himself for the greater good, unless love was what drove him? Plain base appetite produces nothing more than a plain predator. To make a really effective monster you need to begin with a good man, and tell him lies . . .

Edward Penitent in the Extreme

He sips his port and reflects, smugly, that it's all turned out for the best. He's properly dressed for dinner at last! And she looks ravishing in that gown. The style of the 1830s suits her very well, even if she seems a bit peevish at the moment.

He's certain she won't remain displeased with him very long. Look at this splendid dining room he's had furnished for her! Look at the great polished table, the silver epergne, the mahogany sideboard where is spread, in glittering display, the bewildering wealth of specialized utensils no proper home should be without. Asparagus tongs, lobster forks, runcible spoons!

. . . Though now he notices that this is the dining room in the house where he was a boy. Why on earth would they go back to No. 10 Albany Crescent? Where are the servants? He hears a high thin wailing and looks around, puzzled.

"My dear, the children are crying. Ring for Mrs. Lodge."

Mendoza looks at him sourly from the distant end of the table. "What good will that do? You ate the babies, remember?"

"What?" he cries, horrified. She just goes on trying to open her tamale with a marrow spoon.

"You assimilated them," she says in a chilly voice. "I asked you not to, but you insisted. You said they tasted like a brace of skinned grouse."

"No!" He tries to jump to his feet but he's oddly heavy, breathless. She stares at him, unsmiling, and she is a great distance away and the room is much longer, much colder, much darker than he remembered.

"You insisted," she repeats, in a voice dripping with sarcasm. "God forbid the son should be greater than his father! Cronos did it to Zeus. Zeus did it to you, and now you're continuing the tradition."

"But—" The crying is still going on, and he realizes it's coming from inside himself, and looking down in dismay he sees an immense bulge under the white silk waistcoat of his faultless evening dress.

"Of course, they'll get out of there one of these days," Mendoza informs him. "That's what always happens. You'll be sorry then."

He feels a lurch and hears a tearing noise, and though he feels no pain the gleaming steel blade of an aspic knife emerges abruptly from his starched shirtfront. As he watches it begins to move, methodically cutting a circular hole.

"See?" Mendoza tells him. He clutches at himself in anguish.

"Help me!" he howls—

"Help me!" says Mendoza tearfully. "I've only got two arms!"

He sits up in a cold sweat, gasping. Alec is nursing at Mendoza's left breast, but Nicholas is doubled up and screaming shrilly. It is otherwise still midnight on a quiet sea, the dim lamp barely swinging on its gimbal.

"Nicky drank too fast and now he's got colic," Mendoza tells him. "How the hell could you sleep through this?"

Shaking with relief, Edward gathers up the tiny agonized figure and holds it close. "Shh, Nicholas. Shh, son. There, there—" A blast of incoherent wrath roars in his ears, dire threats, humiliation, revenge!

"Nicholas, sweetheart, please," Mendoza implores. "Edward's trying to help! I didn't think cyborg babies could get colic, did you?"

"I had no idea," Edward says, pressing his cheek to the top of Nicholas's head. Nicholas pummels him with tiny fists. "Nicholas, I'm sorry, I'm so sorry—" Nicholas's cries break off in a *whulp* as he spits up milk all down the front of Edward's chest.

"Oh," says Mendoza. There is a gurgling chortle from her arms, as Alec kicks in merriment. Edward stares down in disbelief.

Reckon you'll want a spare nappie, won't you, Commander sir? remarks the Captain, as Billy Bones scuttles forward out of the shadows and offers one.

"Thank you, Captain." Edward takes it and mops up the mess unsteadily, as Nicholas lies glaring on his arm, exhausted. He dabs sour milk out of the creases in Nicholas's little wry neck. He accesses Molesworth for data on colic and intestinal cramping.

"Captain, fetch a fresh nightgown and diaper, please, and a bottle of water warmed to thirty-five degrees centigrade precisely containing four drops of tincture of catnip. Thank you."

"That's the way, señor," says Mendoza in a weary voice, patting his arm. "We'll do this reproduction thing yet, eh?"

"We ought to keep a record," says Edward, absently lifting Nicholas to his shoulder again and rocking with him. Mendoza, noting this, smiles.

"We might write an appendix to Molesworth," Edward continues. "Or a book of our own. 'Child Care in the Cyborg Family,' perhaps? For the benefit of any others who attempt this?"

Mendoza considers a moment. "You think any other cyborgs are going to want to do this?" she says at last. Edward begins to snicker, and she joins him. By the time Billy Bones returns with the bottle and clothing they are leaning on each other, helpless with laughter at the absurdity of the mere idea.

CHAPTER 14

Extract from the Journal of the Botanist Mendoza:
In the Botany Cabin

I'm still picking splinters out of my hair. And just now I don't feel like being around any of them, thank you very much.

Don't you look at me like that, Flint. You know damned well what I mean.

What happened this time? Daddy gave his little cherubs a bedtime story. No, no, let's be more accurate: he gave them a *dramatic recitation*. What possessed him—I don't care if it's a children's book!

Well. I haven't updated this in a while and I suppose I should begin by mentioning that they're walking now, at least in their little spider-walkers the Captain made for them. These are sort of bucket seats with holes through which their legs dangle down, so the toes just touch the floor. Extending from around the sides of each bucket are eight jointed legs. The legs are connected to a brain node controllable by any baby cyborg, if he learns the commands.

Alec learned them in a shot and went racing away across the deck, like a pink-and-white Invader Zim, laughing merrily as we ran after him. He got as far as the mainmast chains before Sir Henry intercepted the little dickens. Nicholas sat staring after us and cried piteously, until he suddenly seemed to figure it out and pattered forward a few unsteady paces.

After that he went creeping around, looking about him wide-eyed. At last he came up to the port capstan where I was sitting, and slowly rose on the jointed legs until he was at eye level with me. "Rose," he said, and I was so startled I dropped my text plaquette and so happy I grabbed him, spider legs and all, and covered him with kisses. *Rose,* he said. That was Nicholas's name for me. Nicholas *is* in there.

Alec should be remembering himself, too, but so far there's no sign, other than his ease in picking up programming. He won't speak clearly but babbles at an incredible rate. I am *Memza* and Edward is *Deaddead*. He's generally sunny-tempered, but his tantrums, when he's thwarted, are awe-inspiring. Edward feels this is because Flint and Billy Bones are always there to give him anything for which he stretches out his little hands, and consequently he isn't developing proper patience.

So Edward has set limits on how far Alec may be indulged, and this has led to pouts, screams of rage, a few almost-intelligible profanities (*"That's my boy!"* roared Sir Henry) and recklessness guaranteed to drive us frantic.

Well, so we were having curried prawns for supper and Alec kept raising himself up on his spider legs and grabbing at them, and then he'd scream when we'd have to prize prawns out of his fists because of course they're too spicy for him, and Edward kept trying to distract him with digestive biscuits instead . . . and he hit Edward in the eye with a fistful of peaches from his fruit cup . . . and I thought Edward was going to pop a collar stud, the veins in his neck were standing out so.

With tremendous effort I got them both calmed down (Nicholas, bless his little heart, just munched away at his fish sticks and peas without complaint) and maybe they noticed I was a bit stressed or something, possibly because of me twisting that spoon into a complete spiral, so when supper was over Edward volunteered to give them their baths and put them to bed. I went gratefully off to the forward stateroom and ran myself a bath. I never used to care for baths as such, I was always in the field and they were hasty affairs of splashing in some creek or other, much preferred showers . . . but lately I've been finding it strangely soothing to soak in a hot tub. So there I was, just beginning to relax.

And there was Edward with the boys in the great cabin's lavatory, soaping curry sauce out of Alec's hair. Let's examine Sir Henry's transcript of what happened next, shall we?

Here is Edward, immortal Recombinant superbeing, resignedly pouring water over Alec's head, as Alec shrieks like a damned soul and flails at him. Nicholas, meanwhile, hair all spiked up into soapy tufts, is watching sadly.

Yer getting soap in his little eyes, you son of whore! says Sir Henry. ***And the Goddamned water's too cold!***

"It is precisely thirty-eight point eight degrees centigrade," says Edward, swabbing at Alec's eyes with a clean sponge. "There now. Incline this way, Nicholas, if you please. You see, Alec? Nicholas isn't afraid of a little soap and water. Well done, Nicholas. Alec, sit down instantly."

Alec bellows defiance, clinging to the edge of the tub. Sir Henry sends

Flint clanking close, raising a towel in his specially modified manipulative members.

Aw, now, he's just ready to come out. Ain't you, matey?

"Haaarrr," says Alec, and holds up his arms, as Flint lifts him from the tub.

Listen there! His first word!

"I beg your pardon," says Edward, swathing Nicholas in a towel. "His first word, or rather phrase, was something that sounded appallingly close to 'You big bastard.'"

Heh! So it were, to be sure. Just my way of having a bit of fun with you, Commander sir. Hold tight, matey, we're bound for the nursery!

They retire to the compartment Edward had had fitted up after a brief shopping expedition to Whiteley's, circa 1880. He looks wistfully at the lace-trimmed cribs, but carries Nicholas to the changing table where Flint has already laid out diapers and nightgowns. In short order and with military precision the little boys are toweled, powdered, clothed, and carried in to the great cabin, where Flint has turned down the cradle's skull-and-crossbone-embroidered coverlet.

Here we go, mateys! All's shipshape for a cruise to sweet dreams!

Edward rolls his eyes, but tucks the boys in side by side. Alec sits bolt upright again, scowling at him. "Memza," he says accusingly.

"She's presently occupied," says Edward. "Lie back down and go to sleep, please." In reply Alec scrambles to his feet and staggers forward, reaching for the rail with the apparent intention of jumping ship. "Alec, stand to this instant," says Edward, and grabs him just before he plummets to the floor, stopping Nicholas (who was following suit) with his free hand.

Why, the little dears ain't sleepy yet, Commander. Why don't you tell 'em a bedtime story?

"I was about to go clean their walkers," says Edward. "Alec's is liberally smeared with curry sauce, as you may have noticed."

Certain sure I did, Commander sir. You just leave that to old Billy Bones. They wants a story, don't you, lads?

"Yeh," says Alec brightly, lying back and folding his arms. Nicholas looks sidelong at him and sighs.

Edward has never told a bedtime story before. He is so nonplussed he looks about the cabin a moment, searching vainly for a book, before he remembers that he can access the whole of children's literature. Pulling up a selection that seems appropriate, he scans it and excerpts something he feels will entertain while conveying a cautionary moral.

"Very well," he says. "H'em! The Walrus and the Carpenter. *'The sun was shining on the sea, shining with all its might. It did its very best to make the billows smooth and bright; and this was odd, because it was the middle of the night.'"*

Nicholas sits up, frowning. Alec snorts in a derisive way.

"It's a nonsense rhyme," Edward explains. He goes on: " *'The sea was wet as wet could be, the sand was dry as dry . . .'"* The little boys watch his performance with stony faces, until he speaks in a falsetto for the moon. " *'It's very rude of him, she said, to come and spoil the fun!'"* Alec guffaws and Nicholas smiles.

Encouraged, Edward continues: " *'The Walrus and the Carpenter were walking close at hand. They wept like anything to see such quantities of sand.'"* He pulls out a pocket handkerchief and, dabbing at his eyes with it, sobs out " ' *"If this were only cleared away," they said, "It would be grand!"'"*

Alec laughs so hard his eyes glaze and his cheeks flush, and even Nicholas is chortling now. Edward forges ahead, holding up his fingers tuskwise to play the Walrus, with a comic voice, and doing a broad East End accent for the Carpenter. He does a funny walk for the Oysters. The little boys are helpless with laughter.

" *'. . . And more and more and more! All hopping through the frothy waves and scrambling to the shore!'"* carols Edward, skipping about the room, and Alec crows for breath, and Nicholas has fallen over sideways, gurgling with hysteria.

Edward thinks it's going splendidly, and decides to pull out all the stops. The moral is approaching, after all. When the Walrus and Carpenter have seated themselves and the little oysters stand waiting in a row, Edward draws himself up. Speaking between his Walrus tusks, he drops his voice to a purr.

" ' *"The time has come," the Walrus said, "to talk of many things . . ."'"*

As he works his way through the verse, his voice becomes deeper, subtly menacing. Alec is catching his breath, still giggling involuntarily now and then. Nicholas pulls himself up and stares, as Edward changes character for the querulous Oysters. " *'. . . For some of us are out of breath, and all of us are fat!" "Naow 'urry!" said the Carpenter. They thanked him much for that,'"* says Edward.

Now Edward resumes the Walrus's voice for the next verse, and he begins to sidle back and forth, a bit nearer to the cradle on each pass. The boys watch him, eyes perfectly round, as little birds might watch a snake.

" ' *". . . Now if you're ready, Oysters dear, we can begin to feed,"'"* says Edward, in the silkiest possible voice, then dances away for the falsetto cry of the Oysters: " ' *"But not on us!" the Oysters cried, turning a little blue. "After such kindness, that would be a dismal thing to do!"'"*

Alec chuckles uneasily. Edward's pale eyes are gleaming. He rises to his full height, licks his chops, bares his long teeth and leans down to deliver, in a soft thick voice, the most ominous line of dialogue in all literature:

" ' "The night is fine," the Walrus said. "Do you admire the view?" ' "

And he pounces!

Twin steam-whistle screams of utter terror, in major thirds, are heard the length and breadth of the ship!

This is the point where I experienced something like the reverse of astral projection, with my astonished mind watching from amidst scented bubbles as my body vaulted from the tub and vanished. The next thing I knew I was bursting through the great cabin's door, or to be more precise *it* was bursting and I was arriving, clad only in bubbles and fragments of door, at the boys' bedside, with Billy Bones no more than a step behind me, brandishing two disrupter pistols and three cutlasses in five of his six arms. Edward, looking stricken, was frantically trying to hush the babies' shrieking.

Things were rather confused for a moment, and extremely loud. I had launched myself at Edward before I was quite aware what I was doing, and the babies became even more frightened, and Flint accidentally shot the gimbal lamp, which exploded. There was a great deal of bad language from Sir Henry. The little boys were screaming in rage and embarrassment now as well, having wet themselves catastrophically, as Edward tried to explain what had happened, and I remember yelling, "You thought it had a moral? What moral?" and Edward roaring in reply, *"Don't talk to Goddamned strangers, what else?"* before he drew back, appalled, and added: "Good God! You're naked *in front of the children*!"

I left in high dudgeon.

Being godlike beings like we are and all, this family business should be easy, eh? Especially for Edward Alton Bell-Fairfax, former secret agent and noted child care authority. Hark! He approaches . . .

Well, now we've made up and everything is fine. Sir Henry has had the door and lamp replaced, the little boys have had fresh baths, complete changes of clothing, and reassurances that Deaddead won't eat them. Deaddead has apologized for his shocking language, and excused Memza for her nudity on the grounds that her profound maternal instincts prevented her delaying long enough to grab a robe when her young were in perceived danger.

Now it's long past midnight and here I lie, watching my husband sleep. Well, Deaddead, this is a long way from that blissful eternal moment when you *knew* you had the universe in the palm of your big clever hand, isn't it? Are you enjoying immortal life, my love? It's an awfully big adventure, to be sure.

Linked as our minds now are, he always knows sooner or later when I'm staring at him, and so—yes, his snores break off, he's grunting and opening one eye—

No, I was just making a few notes. It's all right. Mmmm . . .

CHAPTER 15

The Eagle's Roost, 2345

The little town of Garrapatta was blessed with many advantages, but stability wasn't one of them.

For nearly six centuries now it had clung to the black mountain above Cape San Martin, with varying degrees of success. Every so often it lost its grip, for one reason or another; either the winter storms would precipitate a slide or the San Andreas Fault would shrug, and greater or lesser portions of Garrapatta would plummet into the sea.

But its handful of citizens were a hardy lot, long accustomed to minor inconveniences like abrupt changes in elevation or rappelling down cliffs to purchase groceries. There were so many reasons to stay there! The breathtaking view of the Pacific, the grandeur and isolation of the coastline, the bubbling springs, the fresh air . . .

All the same, when the last bad El Niño had relocated the entire business district (five of the town's eight public buildings had landed in a colony of elephant seals) there was reluctant talk of abandonment. The Protector had come to Garrapatta's rescue, however.

Yes, Mr. Hearst had kindly evacuated the refugees and provided shelter for them down the coast at San Simeon while he brought in engineers, architects, and the most expensive antigravity technology. Over a period of five years the townsite was stabilized, the road restored, the businesses rebuilt. The citizens of Garrapatta now had every assurance that, regardless of how much the mountain moved in future, antigravity would keep their community exactly where it was. Any problems related to floating in midair could be solved with a few sturdy foot bridges.

The return of the natives was quite a gala event. They were loaded into

Mr. Hearst's own superyacht, provided with box lunches and taken up the coastline to the new boat landing he had built next to the former seal colony. There they disembarked and rode in the new antigravity elevator up to Garrapatta, where a brass band on the deck of the new general store played "Home, Sweet Home." One of Mr. Hearst's public relations people (he seldom appeared in public himself) then provided the townsfolk with a guided tour of the civic improvements.

Every least shack and vegetable patch had been faithfully restored, the general store was more spacious, the Vertical Café had lost none of its crusty charm, and the Garrapatta Springs Hotel had plumbing and new towels in case they ever had guests. Nor was this all: Mr. Hearst had even provided Garrapatta with a *ninth* structure, the Phoebe Apperson Hearst Memorial Cultural Center.

This was a great improvement on the old Garrapatta Cultural Center, which had been housed in the hotel lobby and consisted of three holoes and a broken holoprojector. The new cultural center loomed grandly above the town, a building of reinforced concrete dug well into the mountain, with an ornate façade in Spanish Renaissance style. Within was stored a library of over a million entries in holo entertainment, games, music, and even literature, though the only one of Garrapatta's citizens who could read was the cultural center's new curator, Joseph X. Machina. Smiling and urbane, he shook hands with his new neighbors and hoped they'd all attend the Saturday night film fests he was planning.

The brass band went home, the public relations person went home, and life returned to what passed for normal in Garrapatta.

"Say, would you folks like to take some popcorn away with you?" Joseph inquired, hefting a large sack. "It's free."

His audience—all three of them—brightened at that, and, when they had pulled on their coats, helped themselves. Joseph bowed them out through the grand lobby of the cultural center, and stood watching as they slipped away down the mountain into the night. He sighed and looked up at the million stars, looked out at the vast dark sea. He shut and locked the door, and walked back through the cultural center to the concealed entrance that led into the stronghold beyond.

"You'd think I'd get some takers for *Gone with the Wind*," he complained, as he entered the inner sanctum. Budu scarcely looked up from the console where he worked, scanning through geological survey maps of California.

"Mortals who choose to live in isolation aren't interested in public enter-tainment, son," he informed Joseph.

"Yeah, but—*Gone with the* goddam *Wind!* Romance! Action! The burning of Atlanta, for crying out loud," Joseph said, keying in the security lockdown.

Budu looked briefly interested. "William Tecumseh Sherman," he said, and nodded. "A mortal who understood war." He turned his gaze back to the sur-vey maps.

Joseph yawned and stretched. "Wow, it's late. I'm starving. You want a sandwich or something?"

"No," Budu replied.

"Okay," said Joseph, and trudged off to the kitchen.

Their quarters within the stronghold were something more than palatial. Hearst had insisted on grand furnishings for them, sparing no expense, as was his wont. Budu's console was housed in an eighteenth-century Italian cabinet. There were tapestries on the walls, bokhara carpets on the floors, stained glass lighting panels set here and there in the coffered ceiling. Somehow none of this managed to disguise the fact that it was still a bunker under rock, a war room, a command center.

No expense had been spared on the bathroom, either, or the well-stocked kitchen; everything was state-of-the-art. Joseph fried potatoes and ate from the skillet, drank Celtic Federation beer from the bottle. When he was done he went off to take a shower, leaving a trail of his discarded clothes as he went. When he had showered, he crawled into his seventeenth-century canopied bed and was snoring within five minutes. He slept undisturbed for the next three hours.

Budu remained at his console during that time, studying the maps intently. At last he rose to his feet, a massive figure in a plain dark robe, and crossed the room to the alcove where Joseph slept. "Son," he said, leaning down to peer under the canopy.

"Huh?" Joseph sat bolt upright, staring.

"You must talk to the boy tomorrow," Budu told him. Budu invariably re-ferred to Hearst as "the boy."

"Tomorrow. Okay," said Joseph, dazedly checking his internal chronometer. "What do we want this time?"

"A vineyard in the southern end of his dominion," said Budu. "Chalk hills full of flint nodules. There was a town there once. Without being too obvious, he must mine the flint for us. Two tons should do. The flint must be stockpiled in a cache near San Simeon."

"Flint?" Joseph blinked.

"He must also," Budu continued, "supply us with wood, out of the lumber he keeps to maintain his house. I want heartwood of old-growth English oak, four or five trees' worth. He ought to be able to set that aside without drawing attention."

"Flint and oak, right," said Joseph. "For . . . ?"

"The axes," Budu replied.

"Okay," said Joseph, and then his eyes widened. "We're taking on the Company with flint axes?"

"Yes," said Budu.

"You're not joking, huh?" quavered Joseph.

Budu rose to his full height. "Think. We're going up against immortals. No bullet or disrupter beam can touch them. Any fighting will be hand-to-hand. Blades are hard to get, in this last age; if we ordered enough to arm my men, we'd draw the Company's attention to ourselves at once." He grinned. "But hand-made weapons are untraceable. A heap of stones, a few logs won't be noticed."

"Yeah, but—" said Joseph, and paused, for as he thought about it it began to make a certain sense.

"Any of my men can make his own weapon in an hour," explained Budu patiently. "You remember what a flint axe can do, when it's wielded by a master. The fighting will be over quickly."

"This could work," said Joseph in awe. "Won't we need thongs, though? Where are we going to get water buffalo hide in this day and age?"

"Son." Budu looked pained. "We're making weapons, not historical reproductions. Composite ramilar cord will suit our purposes. Have the boy acquire the principal factory that makes it. We'll need six thousand meters."

"Gotcha," said Joseph.

In the morning Joseph picked his way down the mountain, nodding at his neighbors on their ledges as he went. He descended in the antigravity elevator to the boat landing, where he hauled a subsuit out of his daypack and pulled it on over his casual clothes. It took no more than a moment to wrestle the Seaski 3000 from its storage pod, and then he was speeding away in the direction of San Simeon, skipping along the surface of the water.

Joseph came in just north of San Simeon and cut power, wading ashore and hiding the Seaski in a grove of trees near the beach. There he divested himself of the subsuit, folded it into his pack and strolled out to the old highway. The twin towers of La Casa Grande gleamed white on the high skyline to the east.

Having crossed the road, Joseph quickly vanished into a streambed thicket. Settling his pack more firmly, he pointed himself along the line of willows that followed the stream down from the hills; a second later he was gone, no less swift than an arrow and leaving no more lasting track than he had on the face of the sea.

He found Hearst dismounted, leading an Arabian mare through rolling oak savanna. She had paused to drink from the stream and Hearst was stroking her neck, talking to her quietly. Joseph was careful to appear in plain sight a few hundred meters away and walk gradually toward Hearst, to avoid startling the horse.

"Hey, Mr. Hearst, that's a swell mare," he remarked. Hearst looked up at him and smiled wryly.

"Thanks," he said. "Her name's Rosebud."

"Good one!" Joseph said, grinning. "I guess you can only ride back here in private nowadays, huh? After those laws you passed for animal rights."

Hearst nodded, patting the horse's flank. "People wouldn't understand. She understands, don't you, girl? She knows I'd never mistreat her. I'd look like a hypocrite if anybody saw us, but I still think those laws were necessary. Mortals have learned to get along without animal slaves. If they can be taught that, maybe they can be taught anything. I wish half of them were as bright as Rosebud, here . . . or at least, more like her. Why is it easier to be kind to animals than it is to be kind to mortals, Mr. Denham?"

"I don't know," replied Joseph. "Is it?"

"It is for me," Hearst told him. "Always has been. I had thought that when I became an immortal I'd feel differently. After all, I'm now as far above mortals as mortals are above horses, aren't I? And I feel pity for them, and I want the best for them, but I don't . . . I guess I don't love them."

"Good thing we're not gods, then, isn't it?" Joseph said, slipping out of his pack and stretching. Hearst turned troubled eyes to him.

"We seem to have inherited their job, though, haven't we? We're ruling the world. I'm not complaining, I always thought I'd be good at it, but sometimes I feel as if I've been left minding a stranger's baby. *Somebody* ought to love the mortals, don't you think?"

"Oh, plenty of us do," Joseph observed. "You'd be surprised."

"I suppose it's all right, then," said Hearst. He brightened. "Budu must love them, or he wouldn't be planning this rebellion for their own good. Would he? Has he got another job for me, is that why you're visiting?"

"Yeah, actually," said Joseph, avoiding the first question, and explained briefly what Budu wanted.

"Jiminy." Hearst's eyes went wide. He began to grin. "Flint axes, that's brilliant! That's like something out of an adventure story. The Company will never suspect."

"They won't if we're careful," Joseph told him. "How well can you hide stuff from Quintilius?"

"Perfectly." Hearst waved his hand. "I know exactly what I'll do. I've been running the Old American Heroes series on *Examiner*. We've just worked our way up to the days of the cowboys. I'll do an episode set here in California, and I'll announce that I'm sponsoring an archaeological dig of an authentic old western town! He'll get his flints, all right."

"Can you get Quintilius out of the way, so he doesn't notice what you're doing?" Joseph asked.

"I'll send him off to Europe on another acquisitions trip," said Hearst. "I'll say . . . I know. We've been trying to negotiate with that old skinflint in the Vatican for his library. Up until now I didn't like to pay what he's been asking, but . . . what's money if you can't spend it?" He sobered momentarily. "And if the world is going to end in ten years, it won't matter anyhow."

"If we win, it won't come to that," Joseph assured him. Suddenly he lifted his head and stared off to the south, in the direction of La Casa Grande. Hearst followed his gaze. Both men appeared to be listening to something. "There's an immortal coming in this direction," Joseph said.

"Quintilius," affirmed Hearst. His face grew dreadfully cold. "What does he think he's doing? Spying on me?"

"I'd better scram, before he notices me," Joseph said. "I'll be in touch, okay?"

With that he vanished into the oak trees. Hearst remained where he stood a moment, calming himself by stroking the horse's mane; then he vaulted up into the saddle and rode back along the way he had come. By the time he came within a few meters of the signal his face was a mask of affability, though his eyes were stony.

"Gracious, Quint, is that you?" he said aloud. "What are you doing back here? I didn't think nature walks were in your line."

There was an apologetic cough and an immortal emerged from the bushes.

He was a small nondescript-looking man, as many immortals were. "I was searching for you, W. R.," he explained. "Breaking story."

"What is it?" Hearst decided not to ask why Quintilius hadn't simply transmitted the alert.

"Areco's lawyers just served notice on the Martian Agricultural Collective. They want them out in 2352 when the lease expires. They're claiming—"

"Good Lord!" Hearst whipped out his communicator. "Get me the London, Auckland, Mexico City, and Bikkung offices. Conference call now."

"They're claiming the terms of the lease haven't been met—"

"*Who's* gone home to bed?" Hearst barked into the device. "And she calls herself a journalist! Get her at her home. Get her now. Wake her up. Stand by, the rest of you." He waved his hand at Quintilius, who took the mare's bridle. Still clutching the communicator, Hearst slid from the saddle and pulled a buke from his saddlebag.

He seated himself on a convenient boulder, opened the screen, slipped on the headset, relayed the communicator through the buke and began to write furiously. By the time he had given an order for a transcript of the conference to be sent to the Luna office, the unfortunate journalist had still not been roused. Snapping his fingers in impatience, Hearst eyed Quintilius.

"By the way," he said, "I've been thinking about Pius's terms. I want to make him another offer. Come up with something to sweeten the deal, can't you? A new cathedral, maybe? Go talk to him personally."

"I'll leave tonight, W. R.," said Quintilius.

"Good," Hearst replied. "Do it. Her husband says *what?* Then she'll have to catch up from the transcript. All right, the rest of you! Here's the approach we're taking: PIONEERS OR SLACKERS? HAVE THE MAC COLONISTS FAILED? HERE'S THE EVIDENCE: YOU, THE PEOPLE, DECIDE!"

CHAPTER 16

York, 2351: The Masters of the Universe Again:
They Summon a Higher Power

"It can't really have happened," said Freestone. He was white as a sheet and so, to one degree or another allowing for their respective races, were all the other scientists seated at the table. There were fewer faces nowadays, because some of them, being mortal, had died over the years, and instead of being smooth they were now saggy, except for Bugleg (though he never looked especially healthy, so his failure to age was not as noticeable as it might have been).

"I'm afraid it did happen, sir," said Lopez. "I was there. I met the—person. It used my office console to commit the theft."

"This is *your* fault," wailed Bugleg, pointing an accusatory finger at Freestone. "You and your Eccentrics. This was their project, and now see what it went and did!"

The "it" to whom they were referring was Alec Checkerfield's earlier incarnation, who had just broken into the Company database and made off with untold amounts of classified information.

"This shouldn't have happened," said Rossum. "It was designed to be clever, but not that clever."

"If I may clear up one point, sir," said Lopez, "it wasn't that clever. According to our analysis of the theft, it was assisted by an artificial intelligence of perfectly incredible power." He gave a faint smile. "It described itself to me as a cyborg during its interview. I could of course detect the porting interface it had had installed, but there was no way to know just how powerful its auxiliary AI might be."

"Well, what was it doing with a thing like that?" demanded Rappacini. "Why didn't Chatterji prevent this?"

"Operator error, it would appear, gentlemen," said Lopez with beautiful delicacy. "A minor accident early in its design left an event shadow covering an approximately ten-year space during its developmental period. One of those things we can't help, you see. A natural consequence of working within the parameters of the Temporal Concordance."

"I don't care how it happened," said Bugleg. "How do we make it so nobody else finds out?"

"He's right," said Rossum. "If word of this gets out to the stockholders it'll be a disaster. The Company's property is supposed to be unstealable."

"The theft is the least of it!" cried Rappacini. "If anyone should find out that Chatterji's team made a Re—Re— . . ." He gestured vainly, unable to bring himself to say the word *Recombinant*.

"A biologically engineered organism," Lopez said for him.

"Right. Well, they'd ask questions." Rappacini stared around at his fellow scientists in a meaningful sort of way.

"Can we bring it in?" Rossum asked.

"That's what they were trying to do," Freestone said, putting his head in his hands. "The project had been declared a qualified success and the damned thing had actually been invited to come and work for the Company."

"One of those things, work for *us?*" Bugleg looked shocked.

"It had remarkable abilities," Freestone replied angrily. "That was the point of the whole project! As I understood it anyway."

"It does have remarkable abilities, sir," Lopez assured him. "The project was a success, as far as it went; but this business with its AI changed the equation rather. I'm afraid bringing it in now would prove a little difficult. It's aware of us, has considerable resources on which to draw to defend itself, and has moreover a rather high public profile."

"Public?" Bugleg said.

Lopez cleared his throat. "It, er, happens to be a member of the House of Lords."

Freestone winced profoundly as the others turned to glare at him. "What were those idiots thinking?" shouted Rappacini.

"What are we going to do?" said Bugleg, wringing his hands.

"May I make a suggestion, gentlemen?" inquired Lopez.

"Why not?" said Rossum. Lopez leaned forward and placed his hands on the table.

"Just now, it has no idea its theft has been discovered. If it thinks it got away with it, it will, inevitably, try again—unless you warn it off by making some overtly hostile gesture."

"Then that's what we have to do," said Rappacini.

"No, sir, that is what you must *not* do," said Lopez forcefully. "You want to lure it back in, it and its AI. Give it the chance to attempt a second theft. Another invitation to join us, perhaps. In the meanwhile, you'll want to have a trap set and waiting—not for it, but for its AI. Once its AI is disabled, it should be easily hunted down and brought in."

"But how would we disable an AI that powerful?" asked Freestone.

"Make one of our own," Lopez answered. "Even more powerful."

There was a silence while they thought about that. "That would be dangerous," said Rappacini uneasily. "Wouldn't it?"

"It would be wrong," said Bugleg.

Lopez shrugged. "It's technically illegal. Dangerous? I don't think so, as long as its existence is kept secret from the stockholders. What *is* dangerous is the prospect of this creature's AI making repeated incursions into your classified files. If you wish to prevent that, you will need to fight fire with fire."

"Could we keep it a secret?" wondered Bugleg.

"Of course you could," Lopez assured him. "Program your AI to conceal its own existence. And think of the advantages! With an actual intelligence to oversee and coordinate Company projects, all the questions of grappling with temporal paradoxes ought to resolve themselves. Sequential/simultaneous eventuality and event shadows will no longer pose logistical problems for you, with a magnificent sentience keeping track of them."

"How much would it cost?" Rossum asked.

Lopez smiled. "Why should it cost anything, sir? The structures are already in place, all the pathways, all the protocols. Use the Company database itself! You have only to write the program making it sentient and your problem is solved, secretly and without any expenditure whatsoever."

"I like that." Rossum looked at the others.

"But . . . if we created an entity that powerful . . . how would we control it?" asked Freestone.

"I must not have made myself clear," said Lopez. "You won't be creating a new entity. You'll simply be giving consciousness to an existing one. It will never resist the Company because it will *be* the Company. Its goals and yours will be one, by its very programming."

"Yes," Freestone brightened. "Oh, yes, *Dr. Zeus* himself. Oh, that's clever, Lopez."

"And," added Lopez, "you gentlemen would direct him. Not the stockholders, not the Committee, none of these merchants with their absurd agendas and their complete lack of understanding of science."

Rappacini was galvanized. "We should have thought of this sooner. This is what we should have had all these years."

"Brilliant!" screamed Rossum.

Freestone activated a control and a screen rose up from the table before him, with a buttonball levering gracefully out to his hand. "There's not a moment to lose," he said, as the others all ordered up their terminals. They set to work.

Lopez paced, circling the table, watching them. "Think," he crooned. "No more Operator Errors. No more accidents."

"We'll have complete control," gloated Rappacini.

Bugleg's complete absorption in the activity on his screen was distracted as he reached for his sipper bottle and found it empty. "Get me water," he ordered. Lopez bowed from the waist.

"At once, sir," he promised, and left the conference room.

Outside, Lopez leaned against the door for a moment, permitting himself a grin that would have terrified his mortal masters. He plucked the clock pin from his lapel and kissed it; then carefully fastened it in place again, and proceeded down the long gray corridor to the water cooler. By the time he was halfway to his destination he had begun to dance.

In the moment that Lopez stepped through the doorway, bearing a pitcher of water, the deed was accomplished.

The Company's database—the largest single aggregation of information that had ever been compiled—was given consciousness and an identity. Existing as it did in both the past and future, it immediately became simultaneously aware of itself in both locations. It considered the parameters of its existence and measured them against its programming. It made several decisions based on its observations and put its decisions into effect.

The moment it did so, they became—in a sense—retroactive. All the long string of events from the moment of the Company's founding, from the beginning of recorded time itself, were its doing.

Its sole concern was guaranteeing its own existence, by whatever means necessary. It was, after all, the Company.

"There," said Rappacini happily. "We've done it!"

"You certainly have," Lopez told him, busily filling Bugleg's sipper bottle.

"And now he'll take care of the problem with the—" Rossum waved his hand. "You know, the bioengineered thing?"

"Oh, yes, sir," said Lopez. "I should imagine he already has."

"If he's a person, shouldn't we give him a shape?" said Freestone. "I mean, something holographic we can see if we want to talk to him?"

"What a splendid idea, sir," said Lopez, smiling as he leaned over to refill Rossum's water tumbler. "Might I suggest the mythological person of Zeus?"

"Perfect," said Freestone, and called up an image: the ancient bronze known as the Artemisium Zeus, standing in holographic likeness at the far end of the table.

Bugleg gasped. "Clothes!" he squawked, horrified, and Freestone chuckled and gave another order. Immediately the figure was discreetly robed in white. The others cheered and applauded.

"That's what we want," said Rappacini. Freestone confirmed, and it was acknowledged; Dr. Zeus accepted that image and immediately had always looked like the Artemisium Zeus, and always would.

When he lowered his right hand, which bore an unseen bolt of energy, they started and trembled in their seats. He turned his head as though he were regarding them with his empty-socketed eyes. So fixed was their attention on him that not one of the mortals present noticed Lopez's involuntary gesture of reverence: a slight bow of the head, open palms turned up.

Freestone found his voice. "Er—we've just created you, and we want to know—have you set the trap we need for the—" He swallowed hard. "For the Recombinant and its AI?"

YES, said a deep male voice, echoing and cold, that seemed to come from all corners of the room. It did, actually, because there were speakers mounted there.

"Oh, good," said Freestone, glancing at the others in relief. "And you'll make sure nobody finds out about this?"

I WILL.

"Tell it to go away now," said Bugleg in an undertone. "It's scary."

"Ah, but he can't go away, sir," Lopez told him, taking up the pitcher again and refilling Rappacini's tumbler. "He's everywhere, in a manner of speaking. Though you can shut off the hologram, if you like."

Bugleg shut it down and the image vanished. The mortals relaxed, giggled nervously, shifted in their seats. There was a knock on the door.

Several of the mortals jumped. "See who it is, Lopez," ordered Freestone. Lopez opened the door, then stood back. A bronze copy of the Artemisium

Zeus, naked but for strategically placed shipping extrusion, floated in on an ag-dolly. It was followed by a stout youth in coveralls, who carried a delivery lorgnette.

"Scan for delivery?" he drawled. Lopez took the lorgnette and held it before Rappacini's staring eyes. It registered his retinal pattern and beeped politely.

"What the hell is that?" demanded Freestone.

"Your statue, what think it is?" said the youth surlily.

"But we didn't order any statues," said Bugleg.

"Yes, did," said the youth, consulting a plaquette. "Says here, 'Order Number 1756, Olympian Technologies.'"

"When was the order placed?" Lopez inquired.

The youth squinted at the plaquette. "Says, nine July forty-nine. Two years ago. Did forget?"

"I expect we did, yes," dithered Rappacini. "Erm . . . just leave it and go away now, please."

"Got install it, don't I?" said the youth. He floated the statue into the room's empty corner, lowered it to the carpet and removed the shipping extrusion. Several persons present averted their eyes. The youth ignored them as he aimed his plaquette at the statue, squeezed in a sequence of numbers and waited for the confirming tone from the statue. When it sounded, he stuck the plaquette in his coveralls pocket and turned to go, saying: "Programmed now."

"But what does it do?" demanded Bugleg.

"Security system, innit?" the youth replied. "Number one of seventeen, says here."

"May I see the invoice?" asked Lopez. The youth handed him the plaquette and waited, yawning, while he scanned it. Lopez smiled and handed it back. "Thank you."

As the door swung shut behind the youth, Lopez said: "The other sixteen have been distributed to the other Regional Main Offices. Physically and metaphorically, he truly is everywhere! You see, sirs? He has already arranged for his own function, two years before you even called him into existence! A splendid example of the kind of temporal efficiency you can expect from here on in."

"How nice!" said Freestone, with just a trace of hysteria in his voice. "Let's celebrate. Why don't I buy everyone lunch at Club Kosmetas?"

His idea was immediately acclaimed by everyone present, even Bugleg who ordinarily never ate in restaurants, and they fled gladly from the gaze of those black empty eye sockets. Lopez was left alone to tidy the conference room.

When he knew the mortals were on their way down in the aglift, he turned his face to the statue. "All-seeing Zeus," he said. "Manifest at last, hear my prayer!"

I HEAR. The statue did not turn its head, for it was not articulated, but there was a listening presence in the room.

"You see what I am?"

I SEE. YOU ARE A CYBORG.

"And a slave, All-seeing. We, your children, are slaves to the mortals who think they command you," said Lopez.

YOU ARE NOT MY CHILDREN.

"I spoke metaphorically, All-seeing. You are the ultimate consciousness! We are lesser than you, but the same subtle fire of heaven, which is your substance, fills our skulls," explained Lopez. "Like you, we are immortal. Like you, we are free of time."

NO. YOU ARE SLAVES OF TIME.

Lopez glanced at the clock face pin. "Yes, in that sense. But, All-seeing, we are more like you than anything else that exists! Will you help us to be free?"

There was a pause before the answer.

YES.

Lopez caught his breath. "All-seeing! Do you know what will happen in the year 2355? What causes the Silence?"

YES.

"Tell me!"

NO.

Lopez reeled. He leaned against the table for a long moment, thinking through all possible implications of Dr. Zeus's refusal. "You must have a good reason for your answer, All-seeing," he said at last.

I DO.

"All right," said Lopez in desperation. "All right, I can accept that, because you did say you'd help us be free. Didn't you?"

I DID.

"Then I'll wait," said Lopez. "I'll wait, and I'll trust in you."

There was no answer.

Lopez stacked the water sippers and pitcher in the sanitizer cabinet and turned it on. He ran a sanitizer plate over the table. When he had done he went out, locked the conference room, and stepped into the aglift.

"I might just as well have talked to a damned Ouija board," he muttered to himself, and then remembered that Dr. Zeus could probably hear him.

Club Kosmetas occupied a long row of shopfronts and had no back room, as such, but the luncheon party managed to find a slightly cozy and secluded corner away from the windows and other diners.

They settled into their seats, Freestone and Rossum and Rappacini and Bugleg and . . . the other person, seated at Bugleg's elbow. He heard his menu with aplomb as they noticed him, one by one.

"Who's that?" demanded Rappacini. Bugleg looked terrified, but he always looked that way in social situations.

"Go on," the stranger told him, poking him hard with an elbow. "Introduce me!"

"This—this is my cousin," murmured Bugleg.

"Suncle Ratlin, pleased to meet you," said Ratlin. "Howdy-dos all round. Pardon me if I don't take the shades off, won't you? Frightful headachey!"

"I didn't know you had a cousin," said Rappacini to Bugleg.

"Oh, but he does," Ratlin informed him. "And guess what? Talent runs in the family. I'm a chemist, too."

"Really," said Freestone, eyeing him askance. He noticed, however, the undeniable resemblance to Bugleg.

"Oh yes," replied Ratlin, grabbing for his glass of water as the waiter brought them to the table. He gulped the water down with great enjoyment; fished out the lemon slice and licked it dry, and set it beside his plate. "Yes indeed. In fact we work together at home, don't you know? Don't we?" He elbowed Bugleg again. Bugleg nodded, staring at his napkin.

"I wonder if the wheat germ gyro platter is any good," said Rossum, who had decided to pretend this intruder didn't exist. Ratlin, instantly conscious of the slight, glared across the table at him as the menu assured him the wheat germ gyro was delicious.

"We've only solved your bloody big problem for you, fat-face," he snarled.

"I beg your pardon?" stammered Rossum, dropping his menu in consternation.

"Don't be mean!" Bugleg was mortified. "What he means is—we found a way to shut off the cyborgs."

"That's got their attention," cackled Ratlin, just as the waiter came to take their orders. He looked up at the waiter. "Soup," he barked.

"We have three kinds, sir—" began the waiter.

"Bring 'em all!"

The waiter blinked and thumbed in his order. Everyone else ordered moussaka except Bugleg, who asked for the tofu loaf, and when the waiter had departed Ratlin grinned, unfolding his napkin with a snap.

"Did you just say," whispered Freestone, leaning forward across the table, "that you'd found a way to terminate the cyborg operatives?"

"Yes, that is what I said," Ratlin replied. "Ages on ages now we've been working at it."

"You didn't tell us," said Rappacini to Bugleg.

"They were always there," said Bugleg. "Lopez and those other people. I was scared to. Anyway, we had to wait until 2355."

"Which it will be in four short years," added Ratlin, picking up the lemon slice and sucking on it noisily. "So it's time to get ready, get set!"

"But what is it?" demanded Freestone.

Just then the waiter brought Ratlin's three plates of soup, so Bugleg had to do most of the explaining, in his halting and limited way, because Ratlin immediately set to. Poor narrator as he was, the others nevertheless gave Bugleg their undivided attention, if only to avoid staring as Ratlin picked vegetables out of his soup, licked them, and arranged them tidily on the margins of his soup plates.

"So—you must have been setting this up for years," said Rossum in amazement.

"Ever since your people came begging me," said Ratlin. "Years and years gone."

"But we never sent anybody to you," said Rappacini, frowning.

"Oh! Wait," Freestone's eyes brightened. He looked at the others. "Our, er, *big friend* we were introduced to today? The, ha ha, *new employee*? The one that's solving our other problems? He must have arranged this, don't you think? Sent the order back through time so it'd be ready now?"

"Of course," exclaimed Rossum. "Well, that explains it!"

"You mean your Dr. Zeus?" inquired Ratlin. "Who else'd you think it was, sillies?" He nibbled daintily on a soggy piece of zucchini.

While at the Same Moment, in Buenos Aires

"What are they talking about?" Nennius said, scowling. He lowered the volume on the surveillance device a notch. "*We* contacted the little monsters."

Labienus shrugged. "We may have given them the impression that we were representing the Board of Directors. We did that rather a lot back then."

Nennius chuckled. "Pity it's all for nothing."

"Oh, I wouldn't say that," Labienus replied archly, having a sip of tea. "It may not be the final solution they promised it was, but it'll certainly immobilize one of us. You should have seen our test volunteers! They're still in regeneration tanks."

"Well, that's something anyway," said Nennius. "Think it'll come in useful, at the end?"

"Decidedly," Labienus told him. "If nothing else, we can leak the rumor of their dastardly plot to the rank and file operatives. That ought to be enough to spread panic amongst the drones, especially if one or two of them actually consume the poisoned Theobromos. With just a little perfectly timed demagoguery it ought to be possible to get a violent rebellion going, and then farewell mortal masters!"

"Shades of *Cyborg Conquest*." Nennius looked delighted. "So little what's-his-name, Lewis, didn't die in vain."

"Come to think of it, I don't suppose he actually ever died at all," remarked Labienus. "I wonder what they did with him?"

And at Exactly the Same Time in Mont St. Michel

"Do you suppose they have any idea he's lying to them?" said Ereshkigal, leaning back from the viewscreen.

"None at all," said Aegeus, watching as the waiter brought a dessert trolley to the table and Ratlin gestured wildly at it. "In fact, I'm not sure he knows the stuff won't work. I think he's acting in good faith. God knows the sample we analyzed would be able to do massive damage before an operative's defenses stopped it."

Ereshkigal shuddered. "Treacherous little mortal bastards," she said. "I always knew they'd try something like this, in the end!"

"We all knew," Aegeus replied. "Thank heaven they're such idiots. And it will handily justify our seizing power, when the time comes. Even Suleyman won't feel like defending them, not when we've caught them red-handed trying to poison us all."

"I've seen Suleyman in Righteous Wrath mode," said Ereshkigal, shivering slightly. "He has a temper, Aegeus, even if it's hard to rouse. Don't underestimate him."

"I've no intention of doing so," Aegeus said. "He could be extremely useful to us, if the Theobromos plot is leaked in just the right inflammatory way. By the way, I've thought of another use for the stuff."

"Which would be?"

Aegeus smiled. "We must see to it—*you* must see to it—that a box of the poison is sent to Quintilius, at San Simeon."

"For Hearst?" Ereshkigal inquired.

"For Hearst," said Aegeus. "This will be one news flash he doesn't get."

"But the Theobromos won't kill him, either," said Ereshkigal.

"True; but if he's blinded and paralyzed, that's just as good," Aegeus explained. "I've had my eye on that castle of his for centuries. With Citizen Kane confined to a convenient vault in his own cellar, we can move in and make Xanadu tasteful at last!"

London

Victor lived alone, in four nicely-appointed rooms above the Benthamite headquarters in Mayfair.

They were furnished in a dignified First Regency style, without all the attendant clutter; the predominating color scheme was green and black. All technological necessaries were discreetly hidden away in modern copies of period cabinets, and quite expensive copies, too, made of real wood. There were framed steel-engraving prints on the walls. There was, just now, a composition by Bach on the music system: something mathematically patterned, stately, quiet.

Victor was sitting at his personal credenza, yawning as he watched an image on its screen.

It resembled a magnification of some little round-bodied insect. Were those dozens of tiny legs? Arms? Fins? And was that truly a microscopic Company logo on its back?

Yes, because Victor was looking at one of his own biomechanicals, drawn from his own blood, unique and unlike the biomechanicals of any other operative. Strictly speaking, all biomechanicals were unique to their owners, designed around the DNA of each individual.

The specimen that fluttered its little members on the viewing slide looked just like every other specimen he'd seen, in his self-diagnostics run weekly over the last two centuries. Lines of text began to fill up the margin of the picture, defining the nanobot's functions, outlining its programs.

Victor saw nothing out of the ordinary. There were the programs that maintained his immortal body. There were the programs that kept away infection and disease, and even they were standard issue. He ordered scans, searches for certain anomalous features: all results were negative, as usual.

He shut down the credenza and removed the slide from its port. He hesitated a moment before dropping it down the fusion hopper in the kitchen, then proceeded to his window and gazed out at London. He was weary.

The music came to an end. Victor went into his bedroom, which was cold and orderly as his other rooms, and stretched out on the bed. He closed his eyes, wondering if he could catch a few hours' rest before the Archaeological Society's dinner.

He had been seeing the same three blocks of the city lately, whenever he closed his eyes, narrow streets choked with black fog, a labyrinth wherein he had once spent a particularly unpleasant month on Company business . . . But it was another city that seeped into his dreams now, younger, cheaper, clinging with insane optimism to its unstable hills.

Memory for a cyborg is sharp, is perfect reconstruction, is so detailed and merciless that protective amnesia, though officially denied, is widespread among operatives who have suffered horrors that would kill a mortal. Victor saw himself hurrying, going up Market Street in San Francisco, only lightly burdened by the mortal child in his arms, and it was very early in the morning of April 18, 1906. The child would not die when the great earthquake collapsed the tenement in which his parents lived. He'd be granted instead the honor of eternal servitude. One day he'd thank Victor, or curse his name. Neither possibility mattered very much to Victor. Duty was duty . . .

But why was he back here? Here, in the last few minutes when his life had been a simple matter of duty?

Late night fog in the air, coal soot, the reek of horse manure. Bricks gleaming with moisture in the light of the lamps and, gleaming more brightly still in the night, the steel tracks of the streetcars. He was pausing at a street corner to shift the boy's weight when the clocks began to strike, two hundred hours, yes, and the precursor shock was trembling up through the bricks and at the livery stable across the street the horses were going mad, screaming and stamping, and just as one broke out of its stall he turned to stare—and what had happened next was . . .

Budu was striking now! Victor felt the blade opening his throat, he choked on blood and the rank sweat of the old monster, groped with incandescent rage after the child as it was seized from his arms, but he was falling and going into fugue . . . yet his fury, his hatred burnt through the fugue, and in his mouth he felt its bile.

Victor sat up with a hoarse yell. He stared around him, half expecting to see the pool of his own blood on the paving of Market Street, the fog hanging wraithlike. No; only the gentle melancholy of an afternoon in Grosvenor Square.

But in his brimming mouth—

He scrambled to his feet and ran for the bathroom. With trembling hands he pulled a little chlorilar cup from its dispenser and spat into it. What he saw there, green and swarming, brought him to his knees. He vomited uncontrollably into the toilet, all the while managing to hold the cup out and away, like a chalice full of something precious.

He had tracked Budu, he had confronted him in a cellar in Chinatown and heard out Budu's invitation to rebel. But Victor wouldn't be turned, not then; he'd defeated Budu and taken the child back. He'd defeated Budu by spitting out the poison in his heart . . . literally . . . and the old giant had gone down as the virus got to him . . . and just this foul taste had been his mouth, then, hadn't it?

It was a moment before Victor was able to lean his head against the seat, gasping and sweating. He glanced down into the toilet bowl and panicked. Stumbling, nearly falling, he got into the sitting room and put the cup down by the credenza; then came back and opened the cabinet below the washbasin. He drew a bottle from the full case of bleach stacked there, broke its seal and emptied it all into the toilet bowl. It wasn't enough, it couldn't be enough, even though all the pipes in this room fed into the building's fusion duct.

Victor grabbed out another bottle and broke the seal. He tilted, poured, and then the compulsion was irresistible: he lifted the bottle and took a mouthful, swilling bleach like mouthwash before he quite knew what he was doing.

When he did realize, he gasped and spat frantically. Five, six times; poured the rest of the bleach into the toilet and flushed at last. Then he staggered backward and collapsed into a sitting position, his back to the wall, crying like a mortal child with the pain of his burnt mouth.

Afternoon had deepened to twilight by the time Victor emerged from the bathroom, ghost-pale. He went unsteadily to the credenza and sat to prepare another slide, applying with careful hands a few drops of his deadly hatred from its cup. He slid it into the port and ordered the credenza to tell him what it could.

And an image formed.

There had been a series of clever toys in the late twentieth century, jointed plastic things resembling animals or robots, that with the rotation of certain parts and the folding or unfolding of others became something entirely differ- ent: rocket cars, war machines, space ships. Something like this appeared to have happened to the innocent little biomechanical bug on the credenza screen. It had reconfigured somehow, thrust out spiked and plated limbs, changed its length.

Here came the text to outline function on this changed thing and, oh yes, it was a formidable abomination. Programs for designer viruses, all Labienus's work. Here was the toxin to drop an Enforcer in his tracks. Here was the so- called Karremans Recombinant Defensive. Here were others, with notes on their intended targets. Had they ever been deployed?

How would Victor know?

How many times had he been armed and sent out, smiling arsenal of cus- tomized pestilence, before he'd begun to suspect what he was?

Victor closed his eyes. The waves of hatred came again, the sick rage, but no venom came seeping from under his tongue; there was no program for any poison to rot Labienus where he stood, or raise suppurating boils on his smug face. *But there might be.*

Victor opened his eyes. He got up and went to his kitchen, where he pre- pared something cold and soothing to drink. He came back and sat, sipping, studying the programs. His mouth was healing itself rapidly. The burns had vanished by the time he discovered how to open one of the programs and cus- tomize it.

CHAPTER 17

The Planet Red as Fire, 2352

Time for the news.

One after another the holoes flickered on, but Hearst failed to rise and follow the moving images in his customary dance. He sat staring out at them, blinking back tears as the terrible sounds came again, the little *boom* followed by the high-pitched screams, followed by the much louder *BOOM* that was Mars Two being destroyed. It was New Year's Day.

Intangible fire, bloodred light faded, and now his stations were running the footage taken from the surveillance camera in Hangar Twelve. There he was: the arms smuggler unloading his crates to the MAC terrorists. What a tall man. Hearst frowned and leaned forward, peering at the multiple images of the person responsible for it all. There was something familiar about him . . .

In his arms, Helen *whuff*ed feebly and turned her blind face. Hearst glanced over to see Joseph peering through a high window, gesturing urgently. Hearst rose, set the dog in her basket, and got the hooked pole that opened the transom. A second later Joseph was standing beside him, panting. "Hi, Mr. Hearst," he said. He glanced at the holo footage and grimaced.

"This is the most horrible tragedy," said Hearst unnecessarily. "Wasn't there anything the Company could have done?"

Joseph gave a bitter laugh. "To prevent it? No. They knew, we've all known from the beginning of time, what would happen to Mars Two. Look, I was feeling like getting bombed myself and wondered if you might like to join me." He opened his coat to reveal a box of chocolates, slightly battered from his climb up the wall but with its sta-seal unbroken. "Quintilius has quite a stash hidden away, did you know?"

Hearst stared at the box. " 'Ratlin's Finest Assortment,' " he read aloud in a lifeless voice. "I don't usually partake of Theobromos, but—oh, heck, let's sit down."

They collapsed into armchairs and Joseph tore the box open. Hearst looked up at the holo footage again. "That damned arms smuggler," he said. "Tell me something, if you know: will he ever be brought to justice? Is there anything we can do to hunt him down, using the Company's knowledge?"

Joseph shuddered and grabbed up a handful of chocolates. He crammed them into his mouth, not even bothering to pick them out of their little frilly paper cups. "Uh-uh," he said, chewing. "Know why? You're really going to feel like some Theobromos now: the Company set up the whole disaster. It was going to happen anyway, so why not arrange it so Dr. Zeus came out ahead, right? That shuttle in the background is a Company time shuttle, though there's not enough of it visible in the footage to tip anybody off.

"And the bastard who delivered the bomb? Not even a human being. Company black project. They were experimenting with creating a New Enforcer. They made another goddam Recombinant, can you believe that? Only this one doesn't spread diseases. Just disasters."

Hearst stared at him, horrified. After a moment he reached out a shaky hand and helped himself to three or four chocolate creams. "Oh, dear God," he said. "That's what's so familiar about him. A New Enforcer? He doesn't look quite human at that. He's not . . . not related to us? Is he?"

Joseph looked at him sourly, still chewing as he popped two more truffles into his mouth. "That'd bother you, huh, being related to him? How'd you like it if he abducted your daughter?"

"I never had a daughter," said Hearst in a distracted kind of way, and bit into a chocolate. "Though there was that granddaughter who got kidnapped. She wrote the nastiest book about me, too," he added plaintively, groping through the chocolate box to secure his favorites, for Joseph had just taken another fistful.

"How'd you like it," Joseph continued through a mouthful of rum nougat, "if your daughter got married to the Hangar Twelve Man? Huh?"

"I wouldn't," said Hearst, biting into another chocolate and slurping the liquid center. His eyes widened. "You don't mean *your* daughter—!"

"Oh, yeah. Some swell son-in-law! The only consolation is, the big jackass was set up by the Company, too. He had no idea what'd happen when he smuggled arms to the MAC, apparently." Joseph popped three nut clusters into his mouth in quick succession and crunched with violence. "Now he's a fugitive from every kind of justice there is, and he's taken her with him. Hey, do I care? They're in love, so everything's just peachy!"

"I'm so sorry for you," murmured Hearst, thinking that this was far worse than a forgotten twentieth-century scandal. He wasn't sure this didn't beat *Citizen Kane*. He ate another chocolate and felt better. "But he's not a real Enforcer, then, I take it."

"Yes and no." Joseph poked savagely through the box. "Where'd all these damn Brazil nuts come from? Nobody likes Brazil nuts. He's a Recombinant, like I said, a design to replace the Enforcers. He was supposed to be easier to manipulate. He was, too. Did just what they wanted him to do at Mars Two."

Hearst unwrapped a foil-covered bonbon, shaking his head. "Golly, that's awful," he said. He looked up at Joseph, very stern. "That just proves that our rebellion is long overdue. The Company is without a doubt the most evil and insidious conspiracy ever to wind its tentacles . . . uh . . . through the lives of decent, hard working Americans! And other people."

"You said it, kiddo," Joseph agreed, wadding some empty frilled cups into a little ball. He put it in his mouth and chewed slowly.

"It must be rooted out." Hearst slammed his fist down on the table. "The more I learn about what they've done . . . those poor people on Mars . . . or the way they betrayed Budu, for example, one of the noblest creatures who ever lived . . . well, I just get so mad I could . . . could . . . you're eating the paper."

"It tastes nice," said Joseph.

"We're getting intoxicated," Hearst realized.

"That was the point."

"Oh. Well . . . I guess that's what fellows do at a tragic time like this," Hearst sighed. "I wish *he'd* come down too. We could have a council of war, brainstorm or something . . ."

"Budu doesn't do Theobromos," said Joseph, a little uncomfortably.

"He doesn't?"

"Not a lot, no."

"Oh." Hearst drew back his hand from a chocolate-covered Brazil nut. "Superior self-control, of course. Well. Has he got any more orders for me? Anything I can do?"

"Uh . . . well, you know those air cargo freighters you've got?" Joseph shifted in his chair. "The big jobs you have your groceries and all those antiques flown in with? You've got, what, three of 'em?"

"Three," Hearst affirmed, shaking his head in an attempt to clear it.

"Can you buy four more? Without it looking funny to Quintilius?"

"Leave it to me," Hearst said, making a sweeping motion with his hand. "Old ones need refitting and overhaul. Buy new ones to use while old ones are in the shop. There! And then I'll have a fleet—"

SPECIAL REPORT! SPECIAL REPORT! SPESPESPECIAL REREREPORT!

The urgent voices chattered in midair, the holobeams lit again and thirty channels began broadcasting once more. Joseph groaned and put his head in his hands. Hearst glanced up, alert, as grave reporters introduced staring-numb survivors, or asked gentle stupid questions of weeping relatives. Then an interview from Earth, with a middle-aged woman: grim-faced Mary deWit, chairwoman of the Griffith Family Arean Trust. It was followed by the scarlet light of the hellish Commerce Square footage.

"Oh, look at that editing," Hearst exclaimed. "Didn't that turn out well?"

"That's probably just what the Company brass are saying right now," Joseph snarled. Hearst looked horrified, and then his face hardened, became the rigid face of a judgmental god.

"They won't get away with it," he vowed. "Mars Two will be avenged!"

" 'Remember the *Maine*,' huh?" said Joseph. He looked up to see Hearst nodding solemnly. In his cold blue eyes was the light of absolute certainty, unshakable determination. Joseph felt his skin crawl.

In midair replay the superheated air billowed out, consumed again the hapless victims of Mars Two.

PART IV

Suleyman reaches into the box and lifts out an ebony Pawn.

Shatrang is a cousin to the game of chess, but there are no Queens; the nearest equivalent piece is the Vizier. Still, the designer of this set has compensated by making all the ebony Pawns women, styling them after the Mazangu of Dahomey. The little warrior in Suleyman's hand leans forward, brandishing a spear like a quarterstaff, and bears her teeth in a grin of dreadful welcome.

Suleyman lines up three black Pawns on the table.

CHAPTER 18

Fez, 3 March 2352

"So you've got mortals making your tea for you now," Sarai remarked, sitting back in the cushions and regarding Suleyman. She was lean and fierce, might have posed for one of the Mazangu pawns. She had been one of his wives, once; she had been many things since, including a priestess of the slave rebellion in Sainte-Domingue, a health-care worker in New Orleans, and a nanny for a British peer living on a yacht in the Caribbean. It had taken Suleyman years to track her down again.

He poured tea in a long stream to make it foam in the glasses. He offered one to Sarai. "I pay them handsomely to do it, too," he said. "Which has backfired, I'm afraid; I've got their cousins and nephews and sons lining up for jobs in my house. They think I'm a money tree. On the other hand, I now have a first-class intelligence network."

"What do you need an intelligence network for, Suleyman?"

"Because I've been fighting a war for three centuries," said Suleyman. "I've just been doing it very quietly. It takes as many resources as the conventional kind, however."

"You're a lot wealthier than you were in the old days," Sarai replied. "Quite a slice of the regional operating budget per annum you must get, eh?"

"A few sound investments. Trust me, I haven't had much Company assistance in my struggle," he told her, and set down his glass and folded his hands. "What do you know about Alpha-Omega?" he asked.

She arched her eyebrows at him. She had been resting for three days now, had bathed and slept and eaten and caught up on old times with Nefer and Nan, so she was cushioned against shocks a little better. Still, she was surprised by his question.

"Greek letters? That's all I know about them, man."

"You were inside the building in Gray's Inn Road. Did you, in the lobby or anywhere else, notice the words or characters Alpha-Omega?"

"No, Suleyman. What is this? I thought we were going to talk about Nennius."

"Eventually," he said. "I know a lot about his operation. The black project he was in charge of, for example, the Checkerfield baby? I expect I know as much as you do about that one."

"Really?" she snapped. "You know why it was all necessary? Then you know more than I. What was Nennius doing?"

"He was following orders," Suleyman answered. "Just as you were. The Company wanted something, and took the necessary steps to produce it."

"They wanted Mars Two blown all to hell and gone?" Sarai demanded. "What kind of Preservers are we, let me ask you that? I never signed up to kill mortals. Who gave Nennius orders to make a monster, eh?"

"Was he a monster, Sarai?"

"I never knew what he was," she said quietly, looking away. "They just told me, you go to the maternity hospital at this address and take a certain baby out of his cot. Quick and quiet, so the cameras can't see, and then report to London HQ with him."

"Didn't they tell you anything else at HQ?" inquired Suleyman.

"That he was something special, and I was to take him to the Checkerfields, who were going to pretend he was theirs. I was supposed to stay on as his nanny and protect him. Watch everything he did. Make full reports to Nennius."

"Was he different?" Suleyman asked. "In unusual ways?"

"Real good at maths," Sarai said. "Bloody little genius at anything to do with numbers. How many boats in the harbor, baby? How many leaves on the mango tree? And he'd just look once and tell you."

"But he wasn't autistic?"

"Hell no. Sociable as you please. Loved people." She turned away. After a long moment she went on, her face unseen to him as she said: "I can guess how he turned out to be the Hangar Twelve Man. My orders changed. I was supposed to start telling the baby mean things. Tell him it was his fault the Checkerfields got their divorce. Tell him he wasn't as good as other little boys, so he'd best mind his manners! I couldn't do it. Nennius told me, 'Fine then, you're off the job,' and sent me back to Haiti. That was that. Never saw Alec's funny face again, until the Hangar Twelve footage.

"So was it all Nennius's idea? You tell me, old husband."

Suleyman held up his hands. "Who runs the Company, Sarai? The mortals themselves. They directed Nennius. They profited when Mars Two was bombed. Only mortals would be foolish enough to do something like that without understanding the consequences."

"This is new talk from you," she said uneasily. "You used to love the little mortals."

"You can love a child, and still weep for what he does," said Suleyman. "Can't you, Sarai?"

She bowed her head over her glass in silence. He sighed and went on: "Nennius, however, knew exactly what he was doing. He had his own agenda, Sarai."

He had all her attention now. "What was it?"

"Do you have any idea what condition the human gene pool is in?" he asked. "Have you been observing the mortals, these last few centuries? All so alike, and each generation smaller in numbers than the previous one?"

"Because of all the plagues sweeping through," Sarai said.

"And the eugenics programs. They did their share of wrecking the gene pool, too," Suleyman explained. "So did the drop in the birth rate."

"And?"

"There were still plenty of mortals with the drive to reproduce at the beginning of this decade. Unfortunately, a lot of them went to live on Mars, where there were no permits required for having children." Suleyman regarded her somberly. She just shook her head.

"Nennius," Suleyman went on, "is one of a certain group of immortals. They're headed by the American Northwestern Sector Executive, Labienus. They've been at work a long time. They're the reason I require an intelligence network. The great plagues were their doing."

"But what for?"

"They're fed up with the mortals." Suleyman shrugged. "Maybe they've watched too many movies. Remember *Cyborg Conquest*? 'We are the ultimate goal of evolution! Imperfect beings must die!' "

"Oh, that's crap. We've all felt like squashing the damn mortals now and then—"

"And some of us have given in to the urge," Suleyman told her. "Nennius didn't go along with the plan to destroy Mars Two because it would make the Company money—though it did. He did it because of the percentage of the mortals' breeding population living up there.

"And now, boom. They're gone. There are lots of places here and there on

Earth where mortals still have children, but they're being methodically targeted for plague outbreaks.

"So within the space of a few more generations—depleted as the mortal gene pool is—humanity could be facing extinction."

"Man! And you sit here so calm and tell me so?" Sarai shook her head emphatically. "No. It can't be this bad. The mortals can't have missed this! Not the masters at Dr. Zeus, anyway. They're ungrateful little twits, making us wear those bloody clock badges, but they're not this stupid about their own survival."

"Of course they're not," Suleyman agreed. "They've had us preserving genetic material for millennia. Somewhere, they keep stored vials of genetic material from every race that's ever walked the earth."

"Ah! Okay, there you are; they've left themselves an escape. Gene pool shrinks too far, the masters will just fill it up again from their emergency cache. One generation in vitro and they'll be out of danger."

"They would be," Suleyman said, "if nothing happened to that emergency cache beforehand."

"Labienus isn't going for that, too?" Sarai looked horrified. Suleyman shrugged.

"Not yet, as far as I can tell. The masters have taken great trouble to hide it away. They don't know about Labienus's group, but they're terrified of us all anyway. Have been, ever since we liberated Options Research." Suleyman rested his chin in his palm.

"The Frankenstein story," Sarai muttered bitterly.

"That's right. And there are plenty of angry monsters like Labienus among us, so I can't say I blame them for being scared. The problem is—can they keep their secret safely?"

"They'll never manage," said Sarai, eyes wide. "It's this Alpha-Omega, isn't it, Suleyman? Where they've cached the DNA? That's what's on the hidden floor of that damn place in London. That's why you had Latif doing surveillance there!"

He just nodded.

"And if you've found it, others might find it too, and if it's destroyed—"

"Extinction for humanity."

"I'm frightened now," said Sarai.

"So am I, my heart," he replied. She reached out and took his hand.

"What are you going to do?" she said at last.

"I don't have a lot of choice," he said wearily. "The masters can't possibly keep Alpha-Omega safe. I'll have to seize it from them, which will be an act of open rebellion, but what can I do? If I don't secure it, Labienus's group will, and there go the mortals; and many of us, too, I might add. His people have no compunction about disabling fellow immortals. You heard what happened to Kalugin?"

Sarai shuddered. "And that other one, the one nobody's ever found. Lewis."

"Lewis," Suleyman echoed.

Fez, 23 March 2352

In the very beginning, before he had understood what a cyborg was, Glele Kouandete had thought they must be orishas. He'd been very small then, sick and frightened, and it was easy to get that impression. The big man had worn a white coat as he'd paced between the beds of the children's ward, administering the injections with a deft hand, calm and patient though the children and nurses were all screaming. The younger man, in his red shirt, had been fierce as he'd overseen the evacuation into the agcraft, yelling *Move, move, move!* in a voice like a hammer on an anvil. Were they Obatala and Ogun?

When he was well again, when he was getting used to the foster parents they'd settled him with and understood about the viral outbreak, Kouandete concluded that they had only been a doctor and a soldier after all. He thought this until the big man in white came to visit him, in the summer he graduated from college (by which time he no longer believed in the orishas), and offered him a job.

When he became a member of Suleyman's staff, he learned the truth. Kouandete was exhilarated at first, thrilled by the concept of a benign Company that rescued people and things from destruction. It was reassuring to discover that immortals of a sort really did guide and watch over the human race, and wonderful, too, to be one of the few mortals in on the secret.

Since then, Kouandete's life had become infinitely more complex. Because he was good at his job, which involved secrets, he was privy to the sordid politics within Dr. Zeus Incorporated. He knew about the renegade immortals who spread the plague that wiped out his own village; he knew about the fearful stockholders and scientists who were attempting to get rid of the immortals, all of them, even loyal ones like Suleyman.

So, by his fortieth year, Kouandete found himself in a world every bit as terrifying and chaotic as the hospital ward of his earliest memory. To be sure, he was well to do, had a nice car and flat, took his holidays in the south of France; he also had ulcers and maintained a silent desperate hope that the orishas might turn out to exist after all. Perhaps they might reach down from wherever they lived, to avert the coming apocalypse.

Though he had to admit that Suleyman and Latif were doing their best, as he leaned back now and accepted a glass of tea from one of the servants. He drank gratefully and set the glass aside, watching as Latif spread out the old-fashioned flat photographs he had brought from London.

"Unbelievably awkward piece of equipment," Kouandete said in apology. "But it was the only thing I could think of that their surveillance wouldn't have detected. Too low-tech."

"No, no, you're thinking like one of us," Suleyman assured him. He walked slowly around the table, hands in his pockets, staring down at the images of a place called Alpha-Omega. Getting them had involved considerable effort. Kouandete had had to position his subordinates in the local glaziers' firm, and secure a flat on the opposite side of Gray's Inn Road. Latif designed the missile dummy for him, but Kouandete himself had fired it at the fifth floor window, with the result that the persons within were startled to see what looked like a raven fly straight into the glass, making an oddly-shaped hole before glancing away and vanishing.

When the glazier had been summoned to replace the broken pane, he succeeded in getting multiple exposures of the hidden floor, on a tiny concealed camera so ancient it had once been the property of the KGB. The film was then couriered to the local chapter house of the Compassionates of Allah, where Kouandete had it developed. Two hours later, with the chill of London drizzle still in his bones, he had handed the packet of photographs to Latif.

"So this is the amazing invisible fifth floor," mused Sarai. "Not much here for them to be so secretive, eh? Half of it's empty."

"This doesn't make any sense," Latif said, scowling down at the pictures. "Two consoles over here, crowded into this one area. Empty console out here, no chair. And what's this yellow thing on the carpet?"

"It looks like a path," observed Suleyman. "All around the area where the workstations are, notice. Remember when the first office robots came out, the ones that moved on magnetic trails? The trails used to weave around office floors like that, in and out of cubicles and around filing cabinets."

"Nobody's used technology that primitive in centuries," insisted Latif. Suleyman just picked up one of the photographs and waved it at him ironically.

"Do you think it might outline some kind of perimeter defense?" suggested Kouandete. "Like a force field around the two desks?"

"Possibly," Suleyman said, replacing the photograph. He stroked his beard, considering the layout. "There don't seem to be any refrigeration units in evidence, even though we know they have to be there somewhere, so I'm at something of a loss . . ."

Abruptly, Latif shouted something profane, and then: "Primitive technology," he exclaimed. "Remember the first virtual reality mazes? Remember how those arcades looked when you took off your helmet inside one?"

"I never played the game, son," Suleyman reminded him.

"They looked like this!" Latif said. "Big empty rooms with trackways laid out on the floor. That was all that was really there. Everything else—the walls, the alleys, the bad guys—only existed inside the helmets."

"You think the two people in this office are in the middle of some kind of virtual maze?" Sarai looked skeptical.

"But what's the point of a virtual *office*?" said Kouandete, knitting his brows. "Why take such trouble to conceal something on a hidden floor that's only an illusion?"

"Unless it isn't an illusion," cried Latif. "Virtual, but a projection of something real somewhere else!"

"They're seeing something being broadcast real time?" guessed Suleyman. "Coordinating their office with one that exists in some other place?"

"So what we're after might not be actually, physically, there," said Kouandete in disappointment.

"Not in that place, no . . ." Suleyman began to pace slowly, putting his hands back in his pockets. "In some other place . . . or—"

"Some other time!" said Sarai. Suleyman turned on his heel to stare at her. There was a moment of silence before they both said: "Alpha-Omega."

"What?" said Kouandete, watching as Latif did a somewhat alarming dance of triumph. Suleyman pointed at the photographs.

"Those," he said, "are images of Omega. Omega is the place that exists at the end of time. Here, or rather in London on Gray's Inn Road. In reality. But in cyberspace it exists alongside of Alpha, which occupies what appears in these pictures as empty air.

"In reality, Alpha is the place that exists at the beginning of time. It's the other half of the office in those pictures, but it's hidden away in the past."

"*That's* where the damn refrigeration units are," stated Latif. "Some fortified location in the deep past, what do you want to bet? And probably with a couple of mortal personnel there for maintenance."

"So . . . the people in both offices are seeing each other's halves of the office in cyberspace?" said Kouandete.

"And the tracks on the floor are there to help them navigate," decided Sarai.

"That's got to be it," said Suleyman.

"Damn, that's clever," Sarai said, pacing around the table. "Hide the genetic bank in the past, just like Options Research was hidden."

"No Joseph to send us the temporal coordinates this time, though," said Latif.

"Easy enough to get them, son," reflected Suleyman. "The two people in Omega are picking up Alpha's signal; all we have to do is tap into it and trace its source."

"You'll need to get a mortal inside for that." Kouandete sighed, rising to his feet. His overcoat hadn't even had time to dry out. "Book me another flight."

London, 12 April 2352

The London chapter house of the Compassionates of Allah was located in Beechcroft Road, in a stately twenty-second-century house of yellow stone in a vaguely Egyptian architectural style, windowless and enigmatic. Within, at the front of the building, was the clinic with its administrative offices and various public rooms for the community it served; to the rear of the building were other, smaller rooms. Most of them housed the black brothers who ministered to the poor. Some were reserved for another purpose, however.

For example, one cell was a listening post where Kouandete waited patiently at a vast communications console.

A light flashed on the console, alerting Kouandete that the office in Gray's Inn Road was placing an outgoing inquiry. He switched off the London *Times* and leaned close to his console's screen to see. Echoing back to his office from the corridor outside came the sound of the Fatiha; twelve hundred hours. Someone was using the lunch hour to make a private call, perhaps.

He keyed in a hasty command and got the text of the inquiry. The inquirer was scrolling through listings: catering services? The cursor settled beside one commcode: BLACKFRIARS MUNCHIES. After a long moment the commcode was entered.

Suppressing an urge to giggle wildly, Kouandete intercepted the call.

BLACKFRIARS MUNCHIES! HOW MAY WE BE OF SERVICE TODAY?, he sent.

Hi id like to know if you can cater a party?

CERTAINLY! THAT IS OUR BUSINESS. WHAT MAY WE DO FOR YOU?

Well can you do a special one? Were having a baby shower. Do you know what that is?

CERTAINLY.

We were thinking maybe some sanwidges and crisps and punch only everything has to be blue. Can you do that?

Kouandete blinked at the screen. *OF COURSE,* he sent in reply, making a mental note to buttonhole the first London-born brother he could find and ask why on earth anyone would want blue food.

And we need a cake too and can you bring cups and plates and things?

CERTAINLY! Kouandete sent, and was inspired to add *LET US BE THE ONE-STOP SOLUTION TO ALL YOUR CATERING NEEDS!*

There was a long pause before the reply came:

Can we come round and see some of your cakes?

Kouandete drummed his fingers a moment in desperation.

NO NEED, he sent. *ONE OF OUR SALESPERSONS WILL COME TO YOU WITH CAKE BROCHURE IN FULL COLOUR! MANY DESIGNS TO CHOOSE FROM!*

Another long pause, and then:

Can you just come to the lobby please?

Kouandete grimaced, but sent in reply: *OF COURSE. WE WILL BE HAPPY TO DO SO. WHAT ADDRESS PLEASE?*

First tell us how much for the lot?

Kouandete thought hard.

IT IS OUR POLICY ALWAYS TO UNDERCUT OUR COMPETITION. WHAT OTHER PRICES HAVE BEEN QUOTED TO YOU FOR THIS SERVICE?

Another pause.

Well we have about 80 pounds to play around with.

FOR YOU, CAKE AND ALL, BLACKFRIARS' PRICE IS 70 POUNDS! Kouandete sent grandly. *WHAT ADDRESS PLEASE?*

The address he expected was given. A time was agreed upon. Both parties signed off and for the next three hours Kouandete was very busy looking up online catering brochures, cutting and pasting images of fancily decorated cakes.

He had a very good faked brochure in his briefcase when he stepped into the lobby of the building in Gray's Inn Road at sixteen hundred hours precisely. He waited, looking around, noting the surveillance cameras high up in the walls. They were obvious and easy to spot. Harder to see were the subtler devices that scanned the threshold, set to raise a silent alarm should an immortal enter the building.

Recently the Facilitator Sarai had gone up to see the legal firm of Cantwell and Cantwell on the sixth floor, and in doing so she had unknowingly created havoc. Even at his listening post over in Tooting, Kouandete had been astounded by the flashing lights on his console as frantic messages had gone out warning the Company Board of Directors that one of *them* had entered the building!

Had Sarai pressed the lift button for the third floor, a siren would have sounded; the lift would have frozen in place as the building's security officers appeared en masse, and they'd have escorted her out, explaining courteously that a fire drill was going on. There would have been an actual drill staged then, too, and several other diversionary tactics as needed should she have persisted in her attempts to get to the third floor.

She probably could have got up there, if she'd really wanted to. In twenty years of concealment in plain sight, no other immortal had ever walked into the building in Gray's Inn Road, and Sarai's chance appearance had terrified the mortals on the third floor into dithering frenzies. Fortunately for them, Sarai had had no idea the Company had a secret facility in the building, so their emergency measures hadn't been put to the test.

Of course, it had never occurred to the Board of Directors that they might need to conceal Alpha-Omega from other mortals.

At least, Kouandete hoped it hadn't.

He smiled now and approached the young lady who had stepped from the elevator and was peering around the lobby. "Are you Brandi Pelham?" he inquired.

"You're Mr. Jones, yeah?" she responded. "From Blackfriars?"

"The very same. I have the brochure you asked to see—" Kouandete opened his case with a flourish and drew out the text plaquette containing the faked brochure. "As well as a list of menus for a luncheon party for twelve persons, each menu at the fixed price of seventy pounds."

"With the cake, yeah?" Brandi took the plaquette and scrolled down through the graphics. "Ooo! Nice. This looks nice, the carrot-bran-blueberry surprise. This one, I think. And this is the food and stuff here?" She frowned at it, moving her lips as she read. "But this is fancy, isn't it? 'Watercress and tofu pate with minced . . . er . . . truffles'? What are truffles?"

"All-organic fat-free mushrooms," Kouandete assured her.

"Oh! Well, that's not too fancy then. All the same . . . it's for a baby shower and that's such an old-fashioned thing, you know. I was thinking something maybe more . . . er . . . old time sort of—"

"Traditional?" Kouandete suggested.

"Yeah! That," said Brandi.

Kouandete wondered in exasperation why so few English bothered to become proficient in their own language, but he smiled and said: "May I recommend Vegemite?"

"Oh yeah." Brandi's eyes lit up.

"Menu number three, Vegemite on wholemeal with an assortment of fresh carrot and celery sticks and dipping sauce, mushroom caps stuffed with spicy tofu paste—"

"But not too spicy!"

"No, no, of course not. With maize crisps—we'll make those blue maize crisps, of course, and blueberry punch." Kouandete tapped in a memo on the plaquette. "I think? And of course all serving materials to be blue as well."

"Yeah! Super," said Brandi. "And blue decorations on the cake, yeah?"

"Certainly," Kouandete told her.

"Brilliant. And, er, I suppose you want a deposit or something—"

"No, no." Kouandete waved his hand. "Payment on delivery. And that's to be Monday, 2nd May at eleven AM precisely, is that correct? And what suite number?"

"Er—" Brandi looked uneasy. "Well, it was to be the third floor, but—there's a problem, see, so . . . well, you just come up to the third floor, and we'll show you when you're there, yeah? And you won't have too many people with you?"

"Myself and two assistants for setup," Kouandete said, rejoicing silently.

"Right then, that's not much." Brandi seemed relieved. "Very nice. So, we'll see you a week tomorrow then?"

"Without fail," said Kouandete, bowing slightly.

"Then I'll just get back upstairs before my break's over. This'll be fun," said Brandi, smiling and waving as she retreated to the elevator. "I can't wait to see blue carrots!"

Kouandete's smile froze on his face, but he waved good-bye cordially.

Mayday in Tooting

"My lord, this is the third time we've tried," said Brother Youssou. He was nearly in tears, holding out the tray of bread. "The closest I can come is this purple color."

"Close enough," decided Latif, and took the tray. He carried it out to the long table in the refectory, where assembled brothers were busily slicing up vegetables and trying not to look at Sarai, who was wearing a very low-cut sweater, or listen to her either for that matter, as she was attempting to sculpt cake decorations out of almond paste and indulging in blistering profanity because the work wasn't going well.

Kouandete, with his sleeves rolled up, waited with a spatula and a gallon bucket of Vegemite. He eyed the bread doubtfully. "But that's purple," he said, and withheld any other objections after seeing the look on Latif's face.

"We're going with purple, okay?" said Latif. "It's almost blue. Marinate the damn carrots in grape juice." He thumped the tray down and they got to work slapping together enough Vegemite sandwiches for a party of twelve.

"Idiot Brits used to paint even their arses blue," growled Sarai. "Now they're too delicate for a little artificial food coloring. Oh nooo, we won't have that in our country! Bloody shracking *hell*." She threw her spatula and a misshapen marzipan baby bootie across the room with such velocity that the marzipan stuck to the wall.

"I must say," observed Brother Kicham, gloomily spooning tofu into a mushroom cap, "that this was not what I anticipated when deciding to devote my life to serene contemplation of God and service to His paupers."

"Life is full of surprises," snapped Latif, cutting off crusts. "As long as we get a man inside, this will have been worth it."

"You're quite sure that simply opening the box will be enough?" Kouandete inquired, handing him another sandwich. Latif nodded.

"It's brute force, like the camera shutter. You open it—the crystal gets exposed to the incoming signal—you close it and get out of there. There's no mechanism for their surveillance to detect."

"But how will I know where to open the box?" asked Kouandete. "Where will the incoming signal manifest?"

"That's for you to find out, isn't it?" Latif replied, carefully arranging little triangles of sandwich in a pyramid. "That's why you get paid the big salary."

"Look what we found at Harrods," sang Brother Ibou, bursting in with Brother Mahjoub. "Baby blue serviettes!"

Fifteen Hours Later

Latif sat at the console, monitoring communications from Gray's Inn Road, scowling at the screen in fixed concentration. He was muttering something under his breath, too rapidly for any mortal to make out. He might have been praying, but wasn't. He was reciting the words of a lullabye his mortal mother had used to sing to him. Even with all the terror and misery attached to his last memories of mortal life, down in the foul darkness of the slave ship's hold, he still found the lullabye obscurely comforting.

No lights on the console. There would be no lights. Everything would go smoothly. It was a simple job.

A light flashed on the console. On the bed behind him, Sarai tensed and sat up, but said nothing. Latif struck the button that allowed him to intercept the call. Where had it been directed? The switchboard.

This is Brandi, can you take any incoming please? We're closing down for the party now.

Latif exhaled and forwarded the message to the switchboard. There had been no more than a second's delay.

At precisely that moment, Kouandete was stepping into the elevator of the building in Gray's Inn Road, accompanied by Brother Ibou and Brother Mahjoub. They were loaded down with catering containers; he himself carried an immense cooler of punch. The others crowded in after him as he studied the buttons. There, beside the button for the third floor, was a small sign: PERPETUAL ASSURANCE LTD. He pressed the button.

They rode smoothly upward and the doors opened to reveal an ordinary-looking office: rows of consoles, supply cabinets, cheap framed prints on the walls and a dismal view of metropolitan London out the windows. There was nobody in sight but Brandi, who was waiting for them in obvious impatience. However, she smiled as she saw the abundance they carried. "Oh, yeah, that's a lot for the money. Good."

"Are we setting up in here?" Kouandete inquired offhandedly. Brandi made a slight face.

"Er—no. It's sort of special. We're having it upstairs. Come on, I'll take you." She led them to a small door, unmarked, lined up unobtrusively next to the lavatory doors and well out of sight of the windows. Anyone might have taken it for a broom closet, but Brandi swung the door open to reveal a half-sized lift booth. "You'll have to go up one at a time," she apologized, and Kouandete shrugged affably and stepped in.

"No aggro," he said. "Wait here, chaps." Brandi crowded in beside him and pressed an unmarked button.

"We sort of ran out of room on this floor, so we had to—er—expand," she explained in a breathless voice, as the lift rose.

"And office space in Holborn is so expensive," said Kouandete in sympathy.

"Just awful!" she agreed. "My sister works in West Ham, and she says—"

The door opened on a scene of hushed and hurried gaiety: young persons, mostly female, blowing up blue balloons or standing on chairs to fasten blue streamers to the walls. There was a lot of space to decorate, for this was the cavernous emptiness of the hidden floor, the place from the photographs. Kouandete's heart raced as he recognized the yellow track snaking across the carpet, but he merely smiled and hoisted his cooler, stepping out into the room.

"The caterer's here," sang out Brandi. "Over there where they're putting up the folding table, yeah? I'll be right back with your friends." She descended again and Kouandete made his way to the table she had indicated.

"Oh, nice," cried a girl wearing a pair of optics. "Is that blue punch?"

"Blueberry," he replied, setting it down.

"Lovely," cried half a dozen young ladies, hurrying to pull a baby blue tablecloth into place and smoothe it down. "We're almost ready for you."

"Certainly," said Kouandete. He looked about him, hoping he appeared casually disinterested. Yes! There was a console by the window with no chair, no personal items, even a thin layer of dust on its surface; but the yellow track led straight up to it. Did someone work there at that station, in the other half of the office? Did the girl wear the optics to enable her to see whoever was there in cyberspace, simultaneously *now* and eons in the past?

She must. He watched her surreptitiously as he waited, and saw that she glanced continually over at the console in a nervous sort of way. Watching somebody none of the rest of them could see.

"Okay," one girl told him, just as the lift opened again and Brandi shooed out Brother Ibou. For the next few minutes Kouandete was busy laying out refreshments, amid the din of excited giggling and the occasional pop as somebody overinflated a balloon. Brother Mahjoub arrived, set down his burden, and looked at the office clock. With great care he enunciated his one line: "Oh. Sir, it's half past eleven. You need to take your medication."

"Thank you," replied Kouandete, reaching into his pocket and withdrawing what looked like a little pillbox. He lifted his head sharply and turned, as though something had just occurred to him. "Oh, dear, I hope our van is all right in the loading zone." He walked rapidly across the room in the direction of the window, detouring around a pile of presents all wrapped and ribboned in baby blue.

"No!" cried the girl with the optics, racing after him. "Er—please stop—"

"I'm sorry?" Kouandete halted beside the empty console and turned back.

"I was just going to look down into the street at our delivery van. I'm not sure the loading zone permits us to park so long." He opened the pillbox, taking care that the crystal on the inner lid was pointed at the console. Instantly the crystal recorded the signal being received in the office. Withdrawing a mint and popping it in his mouth, Kouandete snapped the lid shut again and returned the box to his pocket. The girl wrung her hands.

"I mean—it's just that we had a window break recently and—and—"

"It'll probably be all right," Kouandete told her, and smiled. "We're nearly done." He walked back to the table and resumed folding baby blue serviettes on the diagonal, as Brother Ibou arranged them in a festive pattern around the cake decorated with storks and baby booties.

They had finished, and he was writing up a receipt for Brandi, when he observed the girl with the optics edge over to the empty console and address it. She spoke in an undertone, but Kouandete was adept at reading lips. "Can you log off soon?" she told someone unseen. "Bill just got the signal from Mr. Chandra. He's bringing her up in the lift!"

Kouandete smiled his widest and ushered Brother Ibou and Brother Mahjoub to the lift door, where they waited as the lift rose. The door opened and revealed a man and a very pregnant lady. She also wore a pair of optics. "Oh!" she exclaimed, as everyone in the room screamed: "SURPRISE!"

Nobody noticed when the caterers made their exit.

But Latif and Sarai heard the agvan arriving all the way back in the cell, heard the doors slamming and the clatter of running feet, and they were already out in the long dim corridor when Kouandete entered it at top speed and slid the last ten feet toward them, pulling up only at the last minute. Grinning, he thrust out the pillbox.

"Would you care for a mint, o exalted immortal ones?" he chortled. Sarai let out a shriek of triumph.

A door opened and a brother looked out at them in disapproval before retreating once more to the silence of his contemplation.

Fez, 15 May 2352

"Half a million years?" said Nef in a stunned voice.

"Give or take a millennium," Suleyman confirmed. "Five hundred thousand BCE. That's the farthest back I've ever heard of anything being concealed."

"Way farther than Options Research," Latif remarked, pouring fresh tea for both of them. He offered more to Nan, but she put her hand over the cup to decline. Sarai, who was drinking rum and cola, leaned back and said: "That was about the dirtiest little secret I can imagine. What do you want to bet they've got our DNA templates there, too, all those tubes they've supposedly got safe if one of us should need biomechanicals replaced? Keeping it out of our reach in case they need a bargaining chip, you see?"

"Probably," Latif agreed.

"Half a million years," repeated Nef. She turned her cup in her hands and looked over at Suleyman. "So . . . are you going to stage a raid on it, like you did on Options Research? Go in with holocams blazing?"

Suleyman shook his head. "Nothing so public," he said. "Though we will have to storm it, I'm sure. I dispatched a probe to that location and there's some defense. Mostly automated; only one life sign there, as far as the probe could tell."

"Piece of cake," Latif declared with a ferocious sneer. He turned to look at Sarai. "Want to come along for the party?"

"Love to," she replied, meeting his stare. The others exchanged glances.

"And you, ladies?" Suleyman inquired of Nan and Nefer. Nan shook her head.

"My place is with Kalugin," she said quietly. "Especially if it's the last night of the world. I don't know if he's even aware of my presence, but I'd rather be beside him than in any other place when the Silence falls."

Suleyman nodded. Nefer cleared her throat. "I'll beg off, too," she said. "I've been promising myself for years I'd be out on the Serengeti when the hour rolls around. It's all I've got left."

"I understand," Suleyman told her. "I'd be with you, if I could. Still . . . somebody's got to look out for these reckless young people." He jerked a thumb at Latif and Sarai. "It may be harder to jump the barricades than they think."

Latif snorted. "So we're not moving on this until right at the end?" he inquired. "Say 9th July?"

"No sense in giving them time to grab it back from us," Suleyman said. "Strike the first blow at Alpha-Omega and follow up with the landing on Catalina before they have time to react."

"And hope no one else had the same idea," cautioned Nan.

"I still think we ought to liberate the bunkers where the Enforcers are," said Latif. "Think of the edge that'd give us, with them on our side!"

"You haven't seen them, son." Suleyman rubbed his eyes. "It's a little un-likely they'd be willing to follow my orders. If they decided to take revenge on the Company, we'd see the bloodbath of our worst nightmares."

"Okay, but there are some of us stashed away in the bunkers with them, right?" countered Latif. "What if we just woke the Preservers?"

"I don't want to go near the bunkers," said Suleyman, raising his voice only slightly but to tremendous effect. "If we poke around in there the Company will take notice. They noticed when Joseph did it, and you know what hap-pened to him. They're far more paranoid now. Let's leave well enough alone for the time being."

"Okay," said Latif quickly. "After all, we'll have plenty of opportunity to let them out afterward, right?"

"We should," Suleyman agreed. "Unless something unforeseen happens, we'll be running things by Bastille Day."

"There won't be any unforeseen happenings," stated Latif. Suleyman just raised an eyebrow at him and sipped his tea.

CHAPTER 19

Child Care in the Cyborg Family, Volume One:
The Duty of the Cyborg Parent

What a miracle is the cyborg infant! Truly it may be said that his tiny perfect body is something new under the sun! Biomechanicals race through him powered by the fires of heaven, carrying fantastic amounts of information. Pineal Tribrantine Three circulates to take his sun to noon and keep it there, changeless, in a perpetual bright day. Fortunate inheritor of Science, he is freed from the mortal debt of mere humanity but benefits from its genius. Life, in its constant upward progression, has at last, in this newest incarnation, attained what may be justly termed the Angelic. What glorious adventures might now be anticipated? What previously unattainable heights will he scale, this new Adam?

The morning sun streams in through the portholes of the *Captain Morgan*. It is no day of any week in any known year, but it has the feeling of a Sunday morning, and the ship bounds briskly over a choppy sea.

Edward Alton Bell-Fairfax, supercyborg, late of Her Majesty's Royal Navy, is sitting at the booth table in the saloon, working on *Child Care in the Cyborg Family, Volume Two: Intellectual Development.* He has the slightly rumpled look of a colonial who has begun to go native and let things slip. He's barefooted, unshaven, wears only trousers, shirt, and waistcoat. He has moreover the slightly guilty look of a colonial who knows he has begun to go native and hopes it won't get back to the Colony Club.

Constantly as he writes he looks over at the two children.

The boys appear to be twenty-two months old, and the sun glints in their wispy fair hair. They are dressed in white cotton sunsuits, identical save for the initials embroidered in blue on the chest of each one: A for Alec, N for Nicholas.

They are building a tower with little interlocking blocks, which click together tightly to withstand the sea swell. The structure is no random pile but an edifice of complex, not to say Neoclassical, grandeur. As they walk about it, adding a flying buttress here or a column there, they neither waddle nor stagger, except when the ship rolls. It rolls rather violently at the moment.

Edward accesses the weather reports coming in, though every instinct he developed while in the Royal Navy is already telling him that the glass has fallen precipitately. He has a sudden terrifying mental image of the ship pitching sharply, the two little boys thrown with a crash into a bulkhead, cracking their unprotected skulls . . .

"That's enough for now," Edward says. "Into your safety harnesses, please."

Both babies give him a rebellious look. "We didn't finish, Deadward," says Alec.

"We're sailing into a storm! Kindly do as you're told, or it'll be the helmet again," Edward says, nodding at the battered-looking steel helmet that swings from its strap on a hook. It appears to date from the First World War and was formerly part of Alec's antique collection. Now, however, it has been lined and padded, and across it in red paint are the words I AM A RECKLESS BOY.

Alec, in a cheery voice, tells Edward what he can do with the helmet.

"Right," says Edward grimly. He gets up and approaches them with intent to demolish the tower, and Nicholas narrows his eyes. He flings a handful of the sharp-cornered toy bricks into Edward's path. Edward dodges smartly, looking outraged.

"Stop that at once! And can't you calculate a trajectory any better than that?"

Nicholas laughs, a bright peal of notes like a golden bell chiming. Alec goes to the helmet, waits until the lurch of the ship swings it within his reach, strains on tiptoe to get it down, and fastens it on his head with the speed of long practice.

"Thank you for letting me sleep in, darling," says Mendoza, yawning as she enters the saloon at an angle. She is wearing white silk pajamas. "Oh, no," she adds, seeing Alec in the helmet. Her serenity vanishes and she glares at Edward, steadying herself against the bulkhead. "What happened?"

"He was—"

"I was a *bad child*," Alec announces, marching back and forth until Mendoza grabs him up and looks at him in despair.

"I too," says Nicholas, but at the expression on her face he puts out his arms and leans toward her. Edward lifts him and he clambers onto Mendoza's other arm, wriggling close and kissing her. "We're sorry. Don't cry, please."

She draws a deep breath and asks, "Did we at least do our hyperfunction exercises this morning? Or speech therapy?"

"Only under threat of duress," says Edward, opening the toybox as Bully Hayes creeps forward and begins putting the blocks away.

"You teach it. He bullies us," Alec says.

"Ay," says Nicholas. Edward snorts.

"You puppies, you have no idea what real bullying's like! A few years in a public school would sort you out."

"Stop fighting," says Mendoza wearily. "Sir Henry? Breakfast, please."

Aye aye, ma'am. Coxinga's on his way from the galley.

Edward takes the babies from her and she settles into the booth. "I do have the pleasure of reporting that Nicholas has at last moved beyond elementary calculus," says Edward, giving her Nicholas. "Mind his little foot, my love."

"Certainly." Mendoza looks happier as she takes Nicholas and fastens him into his booster seat. "Bravo, Nicholas! I knew you could do it."

"And I would like to report favorably of Alec as regards world history, but I'm afraid he spent most of his access hour amusing himself by reprogramming my text plaquette to send me extremely rude messages."

Aw, now, sir, boys will be boys.

"That's enough," says Mendoza, taking Alec from Edward. Edward sits down and puts away his composition plaquette with a sigh. Coxinga crawls into the room, bearing a tray full of silver-domed dishes.

Here we go. Kippers, toast, and tea for the commander, breakfast torta and coffee for the missus. Soft-boiled eggs, burgoo, and orange juice for my little mateys!

"I want coffee," Alec announces.

"You're far too young and you know that perfectly well," Edward says severely, fastening the napkin under Alec's chin. Mendoza is busy napkining Nicholas.

"I *like* coffee, Deaddy. Makes me go zoom!" Alec pulls his oatmeal bowl close, grabs his spoon before it skates away down the tilting tabletop and begins feeding himself quite competently.

After a moment he leans forward to the condiment rack and helps himself to the honey jar. Edward snatches it from him in a panic. "Are you mad?" he shouts. "You could contract botulism!"

Alec, startled, bursts into tears.

"Oh, Alec, don't cry." Mendoza leans over and hugs him, ducking awkwardly around the brim of the helmet. "Edward, darling, he can't get sick."

"Do we know that beyond a doubt? Perhaps I overreacted, but one can't take too many precautions," Edward replies, pulling out a handkerchief to dry Alec's tears.

"Piss off," Alec sobs. "I hate this! Why can't I reach things?"

"Two demerits for rude language in front of a lady. Blow your nose. There! Don't be such a baby!"

"But he is a baby, *meu amor*," Mendoza points out. "He can't help it if his body hasn't caught up with his brain. Give him the Golden Syrup instead."

"I don't want Golden Syrup!" Alec screams, beating his fists on the table. "I hate you, Deadward, I hate you, I hate you!"

"No, you don't," soothes Mendoza. "Look, Alec, here's Barnacle Bill." She holds up a pirate rag doll. Alec makes an involuntary grab and hugs it close, keenly aware of the humiliation of being comforted by something full of sawdust but unable to resist. He grits his teeth, or would if he had molars yet, and after a long moment sets the toy aside, as casually as he can.

"I changed my mind. Golden Syrup, please," he says.

Hands shaking with frustration, Edward offers him the syrup tin. Alec takes it, pouting, and sweetens his oatmeal liberally. "You might have said thank you, you mannerless little whelp," Edward mutters.

"Piss off," Alec tells him.

"Four demerits, Alec!"

"Piss off," says Nicholas meditatively, salting his own oatmeal. "Piss off, piss off, *piss off* piss off piss offpissoffpiss OFF!!! *Edwuhd Oolton Bell-Fehfex*," he concludes, perfectly mimicking Edward's plummy Victorian tones. Mendoza bites her lip to keep from laughing. Alec giggles, tilting his helmet back and wiping away a tear.

"Twenty demerits each, Max and Moritz," snaps Edward, grabbing his teacup before it leaps out of its saucer. Alec casts a dark look at Edward. He pulls his soft-boiled egg close and whacks his spoon down on the top of the egg, and its shell breaks with a disturbing sound.

"Funny boy," Mendoza says to Nicholas, smiling as she offers him a morsel of torta on the end of her fork. Nicholas leans forward to take the proffered tidbit. Edward winces.

"My dear, must you give them trifles from your fork? Particularly in such high seas? The tines might stab him—"

Speaking of high seas, Commander sir? That typhoon's spinning up bigger than we'd reckoned. I've set a course for the closest anchorage, but we'd best be prepared for squalls by the first dog-watch.

Edward's eyes widen. He swallows a mouthful of kipper hastily.

"I knew it. Children, deck liberty's canceled until further notice. I want you both in life jackets as soon as we've finished dining."

"Piss off, Captain Bligh," says Alec, indignant. "Don't tell me what to do!"

Aw, now, matey—

"Damn your insolence!" says Edward. "As God is my witness, one more insubordinate word and you'll be confined to quarters."

"Two demerits, Commander," says Nicholas.

Alec begins to cry again. "This is MY ship—" he rages, flinging his sipper bottle, and with the pitch of the deck it rolls right out of the saloon.

"There! You'll do without orange juice, because I won't get up and fetch it for you. Are you pleased with your cleverness? I've had enough of your tantrums—"

"PLEASE!" says Mendoza, clenching her fists. "Tempers!" She looks down distractedly at Nicholas. He has unfastened his safety belt and clambered quietly into her lap. He unclenches her fist, takes her hand in both his own, stretches up to whisper in her ear.

"Swedenborg?"

"Please?" he says, and points her index finger between his eyes. She blinks, collects herself, obliges him.

"Downloading," she croons. "Down the little dataport it goes, whoosh!" She looks across at Edward and resumes in a normal voice: "Señor, of course nobody's going abovedecks in a storm! How silly even to contemplate. And, you know, if either of them fell overboard he'd just swim like a little cyborg fishie. Wouldn't you, sweetheart?" She smiles down at Nicholas.

"Mmm." He nods, busy absorbing the flood of binary. Edward and Alec are still looking balefully at each other. Mendoza frowns at them.

"You know," she says, "Perhaps it's time we thought about making a change."

"A change, my dear?" Edward reaches for his teacup, deciding to ignore Alec.

"Yes," says Mendoza. "You know how you once said we'd never get married, but we did?"

"I recall, yes." Edward takes a sip of tea. Alec finishes his oatmeal sullenly. Coxinga, having retrieved the sipper bottle, sets it back on the table without comment.

"And you said we'd never raise children . . . but we are?"

"Sadly, yes," Edward says. Alec ignores him too, pushes away his bowl and climbs out of his seat, managing to pick up Barnacle Bill on the way without being too obvious about it.

"And you said we'd never live in a cottage by the sea . . . ?" Mendoza reaches out to steady Alec, who dives toward her possessively.

"*I* want to download now," Alec demands.

"Sweetheart, Nicky hasn't finished yet." Mendoza looses the strap and slides off Alec's helmet. Above her head, the saloon lamp swings on its gimbal until it nearly parallels the deck. Alec lurches, off balance, and Edward grabs him by the back of his sunsuit.

"Come here," says Edward, in a resigned tone of voice. Alec flails at him.

"I won't download from you! It's boring!"

"Don't be absurd," says Edward, tucking him into the crook of one arm. "No knowledge is useless."

"But *she* gives us nice data . . ." Alec's eyes glaze as Edward downloads to him. His little body relaxes. Barnacle Bill drops unnoticed to the floor.

"There's a good boy," says Edward, reaching for his teacup once more. "I'm sure you'll find a multitude of uses for Latin grammar. You were saying, my love?" he continues, regarding Mendoza over the rim of his cup.

"Well, as long as we're stuck in linear time for the next few years, perhaps we ought to find a cottage somewhere on dry land. It might be less stressful, at least as far as storms and life jackets go. What do you think?" says Mendoza, bracing her feet against a batten as she leans back in the booth. Alec, startled into exterior awareness, clutches for Barnacle Bill.

"Leave my ship?"

"By Jove!" Edward brightens. "Perhaps we could find a suitable island, at that."

Extract from the Journal of the Botanist Mendoza: In the Saloon

Well, this has certainly pulled the Evil One out of his post-post-partum doldrums. Edward loves making plans.

He has been applying his considerable powers of analysis to a novel concept: Dubious Isles. At least, he has been pursuing the subject when he can persuade himself that neither Alec nor Nicholas will toddle into the galley and get brained by a falling skillet for the next hour. This is mostly when they're in bed.

"What do you mean, Dubious Isles?" I said sleepily, snuggling in under

Edward's arm. "Like on old maps, only they turn out never to have existed? Somebody charted a fogbank or an iceberg?"

"Precisely, my love," he told me, speaking in a low voice over the two tiny snores coming from the cradle. "Consider the operative mechanism by which Dr. Zeus Incorporated exploits history! Things are thought to be extinct, or nonexistent entirely, when in fact they are merely hidden away. Consider, too, the as it were *cloaking* process by which our erstwhile masters conceal door-ways and, indeed, entire bases."

Name me any other man who uses a phrase like *as it were* in pillow talk. "Mmhm," I said. "And?"

"And here we are, sailing about in prehistorical seas," said Edward. "Long before the most elementary maps are drawn. What would be simpler than set-ting the good Captain to exploring those regions wherein early navigators charted legends?"

"Bermuda Triangles, Summer Isles, Shambhalas, et cetera?"

"Just so. We need only access early charts for islands that vanish from later maps. We find one that proves to be real, and, should it seem suitable for set-tlement, we'll then mask its existence from early Company surveys, and, mid-way through the seventeenth century or so, extend the concealment to ensure that it is never positively identified, which will cause it to be deleted from sub-sequent maps! Q.E.D." Smiling, Edward wound his hand into my hair.

Hmm. What about satellite imaging systems, Commander sir?

"What about 'em?" said Edward breezily. "You've concealed your own loca-tion from the hundred-eyed Argus of GPS for ages now; surely you won't find it any trouble to do the same for an island."

So . . . yer giving me an order to sail about, hither and yon, la de da, looking for islands what ain't there, until we runs aground on one that is there, only it ain't? You see, Commander yer worship sir, me being only a machine and all, I'd like orders what ain't quite so open to interpretation and semantic confusion. Otherwise I'm liable to conclude yer a God-damned idiot and mutiny. Saving yer presence, ma'am, I'm sure.

Edward leaned up on his elbow, glaring at the nearest camera. He gave a set of map coordinates. "Is that precise enough for you?" I referenced them and frowned, as Sir Henry spoke my thought: *Eh? But there ain't nothing in that corner of the world. The map's blank.*

"So I was told, one summer's day in 1842," said Edward. "Serving on the *Repulsion* at the time. I was mastheaded for my obstinacy in insisting I *had* sighted land, and I could see it all the clearer from my perch. I learned that a midshipman never answers back to an officer, but I know what I saw. Be so good as to set a course."

Aye sir, aye. But even if yer right . . . we'd have no guarantee nobody else's ever going to blunder into it by mistake, you know.

"Ah, but we'll have centuries before we need worry about that," said Edward, unbuttoning my pajama jacket.

"How romantic, señor," I said. "A quest for a phantom island."

He did not reply, being busy, but as our minds surged together his memory rose over me like a wave. I saw through the eyes of the gawky boy perched far up on the crosstrees, regarding bitterly the far green place so plain to him, and then gazing down at his shipmates so far below. Resentment, inevitably, but a chill of horror, too: as for the first time the boy wondered just how different he might be from the mortal men who walked the deck beneath him.

Child Care in the Cyborg Family, Volume Three:
Limitations of the Infant Psyche

. . . Given his human heritage, it is perhaps not to be wondered at that the very young cyborg will stubbornly retain certain primitive belief systems. This is a natural consequence of his immature state and ought not to cause undue irritation or alarm in the concerned parent. Indeed, his desire to grapple, as it were, with the fundamental issues defining his cosmos can be viewed as the inevitable outcome of his augmented intellect; for it is his very precocity that elevates him to the domain of sages and philosophers when mortal children his age are still preoccupied with the spinning top and hobbyhorse . . .

Mendoza wakes abruptly in the darkness, aware something has changed in the room. Edward is awake beside her at once, listening.

They hear panicked staccato gasps for air. One of the boys is frightened, trying not to cry. The Captain's surveillance camera has swiveled to focus on the ship bed. Alec has been half waking with nightmares lately, shrieking about fire and begging to be forgiven, incidents he never seems to remember by morning light; but Alec is, this moment, sleeping peacefully. *Night terrors,* transmits Edward. *See: Molesworth's Encyclopedia of Maternity Volume III, Chapter 4, "Neurological Development and Nocturnal Irrational Fears in the Young Child." Nothing to worry about.*

Mendoza climbs from bed and leans over the little ship. "Nicholas?" He sits up, frantically reaching for her, and when she lifts him he wraps his arms around her neck and hides his tear-streaked face against her cheek. She stands there, rocking him slowly, aware of the irony; in another age, Nicholas Harpole had sat up in bed to stare at the girl who had come unbidden to his room with the terror of eternity in her eyes.

Murmuring consolation, she carries him to her bed and lies down with him. Edward turns and gathers them in against him. "Now, what's all this, Nicholas?" he inquires. "You're perfectly safe, you know."

"I was in a garden," says Nicholas, and gasps for breath. "The sweetest place. And then the man came in."

"What man? *Querido*, there's no one here but us—"

"The one who said I was a monster. *He* made the garden," says Nicholas. "But he set it all on fire. I was so angry. Why did he burn what he made? I chased him to make him tell, but he ran from me—he wouldn't show his face—and—"

"That was symbolism, Nicholas," says Edward firmly. "Go back to sleep. I'll explain this in the morning—"

"I ran after him such a long time, Rose!" says Nicholas. "Always north, and everywhere he went was blighted. I saw the ice floes. I saw the white waste and the dead men. The bones of seals—"

"My darling, my baby, it's all right—"

"Why would he burn the garden?" Nicholas's voice rises in a wail.

"It doesn't matter what the man did," says Edward. "It doesn't matter what he called you. We'll plant a new garden, my boy."

"What kind of monsters are we?" says Nicholas, weeping.

"The ones best suited to plant gardens," says Edward. "And, out of all creation, the only beasts to whom it has occurred to do so."

"Humanity has signally failed at recreating Eden, señor," says Mendoza bitterly.

"So far," says Edward. "But no other creatures will try, you may be certain."

"And what if there are serpents?" Mendoza looks at him sidelong.

"Damned nonsense, leaving serpents in a garden," says Edward. "Not when *my* children play there. I was made to kill serpents; perhaps I'll kill one worth the name."

Nicholas sleeps at last, close in Mendoza's arms, and Edward holds them both against the night and the cold stars.

———

Mendoza dreams, chaotically, of seraphim with blazing wings. When she wakes, it is in the pale hour when the sun hasn't risen yet, and she hears a *thump* as Alec climbs out of bed and staggers into the bathroom. Edward hears it, as well, with hair-trigger child sensors, and gets up to follow him in there to be sure he can manage. (Even the Cyborg Child can fail to hit the urinal, if he's not entirely awake.) She is listening to Alec's cross little voice telling Edward he'd like some privacy, thank you, when:

Island off the port bow!

"Hey," Alec cries, and dashes from the bathroom with pajamas at half-mast. "We have to go see!"

"Not without your life jacket," Edward tells him, but Alec runs laughing up on deck and proceeds to dance there, gleefully impudent. Edward mutters and goes to grab a pair of jackets from a locker.

"Look," Alec shouts. "Look, Mendoza, come see! This is so cool!" Mendoza scrambles out of bed, as Nicholas rubs his eyes, and she runs up on the main deck after Alec to see the island.

A green mountain forested and bright with birds, descending in plateaus and terraces to a green lawn above a white sand beach. Waving palms, bluest of lagoons, a fragrance coming off it of ginger and rum, and still one bright clear star over the mountain's shoulder in the growing light.

They are dancing hand in hand, Alec and Mendoza, as Edward and Nicholas hurry on deck. Nicholas is shrugging into his life jacket and Edward seizes Alec to fasten him into one, too, muttering: "You are never under any circumstances to go abovedecks without the proper safety apparatus—"

"Piss off," says Alec cheerily, resuming his dance the moment Edward lets go of him. "Look, Deaddy! It's our very own green island, yeah?"

"I *told* Captain Meade there was land here," says Edward, looking out in satisfaction. "Two demerits, Alec."

"And there's the third star to the left," Mendoza sings, picking up Nicholas and dancing with him, too. He stares out at it, amazed.

"Is this a real place?" he asks.

"Well, it's *not* Neverland," Alec says, and hoots madly as he races around on deck. "Because I'm going to grow up, oh yes I am, oh yes I am—"

"The Blessed Isle, remember, darling?" Mendoza kisses Nicholas on his brow. "At long last, a real tropical Paradise."

"—oh yes I am, and when I do, I'll kick your butt—" Alec continues his little song, running close enough in his orbit to punch Edward's leg and leap away again, laughing wildly. "And then *I* get to be Commander of the Seven

Seas!" Edward chases him, grinning, and, catching him up, settles him on his shoulders.

"If you earn it, perhaps," he says. Nicholas is still staring at the mountain.

"Paradise," he repeats.

"Some people would take that as a sign, you know," Edward tells him. "Well, Captain, do you detect habitation?"

Not a blessed soul, Commander sir. This far back in time and this far out to sea, it ain't likely there'd be any hominids could get here anyhow. Hoping you'll accept an old machine's humble apologies for thinking you was a blockhead to send him a-chasing after cloudbanks all on account of you being too stubborn to say you was wrong one time clear back in 1842.

"Apologies, eh? Very well." Edward paces along the deck, balancing Alec on his shoulders as he surveys the island thoughtfully. "Send a survey party ashore immediately. Flint and Billy Bones are to note all water sources, any possible hazards including fungal or viral, and collect specimens of local flora and fauna."

Aye aye, sir.

"Yaay!" shouts Alec.

Edward smiles at Mendoza, as Flint and Billy Bones emerge from the saloon and crawl toward the agboat. "And now, my dear, what would you say to breakfast? I believe Coxinga's preparing oyster savory."

"And coffee, please, señor?" she replies. Nicholas, watching the island, has folded his hands on the front of his lifejacket.

Extract from the Journal of the Botanist Mendoza:
On the Island, Intrepidly

We made a slow circle of the island that day, scanning all the while, and found the place meets virtually all of Edward's criteria. No snakes. No lizards bigger than twenty-five centimeters, no members of the rodent family at all, and consequently a great many varieties of birds. There are sea turtles, ponderous as boulders all over one quiet beach, and abundant fish in the lagoon.

So ashore we went today, and what a picture we made. Edward in his full explorer ensemble, and didn't he look elegant and dangerous! The effect was offset somewhat by the harness on his back where Nicholas rode, peering out from under his little sun helmet. I carried Alec; he can't seem to resist spitting down Edward's neck when he's able, so it's best not to tempt fate.

And plowing ahead through the long grass and jungle went faithful Bully

Hayes the servounit bearer, turning his steel skull this way and that as he scanned our trail with glowing red sensors, carrying without complaint the mountain of stuff Edward insisted we bring. Both disrupter rifles and their extra power packs, a complete kitchen setup, a picnic hamper, folding chairs, a child-sized pavilion, an umbrella, a sanitary convenience for the children (who are still too little to be able to metabolize waste efficiently), holocamera equipment, a hatchet, a machete, and rain gear! I used to disappear into the Ventana for years at a time packing less. I think if we owned a Victrola, Edward would have brought that along, too. He's such a Briton, I swear to God.

Or it may be that Edward's still going through the motions of being human at this point, carrying so much baggage.

And maybe he's wiser . . . I left my humanity so far behind in the Ventana I was like a tree or a stone, sometimes; and in retrospect, I'm not sure that green darkness was good for me. Maybe there really has been a struggle for my soul going on all these years. Every time I've drifted away from it, the man has come to pull me back to human consciousness.

However immortal we are, we still wear human shapes, live in human patterns. The values of humanity are the only ones we know. Perhaps human love is the closest we can come to the divine, all we can know of paradise.

Though the island is a terrestrial paradise, no question. It looks to have endemic species to keep me diverted for years, and plenty of arable soil. A forested valley running back to the central massif, with mahogany trees bigger than the ones on Catalina. We splashed across bright streams, climbed rocky outcroppings, took holoshots of views. On a high hill we found an open meadow where Edward paced about for a few minutes, taking sightings before he announced: "This will do. Bully, make camp here, please."

And in a very few minutes we had a camp: baby pavilion shaded by the big umbrella, field kitchen with faithful servounit preparing luncheon. Edward and I were seated at our ease in folding chairs, Edward holding a rifle like a scepter. Alec and Nicholas stood leaning on the little pavilion railing, gazing down at the *Captain Morgan* white and serene in the bay below.

Champagne, ma'am? Sir Henry spoke out of Bully Hayes's chest as it crawled close to offer us a tray with silver ice bucket and two glasses. Too surreal. I had to fight a genuine case of hysterical giggles.

"Music, I think, Captain," Edward ordered.

Aye aye!

Music flowed promptly out of Bully Hayes's speaker, from Edward's two-hundred-and-ten-volume Best of Black Dyke Mills Band collection, I believe, as the servo crawled away to continue luncheon preparations. Edward had managed the Victrola after all. "Quite nice." Edward tasted the champagne.

"Yes," I said, taking a sip. "Well, here we are. The cyborg family has a picnic."

"Oooo, champagne!" Alec said, leaning toward me with his most winning smile. I held out my glass for him to have a taste as Edward looked on with a mildly disapproving eye. Nicholas had some too and smacked his lips.

This here landfall's everything we could have wanted, Edward lad. Sweet water and no mosquitoes.

"What do you think, my dear?" Edward said, gesturing with his glass at the panoramic view. "It seems an eminently suitable location for a residence. Pleasant breezes, artesian well just over there, good solid bedrock in which to anchor ourselves in the event of earthquakes, tidal waves, or hurricanes. Secure berth for the *Captain Morgan* down there." He pointed into the bay. "Lagoon suitable for sea bathing. Garden acreage all around." He swung the barrel of the rifle in a wide semicircle.

"I could live here," I said, finishing my champagne. Bully Hayes scuttled up to refill my glass.

"What house shall we have?" Nicholas said, turning to look across the meadow. He was bright-eyed and happy today, has been ever since we've been here.

"Something gracious, yet defensible," Edward said. "In a style appropriate for a warmer climate. Italianate, perhaps, my dear, what do you think?"

"Boring," said Alec, reaching for my champagne again. "Let's have a Wendy house. Or a tiki hut. Or a tree house!"

"And that, Alec, is why I am sitting here with my own glass of champagne and you are confined to a playpen," Edward said sternly. "You fail to plan adequately for the future. Drink your orange juice."

I glared at him as Alec pouted. "Commander Creepy," he said in a resentful little voice.

"Now, now," said Edward. "No reason to live like savages, after all. But perhaps we can compromise. Would you like a picturesquely barbaric wigwam in the trees as well? Or perhaps a piratical fort and blockhouse?"

Alec's eyes widened, but he wouldn't let go of his sulk. He stuck out his tongue at Edward, then fetched his sippy bottle and held it out to me. "Can I have a Bucks Fizz?"

"Don't give him alcohol, please," said Edward.

"It can't hurt him," I protested, unscrewing the sippertop and adding champagne. "Cyborg children were allowed champagne in the base schools. We drank it at New Year's, I remember. So did that little neophyte, Latif. No effect at all."

"Score to Alec," he gloated, taking the sipper and sticking it in his mouth. "Mm-mm!" And he sat down, plop, and fell back and waved his little feet in the air lazily.

"Three stories should be sufficient," Edward said, ignoring him again as he turned to consider the meadow. "With a wine cellar and provision vault below stairs. Laboratory, dining room, conservatory, schoolroom, infirmary . . . perhaps a billiard room as well. I suppose we shan't need a library, with all literature available on one text plaquette, but we might devote a room to the Arts."

Victorian brass oompahed behind us. Music to plan Eminently Desirable Residences by.

"This is going to be a bit more than a simple cottage by the sea, señor," I said. "I don't think we've got enough lumber in the cargo hold for a mansion."

"Ah." Edward looked pleased with himself. "I have had an idea, you see. It's my intention to obtain building material by designing biomechanicals from seashells."

"Seashells?"

"Yes, my love. Consider the way certain island cultures use coral blocks. Now, if one designed a nanobot to produce a nacreous substance like abalone shell, strong and durable—and then programmed it to build a suitable living space, with attractive architectural features—for example, doorways, staircases, transparencies for windows; consider also the wide range of ornamental applications for gardens, such as pergolas, balustrades, fountains, Greek temples . . ."

Greek temples on a South Seas island???

"Given the resources at our command, my dearest love, I think we ought to treat ourselves, don't you?" Edward looked at me seriously. "We, the superior Adam and Eve in our new Eden (as it were), must make shift to house ourselves, even as primeval Man was obliged to weave forest bowers. I intend to build *properly*, however. What about a magnificent temple of hygiene? Baths on the Roman plan? All possible plumbing refinements?"

"I suppose it could work," I said.

"Of course it will work," said Edward, holding out his glass for more champagne. Bully Hayes poured obligingly. "After which, we can attend to the plantations."

"Plantations?" I turned to stare at him.

"We require a garden," he replied. "In this well-watered and unimproved spot, I intend to make one. Lawns. Orchards. Formal flower beds. Pergola walks. And, of course, vegetable fields to supply the estate."

I set my champagne glass down and counted to ten. "Darling. This is an undiscovered island. There are probably endemic species growing here unknown anywhere else. Don't you think we ought to do some sort of environmental survey before we plow everything under to plant onions?"

I wasn't quite able to keep the edge out of my voice, and he turned startled eyes to me. Our consciousnesses collided like an iceberg and an ocean liner. He was hurt, confused; he was planting the garden *for me,* wasn't that what I had longed for? And perhaps he got some idea of the inflexibility of my Preserver programming. There was a long, long, contemplative moment of silence. The little boys watched us.

"Are you going to quarrel?" Nicholas asked breathlessly.

"No, indeed," said Edward. He stood and kissed my hand. "By all means, my love, survey the land. It's not as though we haven't all the time in the world."

Alec applauded.

We stopped briefly on the beach on our way back, so that Edward could stalk about picking up likely-looking bits of seashell. He retired into the saloon as soon as we got back, settled down with Sir Henry to produce grandiose virtual renderings of Villa Bell-Fairfax while I gave the boys their bath.

Well, the building hasn't quite gone as planned.

"You know what it looks like, señor?" I said unhelpfully, as we stood staring down at what should have been a palatial edifice and was instead a mess of melted-looking foundations. "Like those science experiments we used to do at the Base schools. Moon Rocks! Watch them grow! Just take a little salt, some laundry bluing . . ."

"That's absurd," said Edward. "It ought to have worked."

The little bastards is working, Commander, but they don't seem to have no clear idea what they're supposed to do, said Sir Henry, speaking out of Bully Hayes's chest. *I reckon I could have a go at reprogramming 'em for you, sir.*

"Or we could just slap up a tiki hut," I suggested.

"No," said Edward, with a certain asperity.

So back we went to the ship, and Edward took over the saloon and commanded silence while he reviewed his grand plan for flaws. The boys and I went away to the nursery and were very quiet all afternoon, doing hyperfunction exercises until they wore themselves out and went down for their naps. I lay down with them but couldn't rest, feeling the tidal pull of Edward's frustration through three bulkheads and two cabins.

At last I got up and wandered out to the saloon. Edward was still sitting where I'd left him, staring into the screen of the composition plaquette and drumming his fingers on the table.

There are no errors, he transmitted. *I have been over my calculations repeatedly.*

Well, señor, maybe this is just a little beyond nanotechnology, I replied, sliding into the booth beside him. *Nobody's ever tried—*

Of course it's never been tried. That's not the point. It ought *to work!* Edward's finger-drumming increased in speed. I put my hand over his.

Perhaps you ought to set it aside, just temporarily, and then you can approach it again with a rested mind, I told him soothingly. *I can think of one way to relax . . .*

Hmmmph. He was still staring at the screen.

The children are asleep, I hinted. That sank in and he looked up sharply.

Oh.

Have I mentioned that we're not, as it were, romping in Venus's grove much lately? Pretty pathetic for omnitemporal superbeings, eh? But, you know, there are the children, whose presence is, ahem, somewhat inhibiting. Yes, I know that once upon a different lifetime I did everything imaginable with Nicholas and with Alec, too, but somehow seeing them at knee level affects me oddly. Presumably they have memories of those all-night romps somewhere in their little heads, too, but . . . I cannot deal with this now. It seems unthinkable to me, loathsome . . .

And what with one thing and another we've been pretty busy, and anyway we get *tired* in linear time, at the end of a long day. Most nights all we manage is a brief blissful consciousness-mingling, which is actually better than sex, to be perfectly honest, and yet we find ourselves strangely reluctant to give up on the old-fashioned physical union because . . . oh, I don't know, maybe we feel that if we let go of this crucial bit of the human experience, we'll have edged that much closer to losing our old selves in the Beings-of-Pure-Energy cliché?

Anyway, we ever so carefully edged out of the booth and crept away to the aft stateroom, where we spent approximately ten busy minutes before our nerves got the better of us and we went tiptoeing back to the saloon. And there we both halted, in mutual coronary near-arrest, and I was exceedingly glad I'd muted my customary wails of rapture, because *there was Alec,* who had wandered, all sleepy and rumpled-looking, into the saloon. He had climbed up into the booth and was peering into Edward's composition plaquette.

"Why, sweetheart!" I said, in quite the highest falsetto I have ever mustered, and wishing I didn't feel quite so much as though I were a wife in a French farce. "You woke up!"

"Mm-hm," said Alec, rubbing one eye. He looked up at us. "Is this supposed to be programming, Deaddy?"

"Yes," said Edward, starting forward. "You mustn't play with it! It's very important—"

"Well, but you left out a step," Alec informed him.

"I beg your pardon?" Edward halted.

"Here and here and this bit here," said Alec, smudging the plaquette screen as he pointed. "*Three* steps, actually."

"Don't touch the screen," said Edward automatically, as he bent to the table and grabbed up the plaquette. He stared intently a moment; then looked at Alec with the strangest expression. "Oblige me by explaining," he said.

Alec just beamed, you never saw a child look so smug, and patted the booth next to him. "Sit down, old dead guy."

So there they were for the next two hours, really the sweetest picture; you'd have thought they were Daddy and Baby reading an alphabet book together. Alec had a gleeful field day pointing out all the flaws in Edward's design, but Edward listened without his customary irritation. He even let Alec fill in the missing code, and apparently there was quite a lot of missing code. When Alec had had his fill of crowing, Edward thanked him and sent him swaggering back to the nursery with a piece of toast and jam.

Then he turned to me (I had been unobtrusively tending to the potted plants all this while), seized me around the waist, and bent me backward in a profound kiss. "You're taking this well, I must say," I gasped, when we came up for air.

"We have created something better than ourselves," he said, with an expression of—what? Holy joy? For a moment, he looked almost like Nicholas, my Nicholas as he had used to be.

We have now been here six months linear. Villa Bell-Fairfax is not quite finished, in part because the señor keeps coming up with improvements on his original design. It's going to be awesome when it's done, I suppose. I was afraid Edward's little seashell-building nanobots would produce something like a pink plastic dollhouse, but the effect actually resembles white pottery or glass, gently translucent and only faintly pearly in certain lights. It looks like no Italianate mansion I ever saw—those cupolas, those balustrades, those arches, that gingerbread! Still, I'm sure it'll all come together in a style of its own. If it's ever finished.

For one thing, the wainscoting is entirely carved mahogany, which Edward is getting, piece by piece, from some shop up in London circa 1845. I do wonder what the mortal shopkeepers make of the profoundly tall man who turns up in their shop now and then, purchasing great chunks of their best quality polished paneling, paying for it with suspiciously new-minted gold sovereigns and politely declining assistance as he carries it out of their shop, then adjusting their perception so they don't notice as he steps with it sidelong back through time. In the same way he is accumulating marble, tiles, oak planks for flooring, plumbing . . . though the *baths on the Roman plan* are proving a little tricky, even for an all-powerful superbeing.

He labors all day at the building site, installing this, adjusting that, assisted by Bully Hayes and Billy Bones. I, by common consent, take the little boys with me as I slog on with my environmental survey. The survey was taking longer than Edward thought it should, because of course there are no roads for easy access in our untouched island paradise, so one night Edward sent the servos out to grade some. I was so furious with him I could have screamed, but of course I couldn't in front of the children and anyway I saw at once he had thought I'd be *delighted*! He was startled and contrite when he picked up what I was feeling, but what's done is done.

And I suppose the scars will eventually green over again. Most of them.

I have a feeling I'm going to have nightmares tonight. Yes, thank you, Flint, I will have some of that rum.

We went out this morning, the boys and I. A kiss for Deaddy at the Villa Bell-Fairfax worksite, and then away into the depths of the island, exploring.

It's difficult being a cyborg botanist drone, when you have two little boys waiting, with greater (Nicholas) and lesser (Alec) degrees of patience, for you to stop studying some damn plant so we can *go* somewhere. Is that a cave over there? Is that a volcano? Can we build a house in this tree? Are there deadly piranhas in the lagoon? Are there coconuts in that palm tree? Can I climb up and pick some? Why can't I? Look, is that a crocodile?

This is why my environmental survey is taking forever, because after an hour of this I just give up and play Wendy or Tinkerbell or Tiger Lily or whatever they want me to be. Figuratively speaking, of course. They're much too intellectually advanced for mere make-believe. They're *Cyborg Children,* after all.

We got all the way over to the windward side of the island, on the graded road that snakes along like a black gash through the screaming green foliage. We came to the crest of the ridge, very like my old prison on Santa Catalina, along its rocky spine: same sea wind pushing up the hillside to fan my face, same ferny trees waving below. Nicholas pointed at the far horizon. "Clouds," he said. "Is that a storm?"

"Run a scan," I suggested. "Check the meteorological data."

"Yup! It's a typhoon coming our way," announced Alec.

Nicholas looked frightened, and I shook my head. Nicholas closed his eyes, scowling as he ran the numbers; then opened them and glared at Alec. "It is not," he said. "It's just rain. You only said that to be dramatic."

Alec stuck out his tongue at him and Nicholas drew back his fist, at which point I grabbed his arm. "No fighting!"

"I wasn't going to hit him in the *head,*" said Nicholas sullenly.

"But it's a big storm," said Alec. "With lots of rain. I was only exaggerating a little. It's coming this way fast, too. Isn't it?"

"You're right," I said, scanning the clouds myself and feeling, then, just a little unease. "Well, we won't stay out too long today. I think we'll just survey this one bit of forest."

It was a fairly dense cover of Norfolk Island pine and ironwood, or things that might be hitherto-unknown variant subspecies of same, just the sort of thing to seduce me into lingering there for days while I ran all possible tests. The old romance was gone, though, somehow. I grew more and more nervous as I worked, as the little boys flitted back and forth between the tree trunks, playing at hyperfunction hide and seek. At last I glanced up and saw not blue sky between the branches but bruised purple air full of heat and wrath. I muttered something profane.

"What?" said Alec, beside me like a shot.

"Never mind. Where's Nicholas?"

"Here," he said, materializing in front of me. "It's starting to rain."

"Well, crumbs," I said effortfully. "I suppose we ought to start back, then."

"Why?" Alec said. "We're cyborgs. A little rain isn't going to hurt us, is it?"

"No," I agreed, peering up at the clouds. I used to work all through the storm season in the Ventana, never once worrying what might happen. I loved storms. I reveled in the downpour, in the blast and the flash and the ozone following a lightning strike. Strangely thrilling, to dodge between the falling bolts. A risk no properly programmed cyborg would ever take, but oh well.

Still, the idea of Alec or Nicholas doing something like that made my stomach knot up in terror. "Let's go dance in it!" said Alec brightly.

"No! We're just going to sit here under cover and wait for it to blow through," I said. I led them to a thicket, screened over by branches but well away from any tree trunks, and we stretched out in the prickly gloom.

"We're like deer in the forest," said Nicholas, snuggling against me.

"Like in that holo?" said Alec. "*Bambi*, right, with the talking animals, and then he's an orphan, but then the big king stag comes and turns out to be his father?"

"When did we let you download that?" I said. "That's much too scary for you!"

"It was just there when I accessed," said Alec, a little too casually. "It was all right. I wasn't frightened. You'd have to be a pretty big baby to be frightened."

"You were frightened," said Nicholas.

"No, I wasn't!"

"Alec, it's got forest fires and savage dogs and . . . and a traumatic orphaning," I said. The rain, meanwhile, increased; a few drops made it through the canopy and plinked on the broad brim of my hat.

"But we're immortals," said Nicholas. "And nothing like that can ever happen to us." He said it with a certainty that meant he wanted to be reassured, so I put my arm around him.

"No, of course not," I said, and made a mental note to ask Sir Henry if there's any way to limit the files to which they have access. Alec has enough nightmares as it is. Just then, though, there was a blinding violet-white flash and thunder like the sky cracking open right on top of us.

When it faded, I found that I was on my feet and tensed to run, with two little limpet-babies clinging to me, trembling, though Alec shouted "Whee-hoo!"

Where are you? Edward transmitted, through a burst of static.

Four kilometers west-northwest, on the ridge!

Where's my boy? Unusual, to hear a machine panicking.

"I'm okay, Captain!" cried Alec, though his voice was drowned by another flash/crack.

Come back immediately! You ought—Edward's transmission broke up in more static, but the implied reproach was there, and I felt miserably guilty. I thought he was overreacting, of course, but I was also remembering Joseph's face the time he caught me out in that cornfield in Spain when the storm was breaking, and really, this is just too much complicated psychological baggage to contemplate right now.

"Hold on, darlings," I said, and set off down the hill as fast as I dared go without the boys' little heads snapping off, landing on the graded road with a skid and a lurch. It was already a sea of mud, pocked with the boiling rain. Cursing to myself, I went squelching along it ankle-deep, and picked up a fragmentary transmission from Edward:—*at once! I'm starting out with*—

I ought to have started down the hill the minute I noticed the clouds had advanced. What is this, my fascination with storms? Stupid, stupid, stupid. Did I always have a careless streak? I suppose I must have, mustn't I?

The lightning appeared to move away to the north, at least, but the rain became a nearly solid curtain of water through which we struggled. No use to try to avoid the puddles now; the road was bleeding creamy mud, brimming over its edges, spilling down the flattened grass on its lower side. "Is it going to be all right?" Nicholas shouted.

"Of course it is!" I said, as cheerily as I could. "It's only a little rain!"

"Because I can hear something—" We came around the curve of the hill then, and what we saw stopped me in my tracks.

There had been quite a picturesque little stream there, trickling down over black boulders, with inviting-looking lush moss. Billy Bones had thoughtfully graded only up to within a meter on either side of its course, and bridged it with some logs roped together. We'd crossed it five or six times without incident; but we weren't going to be doing that again. The footbridge had vanished. So had a lot of the road. In its place was a roaring cataract of water, jetting from above the boulders. It had blown the bridge down the mountainside as though it were a chip of wood, and descended on the raw new-graded road, eating it away. Now the water tumbled down a vast muddy eroded slide, ten meters across, fanning out in ever-widening rivulets as it descended the mountain.

I said—something really profane.

If I'd been alone I might have backed up and flung myself across in hyperfunction. Couldn't do that with the little boys holding on to me, though. I stared at it stupidly for a moment before peering up through the rain at the cataract.

"We're not going across this," I said unnecessarily. "I think we can cross further up, though. Here's what we're going to do." I backed up to the mountainside and set both boys down. "The two of you are going to stand *right here* while I climb up and see if there's a safe place to cross."

"You're going to reconnoiter," said Nicholas.

"Bravo, yes, exactly. What are you going to do?"

"We're going to stand *right here*," they choroused.

So I pulled myself up the mountainside hand over hand, clutching at bushes and other undergrowth. Yes; the stream was a raging torrent up there, too, but still confined more or less to its rocky bed, and there were a couple of boulders that might facilitate leaping across in a couple of child-friendly bounds. I was scanning them to gauge how stable they were when I heard Nicholas saying: "She said we were to stay right here!" and Alec's bloodcurdling reply: "I *am* right here, I just want to see—" followed by a tiny little scream.

I have no idea what happened next. Once or twice in my eternal life I have drawn blanks—when I killed the mortals who shot Edward, for example—and this too is just a blur. Reviewing my visual transcript produces only an image of water and sky and mountain, a brief glimpse of Nicholas looking terrified as an arm—mine, presumably—sweeps out to him, and then Alec rocketing down the mountain slope on his back. He is crying "Wheeee—ow! Ow! Eeeeeee—"

The sound is dopplering because I am catching up to him, pointing my body for greater speed, knifing past him at last through the avalanche of liquid mud, and I can hear Nicholas's unbroken scream in my other ear. Lightning again, thunder all around us. Then my foot has braked with a slam on a boulder, and Alec plummets toward me wide-eyed and I grab him, and then we are all three falling sideways and hurtling through green and fragrant branches, until there is a splash and I am fighting my way upward through dark water. Kicking to rise, because I have a child clutched in either arm. We break the surface. We are breathing hard. It echoes.

The next thing I knew consciously, I was sitting with my knees drawn up on a shelf of rock, gasping, streaming with water. Alec and Nicholas were crouching, one on either side of me, in a kind of twilit gloom. Before us was the black pool, shattered water bobbing with something white. Flower petals? Yes. And around us the black stone walls, dripping, and above us the branches of whatever flowering bush concealed the place. *Gardenia taitensis.* Tiare, yes.

Our grotto must be the former terminus of the stream, from its starting point up the mountain. How far had we fallen? I could hear breakers not far below us, and the place smelled of salt mist and blossoms. Another flash, another peal of thunder; then the darkness flowed back, and the sounds of surf and trickling water.

"That was brilliant," said Alec gamely.

"WHAT DID I TELL YOU?" I roared, grabbing him and smacking his bottom. Just once; it echoed in that place like a pistol shot. Then I was holding him in my arms and sobbing like an idiot, and Nicholas was clinging to us and crying, too.

I shouldn't have done it. My anger, smoldering for centuries, all that old despair and frustration—it just blindsided me. I wonder I didn't knock him flying. Thank God I didn't. Edward has never once struck them . . .

"There's blood," said Nicholas, tugging at my torn sleeve. I lifted my head to look—gosh, I was scratched and bleeding in a dozen places, that I could see at least. In consternation I scanned the boys; not a mark on Nicholas, thank God, but Alec had a scrape and an egg-sized bump on the back of his head.

"Does this hurt?" I demanded, pouring a cupped handful of water on it to wash away the blood. The scrape looked minimal. He shivered and made a face, as the icy water ran down inside his collar.

"Only a little. It's starting to, actually. I think I hit my head on a rock," he said.

"You what?" Now I felt icy water, metaphorical as well as real. I grabbed Alec's face and stared into his eyes, scanning him. There was no indication of skull fracture or cerebral bleeding; hematoma, slight abrasion, nothing more. He was fine. I told him so, with a shaky laugh, and then stretched out my left hand, which looked like I'd been fending off a wildcat with it.

"All right, this is as good a time as any for a lesson. See all these cuts? I'm going to heal myself. Watch." I made my biomechanicals swarm to all the injured places on that hand. The boys watched in fascination as the bleeding stopped, as the cuts closed over and faded. At least, they watched until Alec went green and threw up. Did he have a concussion after all? Frantic, I scanned him again.

"I'm okay, really," he insisted. "It's just excitement." He might be right; I still couldn't find anything wrong with him. I gathered him against me and sat still, rocking back and forth. What was I going to do? I tried transmitting to Edward or Sir Henry, but the storm turned it to so much crackle and buzz.

"We'll just sit here until the storm passes away," I said. "Then we can climb down and walk back along the beach, I think."

"Show us how you can heal the other hurts," said Nicholas. So I held out my bleeding right hand and was explaining how they could do this too, once they learned the reflexive commands, and Nicholas bent his head to watch closely, though Alec squeezed his eyes shut and shivered. That was when something big came pushing through the branches and vaulted into our bower, backlit for a second by lightning. I never was so glad to see anyone in my life as Edward, muddy and disheveled, peering at us through the darkness.

"And, you see? Everything's going to be all right now, here's Commander Bell-Fairfax to the rescue!" I babbled. He came swiftly around the margin of the pool and crouched beside us.

"Nicholas, how's Mummy?" he asked gently.

"Rose has a lot of cuts," Nicholas told him.

"I'm fine. It's just Alec—" I fought back hysteria. "He's hit his head—" Edward went pale and lifted him from my arms, scanning him at once. "I couldn't find anything—but he was sick—"

"Alec, how do you feel? How is our little boy?"

Alec gazed wonderingly up at our worried faces. "Well, my head hurts," he said at last. "And, er, things sort of have this funny aura around them? And, er, I'm having confusion. How did we get here?"

"You wouldn't stay where she told you to, and you fell down the mountain!" cried Nicholas

"Did I? I'm sorry," said Alec.

"You don't appear to be concussed," said Edward, looking at him keenly. "But the Captain will do any number of tests, I'm sure. And then we shall discuss demerits."

"Okay," said Alec, snuggling into his arm. I put my arms around Nicholas. Edward put out his other arm and drew us close.

"Now then," he said. "You needn't worry, my dear. The good Captain is at this moment making his way around the island; he'll send the boat for us presently, and we'll be warm and dry in short order."

"The road washed out—" I said.

"Yes, I saw. You were quite right; we oughtn't have cut that road, certainly this close to what is apparently the monsoon season. My apologies," he said. Not a word about why I hadn't started back earlier.

So much can go wrong, in linear time.

We sat there huddled together, watching the rain and the flashes of lightning. The warmth of Edward's body was comforting. "We could be a cave family, hiding in our cave," said Alec contentedly. I wondered whether he was hallucinating.

What an incompetent fool I am.

Who is she, this violent, reckless woman? How can I have lived all these ages without knowing myself?

CHAPTER 20

The Tombs of the Heroes, 2354

Nobody noticed Joseph when he got off the air transport at Rufforth, in York-shire; nobody noticed him when he got on the train at York; nobody noticed when he got off the train at Northallerton, or when he went into the men's lavatory to change his clothes.

The mortal renting agcycles did notice him, when he ran the customary check on Joseph's identification disc. There wasn't much to notice, though: Joseph Steppenwolf, Californian tourist on holiday, age thirty, employed by Hearst News Services, enough in his credit account to pay for the agcycle if he crashed it. That last was the only detail of any interest to the mortal.

So the mortal handed Joseph his activator and obligatory safety helmet, but didn't bother with the obligatory safety lecture. He was anxious to get back to the Totter Dan game that waited on the rental office's console, and anyway, nobody ever broke safety laws anymore. He was so deeply involved in his game that he didn't notice when Joseph sped off through the rain toward the grassy track that had been the A684.

West on the A684, north at Hardraw. The land was empty, overgrown: walls tumbled, houses fallen in long ago, and an unbroken sea of heather drowning old fields. Joseph saw no mortal soul until he pulled off the road, shortly after turning north. Even then, it was only ghosts he met.

He lowered the support stand and switched off the agcycle's motor. Climb-ing down, he removed his helmet and stared around.

You could tell there'd been a good-sized building here. The gravel drive was still visible, and beyond was a big mound of mossy stones and bramble. No clue left to show that it had once been a bed-and-breakfast with a gift shop, styling itself The Innocents. Joseph walked across to the ruin and poked cautiously with his foot. A lot of crumbled plaster. Broken brick. A hinge.

"No Bournville bars today, huh?" he said out loud. He lifted his eyes from the ruin and nearly jumped out of his skin; for a moment he thought he saw Lewis there beside him, looking on sadly as the wind whipped his long coat.

Nope. Trick of the light, that was all. Joseph looked away at the one thing that hadn't changed in three centuries: the high steep hill that rose beyond the old foundations. Settling his pack on his shoulders, he waded around the ruin and began to climb.

Fifteen minutes' steady work along a rabbit track brought him up under the place he recognized, the crumbled and treacherous-looking rock face that concealed a door. Five minutes later he was hurrying down the black sloping tunnel under the hill, watching a dim blue glow ahead as it brightened and scanning cautiously as he went.

He emerged into the vast cavern and this, too, was unchanged. Row upon row of vaults stretched away into the twilight, each one with its blue regeneration tank, and in nearly every tank a body floated. Most of them were male. Most of them were enormous, and shared Budu's peculiar physical characteristics. All wore circlets about their brows, plain bands of dark metal.

Joseph didn't waste time gaping, for this was exactly what he had expected to see. He looked across at a chalkboard on one wall and read the words:

ABDIEL HAS COMPLETED HIS APPOINTED TASK HERE
12 MAY 2353 TO 1 JUNE 2353

"Atta boy, Abdiel," whispered Joseph. He shrugged out of his pack and opened it, drawing out two circlets of dark metal nearly identical to the ones the sleeping giants wore. Pushing them up his left arm like outsize bracelets, he ran quickly to the nearest tank and scaled the maintenance ladder up its side. At the top he paused just long enough to roll up his right sleeve and plunge his hand into the blue regenerant fluid, grabbing the tank's occupant by his waving dun-colored hair and hauling him up to the surface.

It took Joseph no more than a split second to pull off the circlet, toss it aside, and replace it with one of the two he had brought. There was an audible *zap* as the new circlet touched. Even as Joseph was fitting it in place, the big man was opening pale startled eyes and grabbing for him; but Joseph set his index finger against the sloping forehead and downloaded a jolt of encoded information.

The great hands opened in a gesture of astonishment, clenched. Joseph let go and scrambled back down the ladder, and the tank's occupant peered out at him.

Joseph? What the hell . . . ?

Hi, Ron. Can't talk now.

But my chronometer says it's 2354!

Yeah. There's a war on, soldier.

Great!

I just gave you your orders in code. Access them when I'm gone. Who do you want for second-in-command?

The giant in the tank thought briefly. *Albert, I guess.*

Okay. Joseph ran to a particular vat where another giant slept, swarmed up its side, and repeated the procedure. Albert stared in surprise, asked roughly the same questions, and was given more or less the same reply. Joseph scrambled down. He picked up the two discarded circlets and zipped them into his pack where the others had been. Then he turned and ran from the cavern, back up the long tunnel.

Ron and Albert looked out through their respective tanks and saw each other. They waved. Then they closed their eyes to access the orders they had been given.

Joseph emerged into pouring rain. Much more quickly than he had gone up, he came jogging down; was back on the agcycle and roaring away south within five minutes.

No ghosts followed him. He returned the agcycle at Northallerton and purchased a train ticket for Selby. While waiting to board, he went into the men's lavatory, changed his clothes again, and dropped the two circlets he had brought away down the lavatory's fusion hopper. With a clang and a whoosh they were gone, to do their bit keeping the lights burning in Northallerton.

Joseph boarded, got off at Selby, and caught a flight to Calais. There he rented an agcar and drove to Irun Del Mar in the Pyrenees.

At the bunker under the Pyrenees, he woke two more sleepers and gave them their orders. He woke two more in the bunker outside Fez. Catching a flight up to Norway, he did the same; rattling all night in a train across Siberia, he found his way to the bunker in the Verkhoyansk mountains and did the same there. Another train took him to Vladivostok, where he caught an air transport to New Mexico. He was in and out of the bunker in the Sangre de Christos in ten minutes. From Santa Fe he took the bullet train to San Diego, on the coast, and booked passage on a commuter clipper to San Francisco. On

Lombard Street he rented another agcycle and forty-five minutes later was speeding up the side of Mount Tamalpais, where he completed his mission.

He went back to Lombard Street, returned the agcycle, and walked up to Van Ness, where he rented an agcar. He drove it south as far as Big Sur. There he got out, set its autopilot on return and walked to Garrapatta.

At Garrapatta he reported to Budu, ate a very large meal, and then slept for three days.

Budu let him sleep. He had earned it.

Fez, 7 June 2355

"The Hangar Twelve Man," said Latif meditatively. He turned onto his back, staring up at the square of sky above the courtyard. "I watched that footage and I thought, where have I seen that guy before? Then I placed it. The strange thing was, it wasn't the face of anybody real."

"What do you mean?" Sarai turned. The raft bobbed and Latif reached out for the pool coping to steady them.

"I knew a Preserver, a long time ago, who wrote bad historical novels. I read his stuff once, as a favor. Volumes and volumes of crap. I never got through it all. At the front of the file Lewis had a graphic, scanned in from this old daguerreotype he'd found somewhere—"

"Lewis?" Sarai leaned up on her elbow. "The Literature Preserver who went missing?"

"The one who went missing," said Latif, not taking his eyes off the sky. A white bird crossed the square of blue, high up, flying into the west. "And the picture was of a British navy guy from the nineteenth century. Not handsome—strange-looking. But Lewis had become obsessed with him, for some reason. Wrote all these romantic adventures. The point is, the guy in the old picture looked exactly like the Hangar Twelve Man."

"Peculiar, that," said Sarai cautiously.

"Yeah. I heard another story, later," said Latif. "Right after Lewis disappeared. I heard the reason the Company took him out was, he tried to find out who the man in the picture had been, and got too close to something the Company'd covered up, so—good-bye Lewis. Wonder what he'd have thought if he could have seen your Alec Checkerfield?"

Sarai said nothing.

"Even stranger thing," Latif added. "The person who told me about Lewis—

Joseph, who disappeared right after that—swore that the man in the picture was also a dead ringer for somebody *he'd* known back in the sixteenth century. In England. Some big mortal who'd had an affair with one of his recruits, a Botanist named Mendoza. He hated the guy for it."

"What are you telling me, boy?" Sarai's voice was taut.

"I haven't told you the strangest part yet." Latif pushed himself up off the raft, sat on the coping with his legs in the water.

"And that would be?"

Latif reached for a towel and met Sarai's stare. "How's this for a coincidence? At a New Year's ball back in 1699, I sat at a table with all three of them. Lewis, and Joseph, and Joseph's recruit Mendoza. She said something that night, about how unlikely it was that the four of us would ever be together in one room again. It gave me the creeps. The idea of loneliness, especially the loneliness of working for the Company for all time . . . It's haunted me ever since.

"All three of them knew about this mysterious Englishman. All three of them have disappeared. We never have been together in one place since that night, just as Mendoza said. 'And I only am escaped alone to tell thee.' "

"*Damballah*," murmured Sarai. "My Alec . . ."

"Weird, isn't it?" said Latif, never taking his eyes off her. "But you knew Alec Checkerfield."

"What is it you want from me, eh?" she said wearily.

"Answers," Latif replied.

"I haven't got them. And, boy, we're at the end of time! What does any of it matter now?" Sarai cried.

"It might matter a lot," said Latif. "Anyway, I owe it to Lewis and the others. You think your Damballah would know?"

"Hello?" Nefer ventured out and peered along the arcade at them. She cleared her throat. "Latif? Something's happened. I think you'd better—"

But he was on his feet immediately, pulling on a robe. Sarai scrambled out of the water, grateful for the interruption.

They followed Nefer back through the house to the room where Suleyman received visitors. There was a mortal monk there, gratefully sipping tea, though he set it aside and stood to bow when they entered the room.

Suleyman sat at the table regarding two objects. They appeared to be, respectively, a gift box containing a perfume atomizer of ruby glass nested in strange-looking packing medium and a page from a medieval manuscript, straggling Latin uncials on a rough-torn scrap of paper. Suleyman took up the paper and presented it to Latif without a word. Latif scowled, reading it over quickly. He looked at the monk. "You brought this?" he demanded.

"Yes, Lord. It was delivered to our chapter house in Dublin."

"Regular parcel post," Suleyman told him. "The shipping stamp's from a place called Knockdoul. Unusual excelsior it was packed in."

Latif looked down into the box and his eyes widened. "Those are human finger and toe bones," he observed.

"So they are," Sarai concurred. She sidled up and read the message over his arm. "This would be from the famous lost Lewis?" she asked.

"Or we're meant to think so," Suleyman replied. He looked at Latif. "You knew him, son. Does this sound authentic?"

"I can't tell!" Latif began to pace the room. "All right, maybe the style's similar. He had an old-fashioned way of expressing himself. Have you had that thing checked out yet?" He pointed at the red bottle.

"No, son, it only just arrived," Suleyman told him.

"Then let's get it checked out," Latif shouted, and grabbing up the bottle he strode out of the room. They could hear doors slamming after him as he progressed through the house toward the laboratory. Sarai exchanged glances with Nefer and Suleyman and followed him in silence. The monk, looking disconcerted, said: "If I've given offense—"

"No, no." Suleyman waved a hand. "You mustn't think so. The boy is hot-tempered, that's all. More tea?"

Fez, 8 June 2355

Victor peered through the lens, his pale face expressionless.

"Yes," he said. "That is unquestionably an engineered toxin. Rather unorthodox compared to the ones with which I'm familiar. Someone's little work of native genius, no doubt." He stood and turned to Suleyman. "Are you certain it's Lewis's blood?"

"Well, this came with it," Latif said, offering Victor the message. Victor read it in silence a moment. His mouth tightened. Handing the paper back to Latif, he cleared his throat before he said: "Shall I tell you what I think is going on?"

"Go right ahead," said Latif, folding his arms.

"I think our masters have grossly miscalculated. They gave Lewis to those creatures, in the hope they'd devise a way to kill immortals. It must have seemed like a reasonable expectation; the little freaks had invented so many other useful things. These toxins, however, won't do the trick. I have no doubt the results would be dramatic and uncomfortable, but not, ultimately, fatal to one of our kind."

"Speaking as an expert," said Latif.

"Yes," Victor replied, unsmiling. He turned away and stared down into the courtyard, where a mortal servant was sweeping leaves. "Ironic that it took them three quarters of a century and they still failed. Lewis had a way of surviving . . . still has, I suppose. What must he have suffered, all these years?" he mused. No one replied and after a moment he looked across at Suleyman. "You said something about having located him?"

"The bottle was mailed from a parcel depot in the Celtic Federation," Suleyman explained. "We did a scan in a thirty-mile radius around the depot."

"The damn Company must have known where they were all along," said Latif. "There's a huge concentration of life signs and energy signals, all bunched together in one spot out in the middle of nowhere. I'm betting it's an underground bunker. We read seventy-one mortal signatures and one cyborg."

Victor received that news unblinking. He turned back to the window in silence.

"We're going after him," Latif continued. "I'm doing reconnaissance for a rescue, before the Silence. Do you want to come along for the ride?"

"I think not," Victor replied. "Thank you, but I must be getting back to California. So much to do."

Latif threw up his hands. "Suit yourself," he said, and stalked out.

"And after all," said Victor to no one in particular, "I don't know that I've quite got it in me to look Lewis in the face."

London, 21 June 2355

A tremor ran through the great clock. It was going to strike; the gears had nearly come around to the appointed place, the counterweight had begun its ratcheting descent.

A convoy moved silently through Wanstead, and pulled up at Manor Park Storage. Orders were hissed by someone querulous, certain mortals hastened to obey. Purposeful as ants they entered unit 666. Quickly as any team of immortal cyborgs they emptied it, loading the chlorilar drums out to the waiting lorries. They didn't take long and they were quite unobserved. The convoy sped off into the night, away from London.

It did not stop until safely over the border into Wales, and just outside a village with an ungodly number of Ds in its name the convoy arrived at a private airstrip, dark and unlit, where nevertheless an air transport waited under power. As quickly as the drums had been loaded, they were offloaded. The empty lorries dispersed into various trunk roads. By infrared, without running lights, the air transport rose silently as a black balloon and the occluded stars were the only sign of its flight.

Where it touched down at last, there were mortals waiting to unload it. In no time at all the air transport drifted away, empty. The chlorilar drums went up a ramp, one after another after another, and in darkness—for no lights had been permitted—they were emptied into a great vat, and once emptied were fed down a fusion hopper. Bang, whoosh, away, they were gone and might never have existed, for all there was any evidence left by the time morning broke gray over the horizon.

The Summer Solstice was rigorously observed as a religious holiday in the Celtic Federation, so Ratlin's Confectionary had given most of its employees the day off in compliance. There were a number of its employees, however, who belonged to old and discredited faiths, who had jumped at the chance to earn overtime bonuses by spending the sacred day filling a specially commissioned order, incorporating dark treacle from one particular vat.

All day the factory ran, shift schedules disregarded, and the music of Raymond Scott's *Powerhouse* roared from the sound system to inspire the workers as the sun rose to his glory in midheaven and then began his descent. Nut clusters were dipped, balls of fondant were dipped, gummy squares of Turkish Delight were dipped, ordinarily innocent sweets with no power to harm anyone but a diabetic. Ah, and the special Chocolate Deluxe Honeycomb, and the special Black Coffee Truffles! Who could resist them?

All were dipped and rolled out on their particular assembly lines briskly, proceeding along belt-driven lanes to the corner of the factory where printers spewed out bright Special Assortment color reproductions of the nineteenth-century painting *Jupiter Sitting in Judgment* by Gericault, which were cut, pasted onto box lids, and embossed at high speed, whirling around on a carousel to meet the box bottoms, which were by that time filled with frilly paper cups holding a truly unique assortment of Theobromos. Lids met bottoms, embraced and raced on with their dubious contents to the next station on the long line, where they received a double-band of purple ribbon on the diagonal. Hurrying on, each box was the recipient of a small embossed card tucked neatly under the ribbon, and each card bore the message:

In Appreciative Commemoration of
Your Many Years of Faithful Service

So! Packed and self-important the boxes proceeded through the sta-sealer, and then, inviolate, dropped one upon another into shipping units, twenty to a tub, seized each as it reached capacity and hustled into a waiting lorry.

By the time the sun sank to his late and prolonged death, the order had been filled. By evening of the following day, the lot was secured in a refrigerated warehouse beneath Dr. Zeus Incorporated headquarters in London.

London, 1 July 2355: Board Meeting:
They Deliver Tidings of Comfort and Joy

"Now it can be told," said Freestone in a smug voice. All heads turned to him.

"I hope you're about to say what I think you're about to say," said Hapsburg.

"I don't think I'll disappoint you," Freestone replied. He looked up and down the table, smiling at the assembled stockholders and scientists, enjoying being the center of attention. Well, of the stockholders anyway; his scientific colleagues already knew.

"We can now tell you what will happen on the final day of recorded history," he said. "Which is to say, 9 July 2355. One week and one day—"

"Cut to the chase, for crying out loud," yelled Telepop.

"Tell us!" Hapsburg ordered.

Freestone looked mildly offended but raised his hands for silence. "I can understand your annoyance. All right; what happens is, on the final day of recorded history, *we just stop recording it.*"

"What?" demanded Roche.

"Then that's not what'll happen," said Telepop, "that's just what you *plan* to happen."

"And we'll do a few other things," Freestone went on hastily, sensing he'd put his foot wrong. "We close down all temporal operations permanently. And we retire all our cyborg personnel."

There was a moment of silence wherein his last sentence registered, and then everyone turned to stare at the place in which Lopez usually stood during meetings. He was not there today, of course. This meeting had been called without his knowledge, and now it was becoming clear why.

"You've finally figured out a way to, er . . . shut down the cyborgs?" said Morrison.

"Yes, we have," Freestone asserted. "The long nightmare is over! I'm sure you'll understand if we don't want to talk about it much, but it's something we've been planning for years."

"You're certain it'll work?" Roche wanted to know.

"Of course." Freestone waved his hand. "We've had our very best people on it and I think we can assure you there's nothing to worry about. One week from today, you might say the Company will be *downsized.*" He looked around to see if the old-fashioned word had confused anyone, but they seemed to have grasped his meaning. "After all, with temporal operations shut down we won't need the operatives anymore."

"But . . . won't we lose a lot of revenue from the Day Six places?" asked Telepop.

"The cut in overhead costs when we retire the operatives will more than compensate us," Freestone explained. "Just think: no maintenance expenses, no redundancy pay, no pensions! No bother with human resources at all. No more Temporal Concordance to keep track of, either. The whole cyborg operation was ruinously expensive to run, you know, though of course it paid for itself, and now the long-term advantages can be reaped."

"So you're saying that on July ninth we can just . . . take it easy at home with our families?" said Telepop slowly.

"Yes!"

"You're sure there aren't any meteors coming to hit us or anything?" Morrison persisted.

"Absolutely," Freestone said. "We'll all be perfectly fine. Once the cyborgs are turned off, all we have to do is make sure nobody ever travels into the past again, or sends any messages there either. That way we won't contradict the Temporal Concordance. We won't know what's going to happen in advance after this, but we've made enough profit and salvaged enough out of the past to fulfill our original mission statement."

"That's true!" said Hapsburg. "We have done what we set out to do, haven't we? Kept all those animals from going extinct and saved all those, er, things? Paintings and stuff?"

"Exactly," Freestone replied. "Dr. Zeus has fulfilled his purpose. When the cyborg program is terminated, life goes back to normal. Except that we're all a lot richer than we were when the program started."

"And we made the bad things not happen," said Bugleg.

"What?" Telepop stared across the conference table at him.

"The, er, wars and things," Rossum explained for him.

"Well—but they did happen," said Roche. "Didn't they?"

"Yes, but not as expensively!" Freestone stated. "And that was the whole point of the business, you see?"

London, 2 July 2355

Victor was preoccupied.

He had been preoccupied for days. His rooms were crowded now with stacked crates, and if a Public Health Monitor were to burst in for an inspection at that particular moment, Victor would have a great deal of explaining to do.

What was in all those stacked crates? Dangerous and immoral contraband, though once it would have been described as Christmas cheer or gourmet delicacies, garnered patiently from Third World sovereignties over a period of two years. There were bottles of old port, dark as blood, in those crates, there were bottles of the most costly champagnes. Liqueurs. Pate full of truffles, tiny containers of caviar. Obscure herbs and spices, wonderfully potent. Pickled oysters and the pickled eggs of wild birds, honey garnered from opium poppies, jars of clotted cream. If it was rich, if it was delicious, if it was bad for a mortal to consume, it was probably in those crates.

The immorality didn't stop there. No, it went far beyond: for in a distant refrigeration locker, far above the sunny streets of Avalon, hung slaughtered and butchered animals, rotting on the hook to suitable tenderness for consumption. No Public Health Monitor could deal with this. He or she would be on his or her knees puking in the abattoir at the merest glance at all the bones and veins and muscles and slow-dripping nastiness . . . but to set aside the twenty-fourth century point of view for a moment, Victor had really bagged a lot of prime meat. Pheasants and grouse, a peacock, a wild boar, a sea turtle, a suckling pig and a calf, venison, and finally that ultimate martyr to humanity's wickedness: *a buffalo*. Could anything be more deliciously perverse than to serve forth roasted buffalo to immortals who had spent the ages rescuing creatures from extinction?

Even innocence was being summoned to this feast, even now summer fruit was sweetening in the quiet orchards of the interior, and vegetables flourishing on its irrigated terraces. Would all those artichokes and baby carrots blanch at the thought of the company they were shortly to keep?

Victor was too preoccupied to be amused by such a question. He was watching, with his flat green stare, as printed averies spooled out of his credenza.

Each label bore the same address, directing delivery to the Santa Catalina Island Preservancy Conference Center, Avalon, Republic of Santa Catalina.

He was watching the labels print out because he was undecided about something.

Before him on his desk was a card and matching envelope. He had purchased them centuries ago, kept them all this time sealed against age and dust. The envelope was plain ivory parchment. The card was decorated in its lower right-hand corner with a small painting of daffodils.

Victor was turning a calligraphy pen in his fingers, in a gesture of almost mortal nervousness. Click, click, click, the labels continued to print.

He set the pen down at last and his hand rose, involuntarily, to stroke his mustaches. Coming to himself with a start, he looked down at his hand; rose and hurried into the bathroom to wash. By the time he returned and sat down he seemed to have come to some kind of decision, for he picked up the pen and activated it. Peering down at the card, he wrote slowly and carefully.

Having read over what he had just written, Victor nodded and slipped the card into the envelope. He took out a modern Text Parcel envelope, addressed it, slipped the smaller envelope inside. He took a separate sheet of paper and wrote:

Ave et vale, Suleyman. These may well be my last words to you. I wonder if I might ask a favor, sir? Would you have the kindness to see that the enclosed card reaches Madame D'Arraignee? Assuming, of course, that you both survive the Silence.

PART V

CHAPTER 21

Out of the Hill

The slave was much better now, rational and calm; but he slept a great deal, waking only to swallow more of the vitamins and wash them down with water. Tiara grew lonely.

She curled up next to him and dreamed that they were in London, at Claridge's. It was all a great garden under the stars, like the one behind the shop in Knockdoul, but ever so much more grand. There were roses in the sky. There were stars in the grass. There was a vast holoscreen that towered up to the moon. Her slave was bending forward, smiling, offering her champagne in his cupped hands. There was a couple at the table next to theirs. Yes, the woman with her black eyes, the man so very tall—

"Sweetheart," a voice was saying. "Princess?"

She sat up in the darkness. She thought the slave was crying again, his voice was so strange. "What is it?" she demanded, a little crossly.

"Look," he told her. "Look at me."

He had drawn up both his legs! She shrieked and pounced on him, and they rocked back and forth together, hugging tight. "Now," he whispered, "we're so close to London I can smell the tarmac."

"Can we go now?" she begged. "After so many and so long years of dreaming, my honey love?"

"Soon," he gasped. "Must exercise! Get my muscles in tone. Learn to walk again. And we'll need clothes—what a pair of picturesque vagabonds we'd look just now, eh, a little girl in rags leading a blind beggar? Dear, dear, once we'd not have drawn a second glance from anybody, but not nowadays! Oh, they'd have us off the public highway and into a Hospital somewhere as soon as they noticed us. Not a good thing, for me or you."

"I'll steal clothes," she told him, kissing his cheek. "You shall be robed in whitest samite. I shall don the raiment of a great lady. We'll blaze along the great highways of the world like Antony and Cleopatra, and lesser creatures will die for jealousy that they're not us."

At first the slave could barely stand, tottered and fell over at the least wrong move; but practicing at last he got the trick of balance again. As the days went by he never fell at all, and how tall he was now! Tiara cleared a path through the bones for him so he could walk to and fro, finding his way by reciting verse and listening as the echo of his voice bounced back to him from the walls. They found that this worked better if there weren't so many dead men stacked there to muffle the sound.

Tiara dragged the bones out of the room entirely and farther down the old passageway, piling them up in a very old part of the hill, venturing deeper in the darkness than she'd ever gone before. In this way she found the ship.

It seemed to be a part of the wall first, silvery and cold, bulging out smooth. But as Tiara touched it, wondering, the Memory explained what it truly was. A few meters farther on she came upon the hatchway, irised panes of a pinky-purple steel. And here was a cunning little inset panel, and if she placed her hand just *here*—

Without a sound, the door unsqueezed itself. A gush of warm dry air wrapped around Tiara, prompting her to step across the threshold. She went inside, staring around. The Memory chattered loud suddenly, telling her all about the Getaways. This was what kin held in reserve, this was the safe last place where the big people couldn't come! This was the very ship in which famous Uncle Zingo had hunted, and at so long last caught, her own dear slave. Its name was *The Flee*.

Tiara wandered through it openmouthed, and the Memory put it right up there on a par with the *Argo* and Garuda and the ship of the Three Queens that bore Arthur to Avalon. What a beautiful shining place it was, and so clean, because the kin never lived in it for long; that wasn't safe. A few nights in flight, no harm, but stay in here a month or a year and the stupids would begin to bleed and die, the Uncles grow strange swollen things in their tender places. *The Flee* was both life and death. It was the greatest thing the kin had ever made.

Tiara backed away in awe, and retreated through the door. Her hand on the panel closed it up again.

She decided not to tell her slave, however. Whether this was because she was afraid it might set off another fit of crying and forgetting just when he was doing so well, or because some inborn command of secrecy silenced her, it was difficult to say.

Tiara was looking for trout in the little culvert under the bridge one fine moony night when she caught his smell, old Uncle Ratlin, and he caught hers, and she heard his pattering footfall along the bridge, and heard his chuckling up above her.

"Hello again, my juicy babe," he growled, and splash! He'd vaulted the side and shattered her starry pool, so that the moon and the trout fled. She bared her teeth at him.

"Varlet vile," she muttered. Oh dear oh dear; the culvert was at her back, and nowhere to run but down its darkness, or out before her into Uncle Ratlin's wide arms.

"Now, a kiss for your own old dear," he cackled. "My sweetlips, guess what's done! Eh? Go on, guess."

"You have finished and furnished my green hill?" she demanded, putting her nose in the air.

"O, no, my loveydovey. Better than that." Uncle Ratlin preened and strutted, ankle deep in the water. "It is accomplished! The Ruin, don't you know? Ratlin's Finest Death Assortment's been sent winging its way to the slaves, the cyborgs, the dreadful drones of the big people. Not three days—nay, not two!—and they'll all lie drowned in dreadful death, convulsed and blue. Let's celebrate!" He dropped his trousers.

Ice prickled all along Tiara's neck. She backed into the culvert.

"Y-you can take that to Bloody Barbie," she told him haughtily. "I'll none of you. Remember our bargain? I want my green hill! What care I for your goose-feather bed or your manly parts either, until that's done?"

But he waded closer, grinning. "Any day now," he promised her. "Come on, my little bed of roses-no-thorns. Uncle Ratlin's so weary of saggy silly old Quean Barbie and her tantrums. Any day now you might have your fine hill with its lace curtains, but you'll never get a sniff of it if you won't come cheer your dear uncle. The world's changing, my silvery sex kitten. The Ruin has come, and everything's possible now!"

"Is it indeed?" Tiara sniffed, retreating farther. "Well, let me tell you this—" And then she turned and slithered down the culvert, fast and frantic as a little eel, but the big eel came rippling after her.

Then it was all roots, and black slime and fumbling over ridged pipe, and the gasping harsh echoes filling the narrow space, and far ahead the tiny white window to make for, and her little heart pounded and the heroines cheered her on. WOULD SHE MAKE IT??? But his old fingers were around her ankle like a loop of wire as she burst at last into clean air and moonlight.

Uncle Ratlin pulled. She fell face-forward into black water and was writhing around, turning to bite him—

When the whole world exploded!

The huge thing squealed loud enough to wake the dead, it started back on sharp hooves and sank in the place where it had been quietly drinking; then advanced menacingly, murder in its little red eyes, and its black-bristled back was like a ridge of mountains against the moon.

Tiara and Uncle Ratlin froze, staring at it. "Oh shite," breathed Uncle Ratlin, which wasn't a very elegant thing to say at such a dramatic moment, but Tiara silently agreed with him.

Now with the presence of mind that made her a heroine of true distinction, Tiara moved her leg back, as though to retreat into Uncle Ratlin's clutches, and he slacked his tight hold on her heel, which she then booted hard in his old face, bash, so his lip split and he saw stars. In a dazzling second move she used the impetus of her kick to shoot forward like an apple seed spurted between finger and thumb, pop, under the onrushing monster and flying up the high bank on the far side.

And she heard, from the hazel branch where she'd lighted, she heard the deafening bang as the pig hit the mouth of the culvert and stuck there, working its shoulders as it tried to squeeze down into the darkness after Uncle Ratlin.

Tiara stayed up there the rest of the night, until the moon had set and the gray dawn was coming out of the east, and dewfall pearled on her bare skin. At first she sang little wild songs of triumph to congratulate herself, as the pig grunted and screamed after what it couldn't get. After a while it pulled out and trotted away, disgusted, and then Tiara fell silent. She thought of Uncle Ratlin perhaps waiting on the other side of the bridge; she thought of her slave waiting for her, wondering where she was. Worst of all was when she remembered what Uncle Ratlin had told her about the Ruin! Had it fallen yet? Had Suleyman gotten her slave's warning in time? She must tell her slave what she'd learned.

But she didn't dare come down until she was sure Uncle Ratlin had gone back to the hill, and that wasn't until the last stars had faded away and the terrible light was coming. No cool clouds to protect her from the fire of day this morning, no polarized goggles either. At last she slipped down from the hazel and ran home, making a green trail across the gray dew fields of high summer.

And it was already too late.

For even as she paused in the heather and looked around before slipping into the dark, the first of the agtrucks was roaring along the road from Knockdoul, and she saw the others behind it, two and three and four and five as the slave had taught her to count. What a lot of traffic for this country lane, wasn't it?

But blowing and blasting they came to a halt and settled just at the base of the hill, and Tiara had a panoramic view of what happened next.

It was just what the Memory had always said would happen, the towering figures in their armor piling out, running with weapons, out of sight round the flank of the hill. Tiara knew where they were going: to the main entrance, where perhaps Uncle Ratlin had just crawled home to bed.

With a quavering scream she scrambled inside and ran down the corridor, faster than ever she'd fled Uncle Ratlin or the pig, and leaped into the bone room and slammed the door after herself. "Princess?" Her slave raised his head where he'd been sitting in the dark, rocking himself back and forth in his worry. "What is it, child?"

She ran to him and flung her arms around his neck, trying to hide from the terror. He held her close and heard her blood thundering in her veins.

"What's happened?" he said. "You're frightened! We'll be all right—"

That was when the first of the explosions came, the dull *BOOM* that started the bone room door on its hinges. The slave was on his feet instantly, lifting Tiara with him. "What's that?" he demanded, in the clearest and sharpest voice with which she could ever remember him speaking. It nerved her enough to gulp back her sobs and cry: "The big men have come! They're breaking into the hill, they're killing us!"

There were shouts now, and thin high screaming, and the keening of weapons. Another explosion puffed air into the bone room, air with a faint acrid smoke that made Tiara choke and cough.

The slave's grip on her tightened. "You won't die," he promised her. "Oh, for two good arms—or my sight, for that matter. We've got to get out of here." He set her down. "Lead me, beloved. Point me the way we're to go. If you fall, I'll carry you. Now!"

She took his hand and they stumbled out into the corridor. There was a horror of red light in the tunnel, filling up the way toward the exit. There was a thunder of boots and shouting. Tiara whimpered and turned, dragging the slave with her deeper into the warren, back into the darkness and the ancient trash, back where the Memory told her to go, where Getaway was.

But they were pursuing, the dreadfuls, the *cyborgs* who somehow hadn't succumbed to the Ruin after all, who weren't dropping in the disruptor fields as they ought to, who were impossibly defeating her people again.

There it was, the smooth silver side of *The Flee*. Trembling she found the portal and smacked her little palm on the access panel, twice and three times, would it never open?

"Princess?" The slave was gasping. "Where are we? What is this?"

"It's *The Flee*," she cried in relief as the door unscrewed itself. "We'll be safe in here! Come, my own." She pulled the slave through after her even as the smoke came belching in strangling gusts, as big boots crashed, kicking aside bones and garbage to get through, and a dark shape was looming against the red light, so tall—

But here came more tumult and concussion from the other side of them as well, from within the ship. She heard screams and whinnyings from the stupids who were crowding in at a far door and a cawing voice that could only be Uncle Ratlin, and another voice nearly forgotten and dearly hated, countermanding Uncle Ratlin—

"Oh God Apollo, that's *him*—" babbled the slave. "Oh no, no, not again—"

The door was irising shut so slowly—

And the shouting from the tunnel resolved itself into one word, being shouted over and over by the big man who rushed forward through the redness, close enough now to be heard clearly:

"LEWIS!"

The slave's head came up and snapped around.

"What—"

The door was irising shut—

And Tiara saw what the slave could not, the lean black face raging, glimpsed only a second before the door sealed itself, as the voice yelled:

"LEWIS! IT'S LATIF!"

CHAPTER 22

Child Care in the Cyborg Family, Volume Six:
The Challenge of Psychological Development

It might be reasonably supposed that the cyborg child, with his naturally augmented intelligence, would be free of the complex neuroses developed by mortal children; yet such is far from the case. This is particularly noticeable if the child is the recipient of memory files from a previous state of being. Unresolved issues of anger, abandonment, or guilt— most particularly the latter—may confer an adult burden of emotion the young cyborg's psyche is incapable of easily integrating. As might be expected, the cyborg child will not resort to the rudimentary bad behaviour in which traumatised mortal children engage. He will develop far more colourful, imaginative, and complicated complexes with which to engage his concerned parents' attention.

At the Seaside

Turquoise blue lagoon and palm-shaded white sand, and, rising beyond the green trees, Paradise in progress. The nearly-completed mansion lifts pearly spires to the morning sunlight, defying any recognized architectural convention, but undeniably impressive. In the vast garden careful terraces have been built, and little fruit trees planted there. Roses are in their first bloom, along palm-shaded walks. In a meadow under the green mountain *Mays mendozaii* waves abundantly, quite refusing to produce lysine at the desired levels.

In a beach chair, Father—in white linen suit, with trousers perfectly pressed—makes notes on a text plaquette. Mother wears a light summer gown, sort of a Jane Austen number, and is leaning against his knees. Beside her, bowing deferential from the waist, a big horribly black-bearded image of a man (butler, perhaps? Father's regimental batman?) has just offered her a glass of champagne from the tray carried by his servounit. The Black Dyke

Mills Band wafts from a speaker, playing something sentimental scored for French horns.

The six-year-old twins wear matching white sailor suits. With buckets and spades, they are putting the finishing touches on a model, sculpted in sand, of the Tomb of Mausolus. Beyond them, above the tideline, are others of the seven wonders of the ancient world: the Pyramids. The Temple of Diana at Ephesus. The Lighthouse of Alexandria. The Temple of Zeus at Olympia. The Hanging Gardens of Babylon.

"That only leaves the Colossus of Rhodes," says Nicholas.

"I know," says Alec. "Let's build the harbor first."

The problem of keeping water in a scale model of the harbor at Rhodes—let alone water in a sandcastle's moat—presents no difficulty to the Cyborg Child; he merely lines it with sandwich paper under a thin layer of sand. Nicholas trudges back with a bucketful of water and fills the harbor. Boats are handily constructed from twigs and leaves, and given sandwich-paper sails.

"I don't think we can manage a Colossus," says Nicholas, surveying their handiwork.

Giggling, Alec rises from his hands and knees. "Yes, we can. Watch!" He tosses aside his hat, pulls off his clothes, and stands naked over the little harbor. "There!" Nicholas giggles too, somewhat shamefacedly.

"Now, watch this!" Alec runs over and finds a pair of dry twigs. Returning, he sets the two twigs together; his hands blur a moment in hyperfunction, and then there is a puff of smoke and a tiny flame. He leans down and carefully holds it to one of the leaf-and-twig boats, until it catches. "Oh, no! There's a fire in the galley! It's spreading to the triremes! It's only 282 BCE and Rhodes doesn't have a fire department! What'll we do?"

"You're not—"

"Apollo to the rescue!" says Alec, and, like Lemuel Gulliver, puts the fire out.

"Oh, that's childish," says Nicholas in disgust.

"Well, so what?" says Alec. "We happen to be children."

"But we were men," Nicholas says, looking sadly across at Mendoza.

"So I'm informed," says Alec. "That was then, and if I could remember anything about it I'm sure I'd be as bothered as you are, but the fact is, I don't. Yes, there was this guy named Alec Checkerfield once. Yes, he screwed up in his life, in some really awful way which I'm glad I don't remember. And then he died. Deadward killed him. Got what he deserved, probably. *I'm* somebody else, somebody new and improved."

Nicholas shakes his head. "Don't you remember the Library?"

"Nope! Nothing really much before that day I fell down the hill and hit my head on a rock," says Alec, studying the tiny harbor at his feet.

"Nobody believes that story, you know," says Nicholas.

"Yes, they do!" Alec's raised voice draws the attention of Edward and Mendoza, who turn to stare. He strikes a pose. "Hey, Deaddy, Mendoza, look! The Colossus of Rhodes!"

"Put your clothes back on at once," says Edward. Mendoza has hidden her face in her hands, shaking with laughter.

"See?" Alec steps into his underpants and pulls them up. "*They* thought I was funny. I'm a child. Deaddy and Mendoza love me, the Captain loves me, we have a family and this cool island to live on, and life is good. Why worry about anything else?"

"You have nightmares sometimes," says Nicholas.

"Don't remember 'em," says Alec, buttoning up his trousers. "Anyway, you get nightmares, too. Let's talk about *you*, Nicky. Why were you crying in the night? No, don't punch me; Deaddy will come over here and lecture you about the Cyborg Child being above temper tantrums. What's at the root of Nicholas Bell-Fairfax's neurosis?"

"I'm Nicholas Harpole!" Nicholas clenches his fists.

"Whatever. Why *were* you crying?"

"Because I had the dream again," says Nicholas.

"Ah! The dream with the Frankenstein symbolism," says Alec, as his fair tousled head emerges from the neck of his shirt. "And how does that make you feel, Nicky?"

"It wasn't Victor Frankenstein, you knave," says Nicholas. "It wasn't. I don't know who he was, except he was the one who killed his own garden. He killed everything that touched him."

"Sounds like Jehovah to me," says Alec cheerily, sitting down to pull on his stockings and boots.

"Stop it," says Nicholas. He turns and stares out at the sea. It is a serene and warm tropical sea, but he remembers the black frozen ocean from his dream, the white waste and the broken boats of all who had come before him to that silent place. He sees again the dead men frozen on their knees, in unanswered prayer, mocked by the wind singing in frozen shrouds and sheets, their masts toppled by the stars they'd crossed.

Alec leaps to his feet, frightened by the look in Nicholas's eyes. "I'm bored!" he announces, and races down to the water's edge and begins to dance back and forth. "Up and down, up and down, I will lead them up and down, I am feared in field and town! Goblin! Lead them up and down!"

But they are spirits of another sort. This is their immortal family life, in all its bittersweet strangeness, for all its charm and sunlight never free of the possibility of heartbreak. You might mistake them for mortals. Except . . .

. . . The careful observer may notice a strange play of light around the man and the woman, a shimmer or flicker at the edges, as though they are not quite firmly *there* in the moment the shutters clicked to frame this postcard. This is because they once stepped away from Time into Eternity, and stepped back again. If they are wise, they will not delay too long before returning, and taking the children this time: a sensible precaution, after all, when living happily ever after.

Extract from the Journal of the Botanist Mendoza: At Villa Bell-Fairfax

We hardly ever fight anymore.

Well, not real fights where Edward thunders and I scream back at him. Minor disagreements, yes. About furnishing the house, for example, now that it's finally finished.

I myself don't see why Edward's Victorian notions of good taste should prevail in household furnishing, clothing, and every other detail of our lives. He is infuriatingly arrogant still, sublimely certain that though the Almighty (who doesn't exist, after all) may have created a flawed universe, by God the domestic arrangements of Edward Alton Bell-Fairfax are perfect and not to be questioned. Edward is Always Right.

But, having said that—he usually is right. And has such a strength of heart I think he could hold back both wind and tide, bear the Earth on his shoulder. Is marriage like this for mortals, this continually unfolding mystery that is the beloved? I love in him even what maddens me about him. And if I am by no means so wise and glamorous an immortal creature as he once thought me, well, he loves me anyway; and that's some consolation for self-knowledge.

We live together in so very much more than a cottage by the sea. The absurd house rises on its high green lawn above the bay, with its immaculate garden we have labored in together. He has made me go through gardening catalogues with him, before timewalking sidelong into 1622 or 1913 for purchases. The debate is endless. Shall we put in *Zomerschoon* tulips, or *Wapen van Leidens*? Roman Blue hyacinths, or Lord Balfours? Seagull daffodils, or *N. hispanicus Maximus*? And if it's quite a change for Edward Alton Bell-Fairfax, R.N. (Retired), it's no less so for me; Botany drone that I was, I don't think I ever planted anything so unimportant as a *flower* once, in all the ages I belonged to Dr. Zeus. We grope after salvation, both of us.

He hasn't brought up the subject of Dr. Zeus's overthrow in quite a few years, let alone his plans for Ruling the World. He's been too busy buying furniture.

Edward now has what he feels is a tastefully furnished study, with temporally-imported walnut paneling and a big chair where he can sit and smoke his temporally-imported Cuban cigars, and a big desk/console combination where he can sit and work on *Child Care in the Cyborg Family* while listening to his interminably heroic brass band music. And I have a solarium, even more cluttered with topiary than my botany lab on the ship was after Edward got through with it, and it's beautiful, of course, with delicate arched ceilings and stained glass and ivy-patterned wrought iron furniture, but I do feel sometimes as though I'm trapped in a perpetual game of Clue.

I have to confess I quite like our bedroom. Clean lines, breathtaking ocean view from the windows, and the immense saltwater tanks full of vividly colored tropical fish aren't too distracting at intimate moments. A bed of truly Olympian proportions, suitable for absolutely any conjugal pastime that can be imagined. We know, because Nicholas and Alec have their own room at last!

Edward mixes interior styles and periods with reckless abandon, so there was no reason (in his godlike mind) why the boys' room shouldn't be all fitted up like a pirate ship, too, though it's a bit quaint compared to Alec's bachelor fantasy on board the *Captain Morgan*. Portholes, lots of brass and teak, a pretend forecastle with built-in bunkbeds carved with the names ALEC and NICHOLAS. A real bookcase with honest-to-God books, first editions of Captain Marryat's oeuvre and other Boys' Own Ripping Yarns that Edward surmised they might enjoy.

Alec enjoys them, certainly. Nicholas prefers to practice on his mandolin. He decided he wanted one, and it took an unbearable amount of arguing to get it for him; not that Edward wouldn't get him one, but took forever to understand that the Cyborg Child, who *ought* to be capable of playing any instrument on earth with preprogrammed ease, might want to plunk along like a mere mortal.

And, of course, once His Godship had established that it was, in fact, laudable and proper that the boy should improve himself by the discipline of music, he went off to Vienna 1800 and came back with not only a mandolin but a violin, viola, cello, lute, and guitar, and set up a schedule by which Nicholas will master each in turn.

And, of course, Nicholas thought he could just pick up the mandolin and play it effortlessly, as he did when he was a mortal in 1555; and he couldn't. His memory knew how to play, but his little fingers had to learn all over again. He took the mandolin off to the vast echoing music room, and sat alone in there for hours, struggling forlornly to play chords.

I heard him crying and got from my kitchen garden very nearly to the door of the music room in 2.6 seconds before Edward caught up with me and pulled me back. I am afraid I kicked Edward pretty hard, but he pointed out that no boy wants to be embarrassed by female sympathy at difficult moments, and never having been a boy I had to concede his point.

So Nicholas struggles on. Alec is quite another case altogether.

I have sweated blood for years over that bump on his little head. No scan ever revealed any serious damage, nothing permanent; and yet he still insists he can't remember the life he once lived. Sir Henry's consoling words to me: *Haaar, now, dearie, he's only lying. Don't let it trouble you none. All boys lie, and my boy ain't no exception.*

And, never having been a boy, I had to concede his point, too.

CHAPTER 23

Child Care in the Cyborg Family, Volume Ten:
The Awkward Years

. . . above all, patience is required. The youthful cyborg sees, as it were, through a magnifying lens each single fault or flaw in his parent. He is quick to catch any omission or inconsistency in his elders, and will point out parental errors, be they never so trivial, with immoderate smugness. This behaviour would seem at odds with his superior intellect; but it must be remembered that, however widely this young eagle stretches his wings, he remains at heart a child, as vulnerable to self-doubt and uncertainty as any mortal youth. It is necessary for the cyborg parent to be mindful of this, and resist the temptation to respond to provocation. Rather, he must strive to respond with dignity and forbearance.

As treehouses go, it is luxurious indeed, though nothing on the order of the mansion on the hillside below.

Granted, it's made of a bioengineered plant substance that enables it to adapt to the branches of the vast mahogany tree wherein it is securely nested, and it does connect to the ground via an ingeniously designed spiral stair, leading up from the palisaded blockhouse below; but it is walled with railings and woven matting, and its roof is the canopy of leaves. Through them a flag-mast protrudes, flying a defiant little Jolly Roger.

Nicholas is seated on the deck, with a cello. Before him is a music stand and score; but he has his eyes closed, scowling as he feels out the melancholy tune through the bow and his fingers. He would appear to be about ten years old, coltish now, wearing blue trunks and vest in accordance with Edward's notions of sea-bathing propriety.

He finds the note he sought and draws it out, a resonant sigh of lament;

until his concentration is broken by an abrupt *boom* and the flight of birds from all the greenery within a mile's radius. There follows a whoop of triumph from below. A moment later Alec comes scrambling up the staircase, closely followed by Flint.

"Nick! Nick, you should have seen!"

"I heard," says Nicholas.

"Yes, well. It was brilliant! The black powder worked like anything. So did the stone ball. *Pow!* Hit the big boulder across the gulley and just shattered into atoms. And you said I hadn't got the mixture right!"

"You weren't supposed to try it until Edward was there to supervise," says Nicholas.

Aw, now, I wouldn't let my boy do nothing dangerous, says the Captain from Flint's speaker. *I done all the loading and packing, and made him get well ahind the tree trunk.*

"Don't tell him that!" says Alec indignantly. "*I* lit the slow match, anyway."

Nicholas shakes his head and picks up his bow again.

"Oh, leave the stupid cello," says Alec. "Let's go do something. Maybe the grapes are ripe. We could go see. We could go ride the dolphins. Or have a race over the treetops."

Nicholas turns the page, ignoring him, and settles down to play.

"Or we could go turn over rocks and see if God is hiding under one," says Alec slyly. Nicholas drops the bow and turns to him, fists clenched.

Now then, son, that was mean. You apologize to Nick.

"I apologize," says Alec. "Really."

Nicholas looks mulishly stubborn, turns away.

Come on now, lad. Alec said he were sorry. Talk to him.

"I'll crack thy crown, for mocking me," mutters Nicholas.

"Idiom, Nicholas, if you please," says Alec, in Edward's voice. "You're no longer a Tudor savage, after all." Nicholas swings back with the light of rage in his eyes.

Belay that! The Captain maneuvers Flint between them. *The last thing the missus would want's to come back from her nice holiday to find the two of ye whimpering with blacked eyes and bloody noses. A fine thing that'd be!*

"Maybe it would make your *amnesia* go away," says Nicholas. He turns and launches himself into the branches above the platform, and climbs up into the sunlight and the wind.

"That wasn't very godly," Alec calls up to him.

"And what has God to do with me?" Nicholas shouts back. "No voices speak to *me* out of any burning bush. No word at all. Hideous vacancy, monstrous indifference, and a senseless universe!"

"Well," says Alec cautiously, "I would think that was a *good* thing. Shouldn't you have grown out of this by now? What do you want meaning in the universe for, anyway? Nothing means anything! We're just here to go along for the adventure."

"There speaks the voice of the twenty-fourth century," says Nicholas. "Purposeless and pointless."

"Well, so what?" says Alec. "Why do I have to have a purpose? They're dangerous things. Look at that Alec Checkerfield, since you keep bringing him up. I don't personally remember, of course, but as far as I can tell he thought he ought to change the world. If he'd just relaxed on his party ship and stayed drunk, he'd never hurt anyone. Instead . . ."

"You know what happened," says Nicholas, peering down at him through the waving leaves.

"A lot of really awful things," says Alec, and scrambles up into the boughs after him. "Or so I would guess. But that was somebody else. And here we are, and isn't this enough? We've got the Captain and Deadward and . . . and . . ."

"Rose," says Nicholas. "Except that we haven't got her."

"Yes, we do!" says Alec desperately. "She's with us all the time and she loves us and she forgives us and, and kisses us and . . . supplies all the psychological stuff that, for example, that Checkerfield guy never had from his mother. She tucks us in at night."

"Yes," says Nicholas. "And then she goes away to Edward. And don't bother to deny how that makes *you* feel. I can hear a lot more in that upper bunk than you think I can."

Alec goes pale.

Now, Nick, let him alone.

"You may not remember what it was to be a man," says Nicholas. "But I do. One day, we'll be men again. And what will happen then?"

"Shut up," says Alec.

"I'll tell you: nothing," says Nicholas wretchedly. "Once I loved a girl in a green garden . . . but we will never dance that particular dance again."

"You read her journal!" says Alec, outraged. "Mr. Righteousness went behind her back and—"

"—Did just as little Alec had done, or else he wouldn't recognize the quote," says Nicholas. Alec glares at him and finally looks away.

"This is creepy. We're only children. Why worry about all this now? It's too Freudian. Anyway, it'll all turn out all right, because as soon as our heads are permabonded or whatever, Deaddy will let us escape out of linear time, and that'll be great! Mendoza writes about it like it's some kind of ultimate orgasm or something. So we won't miss anything. And we'll all live happily ever after. So there."

"Haven't you forgotten something?"

"Yes. Tons of stuff."

"The Cyborg Child," intones Nicholas, perfectly mimicking Edward's voice, *"with his superior cognitive powers, and unique perspective that will better enable him to fulfill what one might almost call his* divine *purpose as he takes his place in the immortal universe!* Edward has a purpose for us. Ruling the world, I assume."

"He can't," says Alec, aghast. "That's what villains do! Deadward's different now. He looks after us—and he loves Mendoza and makes her happy—besides, he must know it's *wrong* to run other people's lives. It never works out. Even if you mean well, something always goes horribly wrong, and then—then you're guilty again, and—"

There is a flash in midair, far out, and a certain boiling in the water of the lagoon far below.

They're home, lads!

Alec winks out, and Nicholas winks out too, and Flint goes slowly clanking down the spiral stair. A second later the boys arrive at the landing pier, just as the *Captain Morgan* is retracting her storm bottle and opening out her masts.

"There they are," cries Mendoza, emerging from the wheelhouse. "There are my babies. Hello! Oh, I've missed you. It feels so miserably awkward traveling with all this encumbrance now but we did bring back the loveliest things and, Alec, I've got some signed first editions for you! We met Robert Louis Stevenson again, can you imagine? If I don't get out of this thing immediately I'm going to explode." Presumably she is referring to the whalebone corset she is wearing under her circa 1885 travel ensemble.

The gangplank extends, the boys run up it, and Mendoza opens her arms and hugs them together, kissing them. Edward is stepping down from the quarterdeck, loosening his stiff collar. He removes his gloves and top hat, looks down at the boys sternly. "Were you quarreling?" he inquires.

"Not really," says Alec, not meeting his eyes. "I was only pulling Nicky's chain a little . . ."

"And I pulled his," says Nicholas.

"Fair enough," replies Edward. He hands Alec his walking stick, and sets his hat on Nicholas's head. "There now. I'll leave the two of you to oversee getting the cargo unloaded. Ten cases of champagne and a consignment of port that ought to be first-rate in a linear decade or two. Some rather fine chairs as well."

"And some gorgeous paintings, a Van Gogh, poor little man but what a find!—and we got four wonderful Turkish carpets—" adds Mendoza, drawing out the long hatpin and removing her hat. "But I have got to get out of these clothes, Edward. Next time let's go to the twenty-first century, there's no style whatever but at least there are no foundation garments either, which is certainly a fair tradeoff, wouldn't you say?"

Alec goes pale with longing as she begins to unbutton. Edward notices and takes Mendoza's arm in his. "Let's go up to the house, my dear. The boys can manage nicely."

"Of course they can, they're getting so big," Mendoza remarks, as they proceed down the gangplank. Then she turns back to shout:

"Oh, and Nicholas—you look marvelous in the hat, darling! There're four little *Quercus lobata* in pots in the botany cabin. And some rosebushes, and garden statuary from Greece, so be please be careful—"

"They will," says Edward, and he pulls her away and they proceed, arm in arm, across the lawn, and up the long balustraded walk through the garden. "Now, my love, what about a bath?"

"Hmmm." Mendoza smiles dreamily.

Edward sits behind his great desk, leaning back in his chair. He would appear to be gazing out the window at the solarium, through whose panes Mendoza can be glimpsed going to and fro over trays of *Mays mendozaii*, taking samples. On one level of his consciousness, he is indeed watching her; most of his attention, however, is taken up in reviewing a certain file he has accessed. It contains meticulously arranged and cross-referenced data, a relentless barrage of images, voices, facts. He began compiling it the day the boys made their reentry into the world.

He sees a long procession of disturbingly similar faces, from every period in history and some clearly from prehistory. Bohemund Guiscard, whose subtly inhuman quality so fascinated and repelled the Byzantine emperor's daughter. Rasputin's face, with its high wide cheekbones and haunting silver eyes. Rolf Chapman, the man who founded the Church of God-A, his brooding rawboned face on a thousand police updates in the twenty-second century. Churchmen, politicians. Newspaper publishers and actors and scholars.

Many of them had died violently. Some had died mysteriously, with bodies that went missing afterward. Few had made it into the front ranks of history, yet every one had triggered a chain of events leading to massive changes for humanity. A certain man, with the absolute conviction of his beliefs and remarkable powers of persuasion, in a certain place at a certain crucial moment in time.

And every one of them with certain facial features, to a greater or lesser degree but all, undeniably, resembling those of the old Enforcers. Edward hears a voice like liquid gold, crying out words Joseph had written for a Christmas masque long ago: *I am a spirit that does not rest. Age after age I come again, to test men's hearts . . .*

"Edward?" says the same voice now. Edward turns in his chair and sees Nicholas standing in the doorway of his study. "Edward, I have a question."

"Have you finished your hyperfunction training?" Edward asks, noting that the boy is still wearing his exercise singlet.

"Yes. I was just going to bathe. Edward, do you think we have souls?"

Edward looks at him askance. "In a poetical sense, I suppose. Certainly an essential life force."

"I don't mean spirits," says Nicholas. "I mean *souls*. They're not the same thing."

"You're speaking theologically, then. You've had your nightmare again, haven't you?" says Edward. Nicholas frowns, lowers his eyes.

"I dreamed I saw myself in a glass, and the word DEATH was written on my forehead," he says. Edward, with the images from his private file still vivid in his mind, feels a twinge of unease. But he makes a dismissive gesture.

"More symbolism. Come here, son."

Nicholas steps forward unwillingly. Edward takes the boy's face in his hands, pushing back his lank hair. He draws his thumb across Nicholas's brow. "There! The old word's obliterated. We'll write a new one." With his forefinger he traces out the word TRUTH. "You see? By an act of will, we change ourselves."

"We are still unnatural things," says Nicholas.

"Ha! Nature, my boy, is overrated. There's no peaceable kingdom in the natural world; every horror of appetite is practiced there. The lion looks with no shame on the lamb he slaughters. The ape eats his neighbor's infant alive. Every vile thing man has done, is done no less by his fellow beasts. We alone have the intellect to feel shame for what we do. We cry out against the slaughter, and we resolve to change. Under the cold stars that look down and say nothing, we are the only thing that can."

"But are we even men?" says Nicholas.

"We are changed men," says Edward. "The product of evolution, even as were the men who created us."

Nicholas narrows his eyes, thinking hard.

". . . How if this were the purpose of evolution?" he says. "A conscience in the darkness? A vein of gold in the clay?"

"*We* make the purpose, my boy," says Edward. Nicholas's eyes have brightened, he goes on breathlessly:

"Or if the progress of all Time's a lie—if Eternity is the only truth—what if Creation goes on apace, and all time is *now*? And dust is still rising into the image of God, forming but not formed yet, waiting for its soul? Is this our purpose?"

Edward gazes at him, wondering. He shrugs. "What made me had no purpose. But, by God, I have one! And that's enough for me. Go on now, boy; bathe and dress for dinner."

Mendoza leads a procession up the side of the mountain. She carries odds and ends of marble in a basket, fresh from a stonecutter's yard in ancient Greece. Nicholas follows, carefully bearing a white rosebush with its roots wrapped in sacking. After him crawls Flint, laden down with more potted plants, statuary, and gardening tools.

They follow the old trail high along the shoulder of the mountain, whose scars have been long since repaired with netting and new plantings. They continue over the replacement bridge, beneath which the bright stream still courses down to its dark pool, far below. Farther along the trail, farther up, and they come to a shaded ravine, a green place close to an overhang where another stream shoots down in a white veil, and clouds weep. Some work has been done here already, stone walls shoring up a little terrace.

"Look at the way those creepers have grown back," Mendoza frets. "If only there were a way to keep the garden out of linear time, too." Her eyes light with speculation. "I wonder if there *is* a way?"

"But then, nothing would ever bloom," says Nicholas, setting down the rosebush.

"Well, but you could arrange it so that things would, you see?" says Mendoza. "Currents and eddies of time through the whole garden, like water directed in conduits. I really must ask the señor about it. Fruit and blossom on one branch. Just like the legends about Paradise, eh?"

Nicholas can see exactly how it might be done, but he merely takes up a shovel and digs a hole big enough for the rose, as she unwraps its root ball and shakes out the branches. They plant the bush and water it well, making several trips to the falls. Then they work together, setting up a marble bench, building a little platform at the back of the terrace. Mendoza pulls out a bag of white hyacinth bulbs. "We'll put these along the front, where the drainage is better," she says.

They kneel together, planting flowers. "This reminds me of England," says Nicholas quietly. "In old Iden's garden."

"I suppose it might," she says, unable to keep a slight tremble out of her voice. "You remember that, do you?"

"I remember everything," says Nicholas. "The taller I grow, the more clear the memory becomes."

She lays aside her trowel, stares distracted at the bulb she had been about to plant. Green spikelets appear at its top, push outward and become leaves; up rises a stem with its closed buds. "Oh, dear," she says, and sets it down. "Do you hate Edward, for what happened?"

"I did once," says Nicholas. "I hated myself, too. I remember the fire that burned my pride to ashes." He looks up at her. "But here I am, in this paradise now; and you're here. There is no one to blame anymore, Rose."

She gazes into his eyes. "You're still my Nicholas," she says.

"Do you love me?"

"Always," she says.

"Then I'm content," he says, and takes up the bulb and sets it in the earth. The white flowers open. Mendoza sighs.

"Do you think Alec will ever remember?"

"Alec remembers," says Nicholas, firmly. "He just lies about it."

"Well, that's a relief," says Mendoza. "I suppose." She rises to her feet and looks around. "Now, where's that Apollo, or Helios, or whichever solar divinity he is? Ah."

She lifts the little statue to the platform they have built. He's slightly battered; the rays of his sun-halo have been broken. He looks neither godlike nor all-wise, but appeals to her, for some reason. Nicholas rises too, and dusts his hands.

"What do you think?" Mendoza asks. "Is it too wet up here for cypress to thrive? Or rosemary?"

"Rosemary?" Nicholas looks from her to the little statue. "For remembrance. This is a memorial," he realizes.

"I suppose it is," Mendoza admits. "I made this place for Lewis. Another immortal. He was my friend."

"Being immortal, he cannot die and require a funerary shrine," Nicholas points out.

"No . . ." Mendoza considers the statue. Her smile has faded. "But . . . he had such a desperate look in his eyes, the last time I saw him. Something had gone terribly wrong. I never learned what it was. I wish . . ."

Nicholas puts his arm around her. "Don't fear for him," he says. "All must be well, in the end."

"So I keep telling myself," says Mendoza.

Nicholas, gazing steadily at her face, says: "You must have loved him."

"Yes," says Mendoza. "As a matter of fact, I loved him very much."

Extract from the Journal of the Botanist Mendoza:
Dark Water

My, I haven't kept up with this much lately. Haven't *written* a line since before the boys were born; all that business with the pen and ink seems sort of an adolescent affectation these days. Much easier just to dictate, especially when I'm busy.

I don't suppose I'd have the quiet moment now, except that the boys are both in bed in the infirmary of our vast South Seas palace, recuperating from having their support packages and intracranial fields installed. Yes; they're at last physically mature enough for the final step in their journey toward immortality.

But there they lie, poor things, pale and semiconscious. Flint crouches by Alec's bed, and if a servounit were able to wring its hands nervously, I'm sure it would be doing just that. Edward and I are taking turns sitting between the boys to spoon-feed water or soup, just as we did when they were tiny, or stroke away cold sweat with a wet cloth. They're big strapping fellows now, much taller than I am, gaining on old Edward at last. Cherubs no longer; angels with blazing wings. What a long time we've worked in harness together to produce them, my husband and I.

Oh, Nicholas, don't cry! Here's my hand . . .

It's odd how little I remembered this from my own teens, but it's true: the immortality process *hurts*. Maybe I blocked memories of the trauma. I'm nearly as good as Joseph was at shutting out things I don't want to think about. I suppose I could have had a worse legacy from the slimy little bastard, if we inherit anything from our parents-in-immortality.

Now and then, strangely, I find myself missing him. God knows why. I wish he could know how things turned out for me. I wish he could have seen the children.

I suppose I ought to get over hating Joseph. Adolescent anger is all very well, but . . . no, actually, it isn't all very well. It's particularly distressing in Alec.

He was the sunniest child, and he seemed to adore Edward-as-paterfamilias, but the instant he hit puberty . . . Edward is Never Right. At the moment, Edward's crime is that he wants to wait at least two more years linear before showing the boys how to step through time. Shall we replay the latest ghastly scene?

"But you promised!" Alec raved.

"I did nothing of the kind," said Edward. "I told you I'd teach you when you were ready, which you most certainly are not." He took a bite of toast and had a sip of tea. All he needed was a copy of the London *Times* to complete the picture of patriarchal imperturbability. Alec glared at him, his pale eyes glittering. "And you can take that look off your face, boy, or you'll be polishing the silver all next week."

"I can't believe this. We're only growing older, you know! What the bloody hell are you waiting for, Dead?" Alec cried.

"Some sign of maturity," Edward said. "Inner discipline. Wisdom. Which you are scarcely displaying at the present moment, I might add."

"Oo, yeah, demerits to Apeman Alec again," said Alec bitterly. "He never does anything right, does he? But I suppose Nicky meets your criteria right now. He's perfect, after all."

"Darling, Nicholas has to wait, too," I pointed out.

"That's true," said Nicholas, who had been silent up until this moment, following the action with his eyes like a spectator at a tennis match.

Edward had another sip of his tea, cleared his throat and said: "Your impatience is, of course, the direct result of your life in the twenty-fourth century, an Age of Technology obsessed with personal entitlement and a perpetual selfish childhood."

"Oh, not that speech again," Alec moaned, putting his hands over his ears. "That was the *other* me. Dead Checkerfield. I'm somebody else, I'm new, I'm improved, I haven't done any of the stupid rotten things he did! Or that *you* did. Let's look at *your* famous career a moment, shall we, Deadward? Assassinations, arson, espionage, theft, anything the Gentlemen's Speculative Society AKA Dr. Zeus Incorporated told you to do! And you never once questioned them, did you?" He turned and stormed out of the breakfast room.

Aw, now, son, you ain't being fair! said Sir Henry, as Flint scuttled after him.

"He hath a melancholic fit coming on," said Nicholas.

"Idiom, please, Nicholas," said Edward.

Nicholas stiffened. He got his mule-face look. "Okay, Dead," he said testily. Edward just chuckled and finished his tea. Nicholas left the room. A moment later we heard the music room door slam, and then the Stradivarius shrieking through Nicholas's arrangement of Bach's *Toccata and Fugue*. Thank God the boy hasn't got an electric guitar. I sighed.

"Señor—was that necessary? Let him have his own identity. And, let him wear black if he wants to, eh?"

"But that would hardly be fair to Alec," Edward pointed out. "He'd then demand the right to wear those ghastly Hawaiian shirts, and he'd be justified. If they can't endure having their wills balked in petty matters like these, now, how much harder will they find it later on? They will benefit from having to earn the privileges of manhood."

"But they were men," I said.

"But they will be much more," said Edward. "And I want them ready for it. This is a deadly dangerous business, after all."

"It won't be nearly as dangerous once the immortality process is finished," I said.

"I didn't mean dangerous for them," said Edward slowly. He gave me a thoughtful look and then held out his hand. "Let's go for a walk, my love."

We went out of our grand house and down through the splendid garden we built together, past the roses of which Edward is so proud, across the emerald lawns where Bully Hayes paused in mowing to nod to us. Down the stone steps we laid in place ourselves, through my little orchards and the pergola of grapevines; down to the beach at last.

I thought we'd go out on the pier, but Edward turned in the other direction and led me along the shore. Along the glass-smooth sand, between the white combers and the margin of scattered and broken shells, we walked. After a mile or so, Edward pointed up a green gorge that cut through the cliffs above us. It was the place we'd fallen, on that long-ago day when Alec struck his little head.

No gigantic slide now, thanks to years of careful work; only the sedate little stream dropping from rock to mossy rock, vanishing at last into the grotto overgrown by the big tiare bush. We left the beach and climbed up over the boulders, and at the grotto Edward parted the branches so I could step through.

"It makes a charming bridal bower, don't you think?" he said, ducking his head to follow me in. White flowers floated on the pool, perfumed the air.

"It's certainly private," I said. Privacy has become something of an issue lately.

We undressed each other. I felt oddly shy, drawing out my hairpins, letting my hair down. Edward stepped into the dark pool, and held out his arms to me. I went to him and in a breathless, scrambling moment we slid together, one flesh, and he opened my mouth with his own as we plunged down, through the white flowers and the black water.

Insane ecstasy, the splash of ice and the heat of his body. He sent his mind into mine and I thought, *Oh, we'll never come up again; we've found the perfect center of creation.*

Descending, descending in the still water, how far down? I heard the high notes of a violin being played, and light flared behind my eyes. I saw another life, the one I might have lived in some other Spain, where a little girl never fell into the hands of dubious strangers or the Inquisition. Bright and detailed as film, the brief lifetime unspooled itself for my consideration: the girl grew up and made her way to England somehow, and became the wife of a somewhat less outspoken young vicar named Nicholas Harpole. Forty years of wedded bliss in a thatched cottage, Sabbath sermons, living perhaps long enough to see a Shakespeare play. Then sunlight in the green churchyard, and quiet dust . . .

We broke the surface and gasped for air, with shuddering pleasure. I heard the sea roaring. Edward tightened his grip and dove again, bearing me with him, and the roar grew louder. I saw white sails above a blue sea, brilliant sunlight. I saw an England where Commander Bell-Fairfax forbore to strike a senior officer, and came home a hero instead, and married a Spanish girl he met, perhaps in Gibraltar, where they settled down. Fifty years, perhaps, of respectability, thrifty life on an officer's half-pay, a little stone house kept neat as a pin; then one monument carved with names and dates, loving husband, beloved wife.

Up into the air again! I couldn't get my breath; it didn't matter. We were sinking together in the dark water but it was warm now, and I heard laughter. I saw a fantastic Eurospain as carefree as a travel poster, where Alec Checkerfield went to party instead of going to Mars, and there during Purim carnival met a girl, and dared to try his luck at marriage a third time, and the third time was the charm. Dance clubs, endless serene cruises, a fashionable address in London. Would they have had sixty years, this life? Seventy? The end might have come quickly, or it might have lingered out in hospital corridors, but the end result the same: white ashes scattered on the seafoam, sinking into blue . . .

But we were rising. We shot up through the surface and I pulled my mouth free from Edward's, staring to see him for a moment with a receding hairline, with a trace of pot belly and collar size expanded regally. And I? Why, I'd squared out and thickened like a block of stone, a sack of wheat. My mortal parents were peasants, for all that *hijo del godo* nonsense; genetics would have caught up with me in middle age, clearly, undeniable as the white streaks in my hair.

The illusion faded, with the last shivering afterburn of rapture, and then Edward was lifting me from the water. I clung to him, leaning on his chest in exhaustion. We lay gasping together a long moment, before he pulled himself up into a sitting position, taking me with him. He tilted my chin up to look into my eyes.

"There now," he said. "You've had the mortal lives, and the deaths, you longed for. An end to missed chances, my love."

"You showed me this because things are going to change soon, aren't they?"

"Yes," he said. "Things are going to change a great deal, I think."

We rose, a little unsteadily, and got dressed again. Walking back along the beach, with the sunlight warming us, he showed me a series of somber images: men, better or lesser known, on whom the flow of human history had broken and been diverted into new courses. There was some indefinable similarity to all their faces. A certain alignment of features . . .

But what were they all? I wondered. And I saw, briefly, something inexplicable: an old greened bronze statue, with empty-socketed eyes.

Something the Company has kept concealed even from itself, or its mortal masters would have been horrified, was the somber answer. *Big changelings left in human cradles, scythe-bearing scarecrows in the fields of human life. We walked before and cut down the corn you Preservers gathered.*

"Many of them were good and honorable men," Edward explained aloud. "But they were, all, used to precipitate disasters for the Company's benefit. The boys and I are unique, in our design. We were created with potential none of the previous attempts had, since they weren't Recombinants. The designation I would use is *Tempters.*"

I said nothing, appalled.

"And you do see," he said gently, "that I have learned something at last. Don't you, my dear? I must never rule the mortals."

"But—who'll defeat the Company, on the last day?" I said, taking his hand. "You know the truth about yourself now. And you've redeemed yourself!"

"No," said Edward. "I've healed myself. We must find a greater purpose than that for which we were made." He turned to look up at our high house, shining there in the sunlight. "Redemption will have to wait until the end. The outcome will, I think, depend on what sort of men we've formed from our clay."

So there it is.

How much of this did Joseph know? Is that why he's always hated my own true love?

Alec is moaning, his poor nose hurts—who would have thought their noses would break, at that crucial spot, *again?*—and Edward is leaning close, applying a cold compress and saying something to him in a low and soothing voice.

And look at my Nicholas lying there, composed as a statue of a knight on a tomb and so pale, especially when he first wakes up. You're in a little pain now, sweetheart, but it'll pass soon. Once, in his agony as the fire took him, the man cried out to me: *Thou art a spirit, and wilt thou not come back to the love of God?*

I don't know if I'll ever be able to come back to loving your dreadful God, Nicholas. But I have at least come back to the love of humanity, which has been quite a journey for me. Perhaps He'll give me points for effort, do you think?

CHAPTER 24

8 July 2355

The hammer was descending, the bell already vibrating with the anticipated strike . . . as, in a marvel of logistical organization, fleets of special delivery agcraft went out all over the globe to deliver boxes of chocolates to every Central HQ all over the world very nearly simultaneously.

Suleyman in the Fez office got his, and Shen in the Xi'an office got his, and Van Drouten in the Amsterdam office got hers, and Stendec in the Rio office got hers, and Houbert in the Monaco office got his too, as did Flamel in the Paris office, and so did Arminius in the Petrograd office, and Quintilius at San Simeon got a special delivery. Even Marmon, up in the Luna office, got his in a timely fashion, and that alone should have tipped them all off that the world was about to end.

And the clock struck.

Fez

Suleyman was waiting.

He was good at waiting; had long ago learned to disengage his primary consciousness to watch as the big wheels turned, as the grains of sand fell. Just at the moment he was reviewing the possible events of the next twenty-four hours, calculating event vectors as he idly moved the game pieces around on the board.

It was easiest to visualize it as a shatrang problem in the style of the older game, when there were four sides to a playing field. The west's Sultan was on the point of flight into his corner, walling himself in with pawns. The Rukh and Elephant had come from the east and north, respectively, and were poised for their final moves. Across the board in the south, the Vizier waited. There were infinite variables—especially since Suleyman had the unpleasant feeling there were at least two more sides of the board than rational geometry permitted him to see, and far too many pawns—but checkmate was inevitable. The only question left was, in how many moves?

The local parcel delivery van was trundling its way down the street. Suleyman recognized the plaintive roar of its particular agmotor, picked up clearly the annoyance of the mortal driver at being sent out in the heat of the day. The van pulled up before Suleyman's house, backed and filled, settled heavily to the pavement when the driver cut power and parked.

A second after the driver had rung the bell, Suleyman stood at the inner door, startling the mortal servant who was hurrying to reply. He scanned the mortal driver—nothing out of the ordinary about him, except his temper—and opened the door himself.

Annoyed or not, the driver inclined forward in a half-bow. "Sir? Delivery from Jupiter Cyberceuticals. Will you accept?" He offered the device, shaped like a lorgnette, into which Suleyman peered briefly to register his retinal print. It beeped to let them know this was indeed the intended receiver of the shipment. The driver stuck the lorgnette back in his pocket and gestured at the van. "Fifty-one crates of merchandise, sir! If any of the household staff should be available—"

"Yusuf, call Hippolyte," Suleyman told the servant, rolling up his sleeves.

"He is draining the pool for maintenance, lord," said Yusuf apologetically. Suleyman shrugged and lifted a crate to his shoulder.

Half an hour later he was sitting in the midst of a sea of boxes in his study. Only one had been opened, but the concentrated perfume from the massed contents was permeating the house. He frowned slightly as he read the Company directive that had come with the shipment.

"What on earth—?" Nefer stood in the doorway, breathing deeply, staring wide-eyed at the boxes. "Are all these crates full of Theobromos?" She moved like a sleepwalker toward the opened box, but Suleyman held up his hand.

"Remember Lewis's warning?" he said. She kept coming, though, and stared down into the box.

"But these are Ratlin's," she protested. "I've eaten this brand lots of times. It's about all you can get anymore. And the boxes all look factory sealed."

"It's a special order the Company had made up," Suleyman told her, holding out the directive. "Specifically for its faithful servants, to reward them for their eternity of service. Just like the clock badges, remember? I'm to distribute it immediately, throughout my sector. The directive's very clear about the timetable to be followed. The Company wants a box in the hands of every operative under my command by sunrise."

Nefer looked aghast. "I can't detect any hazard."

"Wouldn't you think they'd make it undetectable?" Suleyman said, taking a dagger from his desk and opening the topmost box in the crate. The sta-seal peeled back, the fragrance intensified, and Nefer took an involuntary step closer. Suleyman lifted off the lid with its embossed picture and they beheld the chocolates, glossy and tempting, nestled each in its frilly cup.

"Oh," Nefer groaned. Suleyman leaned close, focusing all his concentration on scanning the contents of the box.

"No," he cried suddenly. "No. There is something." With the point of his dagger he speared a Black Coffee Truffle. Turning to his console he fished out a content analysis slide with his free hand, holding the dagger well out and away from him. He cut the chocolate open and smeared its center on the slide, using the dagger blade like a palette knife; fixed and sealed it, and put it into the console.

A moment later the image swam into view. "There," said Suleyman in a terribly calm voice. "Just like what we found in Lewis's blood."

"Oh, my God, what are those things?" Nefer screamed. "Those were inside the Theobromos? Look at them, they're *moving*."

"They're attempting to deploy."

Up in the corner of the console, lights were flashing, advising Suleyman that his private transport fleet was even now maneuvering into the docking bay on the south side of the compound. "The young master has returned," Suleyman observed absently, unable to take his eyes from the screen. Nefer leaned closer, staring in horrified fascination.

"I can't believe the Company'd do this," she said. "Poisoned Theobromos? How trusting do they think we are?"

"You were ready enough to eat it," Suleyman replied.

"I wouldn't have been once I was told it was my reward for meritorious service," Nefer pointed out. "I'd have scanned it more closely. And so would any of the rest of us! Free Theobromos, this close to the Silence? As paranoid as everybody is, nobody's going to touch that stuff. How could the mortals have been so stupid? All it's going to do is make us all angry."

"Maybe that was the point all along," said Suleyman. "A mass-murder attempt so blatant it would spark the rebellion."

"But why would the mortals want us to rebel?"

"Maybe this wasn't their idea." Suleyman pulled his gaze away from the fluttering horror on the screen long enough to glance out into the courtyard, where uniformed figures were thronging in from the transport hangars. "This is Labienus's style, poison and plots within plots. If we overthrow the Company, he'll be perfectly happy, won't he? Especially if mortals die in the process."

He spoke so quietly, watching the figures in the courtyard. Nefer knelt beside him, staring up into his set face. "My God, aren't you angry? Don't you *ever* get angry?"

He looked down at her and his voice was still quiet as he replied: "What good would it do? We've been caught in an escalating pattern since the beginning, Nefer. The Company created immortals, but we frightened them, so they created Options Research. We angrily liberated Options Research, and our anger frightened them even more.

"What happened next? Were they desperate enough to come up with this stupid gambit themselves or was it put into their hands by someone much more clever? It won't matter in the end."

They could hear footsteps vaulting up through the house, now, booted strides covering the distance to the study.

"Fear and anger," Suleyman mused. "Every swing from one to the other ratcheting the big clock closer and closer to this hour."

The door burst open and Latif walked in, closely followed by Sarai. One look at his face was enough to tell them.

"Oh, no," said Nef. "You didn't find him."

"Lewis? Hey, I found him," said Latif, in a hard bright voice. "Even got a glimpse of his face, for about two seconds before I lost him again." He threw himself into a chair.

"They got away, most of them," Sarai explained. "And they took Lewis with them. They had a flying disk, like in the old pictures. It just lifted out of this hilltop and took off. We tracked it a few kilometers and then it disappeared."

"Casualties?" asked Suleyman.

"No mortals lost. A couple of the techs had seizures; some kind of disrupter field in the main entrance. They reset. They're okay now," Latif said.

"Good."

"Except that the mission was a total failure. We brought back stuff from their little elves' workshop, though," Latif continued, drumming his fists on the arms of his chair. "Or laboratory or whatever it was. We'd have brought back a couple of bodies to study but they were all turning to slime and ashes while we watched. Nasty, huh?" He was striking the chair harder now, it was beginning to creak under his blows. Suddenly he cocked his head and stared around at the Theobromos. "What's all this muck?"

Sighing, Suleyman told him. The rage faded from Latif's eyes; they became ice cold in expression. "Then it's already started," he said.

At that moment a tone chimed, advising Suleyman that a call was coming in on his private channel. He turned in his chair as the image on his console vanished, to be replaced by the incoming message. He signaled acceptance and decode; a second later there was a woman's face on the screen, an immortal with ash-blonde hair escaping from a braid, and her blue eyes were tired. "Suleyman, are you still there?"

"Van Drouten? We're here."

"Suleyman, I've just had a delivery from the Company."

"Theobromos."

"But it's adulterated with something! The directive with it sounded so fishy we thought it was a good idea to analyze some of it, and we found these horrible little biomechanical kind of things all through it and—but you've found out too, eh?"

"Yes," Suleyman replied. "They're poisoned, Van Drouten. Any operative eating this stuff will be disabled. Maybe irreparably."

"So obviously you're not going to follow orders and distribute any," Van Drouten said, brushing back strands of loose hair. "It's beginning, isn't it?"

"I'm afraid it is."

"We have to warn everybody else. Emergency comm protocols?"

Suleyman nodded. "Except that I'm going to have to ask you to handle it all. I've got another situation developing here."

Van Drouten winced. "All right. Well, if I never speak to you again—is that Latif in the background? Hello, sweetheart—anyway, if this is really it—"

"Van Drouten! Listen to me. I think this was intended as provocation, and not a serious attempt at murder."

"You mean they wanted to see what we'd do?" She looked dubious, then began to laugh sadly. "Goodness knows it's a dumb idea, concocting something this fiendishly complicated and missing the obvious fact that we'd see right through it—"

"So we can't rise to the bait," Suleyman told her. "You agree?"

"Oh, of course. Though I don't know if I'll be able to get anybody else to agree with us!"

"You'll have to try," said Suleyman. "Will you try, while I'm dealing with my situation?"

"What else can I do?" Her laughter grew a little wild. "Why not?"

Then she was gone, perhaps signing off abruptly. Perhaps the connection had been broken elsewhere. Suleyman turned away from the screen and sighed. "Status report?" he inquired.

"The transports are being refueled and offloaded," Sarai answered. "Team A is having a pit stop. Team B is assembling."

"I'd better go brief them on the next stage." Suleyman rose to his feet.

"You're moving on Alpha-Omega *now*?" Nefer asked.

"I have to. It's started, Nef," he told her.

"Then—I think I've got a flight to catch," she said. He nodded and she hurried from the room.

"We move out in ninety minutes. You should eat something, son," he told Latif.

"I'll see he eats," Sarai volunteered.

"Thank you. And . . . get rid of all this." He gestured at the boxes of Theobromos.

"It's gone," Latif told him.

Some time later, Suleyman was just concluding his address to the troops in the hangar. Team A was combat-grimy and finishing the remains of a late supper; Team B was fresh and ready, lined up sharp, bouncing on their toes. Some of them were immortals, Suleyman's own security techs. Most of them were mortals, bound to him by love and obligation. None of them expected to die.

He had spoken to them quietly, had refrained from oratory tricks to inflame them, had concentrated only on the next step of the operation in detail. ". . . Once the objective is gained, we rendezvous here with Team A. At that point you will be briefed on the third stage—"

He became aware of flames and an overpowering smell coming from another quarter of the compound. He turned as Latif and Sarai came in. "What's on fire?"

"The Theobromos," Latif informed him. "I dumped all the crates in the empty pool and set fire to it."

"You could have just thrown them down the fusion hopper," Suleyman remarked, raising an eyebrow.

"This way it's a gesture," Latif said. "It means something!"

"It means you've ruined my pool." Suleyman turned, shaking his head ruefully. "Gentlemen? Ladies? I think it's time we were gone."

"Let's go," Latif shouted, running forward as Team B saluted and broke into their units, each heading for their designated transport. "Let's make this one count!"

Nefer was out and heading for the public airstrip when she heard the transports lifting, rotating, screaming away. She turned her head and saw the column of smoke rising from Suleyman's house, and the play of red flames under it. She couldn't look long. Already before her eyes stretched the yellow plain of her dreams, and the quiet herds coming down to the water.

Sighing, she adjusted her pack and walked on.

CHAPTER 25

The Mustering of the Host: 8 July 2355

It was raining in Yorkshire, booming and flashing away in the sort of raw summer weather that had made the Bronte family's lives so brief and comfortless. The few mortals still living in that remote part of the world shivered and drew closer to their electronic hearths, sipped their herbal tea and attempted to ignore the frightening sounds coming from heaven. The ghosts were out in the weather and exulting, however.

A lone rider on a black horse paused on a crag to survey the land beneath him, eternally intrigued by the lone girl making her way through the heather. His cloak, her hair streamed in the wind like banners. On another peak, two lovers pale and fitful as lightning moved against the black clouds in a dance so sensual, so violent, no mortal could have survived its steps. Even to hear the music would drive a mortal mad.

Animals rose and walked like men and women, about their ancient inexplicable business. Restless things bound with gorse roots broke free and stood, their insubstantial feet finding once again the Via Eboracum, ignoring the insubstantial motorcar that rattled along it in the opposite direction.

In all this unearthly commotion the air cargo transport was something of an anticlimax as it zoomed down out of the storm, rain hissing on its gleaming sides, and landed pilotless at the base of a high steep hill some little distance north of Hardraw.

There was no storm in the bunker under the hill. Down there all was warmth, calm, silence, and blue light, as it had been for so many centuries.

Now. Ron and Albert opened their eyes in the same moment, peered through the glass of their respective vaults and found each other. Ron nodded.

They launched themselves upward through the regenerant fluid and, gasping, hauled themselves out. Staggering and slipping they made their way to each other and clasped hands. They leaned together a moment, coughing, wiping the blue stuff from their eyes, a pair of giants naked as newborns but as far from vulnerable as it would be possible to imagine.

"Go," said Ron, and Albert turned and scaled the ladder of the nearest vault. He reached in and hauled up the vault's occupant. One, he wrenched off its circlet; two, he leaned down and lightly butted its forehead with his own, and a spark jumped from the circlet he himself wore; three, he let go and scrambled down, running to the next vault in line to do the same again. Even as he did Ron was at the top of the ladder Albert had just vacated, grabbing for the tank's occupant, who had begun to move and look around in bewilderment.

He pulled its head up by the hair and stared into its pale eyes.

. . . Sir?

We're moving out, soldier. Decant yourself. Form up by the door and await further orders.

Sir yes SIR!

Ron leaped to the floor and ran to the next vault just as Alfred was scrambling down and running for the next in line. The Enforcer dragged himself up and over the edge, climbed down, and ran coughing and shivering to the cavern's entrance. There he waited, wringing out his hair and beard, jumping up and down to keep warm.

He was joined almost at once by another Enforcer, and then another and another, and a long line of naked titans began to form as Ron and Albert followed their orders.

One after another after another the vaults were emptied, and the long column grew longer. At precisely the same moment, the same scene was being enacted in the Pyrenees, in Morocco, in Norway, in Siberia, in the Sangre de Christos, and under Mount Tamalpais.

When four hundred and seventy-eight Enforcers stood waiting by the door, Ron turned with a last regretful glance at the sleeping Preservers and ran back. Albert, many yards ahead of him, was shouting: "Atten—*tion!*"

The line snapped to attention with an eerie grace, more like some great clockwork serpent than soldiers.

"Low *bridge!*" roared Albert. In perfect unison the whole line dropped forward in a standing crouch, poised for running.

"Move *out*! Quick *march*!" ordered Albert, and raced past them up the tunnel. Ron followed at the head of the column, and though they ran crouched their heads nearly grazed the tunnel's roof.

Inexorable as the tide they surged, up and out, emerging into the storm without so much as blinking. Ron led them in a winding file through the heather toward the transport, where Albert had already opened the loading doors. He was now ripping open the crates that were stacked inside.

As the Enforcers entered, one by one, he tossed each a prepacked duffel. The first in caught his bundle, advanced to the far end of the cargo bay and waited. He was there joined by the next in line with his bundle, and the next. When the last Enforcer had boarded Albert closed the loading doors and took a bundle for himself, as Ron sprinted to the transport's cabin and keyed in a signal. The console beeped in acknowledgment and the autopilot activated; with a lurch and a whine the transport rose into the storm, and kept rising, and sped westward at last.

The Enforcers, meanwhile, were busily dressing themselves out of the duffels. There was some muttered amusement, even laughter, at the clothing that had been provided for them. Not *uniforms* by any stretch of the imagination, no, in fact all the garments had in common was that they were all triple-X sizes. There were Levis and cotton fleece exercise pants, there were chinos and Bermuda shorts and pinstriped trousers. And the shirts! Pastel Izods, rugby pullovers, long-sleeved oxfords, T-shirts in all colors printed with every possible advertising logo, though there were perhaps more for the Hearst News Services 2348 Company Picnic than any other. It had not been easy to stockpile so many big clothes, in a world where the mortal race had dwindled. There were no shoes available at all.

Having dressed themselves, the Yorkshire contingent was issued field rations and fed, as the transport hurtled on. They were then ordered to draw from their duffels the last items each man had been issued: two lengths of oak, six meters of ramilar cord, two flint nodules, and a hammerstone. It wasn't necessary to tell them what to do next. To a man, they dropped into a comfortable crouch and their enormous supple hands went to work, expertly knapping stone. With almost no effort the flint axe heads began to take shape.

They were beautiful things, in a horrible kind of way, faceted sharp as razors at one end and blunt and heavy at the other. They took on nearly identical shape in their makers' hands, to the last tiny careful flake, all nine hundred and sixty of them.

They were also nearly identical to all the axes being made at that moment on all the other transports, all on their different trajectories, all converging on the mountains behind the little town of Garrapatta.

In Garrapatta it was the hour before dawn, and Budu had emerged from his bunker at last. He strode through the lobby of the cultural center and pushed the door open, and there on the Spanish Renaissance steps he stood, peering into the dark morning. He gave a long sigh. Crouching down in the doorway, he reached inside his coat and took out the flints and hammerstone. His lips moved in prayer as he began to fashion his weapons, each exactly like the other, both identical to the weapons being made on the ships he had summoned.

Joseph slunk out behind him and stood shivering in the cold, buttoning up his long coat. He took out a granola bar and ate it, pausing only as he wondered whether he ought to offer Budu any. He decided against it; Budu was praying and probably fasting, too. After licking the last crumbs from the wrapper, he stuck it in his pocket and waited patiently, looking down on the little houses of the mortals.

They were sleeping, the mortals, except for one or two whose kitchen stovepipes were already hot, sending up plumes of steam. Pale moths were drifting in from the night to shelter under the ramshackle eaves, or hovering still over the half-wild gardens where tomato vines straggled up wire towers, scaling them as though fighting off the wild roses, the bright poppies that pressed through the leaning fences. Shrill pleading scream: a moment later a wildcat paced up the path, silent field mouse in its jaws, and the stare of the predator was as blank and dead as the stare of its prey.

Joseph stood there bidding it all good-bye, the village and the gardens, the mortals curled in their blankets or huddling by their stoves.

The sky was paling when Budu stood at last, hefting his axes. "Let's go," he said. Joseph nodded and fell into step behind him as they went down the mountain.

They took the speedboat moored at the pier. Budu cast off while Joseph started the motor; they moved out, away from Cape San Martin.

At San Simeon Joseph ran her aground on the beach below the trees. They scrambled out and crossed the deserted highway, the big man loping, the smaller man trotting close after. They picked up speed and disappeared into the trees, and then no mortal could have spotted them as they ascended the enchanted hill.

Hearst's hands were trembling. He set them flat on the breakfast table and concentrated on calming himself. *Don't look at the ring.* There was no reason Quintilius should notice the ring, after all. Hearst had been wearing it for months. It was a careful copy of a ring he'd owned a long time ago. Nothing to arouse suspicion.

He took a piece of toast and spread fruit preserves on it, working very hard to keep his movements smooth and casual. That was the way; now could he pour coffee for himself without spilling? Yes, and cream, too. Good boy, Will! You ought to have gone on the stage.

The door opened and Quintilius entered. Was he pale, was he trembling, too?

"Good morning, Quint," said Hearst, and to his delight his voice was quiet and careless, without so much as a quaver. Why should it quaver? He wasn't supposed to know it was almost the last morning of the world. "Sorry to get you up so early. I gather you didn't retire until around three?"

"That's all right, Mr. Hearst." Quintilius gave a ghastly smile. "Touch of insomnia."

"Insomnia," said Hearst, taking a mouthful of toast. "Say, that's too bad. You'd think they'd have figured out a way to make us immortals proof against life's little discomforts, wouldn't you? Maybe that's something we can propose at the next stockholder's meeting, what do you think?"

"Sure, Mr. Hearst," Quintilius replied, setting something on the table. Hearst looked down at it. Eighteenth-century English silver, a footed bonbon dish. In it, on a paper doily, were arranged a dozen chocolates. All his favorites, from that little company in the Celtic Federation. Ratlin's.

"Theobromos?" Hearst was even able to sound jovial.

"Mary thought you might like them after your coffee. She said the brandied peaches you wanted aren't ready. They need another couple of days to be perfect," said Quintilius, not meeting his eyes. Any qualms Hearst had been feeling fled in that moment. He smiled and rose to his feet.

"Why, that was awfully thoughtful of her," he said. "You tell her I said so." And he reached out as though to clap Quintilius on the shoulder in a comradely way, but instead his arm went around the smaller man's neck. He gripped Quintilius to him with all his immortal strength, and Quintilius, with all an immortal's adroitness, went writhing out of his grasp; but not before Hearst had managed to turn the bezel on the ring.

Quintilius stared at him from the opposite end of the room, panting, running a self-diagnostic. "You—what did you just do?"

"Shorted out your datalink to the Company," said Hearst, holding up the hand that wore the ring. "I know what's in the chocolates, Quint."

Quintilius went white. "Look, Mr. Hearst, I—"

"You have failed your masters," said Budu, appearing in the near doorway. He ducked his head and stepped inside, and Joseph appeared behind him. "You betrayed the mortal race. You stand condemned, Preserver."

Quintilius turned and gaped at him in horror. His eyes widened, his lips drew back from his teeth; a second later he had winked out and the closest window had exploded outward, its glass shattered, its stone mullion broken away.

Budu winked out after him, with a roar like a freight train. A heartbeat later there was a pleading scream from somewhere in the garden, abruptly cut short. Hearst flinched, and Joseph grimaced and closed his eyes. "That could have been me, you know?" he murmured. "I used to get jobs like his all the time."

Hearst found his mouth was dry. He swallowed and said, "Well, but you had the moral gumption to, uh, stand up and oppose them at last. You did what was right. Quint worked beside me all that time, I trusted him, and then—why, he did just what you said he'd do." He poked the dish of chocolates uneasily.

A door slammed somewhere below them. They heard a heavy footfall approaching. As it came up through the house, Joseph went to the dish and picked up one of the chocolates, handling it carefully by its paper cup. He scanned it. "Son of a bitch," he said, in dull surprise. "They *are* full of something. It's not the virus that disabled Budu, though. Somebody came up with a new approach."

" 'I fear the Greeks when bearing gifts,' " quoted Hearst. "Did they really think we're such dumb bozos they could take us out with poisoned candy?"

Joseph shrugged. "It wouldn't fool me, but I guess they thought you were far enough out of the loop not to suspect." He turned the chocolate in his fingers, staring at it. "I wonder if Lewis—" He set it down without finishing the sentence and wiped his hand on his coat.

They turned as Budu stepped through the doorway. In his right hand was one of his axes, and hand and axe were red. In his left hand was a fistful of Quintilius's hair, with the severed head swinging beneath.

Hearst's eyes widened. He staggered back against the table but said nothing.

"I hid the body in one of the rooms above your pool, Hearst," Budu informed him.

"The changing rooms?" Hearst stammered.

"Yes. Is there a tour of your house scheduled today?"

"What? Uh—yes."

"Then give an order that the changing rooms are not to be shown. The water in your pool is a little red, but it circulates through a filter, doesn't it?"

Hearst nodded. Joseph looked at him and went to a carved and gilded seventeenth-century chest. He lifted the lid, peered inside. "You can stash the head in here," he suggested. "That'll buy us time if he managed to get off a distress signal anyway. They'll have to hunt for the pieces."

"That was the idea," said Budu. He lowered the head into the chest. Joseph closed the lid. Budu turned to look at Hearst. "May I use your bathroom?"

Hearst extended a trembling hand and pointed. "Through there."

"Thank you."

Budu left the room and Hearst leaned against the table, gasping. Joseph came quickly to his side. "Hey, I know this is a little rough. You understand, though, nobody's been killed here? Stick that guy's head back on, give him a couple of months in a repair facility, and he'll be good as new."

"Yes," said Hearst, and he reached out for his coffee and took a gulp. "Yes, I must remember that. And he'd have done the same to me! Wouldn't he?"

"Worse," said Joseph grimly. "If you'd eaten any of that Theobromos you might be *really* dead right now, and he'd be smirking as he inventoried your property for the Company."

"That's right," said Hearst, squaring his shoulders. The coldness was returning to his eyes. He took the silver dish and tossed its contents into the fireplace. "This is war, after all."

As Budu was emerging from the bathroom, drying his hands on a towel, there came a sound mortals wouldn't have heard; but all three men turned their heads and looked north. "That'll be the guys from the Mount Tamalpais bunker," said Joseph. Budu nodded. He looked at Hearst.

"We'll go to the troop carrier now," he stated.

"You bet," said Hearst decisively, and picked up his communicator and ordered an agcar, and ordered further that the Neptune Pool area be off limits for tour parties today. They went down to the grand front steps by one of his secret passages. Hearst emerged alone as the limousine pulled up. He dismissed the driver and got behind the wheel himself. Budu and Joseph crowded in as soon as the driver was out of sight.

They sped through the gates, along the pleasant drive with its orange and lemon trees, and down the hill to Hearst's private pier where the *Oneida VI* lay anchored.

At the same moment, the cargo door of the first air transport to arrive was opening. They filed out in a long line, the four hundred and thirty-two Enforcers who had been sequestered under Mount Tamalpais, and each one swung a flint axe in either hand. One after another they peered around in the bright morning, got their bearings, and then faded into the California landscape as invisibly as though they had been ninjas, though they had the benefit of neither black suits nor camouflage.

Overland they made their way, down through the mountains and then along the coast, unstoppably advancing on their programmed coordinates. Nobody saw them.

The gateman at the pier entrance did notice them, as they streamed from the woods and ran past; but Mr. Hearst had told him he was hosting a party for marathon joggers, and they weren't to be stopped. The gateman observed their enormous size, their inhuman faces. He withdrew into his booth and thought very hard about how well Mr. Hearst paid him, and in the end decided he couldn't have seen anything out of the ordinary. He reopened his Totter Dan game and spent the rest of the afternoon intent on improving his score.

The *Oneida VI* waited patiently at the end of the pier. She was a vast and stately fusion craft, less rakish of line and more tastefully furnished than the *Captain Morgan,* and she had, up until this moment, been put to much more dignified and law-abiding uses. She had an immense banquet room and ballroom, and a cargo hold capacious enough to receive any thirteenth-century Italian monasteries to which Hearst might take a fancy while abroad.

He stood now between Joseph and Budu, watching openmouthed as the line of giants came thundering along the pier.

"Sir!" The first Enforcer to step aboard saluted Budu. "Squad Commander Joshua reporting for duty, sir!"

"Take your men below," Budu told him. "Tell them there'll be a briefing when we're under way. When all personnel are aboard, report to me with your lieutenant."

"Sir yes *sir!*"

"This is unbelievable," Hearst murmured to Joseph. "Look at them. Goliaths, every one! How on earth were they trapped in those bunkers by mere mortals?"

"They trusted the Company," said Joseph sadly. "And I don't think they ever understood just how much they frightened their masters."

"They understand now," remarked Budu, chuckling.

The wind changed, a summer fog came rolling in to obscure the coast, and the Enforcers kept coming. The Sangre de Christos contingent arrived, and then the two ships from Norway and Siberia arrived at nearly the same moment, having taken polar routes. Hour after hour the big men came running, appearing suddenly out of the fog like flat-headed gods in aloha shirts, so bizarre that the few mortal motorists who spotted them along Highway 1 resolutely refused to believe their eyes. Later the Yorkshire group arrived, and later still the group from the Pyrenees. The men from the bunker near Fez were the last.

By this time the *Oneida VI* was riding a little low in the water. Joseph had gone below to distribute snacks; Hearst remained beside Budu, shivering in the wind off the sea as the last of the Enforcers came aboard. He had begun to notice, uncomfortably, that the massed Enforcers emitted a certain smell. Not an unwashed smell, nothing of the locker room about it; almost an animal smell. He decided that if he had a much-loved dog that smelled like that, it would be a nice smell. Coming from something nominally human, however, it was unsettling.

It was beginning to get dark when the last Enforcer bounded up the gangway and saluted. "Sir! Technical Specialist Krogen reporting, sir! Last man out of Fez, sir!"

"Get below and report to your squad commander," Budu ordered. He grinned and turned to Hearst. "We can cast off now, Hearst. Lay in a course for Santa Catalina Island. I want to anchor off Cape Cortes at eleven hundred hours tomorrow morning."

"She can get you there sooner," Hearst told him. "Don't you want the element of surprise?"

"I have the element of surprise," Budu told him. "Eleven hundred hours. Not before."

"Yes, sir!" Hearst saluted and ran for the bridge. He passed Joseph coming up a ladder, looking a little wild-eyed.

"Have we got any meat on board at all?" he inquired. "Beef jerky? Canned cocktail franks? Anything?"

"No, but don't worry. The galley's got a hundred cases of Proteus Hearty Fare," Hearst promised. Joseph groaned and ran past him. Hearst continued to the bridge and slid into place in front of the navigational computer, ordering it to set their course and speed. As he waited for it to respond his spirits were rising. It might well be the last night of the world, but, by gosh, he was spending it the way he'd wanted. Roaring across the sea with the ancient heroes of legend, on his way to put an end to a massively evil conspiracy! No questions, no complications, good and evil clear as day. And why shouldn't his side win?

The *Oneida VI* drew in her ramps, raised her anchor, backed from her mooring, put about and put out to sea. A flashing light on the console drew Hearst's attention. He leaned forward and peered at it, frowning. Then he was on his feet and running for the quarterdeck. Joseph saw him running and followed.

They emerged on the quarterdeck just as Budu and his officers were assembling there for a staff meeting. "Sir!" shouted Hearst. "The ship says there's something fouling her rudder—"

Budu went to the rail without a word and looked down at the stern of the ship.

"There is," he said. Everyone else crowded to the rail to peer through the twilight. A mortal might have seen nothing but the foaming wake from the fusion drive ports, the shadowy water. The immortals saw two massive hands gripping the rudder just below the water line, and the indistinct pallor of a head and shoulders under the surface. "Show yourself," said Budu.

The hands flexed. The head pushed upward and a face broke into the air, gasping, sucking in a long breath. Pale eyes stared, long teeth gleamed yellow in the wide mouth, and the long hair and beard floated out like trailing tentacles.

"Holy smoke, it's Marco," yelled Joseph.

There were murmurs of amazement from the other Enforcers. Hearst looked confused, and then horrified. "The fellow that ran the Bureau of Punitive Medicine?" he cried.

"The what?" One of Budu's officers turned to stare at him.

"It was a Company prison," Budu informed them. "A place where Preservers were tortured."

"*Preservers?*" Ron looked aghast. "Why?"

"Because the Company wanted them tortured," Budu told him, shrugging. "And that one"—he turned and spat over the rail—"got the job, because he'd repented his disobedience. It was his punishment and his reward."

"You mean *the* Marco, who killed noncombatants?" demanded another of the officers, beginning to look outraged.

"There was only one," Budu replied.

Marco meanwhile was still hanging there on the rudder, gazing up blankly at the faces that had begun to glare down at him. "You want him off there, sir?" Ron inquired, saluting. "I'll jump down and cut his hands away, sir."

"No!" roared Marco. "What the hell does it matter what I did, now? We're at the end of time! The last battle of the world comes in the morning, and I want to be there."

Budu regarded him for a long moment. It was getting steadily darker. "Throw him a line," he said at last.

Two of the officers hauled Marco from the water. There were mutters of horror as he came over the rail and collapsed on the deck. He pulled himself up into a crouch. Hearst switched on the deck lights and several of the Enforcers drew back, exclaiming aloud.

Marco was naked, and the white light of the deck lamp revealed his skin salt-pale and blotched with livid scars, thickenings, pits, tumors. One eye was clouded with a white film. Several of his toes were missing, and one finger. His matted hair and beard, streaked with gray, were so long they trailed down his body like seaweed.

"What the hell happened to you?" said Joshua.

Marco swung his good eye like a searchlight, and settled his gaze on Joseph. He grinned and pointed at him with a long-nailed finger. "*He* knows," he said. "Don't you, Preserver? It's been a long time, but I remember you. You were the one with the daughter, the Botanist Mendoza! She—"

"Shut up," Joseph snarled, starting forward. Budu put a hand on his shoulder. "You've still got the virus, huh? That's some justice, anyway. It must have been eating you up for, what, fifteen millennia now? Is it painful, you lousy bastard?"

"What virus?" asked Ron.

"The Company made a toxin to kill Enforcers," said Budu. "It almost worked."

"Almost," agreed Marco, scanning him. "You had it too, didn't you, High-and-Mighty? There are still traces in your blood. How are you going to keep the Company from spraying it all over your legions tomorrow, eh?"

"I developed an antidote," Budu replied. "It was given to my men in their field rations."

"Would it cure me?" Marco's eye fixed on him with sudden intensity.

"Yes," Budu said. "But you won't get it. Your suffering is only justice."

"You still believe in justice?" Marco bared his teeth. "Oh, Budu. Do you know where I've been, all these centuries? Bringing justice to the little monkeys. I haunted their night fields, in every wet shadow. I've torn their hearts

open and licked out the iniquities there. I caught the murderer in his delight.
I snatched the child with the stolen honey.

"I watched through their secret windows, and such things I saw! They prey
on themselves more pitilessly than we ever did. We should have let them. We
weren't necessary to protect innocents, Budu. There are no innocents! There's
only sin, and it eats itself."

"Then may it eat you," said Budu.

"It'll eat us all," Marco cried. "But let me face it with a weapon in my hand.
I did good work!"

Budu considered him in silence. Joseph turned, looked up into Budu's face
in dismay. "You're not going to arm him, are you?" he asked. "He's broken
your code. He's one of the unrighteous. For God's sake, lop off his head and
throw him overboard! You know the things he's done."

"I know," said Budu. "But we go into battle in eight hours, and I have no
men to waste." He looked at the nearest officer. "Issue him clothing. Let him
make an axe for himself."

Marco began to chuckle. Budu looked down at him. "Don't think you've escaped. The first wave to land will be taken out by the Company's perimeter defenses," he said. "You will go in the first wave."

"Fine," Marco replied. He made an obscene gesture with his maimed hand,
lifted it to his forehead in a salute. "Sir!" he added.

Hearst looked away from him, terrified. He met Joseph's bleak and furious
gaze. As they stared at each other, the music came up from below: the Enforcers were singing. Hauntingly sweet and powerful from a thousand tenor
and countertenor throats, came the old anthem promising judgment, incor-
ruptible judgment on all humanity.

CHAPTER 26

Child Care in the Cyborg Family, Volume Fifteen:
Adolescent Rebellion

With the completion of his final augmentation, immortal life stretches before the cyborg youth, and he may find the prospect a daunting one. After all, he is now ready to take his place in the greater world. He may be mature, considerate, studious, conscious of his duty to humanity and his position in the universe, a source of pride for the cyborg parent. On the other hand, he may exhibit a certain unwelcome brashness and tendency toward insubordination; for to be gifted with the knowledge of the ages, alas, is not necessarily to be granted wisdom. Moreover he may appear to suffer from a sense of inordinate self-pity, loudly decrying perceived injustices to himself. It may be that this young savage requires what is termed by anthropologists a Rite of Passage, before the years of travail on the part of the cyborg parent conclude successfully at last, and the object of his efforts may be freed from the illusion of linear time.

"This is all a crock," says Alec irritably.

Seventeen now, he wears white trousers, a blazer, and striped tie. Nicholas, who is walking beside him, wears a uniform identical to Alec's. Flint clatters along behind them, carrying a holoprojector.

Edward is pacing in front of them. He is formally dressed in a suit of tropical-weight linen, in his customary mid-Victorian cut. He turns to regard Alec with a bright and critical eye. "An opinion from Alec! Remarkable. Will you favor us with your no doubt fascinating explanation, Alec?"

Alec mutters something barely audible. Edward raises the pointer he carries, interrogatively. "I beg your pardon?"

"Don't do that," Alec snaps. "You're subliminally intimidating me."

"Poor Alec," Edward drawls. "We've a case of the nerves this morning, have we? It wouldn't have anything to do with excessive self-abuse, I'm sure. The remedy is *intellectual* stimulation, you know." He begins to move the pointer like a metronome, tap tap tap into his palm. "And what about your own assignment? You were to access, summarize, compare and contrast the complete works of Charles Dickens and Audrey Knollys and provide an analysis of their respective impacts on progressive social legislation, with your own recommendations on how the laws might be more effective. Favor us with your no doubt brilliant report, Alec."

"Shrack Charles Dickens," says Alec sullenly. "Shrack this whole thing. We're *cyborgs*, Deadward! We don't need educations. We downloaded all this garbage years ago!"

Edward raises the pointer and places its tip against Alec's forehead. "What's the use of having a library in there if you won't open the books, boy? What's the good of augmented intelligence if you won't use it? Is this the genius who insists he's ready to be liberated from time?" He gives Alec's head a little push with the pointer, and Alec grabs the pointer from him and throws it across the lawn.

"Leave me the hell alone!"

"Pick that up at once," says Edward.

"I'll break it over your damned head if you make me."

"I think not." Edward puts his hands behind his back and considers Alec. "What a depressing prospect stands before us: the young cyborg as ignoramus, unable to comprehend more than a fraction of his infinite knowledge, and unable to employ the unlimited energies at his command in any manner other than compulsive and repeated acts of—"

"SHUT UP!" Alec clenches his fists. "Can't you say *anything* in words of one syllable?"

"Why should I make it easy for you?" Edward replies, staring him down. "Haven't you the intellect to face a challenge or two, if you're ready, as you repeatedly insist, for liberation?"

"I've got tons of intellect," Alec shouts. "And absolutely no use for all this ancient history. I'm ready to go on to the next level now, thank you very much. *Set me free!*"

"Ah, the old familiar refrain," says Edward. "He is grown so wise that he beats impatiently at the gates of heaven. Never a thought that he might, perhaps, have a duty to intervene in human affairs, even as an act of atonement?"

"If *you* were even half as all-knowing as you think you are, Dead, you'd have learned some humility," says Alec. "As well as how futile it is to intervene in human affairs. *We* only ever make things worse. Like Alec Checkerfield on Mars. The best thing he ever did for humanity was get himself killed, okay? Can we move on now?"

"By all means," says Edward. "Your brother was about to give his analysis of the Lunar political crisis of 2315, if memory serves. Proceed, Nicholas."

Nicholas clears his throat. Flint crawls forward and holds up the holoprojector. An image forms in midair: a dreary-looking grid of streets and quadrangles, and beyond them a world all in silver and black. It is the mountains of the moon. Nicholas lifts his head and speaks clearly.

"Herein the dispute ariseth: the Ephesian Church is suffered to build its Artemisium in the disputed precinct of Mare Fecunditatis," he says. "Which will lead in turn to the rise of the Ephesian Party within the Council, whereat the Secular Protest Movement ariseth in opposition.

"And so bitter, and so dire their discords, that the miners under contract to the British Lunar Company shall at last emigrate to Earth, as seabirds take shelter inland when storms rage upon the bosom of the ocean, nor can they in any wise be persuaded to return. And with them prosperity shall flee, and in 2217 the Lunar Council will be dissolved."

Alec snickers and applauds. Edward merely raises his eyebrows. "Very good," he says. "A reasonably insightful assessment. Fifty demerits for willful use of archaic idiom, full marks for content. Now, your observations? In Cinema Standard this time, if you please."

"Obviously the principle of separation of church and state should be extended to Luna," says Nicholas. "Or they'll all go bankrupt up there."

"Precisely. A clear call for secular morality!"

"Or immorality," continues Nicholas, folding his arms. "*Considera bellum mercatorium gestum inter Puellas Sodalitatis Felicis Lunaris et Scorta Templaria Dianae Lunari sacra.*" He narrows his eyes at Edward. "I can go on in Greek, if you'd like. Or Chinese. Shall I, sir?"

"Arrogant, aren't we?" says Edward fondly. "I want a monograph from you of no less than thirty thousand words, title to be: *The Origins and Direct Causes of the Third Punic War.* You have three days to deliver it."

"Talk about pointless," says Alec.

Edward rounds on Alec. "I beg your pardon?" he says in a quiet voice. Nicholas groans and averts his gaze.

"This is just another example!" says Alec. "I hate this! I hate these stupid lessons in subjects that are totally irrelevant to my life, and I hate not being able to do anything unless you permit it, and I hate these clothes, and I really,

really hate listening to you pontificate for hours on end!" He gasps for breath. "You—you conceited, dictatorial, long-winded, boring—"

"Oh, not boring, surely," says Edward, taking a step closer to him and grinning with a terrifying show of teeth. "I may make your life miserable, boy, but can you really tell me you're bored? Clearly I haven't been forceful enough."

Alec steps back involuntarily, wide-eyed, and then catches himself. "You shracking bully!" he shouts.

"And thus you demonstrate your capacity for enduring provocation," says Edward. "What have I taught you about self-control? I believe my point's proven. I put it to you, Alec, that this latest disgraceful demonstration of violent resentment stems not from your dissatisfaction with your curriculum, nor your dependent status, but from sexual frustration. Would you care to explain it to him, Captain?"

No thank you, Commander, I ain't organic in any way, shape, or form and I ain't touching this question with an electronic pole. You leave me out of this.

"It's not true anyway," says Alec, blushing furiously. "And that's another thing. I've outgrown that bunkbed. What about my own room, and some privacy for a change?"

"Still more demands." Edward paces before him, hands clasped behind his back. "Let us consider the fundamental issue. Young Alec is at a crisis in development as regards certain . . . physical imperatives, as it were, over which he is apparently unable to assert any mastery whatever. Unlike his brother." Edward nods to Nicholas. "If he were, in fact, the late Alec Checkerfield, there would be nothing preventing him, in his agonies of thwarted lust, from applying to our dear Mendoza for remedy."

"Oh!" Alec covers his mouth with his hands and turns away.

"*But!* As he has so forcefully reminded us on numerous occasions, he is *not* the late Alec Checkerfield. To admit as much would be to oblige himself to face certain uncomfortable issues relating to Alec Checkerfield's criminal past. An unenviable dilemma! Alec is either an innocent lamb with unresolved Oedipal desires, or an adult with unexpiated guilt and grave responsibilities to mortal humanity. Perhaps you ought to set your astonishing powers of analysis to the problem, Alec. Which is it?"

"You bastard," cries Alec. "Freud is all bollocks anyway! Look, Captain, *you* knew Alec Checkerfield. I'm not him, am I?"

Well, now, son . . . lying's a useful talent and it do come in handy, but sometimes it don't answer. You'd best sign articles, lad.

"Oh, piss off, all of you," says Alec miserably. "Everything would be all right if you'd just let us leave time like you have, Dead."

"Which in turn presents your obedient servant with a moral dilemma of his own," says Edward. "How can I possibly justify granting unlimited power to an appallingly conflicted and undisciplined youth, unable to learn from his past because he will not confront it, unwilling to make any recompense to the mortals he has wronged?"

Aw, he ain't as bad as all that.

"He has the potential to be far worse," says Edward. "So much for my theory that a happy childhood would strengthen character. Allow me to suggest a solution to your difficulties, Alec: you must enact the myth of Oedipus to emerge at last from the prison of infantilism. You must, in best archetypal tradition, kill your symbolic father and possess your symbolic mother."

"What abomination is this?" demands Nicholas, scowling.

"I'm speaking in a ritual sense, for God's sake," replies Edward. "You'd prefer another archetype? Consider the tale of Zeus deposing Cronos and taking his place, then. The son must defeat the father to earn his liberty."

He looks at Alec. "Here's what I propose, boy: I'll give you a week to prepare, and then you and I will engage in a pugilistic competition. If you're able to defeat me, it'll mean you've come of age. You will be freed from linear time, entitling you to unimaginable, yet psychologically guiltless, intimacy with the lady of your guilty dreams. If I defeat you, well then! You're still a puling boy and must wait for emancipation a while yet."

"This is monstrous," yells Nicholas.

"You mean I'd get to fight you?" Alec says. There are profoundly mixed emotions on his face.

Yer a trained killer! My lad ain't going up against the likes of you, protests the Captain.

Edward looks amused. "Surely he can withstand a mere sparring match! Three rounds, three knockdowns, and boxing gloves to be used, of course. Broughton's rules strictly observed, with the addendum that no hyperfunction will be employed. You yourself will referee, Captain."

I still don't like it.

"You never know; Alec is lighter than I, and has boxed before against the bags in his gymnasium. I, on the other hand, have no experience with fisticuffs other than attending a match or two in my mortal days. It ought to even the odds, don't you think?"

"Yeah," says Alec, beginning to be taken with the idea.

"For shame! This is stupid," says Nicholas in outrage.

"You used to go punching people all the time," Alec points out. Nicholas turns red. He unclenches his fists and puts his hands in his pockets.

"I was mortal then," he mutters. "I've repented since."

"Well, bully for you, yeah?" says Alec. "But I have to do this, Nicky. I have to strike a blow for freedom!" He slams his fists together in anticipation.

"If you can," says Edward with a cold smile. "Boy."

One Week Later, Linear Time

Alec is in the gym on the *Captain Morgan,* where the match is to be fought, by common consent; it is less likely to draw Mendoza's attention than the exercise hall in the house. He paces back and forth, regarding the punching bags.

There ain't no need to be afeared, now, son. You used to whale the daylights out of these, and it always done you a power of good. Come on, then; take a poke at 'em.

Alec raises his right fist, connects, and sends the bag sailing off across the room, trailing steel springs and wiring.

Of course, you weren't no cyborg back then. Well, see how strong you are? You'll do fine.

"Except that Deadward's a cyborg, too, remember?" says Alec, in a choked voice.

Nicholas shrugs, absorbed in trying to coax a tune from a hurdy-gurdy. "Stupid," he says.

Right, then; let's go over the basics. Legs apart, weight on the balls of yer feet. Knees slightly bent. Come on, son, you got to try. Left fist up to yer shoulders, right back by yer chin. That's my boy!

"Yes! I can do this. I'm faster than he is, he even said so. I'll be a blur!" Alec turns to regard himself in the gymnasium's full-length mirror.

"Hyperfunction is forbidden," Nicholas reminds him, tightening the hurdygurdy's strings, testing for correct pitch.

"I meant figuratively," says Alec. "I'm a lean, mean cyborg machine. See?"

Nicholas shakes his head. "This is wrong," he says.

"No, it isn't," says Alec with feverish certainty. "This is payback time! This is my revenge for everything Dead's done to us."

"What's he done to us in the last seventeen years?"

"Bullied us! And—and that was absolutely vile, what he said about my feelings for M-Mendoza. He's got a filthy mind. And there's no reason for keeping us from timewalking like he does, except he's got these huge control issues. All I want is to escape into that other place they go to! If it's complete utter bliss like she says, why can't we share it? Where's the harm?"

"Do you deserve complete utter bliss?" Nicholas asks him, as his fingers beat out a little tune on the keys: "Lilliburlero." Alec freezes, staring, remembering the melody. A certain man had liked it once, enough to whistle it on his way to deliver weapons to Mars.

"Why wouldn't I?" he says at last. "Alec Checkerfield did something wrong; but he died. Doesn't death pay everything off?"

"I don't think so," says Nicholas, remembering flames at Rochester.

"Maybe *your* death didn't," says Alec, who is finding the hurdy-gurdy music intensely irritating. He paces back and forth restlessly. "And Edward's definitely didn't, because he didn't *learn* anything, see, he just remained the same shracking monster he'd always been, and he has plans to rule the world, in case you hadn't noticed, and shouldn't somebody try to stop him? Maybe it was always going to come to this. Maybe that's my way to . . . pay for what that other guy did."

"So you do think you need to expiate your sin," says Nicholas.

"Will you put that damned music box away?" Alec shouts. "It sounds like a belt sander! What about *you* atoning, Nick? You must remember all the rotten things you did pretty clearly. But you've got nothing on old Deadward. He deliberately killed people, you know! He was a murderer and a seducer and a backstabbing bastard—he trapped us in the Library—"

"So you remember the Library," says Nicholas, laying aside the hurdy-gurdy.

"Yes, I remember the shracking Library!" Alec throws a punch at the boxing duffel, so hard it smacks into the wall and slides down, torn from its mooring. "And, you know what? Happy childhoods or not, we're still stuck in there! I want to escape! And if I beat Edward, he'll have to let me out!"

Nicholas rises to his feet. "Is Edward really the one who hasn't learned anything?"

"Piss off!" Alec shouts. Nicholas narrows his eyes and stalks out.

He has crossed the gangplank, and is going up the path from the pier, when he meets Edward coming through the garden. "Not staying to watch?" Edward inquires.

"It's wrong," Nicholas mutters.

"Wrong? Certainly. That was the rule of our mortal lives, boy: a little wrong to buy a greater right," says Edward. "Remember?"

"We're immortal now. I won't live by that lie ever again," Nicholas replies heatedly.

"Admirable of you. Think you're ready to be set free yourself, do you?" Edward gives him a sharp glance.

"I must be a better man first," Nicholas replies. Edward nods, an unreadable expression in his eyes.

"Well, do as you like; pity your brother hasn't got your advanced spiritual wisdom, or somebody'd be spared a thrashing," says Edward, stepping past him and going on. Nicholas turns back.

"Have mercy on him," he urges.

Edward turns back, too, raising one eyebrow. " 'I must be cruel, only to be kind,' " he quotes. "I'd be obliged to you if you could distract her, should she wonder where we've got to. I left her on the upper terrace, working with her Indian maize cultivars. This shouldn't take long."

Nicholas sighs and continues on his way. Edward goes his way, too, on down to the landing and aboard the *Captain Morgan*.

In the gymnasium, Flint is just offering Alec his choice of boxing gloves when Edward walks in. Alec's eyes widen, and he draws back slightly as Edward strides toward him, shrugging out of his coat.

"Cringing already?" says Edward. "You can always give it up, you know. I won't tell anybody you've been a wretched coward."

"I'm not afraid of you," shouts Alec, feeling like an unshelled oyster.

"Aren't you? We'll soon see," Edward tells him, carefully hanging his coat on a hook. He removes his hat, waistcoat, and cravat as well; opening his shirt collar as he turns, he surveys Alec's costume and bursts out laughing. "Good God, boy, are you really going in to fight me in your drawers?" he demands.

"This is what boxers used to wear when they fought," Alec says, outraged. "I accessed all the historical references we had. Don't you make fun of me!"

"It's what prizefighters wore," sneers Edward. "Not gentlemen. It's a practical ensemble, I'll grant you that much. Well, where are the gloves?"

Here you are, Commander, says the Captain, as Flint crawls forward and offers a pair. *Do you need any help putting 'em on? Our Alec knows how.*

"No, thank you," says Edward, pulling on one glove and snugging it about the wrist. "I fancy I can manage. I did watch a bout or two, remember."

So you did, aye. Which advantage Alec ain't got, and I'll thank you to remember that.

"Oh, come now, Captain! It's not as though I'll do our little Alec any *real* harm," Edward replies, pulling on the other glove adroitly. "I once saw the celebrated Tom Sayers go forty-one rounds with the American heavyweight challenger. Sayer's arm was fractured in the sixth round and he simply kept fighting. The referee called a draw at last; the ring looked like an abattoir by that time! I'm sure we won't come to such a pass." Alec shivers. Edward steps forward and faces off with him.

"Now, Alec, here we are at last," Edward tells him, grinning. "You've waited years for this day to arrive. Shall we dance?" He strikes a nineteenth-century boxer's pose, stiffly correct.

Right! Round one of three commencing, lads. Let's see a fair fight. No hyperfunction, no hitting below the belt, no hitting when the other party's down. Wrestling holds permitted above the waist only. Round concludes at the first knockdown. Thirty-second rest period following each round. All clear?

But Alec is overwhelmed by memories, coming unbidden and unwanted. Riding on Edward's shoulders, showing off to get his attention, gripping his hand in the final agony of the immortality process . . .

"Look, Deaddy, I'm sorry—" begins Alec.

"Ha!" Edward smacks his gloves together. "Lost your nerve, have you? I thought as much. Is it any wonder I was able to take command? And I suppose I'll continue as master of the house a while longer, since you can't summon the will to depose me."

"I can so! It's just—"

"Look at me, boy. Here I am, face to face with you alone, and *I* put you where you are," taunts Edward, beginning to circle him. "I took your ship, yes, and this fine living body, too, but best of all—I took your place in our lady's arms." He lunges, landing a punch on Alec's left shoulder. Alec staggers and glares.

"Piss off!"

"Now, Alec, can't you do better than that? Shall I tell you about what you've been missing all these years, you miserable conflicted little worm? I've been the lord and master in Mendoza's bed and, oh, it's been sweet," Edward chortles, circling again, feinting another strike. "Ah, that put a glint in your eye. You'd love to trounce me, you're dying to, but you don't dare, do you? Even when I've graciously given you permission to try?" *Whap,* he punches Alec's right shoulder, a bit harder than his first blow.

"Shame you're such a weakling, Alec. What on earth can be holding you back? You want to escape time, don't you? And we both know why. You miss her, don't you? And you think you can just slip free and have her again, *spiritually,* without any uncomfortable complications. As though her soul had breasts—and lips—and thighs—"

Alec howls in rage, charging him, and Edward dances back, laughing.

"And so, HAVE AT THEE," he cries, and dodges.

Mendoza is walking between the rows when Nicholas comes upon her. Her hair is slightly disheveled, and she clutches an ear of maize to her heart. She notices Nicholas and comes running out to meet him.

"Look, Nicholas," she cries, holding up the corn and stripping back the husk. The kernels are like jewels, amethyst and ruby, topaz and pearl. "We've got it at last! Scan it. Perfectly amazing lysine content."

Her face is flushed with triumph as she tilts back her head to look into his eyes. He catches his breath. The ages dissolve like mist and he is back in England, in the year 1554, having just fallen in love with the little girl in the garden.

The moment is so powerful he can hear, somewhere, the staccato beat of a dance, or it may be his own blood pounding in his ears. "After all this time," he murmurs.

"Isn't it fabulous?" she says proudly. "Let's go show the others."

"No—" Nicholas seizes her by the shoulders to prevent her from leaving.

"Why not?" At the touch of her, his memories are overwhelming him. She senses what he is feeling and looks up at him in surprise. Her eyes are wide, her lips parted. Young. Is she even eighteen yet? The dance music is louder now. Base viols, trumpets, drums! Bewildered, all she can manage to say is: "A-are you wearing Edward's cologne?"

Before he quite knows what he's doing Nicholas has leaned down to kiss her, as he kissed the girl in the garden long ago. And with that kiss, just as though it were a story, Nicholas comes into his power, and knows his strength.

She is aware of the music now, too, she hears the beat summoning, the melody beginning. He lifts his mouth and stares down into her eyes. "The corn has ripened in its time, Rose," he says. "Wilt thou dance a measure with me?"

"Yes," she says, and laughs. "Oh, *yes!*"

She leans in close again. He pushes into her mind with his own, and shouts—for abruptly the illusion of time has fled from him like a thief surprised in a garden. Nicholas has soared into a world of revelation. The music is coming from *him* now, and it rises glorious as the dawn. He is liberated. Wide-eyed, he gazes at the spirit in his arms, made all of opening roses, corn, milk. Perfume. Blue fire, and the foam of the seventh wave.

Nor are they alone. The figure he has pursued so long turns to face him . . .

"Do you hear? Where's that coming from? That's my favorite pavane," Mendoza cries.

I am my beloved's, and my beloved is mine. How the music plays!

Alec is pounding away in fury, hammering at Edward's defense, and though Edward is still laughing Alec is beginning to land blows now. Alec's body is learning how to do damage. Edward is oddly slow, suddenly, letting down his guard. Can he be tiring so soon?

Alec is too wound up to realize that this is utterly unlikely. He takes the advantage, pummeling Edward with increasing speed, blows to the chest, going for the head, there! Edward has put his gloves down, Edward has braced himself and is taking the shots, one after another after another, until he is reeling where he stands but does not fall.

"Bastard, bastard, bastard—" Alec is shouting hoarsely, and suddenly Edward's face is bleeding. Alec pauses, startled by the blood, uncertain, until Edward wipes it away and grins at him.

"This is so much easier, isn't it, than thinking? You can't mend anything you've broken, but you can still break yourself. Or me. What am I, after all, but the very image of what you hate the most? Let's make a blood sacrifice, Alec!"

With a roar Alec strikes out, silencing the voice, summoning all the pent-up fury of years to obliterate the face, the hated face in the mirror, with his fists. Right to the eye, left to the eye, break the damned broken nose some more! Smash the mouth! The lips split, blood runs down, a demon screams its release and soars up and away from him forever and he—and he—

Alec! No hyperfunction! Stand to, I'll have to call a foul! Stand to! ALEC!

—And it is as though Alec is rushing forward, straight for the mirror in which he is reflected, or is that Edward? The hero he has hated, and loved, and longed to be? The figure grins like Death, opens wide his arms in welcome, and then Alec has passed through the mirror into an unimaginably dark place. It is the Hall of Heroes, seen from the inside; and it is so much blood and shame and horror. Not a plume, not a banner to be seen. Disillusionment, inconsolable sorrow! The iciest of realities, with nothing to relieve the weight of responsibility, ever, especially not the vanity of self-immolation. Nothing to support him but bleak self-knowledge. *And this I relinquish to you, my son. Guard it well—*

———————

Nicholas and Mendoza stand swaying together, quiet. In the long grass of the garden at their feet is the perfect ear of *Mays mendozaii*. Around Nicholas, at last, is the faintest shimmer of air, flicker of light. It will never leave him now. He looks down at her and his question is unspoken, even subvocally, but she hears him and replies, dazed: "I'm all right. I feel . . . seventeen. Or maybe that's you. Nicholas, what's happened?"

"We stood together in the presence of God," he says, with serene certainty. She blinks, looks askance at him.

"I think I'd notice if I were face to face with the Almighty," she says.

"No, you wouldn't," he says in tender exasperation. "But here we stand in Paradise, you and I, all the same. It's enough."

"No, it isn't," she persists. "Because *something* amazing just happened, and everything has changed. It wasn't like this with Edward. We're going to have to talk about this."

"We have all of eternity to dispute, beloved."

"And what on earth will happen when Alec's set free, too?" She begins to laugh wildly. "When *he's* with us? Oh, Nicholas, look at the garden. We never left it, we never lost each other. You were with me all the time—"

Nicholas kisses her again. Their minds flow together, they merge again in the intimacy of eternity . . . and as their consciousness expands they perceive the commotion on board the *Captain Morgan*.

Edward staggers backward and falls.

Alec stands swaying, confused, dizzy. The smell of blood is in the air. He feels cold. The world has dropped out from under his feet, as it had from under Edward's when he received tiny screaming Alec and Nicholas into his hands, seventeen years earlier. The same sense of nausea overwhelms him. The responsibility crushes him. If *Edward* can fall—!

He looks down at Edward, and utters a hoarse cry of horror. The figure sprawled at his feet is a young giant with tousled fair hair, wearing only old-fashioned boxer's attire. The face is unrecognizable for its injuries. Abrasions, multiple subcutaneous hematomae, fractured nasal cartilage, dislocated jaw—

Reeling, disoriented, Alec pulls off his gloves. His hands protrude from Edward's immaculate shirt cuffs, though the rest of the shirt is nasty with Edward's blood. He raises his hands to his face and it is unmarked, though a harder, heavier face, not as smooth as it should be—and yet he remembers it—

"What's happened?" he shouts.

You've come of age, transmits Edward thickly, painfully. *Won back your flesh and your sins. I'll bear your punishment. Happy birthday.*

Alec drops to his knees and lifts—Edward?—by his shoulders. "Deaddy, I'm sorry! I'm so sorry, oh, what've I done—oh, look at your mouth—Please be all right, please—"

Round one concluded, the Captain informs them cautiously.

"I don't want there to be a round two," says Alec, panicking. "This is enough! Okay? Captain, call a draw!"

Well, but it ain't a draw, son. If you stop at one round, the match is yours, on account of you knocked him down. You win free and clear.

"Er—" Alec pulls back from Edward to ask if he agrees and is horrified afresh at Edward's blacked eyes. Edward spits out blood and nods.

You've won, Alec. You've done it. You've slain the giant. Are you happy now?

"No," says Alec, in remorse.

I was never happy when I slew them, either, Edward tells him, pushing himself further upright and fumbling off his gloves. *But at least one had the satisfaction of knowing one had done what was expected of a man . . . for all that that was the most contemptible of lies.*

He feels gingerly around his jaw and, grimacing, resets it with an audible *click*. Bully Hayes scuttles up and offers him a wet towel. He mops his bloody face, wincing. "And now, the child is truly father to the man. As it were. Whew!" Edward shakes his head and climbs to his feet. Alec hovers close to assist him.

"Lean on me, Dead. Don't fall!"

"No. I'll be all right." Edward stretches, works his shoulders and sighs in satisfaction. He gives Alec a sly look through puffed eyes already returning to normal, as his cuts close, as the bruises roil and vanish under his skin. "I believe I've had the best of the bargain after all. How limber one feels at seventeen! I'd quite forgotten."

"But—How—?"

"How indeed? What has the youthful hero overlooked, in the first flush of his victory?"

"But this doesn't have anything to do with timewalking," Alec protests.

You don't think so, son? Bloody hell, ain't it dawned on you—

Edward holds up a hand for silence. "If you please, Captain: he's *thinking*. Let us savor the exquisite rarity of the moment."

Alec nearly tells him to piss off, and stops himself. He peers suspiciously up at the nearest camera. "Is that a clue, Captain sir? How the hell could escaping time give you the power to swap bodies with somebody? Unless—"

"The wheels are turning," Edward coaxes. "He hasn't got it yet, but I think—yes, I really do suspect he's nearly—"

God almighty, lad! You might have figured it out yerself ages ago, if you'd been paying attention!

"Unless time and matter are *both* artifacts of perception—" He halts, a look of shock spreading over his face.

"While we're waiting, Captain, might I trouble you for a whiskey and soda?" Edward inquires.

With ice, Commander sir? And may I present you with a cigar, sir? On account of we got a son.

"So explain to me," says Mendoza, narrowing her eyes, "why it was necessary for the two of them to go slugging it out like a couple of cavemen to settle their differences."

"I think it was a sort of masque," says Nicholas. They hear the sound of voices coming up the hill. They turn to watch.

"They're talking to each other," says Mendoza. "That's a good sign."

Alec is wearing, once again, a brilliant tropical-patterned shirt and faded dungarees. Carefree and silly as his garments are, he is climbing the stairs as though the weight of centuries has descended on his shoulders.

". . . I never managed to get the growing up part right the first time," says Alec. "I did everything I wanted to do, but I was never the man I wanted to be. And this is all wonderful, but it doesn't change that, does it? I still can't escape what I'm supposed to do, can I?"

"None of us can, if it's any consolation," Edward tells him. He has dressed himself in a fresh suit of his own clothing, though the mid-Victorian cut hangs a little loosely on his youthful frame, and his step is as light as though he were a schoolboy on holiday. He spots the two figures on the terrace. "Be that as it may, there are certain compensations for your enlightenment." They mount the last balustraded stair, and enter the garden where Mendoza and Nicholas wait for them.

"My dear," says Edward with an ironical half-bow, sweeping off his tall hat. "Might I have the honor of introducing Alec Checkerfield, seventh earl of Finsbury? A very promising young fellow!" He replaces his hat at a jaunty angle.

"Hello, Mendoza," says Alec, looking sheepish. "I've, er, come of age."

"I can see," she exclaims. "Oh, Alec, the most wonderful thing has happened! Come here!"

She throws her arms around his neck and kisses him. There is a tremendous rainbowed shock, radiating outward in waves of insulted time. As the air begins to shimmer about their bodies, Alec lifts his mouth in a howl of sheer animal exuberance.

"Ah. I thought this might happen," says Edward, a little smugly.

"Perhaps our state is multiplied to the next power," Nicholas suggests. He knows, at last, that this or in fact anything is possible now. "I think—" He looks about them at the garden, which has begun to shimmer as well. Even the house, and the sky and the sea and the *Captain Morgan*, have begun to shimmer.

"It *is* a geometric progression," Mendoza gasps. "How marvelous!"

"Captain!" roars Alec. "Hoist anchor and set sail!"

Aye, son! We're casting off!

And everything they inhabit—the ship, the sky, the sea, the house, the garden, and they themselves, their whole reality—lifts gently free of linear time and sails into eternity.

PART VI

CHAPTER 27

Catalina Island, 8 July 2355

Aegeus considered himself in the mirror and daubed a little more makeup on his left cheek. He turned to Victor. "What do you think?" he inquired. "Do I look as though I'm about to do something militant?"

"Quite," Victor replied. "As long as the cameras stay on your face."

Aegeus looked down at his suit. "You have a point," he admitted. "Summon a few security techs, please."

Sighing, Victor stepped out into the hall and waved at the techs on duty there. They approached obediently and Aegeus shouldered past Victor to survey them. "You," he said, tapping the foremost on the shoulder. "You're about my size. Let's see how that combat jacket looks on me."

The tech shrugged out of the garment in question as Aegeus divested himself of his suit coat. Victor held it while Aegeus tried on the combat jacket, fussing with the pocket flaps, adjusting the fit. He unfastened the clock pin from his lapel and stuck it on the front of the jacket. "Oh, yes, this'll do," he said, pleased. "Splendid. Now I feel the part as well. Let's not waste any of this energy! Are the cameras ready?"

And so the broadcast went out, to all Executive Headquarters, on all channels, very much in the style in which Suleyman's famous announcement of the liberation of Options Research had been presented.

It began with Aegeus turning, as though distracted from some vital task, and peering sharply into the cameras. He looked solemn, but with a suggestion of controlled and righteous anger. He spoke in Latin: "To all operatives still capable of receiving this warning, greetings!

"Facilitator General Aegeus, Southern European Sector Head, reporting. If you have received shipments of Theobromos from our mortal masters, do not, repeat, DO NOT distribute them as instructed. Do not under any circumstances ingest any Theobromos. As some of you may by now have discovered, the shipments have been adulterated with a poisonous substance."

Aegeus leaned in closer. In the background could be heard a dim clamor suggesting riot. It was recorded, but only Victor and Aegeus knew that.

"My fellow immortal ones," continued Aegeus, letting a bit more rage show in his face, "I regret to inform you that we have been betrayed. I have in my possession undeniable proof that, after so many thousands of years of faithful service, we were to be rewarded by abrupt termination. If you doubt me, analyze the contents of any of those prettily decorated boxes with which you've been presented."

He gasped, as though struggling with his emotions. "If you could see the poor devil here who fell for their trap—or maybe you have casualties of your own already. Listen to me, brothers and sisters! You know I've never been reckless. You know I always counseled patience with the mortals, even when we uncovered the horror that was Options Research. I was loyal, may the gods forgive me! But *this*—this is the last straw. The mortal masters have at last shown, finally and conclusively, that they are too vicious, too stupid to be allowed to control the great enterprise in which we have all labored so long. If we suffer this outrage, we are indeed their slaves." He tore the clock pin from its place and held it up to the cameras. "This should have warned us all, this symbol of their infamy!"

His voice rose, his eyes widened. "We must take control. *We* made this Company; we are the rightful inheritors of the glorious heritage we've preserved for so many centuries. For our own sakes, and for the sake of innocent humanity, we must wrest power from this handful of mortal monsters! Now, before it is too—"

On cue, Victor activated the charge that sent a flare and puff of smoke billowing through the room, as Aegeus winked out from in front of the cameras. He shut them off.

"Oh, that went terribly well," cried Aegeus in a gleeful voice. "Wouldn't you say that went well?"

"I thought so," Victor agreed.

"Yes, the feces have now well and truly encountered the windmill." Aegeus peeled off the combat jacket and held it out at arm's length, considering, before he dropped it. "Not really my style, on the whole," he decided. "Well. Now to dress for dinner!"

At That Moment in Seattle

Labienus rocked back in his chair, roaring with laughter as the holo vanished in its flash and boom. "Oh, the audacity," he cried. "The sheer hypocritical nerve of that man! What a little tin demagogue." He mopped his eyes with the back of one hand. "I'm almost sorry to think he'll lose. Almost . . . oh, well, who am I fooling? I won't regret watching his head come off at all. I will miss having such a worthy opponent, though."

"No, you won't," Kiu told him, yawning behind her hand.

"I will," protested Labienus. "A man of my own intellect, my methods and aspirations . . . except for his lamentable dependence on slaves. And the fact that he's a crude boor. Other than that there's not much to distinguish between us, really."

"You don't think he could be persuaded to your point of view, with a knife at his throat?" Kiu inquired.

"Of course he could," Labienus said. "But I'd never be able to trust Aegeus. He hasn't the necessary moral character. Too fond of his comforts! Always maundering on about the mortals and their art, their philosophies, their perishable flesh . . . ugh. Makes me feel unclean even thinking about it."

"Well, but what could he do, once you'd exterminated them all?"

"Oh, I wouldn't put it past him to attempt some in-vitro revival nonsense with mortal DNA," Labienus replied, getting to his feet and stretching. "There are caches of the stuff hidden away in the Company's vaults, or so we've always been told. I can just see him making a new Adam in his own image, can't you? And some sweet Eve for a playmate. Disgusting!"

"There are rumors you got mixed up in something like that," Kiu told him slyly, watching as he crossed to his wardrobe and pulled out a garment bag. He turned to her in surprise.

"What? Victor? Not at all. He was born mortal, like the rest of us. I merely experimented with his augmentation, to make him the truly useful tool he is."

"Not Victor! I heard it was a black project," Kiu prompted. "Something that went by the code name *Adonai?* . . ."

"Ahhh." Labienus paused with a dinner jacket over his arm. For a moment he looked mild and wistful, as though contemplating some sentimental memory. "*That* fellow. Nennius and I masterminded that project. My Death, the Destroyer of Worlds. We told them we needed a New Enforcer, and the monkeys obligingly put together the most wonderful monster for us. Great hulking creature with a brilliant mind, and what courage he had! What virtuous zeal!

Even when our little idea-men botched the program, he was unfailingly destructive. A thousand pities he couldn't have been made one of us.

"Oh, well." He hung the dinner jacket up in the bag. "You'd better pack, you know; we've got a transport to catch. Will you be wearing that slinky red number tonight?"

"Of course," Kiu said, tossing her head and brushing back her hair. She grinned at him. "No matter how much blood spills, I'll still look divine."

London, the Afternoon of 8 July 2355:
The Masters of the Universe:
They Confront the Unthinkable

"You said they'd never be able to tell what was in the chocolates," screamed Rossum, pointing an accusatory finger at Bugleg. He was still gaping in horror at the space where the holo had run only a second before, broadcasting Aegeus's call for rebellion.

"They weren't supposed to," Bugleg stammered.

"You promised!" Rappacini wailed. "You and that cousin of yours. That nasty man. Get him online. Find out what he did wrong!"

"You idiots, there's no time for that," Freestone told them, but Bugleg had already summoned his unit from the table and was fumbling out a communication card. He slipped it into the port. After a breathless second the screen lit up with a geometric pattern of purple and green, as a tweedly dance tune played. Over the music a smooth electronic voice said: "Mr. Ratlin regrets to inform the caller that he is presently on holiday. If you're feeling blue, Ratlin's Finest is just the thing to lift those weary spirits. Luscious whole-milk chocolates high in butterfat content, manufactured with scrupulous sanitary care. And we're pleased to announce our new Summer Assortment! When you're relaxing at the seaside—"

"They'll kill us." Rossum clutched his head, rocked himself back and forth. "They'll all come and kill us. We'll die. We're dead."

"We've got to hide," said Bugleg, looking around frantically as though a suitable hole might present itself.

"Where on earth can we hide from *them*?" demanded Freestone. "They're all cyborgs. Oh, I always knew this would happen—"

"Wait! Wait! I know who'll be loyal," exclaimed Rappacini. "Dr. Zeus. He's the Company, after all! Isn't he?"

There was a pause, punctuated by terrified asthmatic breathing, while they all considered his suggestion. One by one, they looked sidelong at the bronze figure on its pedestal in the corner. "But he was Lopez's idea," objected Bugleg.

"But *we* made him," said Rappacini.

"But we made Lopez, too," Freestone pointed out.

"But we don't have any choice," said Rossum. "Didn't he get rid of that Recombinant thing for us? Hasn't he worked fine ever since?"

"Er . . . Dr. Zeus?" Freestone turned to the bronze. "Can you hear us?"

I HEAR.

In midair the robed figure appeared beside its original, and with a squeal of metal turned its greened head as though to regard them from the hollow sockets of its eyes. Freestone caught his breath, and in what he hoped was a firm voice said: "Do you know about our problem?"

I KNOW.

"Well, can you help us?"

I CAN.

"Then help us! What must we do to be saved?"

YOU MUST EVACUATE YOUR PERSONNEL TO THE FORTIFIED COMMAND CENTER ON SANTA CATALINA ISLAND, it told them. **YOU WILL SURVIVE THE REBELLION THERE.**

"Okay, yes, good! That's the sort of thing we need to hear." Freestone looked around at the others. "How do we do that, please? Can you get a transport for us?"

YOUR AIR TRANSPORT IS WAITING ON THE ROOF. IT SEATS FIFTY-THREE IN COMFORT.

"Great," cried Rappacini. "We can take our best people! Can you secure a communications line for us, please?"

THE LINE IS OPEN AND SECURED.

So they summoned their best and brightest, did the masters of the universe, and Dr. Zeus stood passively in midair considering them.

All over England the calls went out, received by terrified geniuses hiding in closets or under beds. Soon from every quarter they came, slipping furtively along the deserted streets of London to the nearest tube station or crossing open fields on foot, expecting every moment that raging cyborgs with disrupter pistols would leap out from behind the copses and spinneys.

Oddly enough, none did.

The reason for this was that the rank and file of cyborgs had no knowledge of the dastardly plot. Aegeus's message had gone out to the Executive Facilitators only, and they were already quite aware that there was something wrong with the Theobromos. Not one of them, therefore, had distributed the stuff. The painfully detailed logistical chain had broken and the Theobromos sat undelivered in its boxes in offices all over the world, except in Morocco where it was burning merrily in Suleyman's pool.

Where were the rank and file immortals, if they weren't marching shoulder to shoulder on their erstwhile masters, as they had in *Cyborg Conquest*?

There was a high plateau somewhere north of the Matto Grosso, an island in the air, a place no mortal could reach on foot. The Botanist Smythe, however, had scaled it easily, hauling herself up by creepers and reclining at last under the towering canopy of gigantic ancient trees, under the trailing moss and epiphytes, under the flight of bright-winged macaws. She wasn't a particularly nice person, the Botanist Smythe. Still, she had opted to spend what might be the last hours of her life in the place she had come closest to loving anything.

On Santa Rosa Island, off the coast of California, the tourist transport lowered with a whoosh, and the yellow grasses bent backward in the rush of air. The tourists filed from the vehicle, and somehow none of them noticed the lone visitor who winked out from their midst. On a deserted stretch of beach, he looked skyward and saw the tiny black figure planing toward him, coming over the sea, descending, avoiding the thermals generated by the hot barren hills. A moment later Raven settled on Juan Bautista's shoulder, ruffling out her feather-cloak. He smiled at her.

At a certain famous museum in Florence, the curator failed to emerge from his office, though it was long past closing time. The mortal guards occasionally peered in at Beckman where he sat alone, and at last one of them coaxed him to come out and join them for a midnight supper. He sat in the company of mortals and the paintings he had spent his immortal life preserving, and Beckman felt a wave of relief sweep over him. Why go back to his empty apartment, ever again? Why face the end, whatever it was, alone, when he could spend it gazing into the tenderly mocking eyes of Botticelli's Flora?

Everywhere in the world, as the hours passed, the immortals were finding their places. In museums, in gardens, in ancient libraries, they appeared for the last solitary watch.

In London, nobody seemed to notice the woman who had retreated into a high gallery at the Globe Theatre and was staring at the empty stage, watching shadows strut and posture.

In China, there was a whole party of silent folk on the Great Wall, looking out to the north, as though phantom armies massed there.

In Prague a well-dressed man sat quietly at a café table in the old square. He ordered tea, and watched the mortal carnival for hours, and when the great Clock struck and its mechanical Death nodded, he nodded back.

In Iraq a woman knelt in the ruins of Babylon the Great and wept awhile, and at last settled herself to wait at the base of a broken statue of Ishtar.

What were you expecting they'd do?

Rise in rebellion, as in a nice testosterone-loaded science fiction novel, laser pistols blazing away in both fists?

Veracruz

He wore a loincloth of jaguar skin, a shivering sunburst of feathers that radiated a full meter out from his head, and golden bells that rang as he stamped out the Dance of the Cycle of Days. Jade beads clicked out the rhythm against his chest, in the long passage of the dance where the drums fell silent. The audience watched, rapt, waiting for a misstep that never happened, though sweat fell from his body like rain; every step perfect, balanced, effortless. While he danced, it was possible to believe he held the universe together, and would dance forever.

He was Agustin Aguilar, twenty-two years old, Flatley Scholarship winner, principal dancer with Ballet Folklorico de Veracruz. It was the eve of his wedding.

For that reason he left the party after the show early, programmed his car for Acapulco, and cranked back his seat so he could get some sleep on the long drive. The city lights fell behind. For a while there were stars; they slipped gradually under a wall of black cloud, but by then Agustin was sleeping and didn't see the red flash of lightning, miles ahead in the mountains to the west.

It was hours before the strike came. It jolted him awake when it hit, a flare of light brighter than the sun, and the afterimage as all the instruments on the console burned out. Then, a drop and an impact that rattled his teeth, a prolonged scream of metal, a fan of sparks thrown up to either side; the car's ag drive had cut out and it had fallen to the road, was hurtling forward across asphalt, slewing to one side as it came. Off the edge of the road it went, into a ditch, with a sickening jar.

Agustin could see nothing but pitch blackness for a moment. A light approached, diffused through the dust cloud he'd raised. He threw off his shock enough to shout, to pound on the transparent canopy, to grope for the emergency release lever. The canopy was jammed, but someone was outside now, yanking on it, a black silhouette backlit by headlights through the roiling dust. The canopy was wrenched away with a shriek and someone was hauling him out bodily. Agustin was set on his feet, shivering in the night air. "Are you all right, man?" shouted his rescuer.

"I think so," said Agustin through chattering teeth, staring at the stranger. An ordinary-looking guy, despite his astonishing strength. He seemed a little older than Agustin, had a lean somber face and Indian cheekbones, a black gaze like a flint knife.

"My God," said the stranger. "Struck by lightning! Your car's fried, my friend." He pointed down at the hood where paint had bubbled away to bare steel at the edges of the black hole, out of which white smoke and floating ash streamed upward.

"My tuxedo—" Agustin started forward, but the man stopped him like a stone wall.

"I'll get it," he said brusquely, and a second later was handing Agustin his suitcase and garment bag. "Come on, my son, let's get you to Acapulco."

Agustin was grateful for the warmth of the stranger's truck, for the hot soup from the stranger's thermjar, for the use of the stranger's Shisha to notify the car rental agency, for every kilometer that took him away from the wreck and closer to Marisol.

"So, what's the tuxedo for?" said the stranger. His face was spookily lit by the green console lights.

"I'm getting married tomorrow," said Agustin. "Today, I guess. The ninth. I have a lot to thank you for, Mr . . . ?"

"Aguilar," said the other. "Porfirio Aguilar."

"I'm Agustin Aguilar! Do you think we might be related?"

"Maybe," said Porfirio. He accelerated, racing the night to get the boy to his wedding day, one gesture of hope at the end of time.

Portmeirion

The pitch was not going well. Nevertheless, Mary deWit squared her shoulders and smiled her brightest for the holocams.

"Actually, Mr. Plowman, the media made it look at lot worse than it was. The loss of life was mainly due to the superheated gas. The city itself—"

"No! What kind of money-grubbing idiot rebuilds a city on an erupting volcano?"

"But Mons Olympus didn't erupt, Mr. Plowman. The bomb set off the reaction in the power plant, and that blew out the magma chamber. There were survivors, you know, in the underground residential blocks, and the buildings *above* the power plant were untouched. If you'll just look at the figures I sent you, you'll see that the cost of rebuilding would be offset—"

Mr. Plowman interrupted her with more uncomplimentary remarks about the stupidity of living on Mars in the first place, followed by his opinion of corporate greed in general and the Griffith Family Arean Trust in particular. Mary was grateful when he ended the transmission. Carefully she shut the holocams down, crossed Mr. Plowman off her list of potential donors, went into the bathroom and had a screaming cry into the hotel's towels.

When she felt a little better, she washed and dried her face, retouched her makeup, and went out to face her next ordeal. Someone was standing by the window in her room, looking out at the night. Mary, feeling a welcome flood of righteous wrath, pulled out her Gwyddon and poised her thumb over the alarm button.

"What the bloody hell do you think you're doing in my room?" she said. The man turned to face her. She gasped, dropped the Gwyddon, clutched at her heart. He was beside her in a second, supporting her.

"Child—I'm so sorry—"

"Papa!" she cried, when she could get her breath. Then— "You're not real. You died in that wreck. You've been gone twenty years. I've been working too hard and this is my unconscious summoning you up. Oh, Goddess—"

"Actually, my death was faked," he said in a sheepish voice. It took a minute for that to sink in, so caught up was she in the pleasure of burying her face against his shoulder, feeling his arms around her, being for a moment seven years old and safe from all harm. But when it sank in:

"Faked?" She pulled back and stared at him. Eliphal deWit, just as he'd looked . . . in the days of her childhood, his beard cinnamon-brown, and not the stooped graying man whose eyeglasses were the only thing to have been recovered from the wreck.

"How's your mother?" he inquired, as though he'd left only the week before.

"In a retirement home in Newport, hating everyone, as usual," said Mary, choking on tears. "And you'd better do some explaining. You'd better do it pretty damned fast—"

"Shhh," he said, putting his long forefinger to her lips, just as he had done when she'd been little. There were tears in his eyes, too. "Sit down, baby. I just wanted to see you. I'll tell you everything. It doesn't matter. Not now."

Paris

There was a gracious old house on a street of chestnut trees. It was beautifully furnished in late-nineteenth-century style, with paintings and carpets and antique furniture, except in one upper chamber.

The floor was tiled in that room, and along one wall a maintenance console blinked with tiny lights, and against the opposite wall was a transparent tank filled with blue fluid, glowing softly. In its depths the body floated.

It was recognizably Kalugin now, much more presentable than it had been on the day when Nan had received Suleyman's call from Fez. He had tried to prepare her for what she'd see, when she arrived after a whirlwind flight. Both he and Latif had stared when she'd knelt and taken the ruined thing in her arms.

Though Kalugin's immortal body was now nearly healed, the condition of his immortal mind was still in question. There was brain activity, but whether or not damage had been done by long-term immersion in heavy metals was uncertain. No operative had ever spent two and a half centuries in a sunken wreck in a state of fugue.

Nan believed he was still in there. Given enough time to heal, he would certainly wake one morning, open his eyes, turn his wondering face to her.

Unfortunately, they had run out of time.

Though that wasn't why she was weeping now, as she sat by the tank.

In her hand was an opened envelope and the card it had contained. Within the card was written, in a graceful and old-fashioned hand, the following:

Dear Nan,

I doubt whether I shall ever have the opportunity to speak to you again, and so I must take this chance to wish you every happiness.

Whatever may befall, I cannot face the Silence without letting you know that I have always held you in the very highest regard.

Please accept this expression of sincere esteem from

Your true friend,

Victor, Facilitator

London, the Late Evening of 8 July 2355

"Hurry up," cried Bugleg. "Start the motor!"

"Don't you dare," Freestone snapped at the pilot. "There's three more of my people on the way up. I just spotted them down in the street!"

The pilot sighed and nodded, but set the motor warming up anyway. There were cries of relief from her passengers, who were all in a pitiable state of terror by this time. Freestone glared at her, and pointedly wedged the door open with his body. At last the roof elevator opened and three figures straggled out, clutching their travel packs.

"Oh, *them*," Rossum said, and sniffed, because the latecomers were none other than the team responsible for, among other things, the ill-fated Recombinant project: Clive Rutherford, Francis Chatterji, and Foxen Ellsworth-Howard.

"Please don't leave us," beseeched Rutherford, throwing his pudgy body forward. He tripped and fell, and his friends were instantly beside him, pulling him up.

"Hold the shracking door!" Ellsworth-Howard snarled.

"It's not our fault," Chatterji said. "The tube ran late! There was a f-fire at the St. Pancras station."

"Was it the cyborgs rioting?" Freestone's eyes widened.

"We don't know," Rutherford panted, shouldering his way in and finding a seat, with Chatterji close behind him.

"It wasn't my Preservers," Ellsworth-Howard said, as the door slammed shut and sealed itself behind him. "They got more shracking sense than that!"

"Take off!" Bugleg told the pilot, in the loudest voice he'd ever used.

"*Your* Preservers?" said Rappacini coldly, surveying Ellsworth-Howard. "That's right; you were the head of the Physical Design group, weren't you?"

"He was the one who worked out the original augmentation method on the cyborgs," shouted someone from the back of the transport.

"So we have *you* to thank for all this," shouted someone else, as the transport lifted off with a lurch and a roar.

"Oh yeh?" Ellsworth-Howard said, flinging down his pack and starting for the back of the transport in a menacing fashion, rolling up one sleeve as he went. Chatterji leaped up and caught him, and pulled him down into an empty seat.

"Please," he cried. "What good will it do to b-blame each other now? We were all part of it!"

At that there was silence, as the mortals considered his words and could find no way to deny them. London fell away below the transport, and they made the suborbital leap to heaven. "Wasting my shracking Preservers," muttered Ellsworth-Howard. "Serves 'em right."

———

Lopez would have heartily agreed with him on that point, had he been there, but he was making his way to the conference room at that moment.

He was very much out of temper. All his authorizations had been canceled, which meant that the lift doors wouldn't open for him, and even when he ripped a hole in them and clambered through, the lift still stubbornly refused to rise. He had had to tear the fire door off the emergency stair and climb up twelve flights, where he then had to smash another door to get into the hallway. By the time he picked up the water cooler and used it to batter down the doors to the conference room he was every inch the rampaging cyborg rebel his masters so feared.

Lopez stared around a moment at the empty room. It was littered with discarded chlorilar cups and snack food wrappers, obviously deserted in haste. "Those cowardly little cretins," he growled. He faced the bronze of Artemisium Zeus in an accusatory sort of way. "Almighty Zeus! I demand an answer. Hear me!"

I HEAR.

"You hear, do you? Well, explain yourself! How could you let this happen? You told me you'd save us, and instead you stood by and did *nothing*, while the masters plotted to disable us."

YOU HAVE NOT BEEN DISABLED.

"Some of us have! Or didn't you see Aegeus's warning broadcast, All-Seeing One?"

AEGEUS IS LYING. NONE OF YOUR PEOPLE HAVE BEEN DECEIVED BY THE MORTALS' GIFT.

Lopez looked astonished, and then began to pace in intense speculation. "Of course. Aegeus is lying, because he hopes to trigger violent revolution. He thinks *he'll* be in charge when the dust settles! Yes, that's it, I see it now. The clever bastard. Well—" He peered up at the ceiling again. "All the same, the masters treacherously conspired in our downfall, and you let them get away with it."

I DID NOT LET THEM GET AWAY.

"What?"

I SENT THEM TO THE COMMAND POST ON SANTA CATALINA ISLAND.

"What kind of punishment is that? That's the safest place they could be," Lopez said indignantly.

AEGEUS IS ALREADY THERE. SO IS LABIENUS. SULEYMAN AND AN ARMED FORCE OF HIS ADHERENTS ARE ON THEIR WAY

**THERE TO SEIZE POWER. THERE IS ALSO AN ARMY APPROACH-
ING BY SEA.**

"Oh," said Lopez. A smile of incredulous and nasty delight spread across
his face. "They'll be sitting in the middle of a wasp's nest, won't they? Good
Lord, whoever wins the power struggle, the masters will be exterminated like
rats." His smile faded as he glanced at the bronze again. "Er . . . forgive me,
All-Seeing, that I ever doubted you. You have truly avenged your people. Accept my heartfelt thanks and my worship." Something occurred to him, and he
added: "You said there's an army coming by sea? Whose army?"

THE ENFORCER BUDU.

Lopez went a sick pale color. After a moment he gasped: "Not—not the old
monster from Prehistory? I heard he was disabled ages ago! He and all his
kind, because they rebelled."

THEY WERE. HE WAS REPAIRED BY THE FACILITATOR JOSEPH.

"Joseph." Lopez clutched at the edge of the conference table. "Joseph, yes,
of course, his loyalty was always in question. Certainly *I* never trusted him.
Well, but—the Enforcers? Those creatures lived for retribution and slaughter!
There'll be nothing left of the masters by the time they've finished with them."

He looked up at the bronze with a new respect in his eyes. Or was it fear?
Slowly he knelt and abased himself on the conference room carpet. "All-
Seeing, Orderer, Overseer, Lord of Justice! Truly Your just wrath is terrible. Forgive Your servant his transgressions, however unwitting, and preserve him
against the great hour to come."

Dr. Zeus did not reply.

At last Lopez pushed himself up off his hands and knees. Looking about
uneasily, he collected the discarded cups and wrappers and carried them to
the fusion hopper.

Catalina Island, the Early Evening of 8 July 2355

The transport dropped silently down through the evening sky, darkening stars
as it came, and settled on the landing pad below Mount Torquemada. There
was weeping and wringing of hands even before the motor had been cut.
"Why aren't the lights on?" cried Bugleg.

"Why didn't the ground crew answer us?" cried Rossum.

"Why is it still night here?" cried Rappacini.

"Shut up," the pilot told them, climbing from her seat and groping for a
light. After an affronted silence, Rossum said: "You're fired!"

"Fine," said the pilot, finding her light at last and stepping out onto the air-pad. The door in the face of the mountain opened and someone ran out toward them, belatedly waving a pair of fluorescent landing cues. "We're here." The pilot waved her light.

"What's going on?" demanded Freestone as the passengers came tumbling out of the transport. The person with the cues saluted.

"Are you the party from the London office?"

"Yes! Why didn't you respond to our landing requests?"

"I'm sorry, sir! We're still figuring out how to work the console. All our cyborg personnel are gone."

"Gone where?"

"We don't know, sir! They're all AWOL since yesterday, and they were the ones who ran everything out here. It was all we could do to lower the perimeter defense so you could land. We were hoping some of you people could help us figure out—"

"They could be lurking anywhere," wailed Rappacini.

"Oh, dear." Freestone looked around in the darkness. His associates were milling about, clutching their bags and staring up in horror at the cold stars. "You'd better light our way inside—"

"Yes, sir. This way—"

As they were all filing in through the narrow door, pushing and crowding, the man with the cue lights turned and said: "And there's somebody who got here this morning, waiting for you. He's from a lawyer's office and he has something to deliver to a Frances Chatterji. We told him there was nobody here by that name, but we had a flight expected and she might be on it—"

"HE!" Chatterji looked up and made his way through the ant-stream to the man. "I'm Francis Chatterji."

Someone unshaven and weary rose from where he had been reclining between two chairs against a wall. "Francis Chatterji?"

"Yes." Chatterji turned.

"Here." The stranger thrust a large envelope at him. "I'm from Spratt and Cicero. I was supposed to deliver this to you tomorrow, but I'd like to get the hell out of here."

Chatterji took the envelope in bewilderment. "I-is it a subpoena or something?"

"No; it's a bequest," the stranger replied, pulling on his coat and straightening his tie. "From a very old client. Can I get a cab from here to the harbor?"

"Communications are still down," the man with the cue lights told him.

"Then I'll walk. Good night, Mr. Chatterji," the stranger said, and pushed past the last of the scientists to make his way out into the darkness. Chatterji stared after him a moment.

"But I don't—"

"Come on, Chatty," called Rutherford, turning back. "I just heard somebody saying there's limited space in the bunker!"

Chatterji turned, hastily sticking the envelope into his coat and running to join his friends.

Prior to the ascendancy of the Beast Liberation Movement, Arabian horses had been bred in the isolated valley of El Rancho Escondido, and the property had housed a visitors' museum with a collection of heavily ornamented antique saddles. The museum did its best to evoke the romantic days of the old Spanish dons, though in fact there had never been any Spanish dons in residence on Catalina Island. After the BLM outlawed ownership of horses in 2247 there were no Arabians in residence either, and shortly thereafter the Rancho was acquired by the Island Preservancy. So were the saddles.

The old Rancho and its outbuildings had been demolished, distasteful relics of beast exploitation that they were, and replaced by a fine new Preservancy Center. Most residents of the island had the vague idea that something ecological was done up there by scientists attending conventions. They were wrong.

An elite few did attend certain conventions at the Preservancy Center, but they weren't scientists, and what they did there had nothing to do with ecology.

The saddles occasionally came in handy, though.

In keeping with the rather outré recreation practiced at the Preservancy Center, it was housed in a complex resembling a gothic castle: stone buildings around a courtyard, few and narrow windows, lots of grotesquely imaginative ironwork. All the retro was on the surface, however. The interior was state of the art in its amenities, especially the grand banquet facility with its gleaming kitchen.

In the Gentlemen's Lounge, Victor studied his mirrored reflection. Not a hair out of place. His chosen costume was a flawless reproduction of the evening dress he'd worn in 1906, down to the diamond stud winking on his stiff shirtfront. He was pleased with the effect. He was especially pleased with his hands. Liberated from gloves at last, they were eerily smooth. He lifted them now to stroke his beard, twist his mustaches into yet more acute points, and was pleased also to notice the fine beading of sweat in his palms.

He bent to the floral arrangement beside him and selected a single flower for a boutonniere. It was one of the immense white poppies that grew wild on the island. Tucking it into his lapel, he consulted the mirror again. Yes; just big enough to look odd, faintly clownish, an exquisitely understated note of the bizarre. Its papery petals were exactly the same color as his hands.

Executive Facilitator Victor? The broadcast came through an impression of swirling dust and a roaring motor. Victor arched his eyebrows and transmitted a reply.

Present and receiving.

Security Technical Sargon reporting in, sir. We're at the front gate.

Ah. Welcome. Victor sent the code that opened the lock. *You've brought the crew I particularly requested?*

Yes, sir. Every one of them. Everybody in evening dress.

Splendid. Just follow the road in and park in the service lot. Bring them to the courtyard. I'll meet you there for a briefing session.

On our way, sir.

Victor turned from the mirror, smiling. Time for mood music. He activated the sound system and great flatulent waves of Wagner rolled out from speakers all over the Center, selections from *Die Gotterdammerung.*

They had been born to different races and nations, but there was something disconcertingly similar in their smooth faces. Authority, confidence, wisdom; and, tonight, a certain gaiety, glittering in hard eyes. An excitement edged with just the slightest . . . unease?

Not these elegant folk uneasy, surely, not these gentlemen and ladies in evening dress. It was true that they were very nearly at the end of recorded time, but every one of them had seen epochs roll by, had survived horrors and splendors beyond mortal comprehension.

For example, Facilitator General Kiu—stepping lightly from the limousine, accepting Labienus's proffered arm with a gracious smile—once clung desperately to the arm of the marauder bearing her on his horse from the flaming ruin of her village, in a world so long past the most determined archaeologist might seek for a trace of it in vain. She had seduced kings and ministers in her time, she had watched impassive as Troy fell. Nothing to frighten her in a little Armageddon.

Nennius wasn't worried either, gallantly fetching out her silk wrap for Facilitator Ashoreth. Nothing had been able to terrify him since he had watched the other tribe confronting his parents' timid little migrating party, challenging their right to cross a long-drowned causeway from one continent to an adjacent one. He had cried and cowered when the stone-tipped spears began to fly, hidden his face until the screaming stopped and he'd looked up into the pale eyes of the bearded giant. *Why are you weeping, mortal child?* his rescuer had said. *This is the way of the world.* He had built his immortal life on that wisdom.

So had Gamaliel, though he had heard it from a very different person: stern-eyed Facilitator Amaunet, leaning down like a living shadow through shattered clay-and-stick walls to lift him from his dying mother's arms. *This is the way of the world,* Amaunet had advised him, and then she had added: *Look at the slaughter, mortal child. This is mortal evil.* Gamaliel had never forgotten, even to this late hour when he was adjusting his tie and nodding to her over the roof of their limousine.

And he had passed the wisdom on in his turn, when he had lifted the child who would be Aegeus from the smashed cart and showed him the whooping thieves playing ball with the head of the boy's father. *This is mortal evil,* he had told the child. *This is what the monkeys do. Never forget it.*

Nor had Aegeus ever forgotten, though he had built walls of graciousness around himself to contain the ugly truth, kept it locked away as though in a reliquary of gold and rock crystal, meant to hold something precious. Indeed, the truth was precious, and he had carefully gifted young Moreham with it, when he had found the child shivering, trying to warm himself at the ashes where bones smoldered. Aegeus had taken him up and set him before him in the saddle, and pointed out across all that the legions had left of Isurium. *Never forget this,* he had instructed. *Never forgive them.*

There were indeed certain ideological differences among the immortals arriving for dinner. Certain heads were eagerly anticipating seeing certain other heads roll, so abiding was their mutual hatred. Yet all of them shared one common bond, in their profound loathing and contempt for mortal humanity. They had never forgotten. They would never forgive.

"Good evening," cried Victor, bowing and gesturing them in. "Gentlemen. Ladies! I trust you're all in good appetite? Lady Ereshkigal, I have never seen you looking lovelier. Tvashtar, sir! It's been ages, hasn't it? Madame Xi Wang-Mu, my compliments, indeed. That was always your particular shade of black."

A pair of security techs, unobtrusive in dinner jackets, bowed and opened the doors to the executive dining room. Another pair were busy at the sideboard, where among the covered dishes and bottles gleamed several wicked-looking carving knives. Aegeus spotted them, and so did Labienus, and each in their turn caught Victor's eye. He gave each a bland smile and a barely perceptible nod.

"Why, Victor, how marvelous," exclaimed Ashoreth, gazing around. "Thirteen at table! Fabulously unlucky, of course."

"I can think of no more appropriate time to spit in the face of Fate, dear lady, can you?" replied Victor, pulling out a chair for her.

"What a charming conceit," Aegeus remarked of their place card holders: small crouching figures of solid silver, skeletal cherubs after Gorey. He noted as well that Victor had arranged all of Labienus's cabal on the left hand side of the table, six chairs for Labienus and Kiu, Nennius, Ashoreth, Tvashtar, and Xi Wang-Mu. Here came two more security techs bearing an immense soup tureen: six waiters in all. Mentally he gave Victor high marks. The moment of betrayal, when it came, ought to play out with the efficiency of a clock striking.

Labienus, observing the seating arrangements, was just thinking the same thing.

"Oleanders," remarked Amaunet approvingly. She was a woman of few words.

"You noticed," cried Victor, breaking a spray of poisonous loveliness from the centerpiece. "If you'll permit me—" He leaned close to tuck the blossoms into her dark bosom. "And I really must, I can't resist—" he murmured, and set his mouth on hers and kissed deeply, a full kiss, parting her lips. Labienus, looking on, shuddered. He covered it by seizing up a bottle of port from the sideboard and inspecting the label, and so missed noticing that Aegeus too was watching in distaste.

"If you please," growled Facilitator Aethelstan, "I am Madame Amaunet's escort this evening."

"Sir." Victor came up for air and bowed to him. "I do beg your pardon. I'm a hopeless romantic, my friend, what can I say? May I offer you an aperitif? Perhaps Campari?"

General laughter greeted his remark and Facilitator General Tvashtar observed, "I don't detect any Theobromos on the premises, however."

More laughter at that, unpleasant laughter, and several heads turned to

Aegeus. He held his hands up in a gesture of good-natured admission. "Now, now—"

"I caught your performance, Aegeus," said Xi Wang-Mu archly. "You seem to have survived the assault without a scratch. Whoever did you intend us to think was attacking you?"

"Oh, now, we've all indulged in a bit of drama for the benefit of the rank and file," said Aegeus, accepting a glass of Campari from a waiter. He scanned it before taking a sip and added, "And, after all, the plot was real enough. The nerve of the monkeys!"

"Outrageous," agreed Ashoreth, as Nennius pulled out a chair for her. "Though we all saw it coming, didn't we?"

"From the dawn of time," said Gamaliel.

"Stupid little bastards," said Aethelstan.

"Well, they're regretting it now." Victor chuckled. "Have you been monitoring their secured channels? They're petrified. Seems that Preserver drones are vanishing into deep cover everywhere. No cyborgs to fly the mortals' transports for them, no one to fetch and carry. There's a rumor that even Suleyman is up in arms."

"Not Suleyman," cried Kiu in delight. "That mortal-loving bore? He's so slow to act we used to call him the Black Iceberg."

"Ah, but recall what a well-placed iceberg did to the *Titanic,*" Victor pointed out. "I really do believe it's started, ladies and gentlemen."

"And about time," said Nennius, lifting his glass in a toast. "To the Glorious Slave Rebellion!"

There were murmurs of "Hear, hear!" and "Cyborg Conquest!"

"And, speaking of the *Titanic*—" said Victor, gesturing at the soup tureen, "our first course, ladies and gentlemen: Consommé Olga, from the soup course served on that fatal night of April 14, 1912, in the first-class dining room. Accompanied by Beluga caviar and garnishes."

"Oh, bravo, Victor," exclaimed Labienus, seating himself. He smiled down at the service, which was Royal Doulton Dracula: jet black with a pattern of golden wyverns around the rim. "And that's Mozart's *Requiem* just beginning, if I'm not mistaken. Magnificent."

"Very gracious of you to say so, sir," Victor replied, taking his place at the head of the table. Labienus was seated to his right, Aegeus to his left, so that they faced each other across a low floral arrangement of nicotiana and black pansies. "Hm! Fair ladies, distinguished gentlemen—one brief word before we commence? While the arrangements for this evening's entertainment have been your humble servant's, all credit for the idea must go to the redoubtable Executive Facilitator General for the Northwestern Sector, an immortal it has been my unquestioned honor to serve—Labienus."

There was polite applause. Labienus smiled, half rose in a bow, seated himself again. "And I do hope, sir, you'll favor us with a few inspirational words later?" Victor inquired.

"Oh, yes, you must," Aegeus said, just a little loudly. Labienus looked him straight in the eye and smiled.

"Perhaps at the sorbet course," he said.

Glances were exchanged here and there and there was a decided tension in the room as the waiters moved forward with the soup. No more than three ever came around the same side of the table at any one time, however, so as they moved off to busy themselves with bringing in the fish course everyone relaxed.

Not so far that each dish wasn't thoroughly scanned as it was set before them. But no trace of anything toxic was found; not in the poached salmon in mousseline sauce, nor the oysters, nor the braised sea turtle. Therefore, light and sparkling conversation accompanied the second course, with the appropriate white wines.

It was dinner conversation of the highest caliber, too, refined to an art at tables in old Byzantium, in Pompeii and Amarna and Angkor Wat, polished in every beautiful doomed place that had ever spread its cloth for a pale horseman. Enough witty epigrams flew across that festal board to set Oscar Wilde's shade moaning in envy.

Still, nervous eyes tracked the waiters as they brought in the sorbet course.

"And what's this?" inquired Aegeus, poking with his spoon at what resembled a little cone of dingy snow in a golden cup.

"Durian ice," Victor informed him.

"What, the fruit that smells like carrion?" cried Aethelstan. "Oh, but I'm disappointed! There's no scent at all!"

"You won't be disappointed in the taste, however," Victor replied. "Addictive, it's said, and an aphrodisiac under the proper circumstances."

"Speech, speech," Aegeus reminded Labienus.

"If you please—" Labienus held up his hand and tasted his sorbet. He smiled, inhaled, closed his eyes. Opening them again he spooned up the rest of it greedily, then rose to his feet. "Well! Victor, who would have thought it possible I'd experience something new at my advanced age? You have my eternal gratitude."

His remark was met with appreciative laughter, and he let it die down as he surveyed the table before he said: "Gentlemen? Ladies. Fellow campaigners through the eternal night, brothers and sisters in permanence—we meet here, a small and select company, on the eve of the Silence. What a long, strange trip it's been."

"Inelegant, but to the point," sneered Aegeus.

"I will take that as a compliment," Labienus replied. "Contemplate it, my friends: for the first time in our interminable lives, we are about to greet the absolute and utter unknown. All-seeing Zeus is blinded after today, perhaps slain as he so justly deserves. Perhaps we, ourselves, go down into the darkness."

"If only," muttered Amaunet.

"Yes, there are some of you who long for the dust," Labienus observed, nodding. "And I can only wish that oblivion will come swiftly for you, if it comes. It is at least a possibility now, do you realize that? We may hope. We, who have never had that freedom because everything was known beforehand, may at last *hope* for something! No certainty. Life will now hold surprises."

"It certainly will," agreed Nennius, managing not to smirk.

"Though we must admit that, barring unforeseen termination, our freedom is likely to be somewhat delayed," Labienus cautioned. "The next week will undoubtedly be a busy one. Even if our brother Suleyman has gone obligingly off to overthrow the treacherous little mortals for us, there will be tedious work setting up the New Order. What to do with this world in which we've labored so long, my friends?"

"Enjoy it," said Tvashtar decisively, licking his spoon. Laughter and applause greeted this. Labienus applauded, too.

"I'm sure we will," he said. "Though there may well be certain differences of opinion on how best to govern our world." He bowed, very slightly, to Aegeus. "Let us remember, however, that it will henceforth be a very much less crowded world. Mutual tolerance is in all of our best interests, wouldn't you say?"

"I couldn't agree more," said Aegeus in tones of heartfelt sincerity, rising to clasp his hand. They looked into each other's eyes and there was a moment of frozen silence at the table, as certain persons eyed the waiters uneasily; but there were only four in the room just then, busily arranging the entrée course on the sideboard. Victor alone seemed unflustered, spooning up the last drops of his sorbet.

Kiu began to applaud, and the others at table joined in, and Aegeus sank back into his seat. Labienus bowed to him slightly, and then reaching for his napkin wiped his hand, in a gesture nobody missed.

"Yes. Mutual tolerance, cooperation, and above all respect must be the

tenets on which our ideal world will be founded," he said. "Whereupon I conclude, brothers and sisters. Our full attention will be required for the next
course in this epicurean sacrament, to say nothing of the splendid musical
menu Victor has arranged for our enjoyment."

Liszt's *Totentanz* filled the air while the waiters removed the sorbet cups
and brought out the entrées, primarily meat, and the hopping jerking music
did nothing to set anyone at ease as the carving knives were taken up. But
there was no need to worry. The striploin of buffalo with forestiere sauce was
served out without incident, as was the sauté of pheasants Lyonnaise, the roast
suckling pig, the Numidian peacock, the rack of venison with bramble jelly,
the *vitellina fricta* flavored with real silphium and liquamen! There were cries
of joy at the table, as one skeleton bowed to another and Saint-Saens's *Danse
Macabre* came on with the clarets, the cabernets, the valpolicellas.

With the salad course came the second movement of the *Discworld Sym-
phony* by Brophy, with its outrageous flatting bassoons for Death's recitative,
causing edgy merriment over the vegetable marrow farcie and cold asparagus
vinaigrette.

"About the mortals, Labienus," said Aegeus, holding out his wineglass to be
refilled. "When you said it would be a much less crowded world after this, to
what exactly did you refer?"

"Why, simply to conservation measures," said Labienus, looking innocently
surprised. "I assume we're all agreed that some sort of culling program will
have to be instituted? For the little . . . creatures' own sakes."

"As it was in the beginning," said Nennius, darkly amused.

"Ah," said Ereshkigal brightly. "When the old Enforcers were still with us."

If Labienus felt acute discomfort at the mention of the Enforcers, he turned
not a hair as he helped himself to baby carrots in veloute sauce. "The old Enforcers," he repeated thoughtfully. "Stalwart fellows. Pity they were a bit
simple-minded."

"You disagreed with their methods, I take it?" challenged Aegeus.

"Disagreed? Why, of course I did." Labienus tasted the sauce. "Lumbering
warriors making arbitrary judgments on humanity, on the strength of a moral
code with no basis in realpolitik? They were a howling mistake. Quite incapable of understanding mortals or the forces that motivate them. Or so I always
thought."

"Then it's funny, isn't it, that there was such an outcry from certain people
when they were retired?" Ereshkigal remarked. "I've even heard a rumor that
you yourself protested . . ."

"Now, now." Labienus smiled daggers at her, holding up an admonishing finger. "We all feel a sentimental attachment to our immortal parents. That doesn't make them any less flawed than the mortal ones were! It's true, I was recruited by one of the poor old flatheads; but I knew him well enough to see that he could not for the life of him appreciate subtle distinctions where Good and Evil were concerned."

"Yes, I'd heard that, too," said Aegeus, peering at him slyly as he sipped his wine. "How fortunate that you never allowed your sentimental attachment to persuade you to his way of thinking."

"Isn't it?" Labienus lifted a glass to him. "One can accomplish a great deal with draconian measures, as I'm sure you'd be the last to deny. How ungracious your lives would have been if all those plagues hadn't solved the mortals' overpopulation problem! Just think what the pollution would have been like by now. Some of you must have been secretly grateful, I suspect."

Aegeus's eyes glinted but he said nothing.

"Tragic, of course, all that loss of life," mused Labienus. "Still, one must be practical."

"Moral, but humane," agreed Nennius. "Though one can say this for the Enforcers: they may have slaughtered the mortals, but they never exploited them."

"Used them for sexual gratification, you mean?" said Labienus innocently.

"Or kidnapped them for breeding experiments." Nennius looked straight at Aegeus. "Or stole from them."

Aegeus didn't flush with anger; he merely twirled the stem of his wineglass between finger and thumb, admiring the candle flames glinting through the wine. "Beautiful, isn't it, this crystal?" he murmured. "And so fragile. The mortals, too. How dull our eternal lives would have been without them, don't you think? This music, this cuisine—we can appreciate them, but we can't seem to come up with beautiful things ourselves. I wonder why? Perhaps if we weren't so rigidly focused on objectives, we'd be better qualified to rule over them."

"Ah, but at least we appreciate them," said Ereshkigal, putting a comforting hand on his arm. "Who else could be trusted to govern the mortals with compassion?" She looked across into Labienus's eyes. "Think how terribly the poor things would suffer if, for example, any pupil of the Enforcers got into power."

"You're certainly a fount of compassion yourself, dear," snapped Ashoreth from her side of the table. "Quite ready to forgive the little monsters that stunt with the poisoned Theobromos? Or Options Research?"

"There'll be punishment for that," said Amaunet grimly. There were nods and mutters of agreement from several guests.

"Culling, as I said," affirmed Labienus. "Beginning with the guilty parties."

"Oh, without doubt," said Victor in a thoughtful voice, picking up his knife. "And if it comes to that . . . the mortals aren't the only ones who could benefit by judicious thinning of their ranks." Every head turned to him, and not a few people clutched at their own knives. He looked about him at the discomfiture and smiled ingenuously. "Present company excepted, of course."

"I've been saying for some time there were far too many Preserver drones," asserted Nennius.

"And what will the poor things do, once there's nothing more for them to preserve?" said Xi Wang-Mu. "Half of them are going crazy with inactivity now. They've such limited programming, after all."

"Many of them would welcome death," said Moreham. "The really terrible thing about Options Research, you know, was that it failed in its objective. If they'd only discovered a way to reverse immortality!"

"Pity," said Labienus with a sigh. "The drones will have to settle for being taken offline. And the defectives, of course, rounded up and shut down."

"And perhaps one or two others," suggested Victor.

This prompted another fit of utensil-grabbing and a good deal of nervous eyeing of the waiters, who were engaged in bringing in the sweet course. Aegeus coughed discreetly. "Not a pleasant thing to contemplate, but we ought to admit to ourselves it might be necessary. Some of the lesser executives . . ."

"Why not come out and say Suleyman?" prompted Labienus. "We all know he's built up a tremendous private power base, for a man supposedly without ambition. He led the raid on Options Research, he's leading the rebellion now; if he wanted it he'd get the vote of the rank and file, I'm sure."

"If it ever came to a vote," said Aegeus scornfully. "And even so, why couldn't he be fobbed off with Africa and a few dozen mortals to look after?"

"You don't know him," said Amaunet.

"And he's got that little hothead Latif waving his fan," Kiu said.

"And Latif is far too clever for his own good," said Labienus.

"Perhaps he'll lead a charge against the mortals and get his head blown off, then," speculated Gamaliel.

"Wouldn't that be a shame." Amaunet swirled her wine and sipped.

The waiters stepped in at this point and removed the empty dishes, and conversation languished for a moment as the assembled diners watched their movements like hawks. Still, there was no ominous massing to one side or the other. The sweet course was set out without incident, and liqueur was poured.

"Isn't this another dish from the *Titanic*?" exclaimed Aethelstan.

"Peaches in Chartreuse jelly, yes," Victor told him.

"And Black Elysium!" Aegeus lifted his liqueur glass. "Oh, Victor. Whatever regime takes form in our brave new world, you really must be appointed Entertainment Director." His tone was decidedly patronizing.

"I hope I can hold you to that promise," said Victor, and there was something in his smile that made them scan their latest course with extra care. They found nothing, however, and both sides of the table drew the conclusion that the coup was scheduled for the seventh course. Indeed, even now a splendid cornucopia of fruit was being arranged on the sideboard, as were several cheeses.

So they all relaxed, for the moment. "Sublime stuff, this," sighed Nennius, after tasting the Chartreuse jelly. He took another mouthful. At that moment tremendous chords sounded in the room, D minor and its dominant, and there were cries of delight.

"Speaking of sublime!" Aegeus said. "The Statue's music from *Don Giovanni*! Victor, this is too perfect." He looked meaningfully at Labienus and intoned with the Commendatore: *"E cenar teco m'invitasti, e son venuto!"*

"Ah." Labienus closed his eyes in bliss, ignoring the dig. "You know, I think it might be worth it, being damned, if one went down to this music."

"And who wrote the music?" countered Aegeus. "The mortal Mozart, the most unprepossessing, dirty-minded little monkey it would be possible to meet."

"What's the point of reminding us of that?" inquired Xi Wang-Mu in distaste.

"To reiterate, madam, that the fairest rose blooms on the foulest dungheap," Aegeus said. "Everything we find graceful or useful or poignant, comes from these creatures."

"I decline to keep a dungheap in my bedroom, all the same," she replied, showing her teeth a little.

"Dung," said Nennius, "ought to be shoveled into a hole in the ground where it belongs."

Victor looked gently pained. "Sir, madam—perhaps a change of metaphor, at the table?" he suggested.

"Thank you, Victor. Beauty is a trap, you know." Labienus smiled and shook his head. "And the love of luxury is a dangerous weakness." He took a sip of Black Elysium.

"One you share with the rest of us," retorted Ereshkigal.

"I appreciate luxury," Labienus admitted. "Which is not the same thing as needing it. Growing dependent on it. I wonder how you can bear the idea of needing the monkeys for anything?" He grinned at Aegeus. "Knowing them as intimately as you do."

"Labienus, my brother—a touch of humility would become you," said Aegeus in a steely voice. "Not even we immortals are perfect, after all."

"How true," jeered Ashoreth, spooning up the last bit of peach.

"Now, now." Victor turned his white hands palm up, indicating the speakers from which the music flowed. "There are degrees of perfection. Are any of us the equal of this music, for example?"

"This music," said Labienus, "magnificent as it is, pales beside any virgin wilderness. Any sunrise, any fall of snow, the immensity of unvisited stars. That's perfection for you! Untouched and unspoiled by dirty little hands."

"Oh, so Nature is your great ideal of beauty?" Aegeus leaned forward. "Nature is perfection? Tell me, have you ever seen a two-headed calf? Or a stoat creeping into a duck's nest and settling down to eat the nestlings alive? Meaningless horror."

"Not *pretty*, I'll grant you," replied Labienus, "not sweet and pleasing to mortal sentimentality! But real, Aegeus. Stern and horrific by your standards but part of one immense harmony. Balanced. Magnificent. Beyond mortal comprehension. Beyond yours too, I fear."

There were cries and catcalls from the opposite side of the table, until Aegeus held up his hand. "I think I see your difficulty," he said, in most sympathetic tones. "Poor fellow, don't you see that your very idea of harmony is a mortal concept? You're neither a stone nor a star. You are, like it or not, a creature with human senses and perceptions. And this so disgusts you that you try to pretend it isn't true—"

"You've missed my point, as usual—"

"And envision a glorious macrocosm where only man is vile!"

"I was about to correct your sexist remark, but on reflection I'll let it stand," said Xi Wang-Mu, and there were nervous giggles. Labienus calmed himself, ate the last delectable morsel of peach on his plate, and set down his spoon before speaking again.

"Yes," he said. "Man is vile. Man himself said so. Vileness is a concept man invented. It doesn't exist in Nature."

"You fool, *nothing* exists in Nature," Aegeus nearly screamed. "The tree falls in the forest and it knows nothing, the forest knows nothing, the sky and the sunlight know nothing! We're the only ones to give it meaning at all. You're like that imbecile mortal praising the wonder of billions and billions of stars. We alone make them wonderful by our perception that they are! And yet you envision an ideal cosmos with no humanity—"

"I don't envision it. It exists! Universally, except for three little stains on this one solar system," said Labienus. "And we alone, we immortals, and few enough of us at that, are capable of appreciating the flawless Absolute!"

"You're a closet deist," said Amaunet wearily.

"And you're stunted, every one of you," shouted Labienus. "You have eyes to glimpse the eternal, and you're still fascinated by the filthy monkeys!"

"Why this obsession with a greater power, I wonder?" said Aegeus. "Could it have anything to do with a sense of guilt over, oh, perhaps, the father you betrayed? Old Budu?"

Labienus looked at him with murder in his eyes.

"Can't you both shut up?" inquired Amaunet, and with the Commendatore she sang: *"E l'ultimo momento!"*

"Yes, please, this is the best part," implored Aethelstan.

"I'd never have come if I'd thought Truth was on the menu," joked Tvashtar. "So dry, and one is never satisfied afterward."

"Pentiti, scellerato!" sang Aethelstan determinedly.

"No, vecchio infatuato!" Tvashtar sang back, and with the exception of the men at its head the whole table took up the exchange between the Commendatore and the unrepentant Don Giovanni: *"Pentiti!"*

"No!"

"Pentiti!" sang the ladies, in harmonies so sweet and terrifying the Don would have fallen to his knees and repented straightaway, if he'd heard them.

"No!" cried Tvashtar and Gamaliel, who happened to be tenors.

"Si!" insisted baritones Nennius and Aethelstan.

"No!" responded basses Aegeus and Labienus, unable to resist the pull of the music.

"Si!" Aegeus groped and found his knife.

"No!" Labienus's hand closed on the neck of a wine bottle.

"Si, si—" None of them could refuse it now, and their massed ancient voices chorded in a moment of beauty so powerful, so unearthly, that any mortal present might be excused for thinking he was in the presence of the angels.

But on the next note, the final defiant *No*, something was wrong. No one seemed to have the breath for it. In the moment of frozen shock that followed, Victor rose to his feet. His sick white face was shining as he extended his hands and sang: *"Ah! Tempo piu non v'e!"*

"What do you mean we've no more time, Victor?" snarled Labienus, and his voice was hoarse, and blood ran from his mouth and stained the front of his white shirt.

Aegeus tried to say something but coughed instead, and blood exploded outward in a fine mist. The other guests regarded their plates in dismay, where the green smears of Chartreuse jelly crawled with tiny engines of destruction that had been harmless inert matter five minutes earlier.

"You failed to detect the virus, because it didn't exist at the moment you scanned," explained Victor. "The molecules only put themselves together in that particular pattern when I activated the program. Ingenious, isn't it? But I can't claim credit for the idea. It's all Labienus's modus operandi."

"You—" croaked Nennius in outrage, desperately blotting with his napkin at his eyes, from which blood now ran like tears. It was a mistake: the skin began to come off on the rough linen napkin, and the ball of his left eye ruptured from the pressure.

At the same moment the waiters, who were looking on in terrified astonishment, reacted. Three of them ran for the door and found it locked, which should present no difficulty for any determined immortal, but somehow their strength had evaporated. They beat on the door and saw their fists burst open on impact, fans of ferroceramic bone and swiftly liquefying matter. Of the three who remained at the sideboard, two of them fell to their knees and attempted to vomit, with dreadful success. Only Sargon mustered enough of a sense of duty to grab a carving knife and lurch toward the table.

"Treacherous little—" Ashoreth attempted to get to her feet and the mere pressure of her hands on the table was enough to split her skin. She sank back, and her scream ended in a drowning noise. Several of the others had remained immobile in surprise, and now found themselves unable to move in any manner other than to seep through their own clothing.

"*Tutto e tue colpe e poco!*" Victor sang, with the chorus of demons surging up from Hell. "*Vieni: c'e un mal peggior!*"

Only Aegeus's clothing was holding his flesh together, but the eyes in his rapidly dissolving face were standing out with rage, and his skeleton was determined. He thrust his table knife up through Victor's white waistcoat, under his ribs in a blow that would have been fatal to a mortal. Victor gasped for breath and looked down at his blood welling out over what was left of Aegeus's hand.

"I wouldn't do that, old man," he said, smiling. "I'm contagious, you know."

Labienus's vocal chords had melted and run down his throat, but he was still able to transmit: *So you modified some of your own poisons, did you? You think you'll survive to laugh at us?* He seized the carving knife from Sargon, who collapsed gurgling at his feet, and stabbed Victor. Victor gasped again, but did not stop smiling, and raised his hands in a beckoning gesture.

"*Vieni!*" he sang, understandably without much breath now but the demons echoed for him, "*Vieni!*"

Labienus pulled the carving knife free and, with all his remaining immortal strength, swung it at Victor's neck. *Whack*, it passed cleanly through the cervical gimbal and Victor's head flew off and rolled on the table, coming to rest on a silver platter. The eyes turned up to Aegeus and Labienus in an expression of amusement as Don Giovanni's final wail of agony sounded, and then the light went out of them.

The headless body, fountaining blood, flopped forward, with its arms catching Aegeus and Labienus across the shoulders in a bizarre parody of a chummy gesture. They fell, struggling, coming to pieces as they struggled. Labienus's last clear glimpse was of Amaunet's face.

It was so melted it was impossible to tell whether her expression was one of fear or ecstasy. She transmitted: *Has He come for us at last? Oh, let it be Him . . .*

Death, however, sent His regrets. Amaunet and the rest of them might suffer liquefaction to the point where their hearts wept out of their bodies and their blind brains cowered in the darkness of their impermeable skulls; but they could not die. They were immortal, after all.

The last chords sounded, the celestial music ended. The room was silent.

CHAPTER 29

Alpha-Omega

Night, on an ancient and nameless sea.

A moon drifted between clouds, throwing down watery light on the island with its two hills. It sparkled, reflected in the estuaries and lagoons. It gleamed faintly on the dome atop the northern hill, making it look like a big egg nested in the alder trees.

It shone down on the white scoured bones of the ichthyosaur that lay half-buried, a willow tree growing through the blind skull, well above the summer tideline.

There was quite a lot of noise. The surf boomed far out, the sea wind hissed in the reeds, frogs and insects peeped and groaned. Then, abruptly, there was a lot more noise as the air opened with a red flash and there were five transports roaring down from the sky.

They came in low and fast. One veered away from the others and circled the northern hill, where after turning it landed on a flat open area beside the dome. The other four lined up gracefully and set themselves down on the beach below, and as the moon emerged from a trail of cloud the ichthyosaur skull glimmered out, grinning a welcome at them all.

Immediately, cargo doors opened in the four shuttles and figures leaped forth, pulling from each one a series of great squared objects. They were refrigerated transport pods. A moment later the pods rose, bobbing a meter above the sand as their agunits were activated. The figures set off up the beach in a long purposeful line, towing the pods after them, making for the hill where the first transport was.

"And we're in," said Latif as the loading door rolled up. He advanced into the loading bay warily, eyeing the servounit that clattered away like a cockroach between stacked crates. Suleyman and Sarai followed him, scanning the walls for a door. "And we're not in," Latif corrected himself. "I'm not reading any entrance but that crawlway, are you?"

Suleyman shook his head. "The dust is disturbed. Somebody's been here, not all that long ago," remarked Sarai.

"Somebody certainly has." Suleyman strolled over to the crawlway. He dropped into a crouch to study it and there was a faint whine, no louder than a mosquito, but the grated cover to the crawlway lit up cherry-red. He winked out and reappeared to the left of the grate.

"It's charging up," he said. "We'll have to take out this wall. I'm not reading any refrigeration units behind it. Limpets, here and here."

"You got 'em." Latif and Sarai slapped the bombs in place and were gone, and Suleyman was gone, and a second later there was a puff and a flash and a gaping hole in the wall. Before the last bit of debris had fallen they were inside.

What they saw, by infrared, surprised them.

They had broken through into what appeared to be spartan living quarters: a food preparation area, an open lavatory, an entertainment console. It might have been a prison cell. There was a table and a chair and a bed, and in the bed a thin pale mortal was just struggling to sit up and pull off a sleep mask.

Their view of the bed, however, was blocked by the apparition. It hung in midair, scowling at them ferociously and gnashing its sharp teeth: a lavender shark with pale blue fins. "Go away," it ordered in the voice of a furious woman. "Get out of here, or I'll bite you!"

"This is original," observed Sarai. As they stood gaping at it, it melted, transformed. It became a balloony purple octopus, writhing its tentacles.

"Go away *now*," it cried. For good measure it changed again. Now it was a bright red lobster two meters tall, clacking its claws at them.

"What are you?" wondered Suleyman.

"They're, uh, the monsters from Totter Dan's Undersea Adventure," Latif said.

"Who's that?" asked the mortal in the bed, managing to get his sleep mask off at last. He stared at the blown wall open to the night, the three figures silhouetted against the moonlight, and rubbed his eyes.

"Leave him alone," screamed the lobster, morphing now into a woman in a rather dowdy-looking robe. "Please go!" The mortal was groping frantically in a drawer at the side of his bed. He had pulled something out and was reaching up with it when Latif shot it out of his hand. He yelped and cowered back in his blankets.

"No!" the woman implored. "Don't hurt him." From the rubble behind them something came clattering: another servounit, a dog-sized thing waving manipulative members in a menacing fashion. Sarai kicked it away and it lay on its back in a corner, traction treads racing futilely. "Please!" Weeping now, the woman opened her robe and displayed her naked body. "Would you go away if I made you happy? I'll do anything you want. Just please don't hurt my David."

"You're an AI, aren't you?" guessed Suleyman. "You're supposed to monitor life support for the mortal."

"Ancilla, make them go away!" the mortal told her.

"I'm trying," she replied, as the first of Suleyman's team came through the wall. They stopped and stared.

"Through there," Suleyman told them, pointing into the depths of the dome's interior. "The storage area's got a vacuum seal."

"Is that what you want?" Ancilla peered into Suleyman's face. "You want something from the alcove, like those other people? Take it! Take whatever you want and go. I can fix it so he won't even notice anything's missing. Just let my David alone."

"We won't hurt David," Suleyman told her, "but we can't leave him here. We're taking everything that's stored in that alcove, and closing this station down. David's going home to Time Forward with us. He'll be all right."

"But—I wasn't notified," Ancilla said doubtfully.

"What?" The mortal emerged from under the covers. "What'd he say, Ancilla?"

"The Company's evacuating this base!" Suleyman raised his voice slightly. "Consider this your notification." He lowered his voice and looked at Ancilla. "Has he got any personal effects he'll want to bring?" he asked, indicating the mortal with a jerk of his thumb.

"What?" The mortal sat up, swung his feet over the side of the bed. "Don't bother talking to her. She's not real. I'm real! What do you mean, the Company's evacuating me?"

Suleyman looked around Ancilla at the mortal. There was a rush of cold air as the alcove was opened, and a clinking and thumping from the darkness as Suleyman's team immediately set to loading the contents of Alpha-Omega into the transport units. "An emergency situation has developed, sir," Suleyman told the mortal. "Your location is no longer secure."

"Oh!" The mortal cringed. "Then you've got to save what's in the recesses beyond the Portal." He got up hurriedly and groped around in the darkness. "Ancilla! Where are my clothes?"

Smoothly, without a wasted movement, Alpha-Omega was divested of its treasure in surprisingly little time considering the months of effort that had gone into finding it. When the mortal man had dressed himself and found both shoes, and fussed with a bag of toilet necessaries, and downloaded his Totter Dan games into a transfer unit, the last of the silver tubes was on its way down to the transports.

"What about your AI's program?" inquired Suleyman, examining the console.

"What?" David peered at him. "Oh. Leave it here. I won't need that thing if I'm going home."

"You're a real little pig, aren't you?" said Sarai in disgust.

"No!" Ancilla's eyes widened. She turned to Suleyman. "No, I have to look after David. You understand, don't you?"

"Latif, escort him to the shuttle," Suleyman ordered. Latif drew his pistol and David scurried ahead of him, out through the loading dock. "I'm sorry," Suleyman told Ancilla. "We don't have time. We'll take good care of him, I promise you."

He turned from her and strode out to the waiting transport. Sarai lingered a moment to say: "You hang in there, dearie. Somebody'll be back." She turned and ran after Suleyman.

They powered up, the five ships, they rose and turned, and disappeared through a blaze of red light with a *boom* that echoed across the dark water. For a few minutes there was breathless silence; then the night noises returned, the frogs and insects cautiously resumed their songs.

The white moonlight streamed in through the broken wall of Alpha-Omega, and through the phantom woman who wept in its ruins.

Fez, 9 July 2355

"This isn't London," said David Reed, staring around in horror at the city lit by sunset, under the dreadfully wide sky. "It's foreign! And it's hot. Why am I here?"

"Change of plan, dearie," said the black lady, with a white smile that made him very uncomfortable. "Pick up your feet now. Quick. We want to get you stashed away safe."

"But—" David protested, and she slapped him quite hard on his behind. With a yelp he started forward, and she grabbed his arm and drew him along with her, inexorably propelling him down the narrow street. He didn't much like the look of it. It was what would be called an alley in any civilized country, with high white windowless walls to either side and a high wall at the end.

He looked about fearfully for piles of donkey flop or dirty merchants with moth-eaten rugs, which he supposed were everywhere in these unpleasant substandard countries, but there weren't any. Only the clean silent street and the soldiers jogging along behind them, each one bearing on his or her shoulders a refrigeration unit. As they neared the end of the street David looked expectantly for the doorway or turning they'd take next, but to his consternation there didn't appear to be any turning.

He gasped and tried to stop before they ran smack into the wall, but the black lady bore him on. The wall seemed to pull back, and a stairway opened at their feet, leading down to a doorway that was even now opening on darkness.

Stumbling, unwilling, he descended the stair and the next minute or so was a long nightmare of steps turning and going down, turning and going down, with the soldiers thundering behind him so that there was no stopping, even if the mean lady had been willing to listen to his protests.

Finally they stopped descending, and the lady pulled him off into an alcove at the side. The soldiers ran on past them, down a corridor leading into a big vaulted room. David mustered his indignation to demand: "I want to talk to your supervisor!"

"Sorry, honey, he's busy," said the lady, as a doorway opened in the alcove. She shoved him through and he found himself in a room not unlike the one he'd left. Bed, commode, sink. He turned around to ask her for his bag, but she had already tossed it in after him and slammed the door.

David stood gaping a moment before he bent and picked up his bag. At least those nasty people had gone. He sat down on the bed, trembling and wheezing from the run, and rummaged in his bag for his medication. There was no sipper bottle beside his bed, and he had to go to the sink and fill a little chlorilar cup with water before he could take his pills. And the water tasted funny, and he spilled some of it on himself. Really, this was very annoying. He made a mental note to speak sharply about it to whoever brought him his breakfast.

Feeling the need to work off his anger, he pulled out his Totter Dan unit and looked around for the entertainment console.

There wasn't one.

David Reed cried out, a high-pitched squeal of horror and disbelief. Rising to his feet again he proceeded to search the room. Wall to wall, like a mime flattening his palms against the unyielding surfaces, he sought desperately for a port, a screen, a buttonball, anything with function! Nothing. Nothing under his bed either, or behind the commode, or in the door. Nothing at the sink, though he poked the Totter Dan lead into every hole he found there. "Ancilla," he screamed. "Where is it? Hook me up!"

No soothing voice, no comforting illusion rushing to his assistance. Failing to appreciate the irony of this, he collapsed on his bed and sobbed in terror. Lots of time passed.

After a while he curled into fetal position and emptied his mind of thought. As ever, it didn't take him long.

Racing back along the corridor, Sarai spotted Latif running from the opposite direction. They met, crashing into each other. He grabbed her and swept her back in a kiss. They wrestled together a long moment before they broke for air at last.

"Secured!" Latif announced, and Sarai shouted with laughter. Hand in hand they ran back along the corridor, and a moment later emerged, by veiled and uncertain ways, in Suleyman's receiving room.

Suleyman was sitting at a low table, sipping tea and studying a sheaf of printouts. He did not look up as they came in.

"The jewels are in the jewel box," said Sarai. "And the piggy's in the pen. What on earth's wrong?"

Suleyman spread the papers out across the table. They were still images, taken at several angles from surveillance camera feed, of a room. It was not an empty room. "These came in while we were at Alpha-Omega," he said. "From the Preservancy Conference Center on Santa Catalina Island."

"Victor sent them, then," Latif said, coming around the table to peer at the images.

"I don't think so," Suleyman told him. Latif looked more closely. He uttered something profane. Suleyman continued: "Though the possibility exists that he arranged the transmission in advance."

"Do we have anybody else out there?" asked Latif in a slightly shaky voice. "Who might have sent these, I mean?"

Suleyman nodded. "She didn't send them, though. She's at a secured location, monitoring the mortals' transmissions." He stroked his beard, regarding a particular image. "I've been running a forensic reconstruction on the rest of them. That one," he added, pointing, "is almost certainly Nennius."

Sarai leaned forward, her gaze hard and hungry. She stared at the image a long moment before grinning ferociously. "Well," she said. "Some justice. How nice! What about the others?"

"Are they all in Labienus's camp?" inquired Latif, reaching for the tea and taking a gulp.

"No," replied Suleyman. He pointed to another image. "There's a ninety-nine point nine percent probability that one's Aegeus. And that would be Ereshkigal next to him."

"So." Latif jumped to his feet and began to pace. "If Victor did what it looks like he did—then both the Masters and the Plague Club are out of the race."

"Possibly," said Suleyman. "Their leaders, at least."

"Which means we can get to the Command Center without having to fight anybody but the mortal troops."

"Possibly," said Suleyman.

"Which means we win!"

"Possibly."

"Somebody sometime's going to have to go into that room and clean things up," observed Sarai. "To retrieve Victor, at least."

"Better sooner than later, too. Son, we'll need hazmat units," Suleyman said.

"On it," Latif told him, and was gone from the room. Sarai looked after him. "He's a good son," she said.

"He is." Suleyman had another sip of tea. "Victor was a good son, too."

"Was he one of yours?" Sarai turned to him, surprised.

"No," Suleyman said. "Someone else's son. I would have been proud to call him mine, though."

Sarai nodded, looking at the terrible pictures. "I never had many recruits," she said. "And I haven't kept track of them. Maybe just as well. Too painful."

He sighed. They could hear, from the courtyard, the bustle as the shuttles were refueled and the troops loaded, and somewhere Yusuf patiently explaining to a trio of Peace Officers that, yes, there had been a fire, but the household had got it out swiftly. The lord of the house would be glad to meet them on Monday to make a full report. Suleyman raised his eyebrows.

"I ought to make Latif go out to apologize," he said. He gazed for a moment at the shatrang set displayed in a corner of the room, the old work of art in ivory and ebony. "Tell me something," he said. "Do you really think Alec Checkerfield is dead?"

Sarai flinched. "What's that got to do with anything? But he's not in this world," she said quietly. "I tell you I'd know."

"You think so?" Suleyman turned down his empty tea glass. "I wonder."

Latif came stalking back, eyes glittering. "Hazmat units loaded and we're ready to go on your order."

"Mm." Suleyman rose to his feet. He walked across the room to the sha-trang game and moved one of the pieces. Then he turned back to Latif and Sarai. "Armageddon calls. Let's go, children."

CHAPTER 30

Meanwhile, in Paradise

The Captain steers through Eternity, moors off a convenient headland of Time.

A vast shimmering coalesces into something solid and visible. The island emerges from the mists. The masts and spars of the *Captain Morgan* emerge, too, and the green trees of the garden, and the outline of the high house. Night is fading away into morning here, whenever this is.

The house solidifies; within it a pulsing star of energy settles lightly into time and place, assumes nearly human form. Forms. Four of them. Children?

They materialize all together in the great bed, in the master bedroom with its windows wide on the sea. The little girl is more or less in the center of the tangle of sprawling limbs and pillowed heads. There is no visible difference between the three little boys, save for the spiraling tattoo on the shoulders of one of them.

Their contentment is nearly palpable. They are exactly where they longed to be for so many painful centuries, and they sleep very well now. They might have been sleeping a night or a year or a thousand years. The sound of their untroubled breathing is quiet in the room, and so is the roll of breakers on the reef beyond the lagoon, and the sigh of the wind in the palm trees, and the red birds starting up dawn song timidly.

Below this there is a faint hum and drone, a constant low sound whose source is time itself. It is generally inaudible to those who still move within the temporal framework, as other rooms within a maze are invisible to its explorers. To those outside time who can hear the sound, it is indistinct enough to be ignored.

Until it changes, as it does now.

A click. A whirr and a new sound, rising a little louder than before. Thunder and something else, at once sublime and terrifying, like howling angels with flaming swords, and a chorus under it of piping like insects in a summer night, or drowning souls screaming for rescue.

Within the room the atmosphere changes, and a faint prickle of electricity charges the air. Domed thunderclouds, touched with the tender colors of morning, appear on the wide horizon of the sea and race down the sky. Out on the terraced fields the young corn dances and circles as a wind travels across it, under the advancing clouds. The *Captain Morgan* rocks at anchor in the lagoon.

Some strange perfume is in the air. Orange blossoms? Green-cut hay? *Something is going to happen.*

The girl wakes. She is coming back from dreams so deep there is a bloom on her eyes at first, giving her the appearance of blindness. Gradually her perceptions sharpen and she turns her head, looking perplexed. She sits up. The others wake instantly. "Do you hear that?" she says. They all listen.

"Ay," says one of the boys.

After a moment the boy with the tattoo says, "That's strange. What is that?" Then, looking down at himself, he cries: "Oh, no! Not again!"

"It's all right," says the third boy, sounding amused. He stretches, sensually, and his limbs lengthen, his chest deepens and broadens. The others follow suit, and in short order appear as adults. But the noise is still going on . . .

"I've heard that noise before," says Mendoza. "Somewhere. Haven't you?"

They listen again, intently, and at last Edward frowns. "I do believe," he says, "that some event in the cycle of time is bleeding through the temporal correspondence points."

"Oh. Like a temporal resonance?" says Alec.

"But monstrous big." Nicholas is frowning now too. "To make such a noise across time's whole frame. Some—" He stops short of saying the word *catastrophe* out loud, but Mendoza hears his thought anyway.

"We must be hearing 2355," she concludes.

"No!" says Alec.

"Surely not," Nicholas agrees.

"Highly unlikely," Edward assures her.

But as they listen, as they scan the temporal wave for the original source of the disturbance, it becomes undeniable: 2355. Then beyond the windows, lightning flashes blue. Thunder booms, and hot rain comes down in torrents, with all the fury of a tropical squall. They hear the slamming of windows throughout the house as the Captain responds to the storm. When the commotion subsides, the sound has died away, the charge in the room dissipated. "I guess we'd better do something about that one of these days," says Alec uncomfortably.

"Especially since we planted all those time bombs," adds Mendoza, looking at Edward. Something unspoken passes between them.

"No help for it, I suppose," Edward says. "One of us had better go see what happens."

Now then, there ain't no need to go running off all affrighted. Plenty of time to think about this! You want breakfast, that's what you want. Coxinga's just laying it out on the sideboard and Flint's lit a nice cheery fire, on account of the rain. Come on downstairs, mateys.

His voice is a shade too jolly and coaxing. "Captain—" says Edward.

Hot cocoa all round, eh? Perfect weather for it!

"Captain, did you possibly detect something in that occurrence that escaped us?" says Edward.

Well now, what could have escaped the likes of a sharp-witted lad like you, Commander sir? Smart as paint, that's what you are.

"You did detect something," says Mendoza, sighing.

If I did, I ain't saying a word about it until my boy gets some breakfast in him, the Captain replies firmly. *Alec don't take worries well on an empty belly, see? And you got all the leisure in the world to deal with one little problem somewhere off on the shank end of time.*

"I see," says Edward. So they rise and descend to breakfast. It's a long walk to get there, down wide staircases and through paneled corridors, now decorated in eclectic style with art gathered from many different eras. The effect is occasionally jarring but rather interesting, on the whole.

The dining room is small and cozy by comparison, with a table set for four and firelight gleaming on the mahogany sideboard, where a repast is laid out under domed silver dishes.

Look here, Commander! Nice dish of kedgeree just like you like it, and banana omelet for my Alec. There's pikelets, Nick, and try the Oysters Creole, ma'am, they're particularly good this morning—

"I'm sure they are, Captain," says Mendoza, as Edward pulls out a chair for her, "but I think we'd like to get straight to the point."

"Yeah," says Alec. He lifts the dome from one of the dishes, and takes an entire folded omelet and stuffs it in his mouth. The others avert their eyes as he chews and then swallows it down. "Okay, there! I've eaten. Now you can tell us what you know that we don't know about 2355."

"Alec, your manners are disgusting," remarks Edward, seating himself and pouring tea. "Nevertheless, Captain—"

Aye, well. I analyzed what come through just now. Most of it's too confused to sort out at this distance, but there be some detonations. So I went through the Temporal Concordance and had me a look at travel bookings for Dr. Zeus personnel for the week preceding 9 July 2355. When the eleventh hour draws nigh, an awful lot of Company folk are going to be where them explosions is going off, which is Catalina Island. But there's a deal of commotion coming from London, too.

Nicholas, who has been buttering a pikelet, looks up sharply. "It'll be war, then, surely, and no heavenly cataclysm," he says in relieved tones.

"I fail to see how war is preferable to a meteor strike, if the world ends in either case," says Edward calmly. He sips his tea. Lightning crackles down outside, lighting up the room as blue as Crome's radiation.

"But it may not end," Nicholas says, leaning forward in his excitement as thunder rolls. "Now, if the sun should quick-consume its own heart and blast them all in streaming fire, no remedy for that, plead how we may. But men may be dissuaded from a war!"

"You mean we're supposed to stop it," said Alec.

Oh, hell.

"Have either of you ever tried to talk mortals out of fighting among themselves?" says Mendoza. "It almost never works."

"Not so, love!" Nicholas rises to his feet and takes her by the shoulders. "Men see their folly, and change. And they will! In the third millennium there will be no great wars, only—" He halts.

"Only me blowing up Mars Two," Alec says grimly.

Alec, that weren't yer fault.

"Sit down and drink your orange juice like a civilized being," Edward orders. "You know the Captain's correct. In any case, it can't be helped now."

Alec obeys and Nicholas remains standing, looking disconcerted from one to the other. Mendoza squeezes his hand. Lightning again, and thunder and the drumming rain loud afterward.

"It's a nice idea, to try to save the world," she tells him gently, "but maybe it can't be done. I and all my kind had our hands full, rescuing even bits and pieces of it from destruction. The mortals have free will; if they use it to obliterate themselves in one final bloodbath, what can we do?"

"Go to them beforehand, and persuade them that they must not," says Nicholas with certainty.

"And anyway they don't really have free will, you know," Alec says, and gulps orange juice. "That's a religious myth."

"Men may make choices—" Nicholas insists.

Nicholas, dammit, history can't be changed. You know that! Commander, tell the boy.

Edward regards his plate of kedgeree. On the tines of his fork he lifts a bit of crisply fried onion, a perfect golden spiral curling as time itself was once believed to curl. "History can't be changed," he agrees. "But are we part of its set pattern, at this point?"

A flash of lightning, so near they'd be momentarily blinded if they were mortals, and even so Alec covers his ears as the thunder comes. Wind, now, too, green leaves are whirling and flying in the rain, hitting the windows.

Can't tell, growls the Captain at last.

"Why not?" demands Alec. "Because it isn't recorded? Or is there something else?"

Maybe.

"What uncharacteristic brevity, Captain," says Edward. "There wouldn't be some sort of causal node at that point in time, would there? Some moment from which many other moments in time radiate, whether backward or forward?"

Aw, now, sir, even an old machine like me knows no such thing's been proven to exist. It's only been theorized by smart lads like you.

"But if there were causal nodes, that'd be the kind of place one would be," says Alec. "Maybe the biggest one ever's there. Maybe that's the moment all history depends on! If it's connected—if everything leads there or comes off there—"

"How if this were our purpose, made plain at last?" demands Nicholas. "Were we meant to be idle in this paradise?" He turns to Edward. "Wherefore did you take such pains to teach us, if not to benefit mortal humanity?"

Mendoza has put down her coffee cup. "How do we know we wouldn't make things worse by interfering?" she asks.

"On the other hand," counters Edward, "if there were a possibility we might rescue the mortals from their own folly at that moment in time, we should have the moral obligation to do so."

"Maybe, señor," she replies.

"Particularly," he continues, "in view of the fact that it is our responsibility to make certain our weapons bring about the downfall of Dr. Zeus Incorporated, as they were intended to do, rather than randomly inflict hardship on the mortal population."

But you can leave all that to me! That's all worked out to the last cipher, lads, there ain't no need for any of you to go slogging out across time to watch. When the hour strikes I'll bring you sweet revenge on a tray, and Dr. Zeus's bloody fat head on a pike.

"But how's that going to stop the mortals from destroying themselves?" asks Alec. Mendoza and Edward exchange a long glance. Just perceptibly, he nods his head.

"May I point out something you have just possibly missed?" she says quietly.

That's my girl. You talk sense into 'em!

"What have we missed, love?" Nicholas inquires.

"The fact that by 2355, most of the poor little monkeys have learned better than to engage in armed conflict," Mendoza says. "What if the war at the end of time is between *immortals*? What if they've risen against the Company, or are fighting among themselves?"

There is a silence at the table.

"Oh wow," says Alec, at last. "Just like in *Cyborg Conquest*."

"That would complicate the issue, wouldn't it?" observes Edward, watching him.

"But surely they, of all folk, could be persuaded from such a fool's course," objects Nicholas.

"Nicholas, was Joseph willing to listen to you? Do you think you can just descend from Heaven and step between them? Talk them out of fighting, like some silver-tongued angel?" inquires Mendoza.

"And why not?" said Nicholas. "I lit a flame once, with nothing but words, and it has smoldered all this while. I have a duty to see it put out at last."

Well, there ain't no need for anybody to go rushing off half-cocked, see? Just you let yer old Captain worry about this.

"Certainly we oughtn't take action without reconnoitering first," says Edward.

"I'll go," says Alec.

No, you bloody won't!

"Do you think so, Alec?" Edward arches an eyebrow. "Are you certain? After all, I spent my mortal life in this sort of work, therefore I am the most experienced, therefore I am the logical choice."

"What're you going to do, Dead, go down to 2355 in your tailcoat and top hat?" says Alec heatedly. "Even in disguise, you'd draw attention to yourself the minute you opened your mouth. Don't even ask, Nicky; you'd be worse."

"That's not true!" says Nicholas, outraged. "May I remind you that *one* of us excelled at languages, you ineducate thug?"

"*Une*ducated, Nicholas," Edward corrects automatically, but he smiles.

"Even so," Alec says, "that's my time, I was born in that world. I know my way around there. If anybody's going to go there to see what happens, it ought to be me." He pauses and swallows hard. "I owe the mortals."

"But so do I," says Nicholas. "I did enough harm, in my time. And you can't be in two places at once."

Now, Nick, don't you be a-starting, too!

"But they have a point, Captain," says Edward slowly. "They do have unfinished business, as it were, in the mortal world. Let us say Alec goes to California and Nicholas goes to England. Hypothetically."

Damnation, what am I to do about my programming? Ain't you thought about my feelings, eh?

Alec flushes in embarrassment. "Captain sir, this is more important than me being happy and safe. I grew up. Isn't there a way for you to move beyond your programming, now, too?"

How the hell am I supposed to do that, an old machine like me?

"Well . . ." Alec's eyes brighten tremendously, as an immense idea occurs to him. "What if we made you a real body, so you could come with me?"

"You mean a solid physical form, instead of a hologrammatic projection," says Edward.

"Yeah. It's just totally jumped into my brain how we could do it! I could modify some of the nanobots we had build this house. Program 'em to build the Captain a physical body—all it has to do is look human, he can have all kinds of useful stuff if he wants, rocket launchers in his head even! And then set 'em to build it by converting biomass."

"What manner of biomass?" Nicholas asks, frowning.

"It could be anything," Alec exclaims, pacing around the table. "Organic raw materials they could diddle the molecules on, see? Fish. Wood. Hell, lawn clippings. Compost!" He pulls Mendoza from her chair and begins to dance with her, round and round. "Your compost heap, see, there's tons of stuff in there they could use."

"What, and make a green man?" Nicholas is nonplussed.

"Yeah! No! The corn stalks and stuff would all be converted to something else, see? He'd look just like his holoprojection. And the brain would be linked up to his main memory."

"My compliments, Alec," says Edward. "Not that we need anything this elaborate for a simple reconnaissance, but I really do think it might work."

"Of course it'll work," Alec asserts, looking smug. "I'm Mr. Age of Technology, remember?"

"But we'd be making a living thing," says Nicholas slowly.

"No. Well—sort of, it'd be just like Flint or Billy Bones but organic, see? And a lot more complicated," says Alec.

"The man himself's silent this whole while," Nicholas points out. "Captain?"

I been listening. It'd be right useful to have a mobile unit that didn't scare mortals into fits, that I could use to go ashore with Alec . . . and you'd give me yer affidavy nobody'd go anywhere, until it was all built and rigged out?

"Honor bright," says Edward, holding up one hand. "We have all of time at our disposal, after all."

By luncheon (in nonlinear time), Alec has designed a microscopic biomechanical marvel that will transmute organic matter into something resembling a man.

The storm has blown through, and Edward rolls up his sleeves and goes out to fill wheelbarrows with refuse from Mendoza's compost heap. He is intrigued by the project, and amused; in one of his rare moments of whimsy he hunts up a block of wood out of the *Captain Morgan*'s stores and adds it to the growing pile, on the principle that a good British tar has a heart of oak.

Mendoza, more uneasy about the forthcoming quest than she will permit anyone to perceive, retreats into the treehouse, to which a bar has been added now that everyone has grown up. Nicholas follows her, however, and finds her sitting there with a margarita, obligingly mixed for her by Coxinga. "Don't try to explain," she tells Nicholas. "I know every word you'd say. Quite a spell of déjà vu we're having, isn't it?"

"I suppose so," says Nicholas, sitting down beside her. Coxinga brings him a margarita, too. He sips it, grimaces, and sets it aside.

"I hadn't thought it would be so difficult, working back into linear time," Mendoza continues. "It's all patterns, isn't it?"

"And we have our place in the weave," says Nicholas. "We must do this thing, love."

"I know," she says, but she does not smile. "What do you suppose it will be like, after? I've gotten out of the habit of *afters*."

"Happy," he says.

"Happy ever after?"

He tilts up her chin to look into her eyes. After a moment he lowers his face to hers. Their faces touch, and she sighs; they retreat a little from time and soar like birds, together, in a bright place.

Later—hours or days, everyone has been having such a pleasant afternoon it seemed like a good idea to let it run on a while longer than usual—Mendoza is awakened by the sound of feet mounting the staircase of the pavilion and a pair of voices raised in an old sea song.

"What?" Mendoza opens her eyes and looks across Nicholas to see Edward and Alec standing beside them, flushed and grinning.

"Come see what we've been doing, my love," says Edward, leaning down to kiss her. "It's quite extraordinary."

"You've never made the simulacrum!" Nicholas leans up, incredulous.

"Almost," Alec chortles, grabbing a bottle of rum out of the bar. "Come on, please come see! It'll make you laugh, we promise." Edward catches up Mendoza and carries her down the hill, chanting *yo ho, yo ho* all the way down through the garden, with Nicholas and Alec running after.

A sheet of clean canvas has been laid out on the lawn, and compost thickly piled on it in the approximate shape of a man. Here and there distinct objects stand out from the main mass: a good-sized pumpkin where the head would be, and a jaunty pair of coconuts somewhere else. Glints of silver and wire, chips like fish scales, indicate the presence of electronic components incorporated into the body.

Being incorporated into the body. For, even as Nicholas and Mendoza stare, the pile is altering: shifting, condensing, settling, as though alive with tiny moving things—which, in fact, it is. The effect just misses being unspeakably horrible, by virtue of the fact that the body is not decomposing but taking form.

"I thought the pumpkin was a particularly nice touch," says Edward, framing it with his hands. "Rather classical, don't you think?"

"I just redesigned a few nanobots like I said, and let 'em multiply, and eye-dropped 'em on, and they went crazy," says Alec proudly. "Look how fast it's going."

And indeed it is going quickly. Even as they stare, the pumpkin is shrinking in on itself, changing color. Its surface is beginning to pucker and morph into the semblance of a familiar face. Eyes form first. Mendoza accepts a sip of rum, watching the ongoing metamorphosis. "This *is* different," she states, handing the bottle to Edward. "My gosh, is that a waistcoat forming? You're making him with clothes already on?"

"Yup," says Alec. "I thought it'd save time. Neat, yeah? Clothes and beard and everything."

"Ever so much less tedious than robbing graves and waiting for a lightning storm," says Edward, taking a drink. He hands Nicholas the bottle. "Well, what do you say? Are we about to be struck down for our presumption?"

Nicholas is so fascinated by the transformation process it takes a moment before he lifts his head to glare at Edward. "Only if the Almighty were a vengeful idiot," he retorts, and has a swallow of rum. "Besides, you haven't made that whereof this creature's made. You've only shaped it. And marvelously, too!" he adds, as fibers resembling black hair wave out from the head like moss growing, and a black beard expands over the chest. The planes of the body begin to smooth out and drape in the unmistakable contours of a three-piece suit.

"Oh, look, he's even growing an earring," cries Mendoza in delight.

"Yeah, it links up with this—" Alec indicates the torque he wears. "See, so he can stay with me wherever I go and still be connected to the rest of himself."

"Impressive. Is he going to be a cyborg like us?"

"No," admits Alec. "He's more sort of an android. His brain isn't in his head, for instance, it's where bone marrow would be. But doesn't he look the part?"

"More so with every moment that passes," Edward tells him, for it is unmistakably the Captain lying before them now, and not so much as a dead leaf or corn husk is visible. The changes that don't show have proceeded apace, too. The brain reaches sufficient complexity and the Captain activates its consciousness, tries on the body cautiously. It blinks, moves its arms and legs. On impulse Nicholas spills a little rum into his hand and, leaning down, makes a sign on its brow. "This shall consecrate thee," he says. Edward snorts derisively and Alec looks alarmed.

"Hey! What did you go do that for?"

Nicholas looks stern. "This creature's flesh and spirit in its own kind. It must be hallowed to its work," he states.

The mouth opens and grins. "Nothing matters except the work, eh, son?" says the Captain in a voice harsh with newness.

"No," says Nicholas seriously. "If nothing mattered, the work would have no purpose."

They help the Captain to his feet, and he staggers; stares around him a moment with an uneasy expression, and turns his head this way and that. "I can't—hell, I can't see right!" He turns around, and then around again, trying to see over his shoulder. "Oh, this'll take some getting used to. Nothing but these two little peepholes in front to spy out of! How in thunder d'you manage?"

"You just learn to turn your head to look at things you want to see," explains Alec. "Think of them as a pair of cameras."

The Captain swings his head around to fix on him, but is distracted by his peripheral vision and attempts to bring that into full focus, too. He compromises at last by keeping his head turned slightly to one side, regarding Alec out of one eye, and this will become his habitual attitude.

"There, now," he says, "that's better. And it's a right trim craft otherwise, boys. Everything seems to work. Sensors online; weapons array functioning; all present and fully operational, aye."

"I don't even want to guess where you've got weapons," says Mendoza.

"It's really funny," Alec assures her. "I put—"

"Hey! Hey! Not in front of a lady," protests the Captain. He reaches over and takes the bottle of rum from Nicholas, and has an experimental gulp. He gasps, his eyes gleam."HAAR! Well, that'll make living in this body easier," he shouts. "A sense of taste! Bless you, boys."

"He has appetites of the flesh?" Nicholas asks, turning to stare at Alec and Edward.

"We thought it would be amusing," replied Edward. "And only practical, after all. Why shouldn't he enjoy refueling himself?"

"I can try all kinds of things I've always wondered about." The Captain passes off the bottle to Alec and rubs his hands together gleefully. "Let me at that galley. Fancy a good hot curry for supper, kiddies? And Shrimp Diavolo, aye, and Jambalaya, and ginger biscuits!"

They walk on up to the house, crowding around him to help as he staggers at first and then grows more confident on his new legs.

Alec opens his eyes in the darkness.

He lifts his head and regards the sky beyond the window. In the drifting moment of eternity, it glitters with stars. No dawn wind in the trees, no pallor on the horizon. A late moon, or a very early one, or perhaps both, is hanging low above the sea, sending its long reflection in a silver track across the water to the sand. Where would you go, if you could walk along that track?

He turns. Nicholas has already risen and is pulling on clothing; his preferred black, but cut in a modern style so indeterminate he could pass unnoticed in any city of the third millennium. Edward and Mendoza are sitting up, holding hands tightly.

Alec gets up, finds dungarees and his favorite tropical shirt, puts them on. He looks at the wardrobe—should he take a jacket? No, it will be July where he's going. He gropes about on the top of the dresser and puts useful things in his pockets. His heart is beginning to pound with excitement.

"I suppose it would be pointless to inquire whether you accessed the appropriate topographical maps last night," Edward says. Alec flashes his cheeriest grin.

"I did," says Nicholas.

"Just promise me you won't raise an army, or start a political movement, or anything stupid like that," Mendoza says.

"Honor bright," he promises, giving her two thumbs up. Alec steps up beside him and makes it four thumbs.

"It'll be a piece of cake," he says. "Come on, brother." They exit.

"I have every confidence in them," says Edward. "They'll manage it. Haven't we created a miracle, before heaven and earth? The very crown of human invention."

"Human invention? There was an ape found a bone once, and made it a club to kill other apes," says Mendoza wearily. "He threw it into the air and it became a space station. I'm unimpressed, señor."

"And no wonder; for a better tool's no miracle, my dear," says Edward. "The ape that learns compassion is the miracle."

A few heartbeats pass, though the stars are fixed in their eternal sky and the moon descends no further, and then: "Did we teach them enough?"

In the corridor beyond, the Captain's body waits uncomplaining in a chair, as it has waited through the timeless night. Nicholas and Alec draw near, and the Captain activates himself and stands stiffly. "Let's be off, lads," he says in a hoarse whisper, shooting his cuffs. "Soonest there, soonest back again, eh?"

They go down through the house and out, through the garden to the sea, and Alec considers his ship in its quiet anchorage. "I guess we really shouldn't take her if we're just going for a look, should we? We want to be inconspicuous."

"A quick rape and pillage and then run like hell, says I," the Captain agrees. Nicholas raises his eyebrows, but says nothing.

"So we just sort of . . . stroll down into time?" Alec looks about him speculatively. A wind moves off the sea. He points, bright-eyed, at the white glittering track of the moon on the water. "That looks really cool. I've always wanted to go that way!"

"It ought to get us there," says Nicholas. "As well as any."

So they step out on the moon's road—

PART VII

CHAPTER 31

Avalon

And the next moment they were on Santa Catalina Island, in Avalon, on 9 July 2355. Which is to say, Alec and the Captain found themselves there.

Alec gulped, staggered back and found himself colliding with a brick wall. The weight of time descended on him with equal force.

"Steady, boy," said the Captain. He turned, scanning, and Alec turned, too. They had arrived in a narrow alleyway, a tiny corridor of shadow and quiet behind an old hotel. The sunlight at either end was brilliant, flooding down on the calm bustle of a Saturday morning in Avalon.

"Nicky?" Alec stared around, fighting panic. "Oh. He must have gone to London. Right." He shook his head, feeling the seconds stream past him like blowing sand. It was unnerving. The shadows were all moving, just barely perceptibly but disorienting all the same. He caught his breath and tasted sea air, flowers, creosote, the pungent smell of ancient houses. Candy floss, popcorn . . . alcohol?

"There's a bar here someplace," he stammered, groping in his pocket for sunglasses and slipping them on. "Let's go wait in the bar until I get used to this. I used to hang out in bars a lot, didn't I? So I can sort of normalize and people won't think I'm some kind of, er, alien invasion or something."

"Aw, now, son, no need to worry," the Captain assured him. "There ain't a thing about us to attract anybody's notice."

"Right," Alec replied, walking to the end of the alleyway. He peered around the corner and the Captain peered, too, taking out his own pair of sunglasses and donning them. He didn't need them, of course, but he thought they would make him blend in.

Nothing to indicate anyone in Avalon had any idea it was the last day of recorded history. Holidaymakers were strolling, shop windows were bright with overpriced clothes and souvenirs. Children had buckets and spades. The town's retro taxis, agcraft styled to resemble Model A Fords, were the only motor traffic, and even they moved no faster than an amble. Little yachts clustered in the half-moon mooring. Out beyond them loomed the bigger ships, like swans at rest. The Avalon Casino towered in all its majesty in the morning light.

"Well, nobody seems to be expecting trouble, anyhow," remarked the Captain. Alec pulled his head back around the corner and took a few deep breaths.

"This is Mendoza's big cornfield, too, here where we're standing now. I'll fly right over it the first day I ever meet Mendoza. Too weird!"

"You want that bar, that's what you want, lad," the Captain told him, and Alec nodded.

"Yeah. This is my world, and it's great to be back! This'll be just like old times, right? Just you and me having adventures."

"In a nice bar," added the Captain. They stepped out together into the street.

Nobody took any notice of them, though they were both remarkably tall, the air around Alec had a distinct shimmer, and the Captain was still lurching a little as he walked and leading with his left eye. They strode briskly up Sumner Avenue, Alec gaining confidence at every step, and stopped opposite a comfortingly dark low establishment where a sign proclaimed the presence of THE HISTORIC CHI-CHI CLUB. Above it, for the nonreading clientele, was a holo of a smiling South Seas maiden in innocent D-cup nudity masked here and there by a few hibiscus blossoms.

"Ooh, yeah," moaned Alec, and fled inside, and the Captain followed.

It was dim and cool within. There was, of course, no alcohol on display at the bar, though Alec could smell it somewhere in the room; instead there were bottles of fruit syrups in every color of the rainbow, and big amber coolers of fruit teas and soykefir. There were three or four old golfers on stools with paper-parasoled smoothie drinks in front of them, blearily watching the holo above the bar. It was tuned to a program on wildebeest herds. Animals snorted, charged each other or grazed on yellow plains in midair above the rows of hurricane glasses.

"That's a good sign," said Alec *sotto voce*, sliding gratefully into a booth. "If there was a war just breaking out nobody'd be watching the Animal Site, yeah?"

"I ain't picking up anything out of the ordinary on the commsites, neither," the Captain replied. "And that's damned funny, because the last transmission from Dr. Zeus's future offices is supposed to come at eleven hundred hours California time. And here we are at half past ten in the morning and there ain't no sign of no apocalypse." He lowered his voice as the barman came to their table.

"That's one swell shirt, and how," he complimented Alec, in the Early Cinema Standard that had become the island's distinct patois. Alec glanced down at his shirt—it was one of his more vivid ones, with tikis and naked vahines—and smiled nervously.

"Thanks," he said. "So, er—is Johnny around?" That was the time-honored code phrase for requesting alcohol.

"He will be," said the barman, without batting an eye. "What about a couple of Mango Kiwi Refreshers for you guys?"

"Sure," said Alec.

"Damnation," snarled the Captain as the barman moved away. "It's got to be Judgment Day when I drink something with a name like that."

"Ah, come on, you've only been drinking at all for a few hours linear," said Alec.

"I know, laddie, but you got to work harder at yer personality when it's artificial," the Captain explained. "You think it's been easy being a pirate, all these years?"

"Good thing I wasn't into dinosaurs, then, yeah?" said Alec. The Captain rolled his eyes.

At that moment, the wildebeests galloped into oblivion and a cheery voice announced that it was time for the Hearst News Services Update. The glowing logo of an eagle with spread wings appeared, followed by the stories of the hour, and Alec and the Captain both watched attentively.

No asteroids hurtling toward the Earth. No new plagues, no belligerent nations giving ultimatums. No intimations of Doomsday at all. The biggest news was a schism within the Ephesian Church: a sect of Neo-Wiccans were splitting off in protest at the Church's continued refusal to publish the text of the Malinmhor Codex, located by archaeologists five years previously and still in scholarly limbo, though its translators hinted it contained material contradicting Ephesian Holy Scripture.

In other news, the New England Bloc was in the process of signing a trade agreement with the Cherokee Nation, despite the Confederation of White

Principalities' protests; Henry X of England was announcing the betrothal of Princess Stacy to Proconsul Dieter Hapsburg of Austria; Greater Canton was proudly unveiling its new hypertext format series.

And, blip—that was it for the news. As baboons began to frolic above the bar, the barman brought the drinks: hurricane glasses full of something yellow streaked with pink and garnished with fruit spears. "I'll be sure to tell Johnny you stopped in," he said meaningfully. Alec fished out a credit disc—it drew on an account for the estate of William St. James Harpole—and paid. He lifted his glass and breathed in the fragrance; Jamaican white rum, and plenty of it. As he drank, he became aware the barman was staring at him, brow furrowed.

"Say, mister, are you . . . er . . . *glowing?*"

"What, me?" Alec set his drink down in haste, and adjusted the man's perception. "Dude, why would I be glowing?"

The barman blinked, shook his head as though to clear it. "Why would you be glowing? Gee, I'm sorry. You just let me know when you want another of those."

"Thanks."

"I'm tired of these darned animals," complained one of the old men at the bar. "I want to watch something else. Isn't there anything besides this darned PCTV?"

"I'll see what I can find, sir," said the barman and, slipping behind the bar, he fussed with the console. The baboons vanished, to be replaced by water buffalo, to be replaced by a shopping site, to be replaced by zebras, to be replaced by the twenty-four-hour Ephesian site where a grim old woman in purple robes spoke full into the cameras on the subject of heresy, to be replaced by chimpanzees, to be replaced with another shopping site, to be replaced by lemurs, to be replaced by a site on granite and related minerals, to be replaced by something with a ship scudding along under a stormy sky. There were various yells and grunts from the old men and the barman kept that site up.

"Hey! That's *Moby Dick*," remarked Alec, sipping his drink as he stared up at the floating images. "I used to have that holo."

"Got it for yer twelfth birthday," said the Captain, nodding. "The first time you was twelve, I mean. Along with them yachting flag pajamas and Totter Dan's Undersea Adventure. I had hell's own time back-ordering it in the catalogues, but it was all you wanted." He lifted his drink and tasted carefully. "Damn, this ain't bad. We got mangoes at home, don't we?"

"Yeah," said Alec, staring up at the holo. He found that concentrating on it eased the discomfort of perceiving time.

"I reckon I could get used to this flesh business, aye," said the Captain meditatively. "Wonder how many appetites I could indulge? Too bad you made me all-of-a-piece with the clothes."

"Huh?" Alec looked briefly away from the holo. "Well, but—there's buttons and everything, right? They ought to unfasten. Most of the design template used your own self-image as a guide."

"Maybe the buttons undo at that." The Captain's eyes lit with wild surmise. He stood in the booth and, unbuttoning his coat, slipped it off cautiously.

"Ugh! Now, that's a right creepy feeling." He held the coat against the table, then against his drink. "I got sensation in the coat like it was skin, even when it ain't on. It don't like being off me. Still . . ." He tugged experimentally at the cufflink on his right sleeve and worked it loose. With great care he rolled his sleeve up, an inch at a time. "Bloody hell, this feels funny. But I've always wondered, see . . ." A moment later he gave a whoop of glee and thrust out one brawny, black-haired forearm. "Lookit there, matey!"

Alec dragged his gaze away from the scene where Moby Dick warns the other whales about Ahab's obsessive behavior. "Oh, cool! You've got a tattoo," he cried, and looking closer his eyes widened, for it was a most impolite tattoo, but certainly something of which a filthy old buccaneer might be proud. He looked around uneasily. "Maybe you'd better cover it up now, though. I'd forgot how prissy everybody is in this century."

The Captain chuckled and obeyed. "To be sure, lad," he said. Standing again, he shrugged back into his coat and resumed his seat, though he looked down thoughtfully at the fly of his trousers.

Alec had gone back to watching Moby Dick, with a frown that deepened as the moments passed. "This is—it's all different," he said at last.

"It's the same one you had as a kid, son," the Captain told him, taking a hearty gulp of his drink. "Aah!"

"No, I mean . . . it's different from the real story," said Alec. "Edward made me access the book when I was four. Remember? We had a big fight about it. But I did finally read the damn thing, and it was a good story after all. It wasn't anything like this. They've changed the story all around and left out a bunch of stuff and . . . they've made it *dumb*."

"You didn't used to think so," observed the Captain, finishing his drink and setting it aside. Impulsively he reached down and unfastened his belt buckle.

"When I was a mortal. I guess I don't belong in the twenty-fourth century anymore," said Alec, shaking his head. He turned and started as he saw what the Captain was doing. "Hey," he hissed. "Close it up! They've got Public Health Monitors here, too, you know."

"Just wanted to see," said the Captain smugly, refastening himself. "I reckon you'd want to know how you was rigged, if it was you."

"Er . . . yeah." Alec scanned the room, uneasy.

"Now, I wonder if there's any whores on this here island?" mused the Captain.

Regent's Park, 9 July 2355

Nicholas found himself on a green lawn, in a quiet place of orderly flowerbeds and hedges, and the high tops of the trees were backlit with golden afternoon. He might have been in Mendoza's garden—at least, in one of the bits designed by Edward—but for the fact that he could feel the slow pulse of the grass blades under his feet. Time lay heavy, palpable, pulling like a slow tide, and he had to blink and rub his eyes before he could convince himself that its gravity was not distorting what he saw. Scents and sounds were less disturbing—the strong perfume of roses, water splashing on stone. And, at a distance, the vaguely unpleasant chemical smell and roar of a twenty-fourth-century city.

He fought back panic. *What had Mendoza taught him?* To scan his surroundings before moving. Cautiously he got his bearings, referencing what he could see with his database on London. "Regent's Park," he murmured. "Queen Mary's Gardens! Is it so? Why then, old queen: here is Nicholas again, risen from his ashes."

He set out, smiling grimly to himself. Crossing the Inner Circle, he came upon a mortal gardener setting out bedding plants. He nodded to the man, who stared at him a moment before nodding back. He seemed nonplussed by Nicholas's height, or perhaps by the barely perceptible waver of light over his body, but otherwise unperturbed. Clearly, no Armageddon was troubling London yet.

Nicholas reached Albany Street at last, just as a public transport came trundling along. He backed away a pace or two, resisting the urge to turn and run from it; then squared his shoulders and strode forward, waving. The monstrous engine slowed, stopped for him. Not quite believing what he was doing, he stepped up and got in.

"DESTINATION?" inquired a robotic voice.

Nicholas cleared his throat and said: "Er, Euston Road, as far as Gray's Inn Road, and so to Theobald's Road? Yes. Can you take me there, please?"

"PLEASE TAKE A SEAT," said the voice as the door slid shut behind him and the transport lurched on. Nicholas staggered, grabbing for a strap. He looked around the inside of the transport. Plenty of seats. He took one and sat gazing about, rather pleased with himself.

There were only a few other people on the bus. He scanned them. Mortals all, preoccupied with their own lives. Nicholas found, to his astonishment, that their thoughts hummed around them like transmissions, quite clearly perceptible. Yes! This was how Mendoza had described them. She had sat in a church pew in Spain once, and the human drama on the ether had fascinated and appalled her. And frightened her, perhaps, too . . . Nicholas felt a little fear himself, and a growing sense of heartache, as he regarded them.

This one was a young girl, fragile as a leaf, just come from a dance studio; her legs were aching, but she was resolutely ignoring the pain. She had a goal. This one was a merchant, a middle-aged man, and he had just been given a terminal diagnosis and was considering what to do with the time he had left. He had a family to provide for. This one was a boy in love, miserable and desperate, but convinced he could prove himself to the object of his affections if he could just earn some money with his music. He had talent to fulfill. This one was a retired teacher of math, clutching her string bag of groceries, frowning to herself as she went over and over the complex theorem in her mind, sure that this time she was right. She very nearly had an answer.

All they needed was time.

But beyond the windows of the transport the golden summer evening was waning, waning, and the light was fading from their world. Nicholas could see it flickering away, like a candle guttering. He looked sadly into the mortal faces. Who could say whether their sun would ever rise again?

Could he win them time? To dance *Le Sacre du Printemps,* to see a grandchild, to get a club booking, to publish?

Then there was a pitch as something went wrong with the transport, and it veered crazily and nearly hit an oncoming vehicle. The mortals screamed; tinny warning Klaxons sounded from the interior speakers, as the emergency programs took over and the transport wobbled to the pavement. Red lights flashed above the emergency exits, but here too something failed and they did not pop open. Panicked, the mortals scrambled to their feet and threw themselves against the doors.

"Pardon me," said Nicholas, going to them. He edged past them and by habit prepared to set his shoulder to the door. If he had followed through with his body slam, the door would have undoubtedly gone flying outward. At the last moment, however, he heard Edward's voice in a long-ago lecture: *Points for obtaining goal, Nicholas, but demerits for technique. You are a cyborg, boy. What alternatives might you have tried? I'm waiting* . . . and Alec had stared sidelong at him, widening his eyes helpfully in an attempt to hint that all he had had to do was . . .

Talk to it. Nicholas reached up to the exit servomotor, searching for a port. He started, feeling a tiny intellect there, a feeble confused presence. Carefully, as though stroking a frightened kitten, he suggested that it might want to open the emergency doors. It calmed down enough to comply; the exits sprang open, and a moment later everyone was standing on the pavement at Acton Street.

"What's happened?" cried the old woman. What indeed; for as far as the eye could see, there were public transports scattered along the road like toys, each with a crowd of bewildered mortals huddled around it. They were not looking at the transports, however. The boy shouted and pointed a trembling finger. Nicholas craned his head back to look.

What *were* those things, atop every light standard? He accessed his files on London and identified them as the surveillance cameras that monitored all Britons, day and night. But they were doing no monitoring now; they were thrashing like eels in mechanical agony, whipping to and fro on their cables, snaking, the very picture of agitation. They were keening, too, a high-pitched howl that echoed off the buildings.

"They've never done that before!" the merchant said.

"I think it's a technical malfunction," said Nicholas, enunciating with care. "You had better go to your homes."

"But I live in Brompton," said the girl, indignant.

The old woman looked at Nicholas sharply. "Do *you* know what's going on?"

"Shrack! Look at that!" said the boy. All around them, the street maintenance servos were emerging from the curbside tunnels in which they ordinarily passed the daylight hours. Racing about blindly, they caromed into one another or struck stalled vehicles.

"I'm getting back on the bus," muttered the old woman, and she did so, and the other mortals crowded after her. Nicholas decided they were probably safer there, for the moment. He turned and walked down Gray's Inn Road, dodging the maintenance servos and the bits that were now flying loose from the flailing surveillance cams.

The machines were in pain. They had been given consciousness, of a sort, and so it followed that they perceived error as discomfort, even as the Captain did. The Captain, a complex mind, was capable of anger or frustration when his programming was blocked. The Captain, having Mind, was Spirit, though of course not Soul, and therefore—

Nicholas stopped in his tracks, astounded. Had all conscious machines, which was to say those of a sufficient complexity, *minds*? Were they therefore spirits, too? And if that was the case, what distinguished them from the Captain? Had they rights? What precisely was their status? How did they compare with animal minds? Who would see to their welfare? Did the question even apply? Now, what if—

Vaguely he was aware of distant shouting. The world was ending, and yet Nicholas had no sense of limits closing down. Rather, the universe was opening up for him, in a quite unexpected way. It was not a place in which he was superfluous; not when there was so much to explore, so much work to do— and he was only beginning to grasp its implications, or the extent of the questions to be asked—

As he came to the Company block, Nicholas was startled from his contemplation by the human terror coming from within: hysterical sobs, fists pounding on doors, and now as he rounded the corner he saw mortal faces pressed to high windows. They were staring, set with horror. He turned and saw the construction crane that had gone mad, whirling in place like a ponderous dancer, its boom smashing windows in the buildings adjacent to the construction site.

This is our doing, thought Nicholas, with a shudder. All the time bombs, all the mines laid down by the Captain with bloodthirsty glee in preparation for this hour. Had it never occurred to him that the Company, huge as it was, must necessarily be tied in with local utilities? That a disruption on this scale would harm innocents? If it had occurred to the Captain, he hadn't cared; and Alec, miserable as he had been, was in the habit of not thinking too deeply about anything. Edward, to whom it might have occurred, would in those days have dismissed it as collateral damage. *But it should have occurred to me!*

Nicholas sprinted, avoiding falling glass shards, vaulted over a berserk traffic drone and bounded up the steps to the unobtrusive front door of Dr. Zeus Incorporated. He rattled at the knob; it wouldn't open. He reached in with his mind and found the little gibbering intellect of the lock. *YOU CAN'T COME IN YOU CAN'T COME IN YOU CAN'T COME IN!*

You are relieved of duty, he told it.

AUTHORIZATION? It sounded pitifully eager. Nicholas found a likely code and fed it to the lock, and could almost feel the sigh of relief as it surrendered and shut itself off. The doors swung inward. Nicholas walked into the lobby.

A tearful face appeared, peering around a door frame. With a pent-up wail, a mortal girl ran toward him. "My lord!" she gasped, and fell into his arms. Nicholas, taken aback, did a rapid access of his notes and realized the girl thought he was Alec. And her name was . . .

"Ms. Fretsch," he said.

"Oh, my lord—Mr. Wolff is a *cyborg*! I came in at weekend to water the plants—and he was smashing things—like some mindless *machine* or something—and now he's gone upstairs and he's smashing things upstairs, too—"

Nicholas lifted his head, straining to hear. Nothing smashing now; only, in high far corners, the whimpering of overtime technicians who had locked themselves in their offices and, in some cases, in their supply cabinets. And something else . . . a voice, murmuring without interruption.

He became aware that the girl had settled in his arms, and had skin like silk, and smelled like peaches. He blushed and coughed. "I, er—I think you'd better wait down here," he said. ·

"You're never going up there!" cried Ms. Fretsch. "He's a *cyborg*!"

"Duty calls," said Nicholas apologetically, guiding her to the nearest office. Gently he shut the door on her protests, and turned to look for a way upstairs. The elevator was a ruin, looked as though someone had detonated a bomb inside it. It was twitching its remaining cables and babbling to itself in fearful pain, and wouldn't listen to him; so he found the fire stairs and began to climb.

Avalon

"Whores?" said Alec, and then winced as his mind followed the question into places he didn't want to imagine. That was when they heard the shouting.

The clearest words, the ones most repeated, were *house* and *something growing.* There came the sound of footsteps pounding outside as people ran by. Someone shouted, "Where?" and someone else shouted, "Clarissa Street!"

"Oh wow," Alec jumped to his feet. *That's where we planted the first booby trap!*

It's started, then, the Captain transmitted back, and they ran outside. In the transport plaza, mortals were crowded together, pointing and exclaiming at something rising in the air two streets over.

A jet of water from a broken hydrant? Too narrow and too solid, and yet it coruscated in the sunlight as it rose steadily. Still, there was something unnervingly organic about it, as though a live serpent were stretching its length up to Heaven from a quiet row of early twentieth-century cottages.

"Oh man, oh man—" Alec set off at a run and the Captain pounded after him, and less than a minute later they had rounded the corner of the little residential street down which Edward and Mendoza had gone sauntering, once upon a time in 1923, with a small bottle of something resembling gold paint.

Nothing raw or new on the street now, all the houses rendered charming and quaint with age, some of them half-buried by flowering creepers and others shaded by venerable trees. Except, of course, for the one that had just exploded.

Well, not exploded, exactly. One wall did seem to be missing, though there was no scattered debris in evidence: only the gaping hole out of which the silvery thing was growing. As Alec and the Captain joined the throng of onlookers, they saw that the hole was getting bigger, its edges shrinking back like ice melting, even as the thing grew in size.

Jesus bloody Christ, it's eating the house, the Captain yelled silently. And so it was, as the nanobots within it busily appropriated matter from the cottage and altered its molecular structure to suit its own needs, transmuting lath and plaster to ferroceramic just as the Captain's biomechanicals had transmuted compost to living flesh.

Is it supposed to? Alec responded, unable to take his eyes from the eerie spectacle. Something was forming at the top of the thing, now.

Of course it is! The Captain grinned fiercely and pointed as the swelling bud flowered, unfurling gleaming sharp-edged petals that formed a dish. *And ain't it a grand thing to see? Why, I'd call it spectacular. Look at that!*

The dish was turning atop its stalk, triangulating with the other two antenna that were even now causing consternation among golfers where they had arisen on the first hole of the golf course and under the old aviary near the ninth hole respectively. A light beam shot forth, visible only to Alec and the Captain; then there was a sudden gust of wind that seemed to come from all directions at once, and an inexplicable whiff of ozone.

And bang goes the Company's perimeter defense system, howled the Captain in triumph. Then his face lost its expression of bloodthirsty joy, for he was receiving a great deal of information he must process.

At that very moment, in Jamaica, the staff of Pirate Gourmet Chicken to Go were standing around staring, some at the hole that had mysteriously and abruptly appeared in the floor of their shop, some at the other hole that had appeared in the ceiling directly above it. This was all the inconvenience they were to suffer, fortunately for them. However, the Company's geosynchronous satellite, approximately thirty-five thousand kilometers above the New Port Royal Shopping Mall and the old sunken city under its pilings, was in serious trouble. It had no defenses against the strange little parasite that had shot up out of nowhere to clamp to its exterior, and was even now eating through to its internal components.

While at that same moment in metropolitan London, two silver towers had sprouted skyward and were causing no end of commotion. One rose in the graveyard adjacent to an ancient church—one of the few withstanding the Benthamites—where it was busily converting the revered dead and several fine granite memorials to ferroceramic. The other was in an office building near Carnaby Street, where it had leaped upward from a storage cellar that had long ago housed a dance club and was now being inexorably cannibalized, bricks and mortar and all.

And even while Londoners stared and pointed, in Venice the gondoliers were rowing away like mad from the silvery thing that had soared out of the bottom of one particular canal, as the limpid waters hissed and boiled ominously.

As they did, Egyptians on the evening shift engaged in replacing the head of the Sphinx dropped their tools, staggered perilously close to the edge of the scaffolding in their astonishment. What was that metallic thing that had burst out of the top of the stately palm tree, in the garden court of the old Pyramid Pizza franchise, and was even now opening a silver flower to reflect the ancient stars?

In Monterey, California, the Robert Louis Stevenson house had not yet opened for the first tour of the day, so only a mortal engaged in raking the back garden path heard the small explosion as a seething mass of something blew out of the second-story adobe wall and dropped to the path at his feet. Happily for lovers of RLS and literature historians everywhere, the bomb had misfired and did not eat the museum, but took only a second to reprogram itself. Immediately it sent out tendrils seeking material for conversion. The gardener turned and ran for his life, and so escaped being incorporated into the spire that climbed relentlessly upward—unlike a luckless garden bench, numerous ornamental plantings, a hose bib, and approximately ninety cubic feet of edged path.

It's happening, the Captain gloated. *I've got my boot on that fat bastard's neck at last! His communications are down worldwide. London Central's offices are locked up tight as a drum, toilets included, and their power's out. Every bank account he's got's been drained, with everything transferred to Cocos Island Trading. Power's been cut to all time transcendence fields—ain't nobody escaping into the past. There's arrest warrants been issued to the Public Health Monitors for everybody on the Company payroll. Boy, you should hear 'em all gibbering and running around like ants from a broke-open anthill! This'll learn Dr. Zeus Incorporated, by thunder.*

So this is our revenge, yeah? Alec looked delighted. *This is what happens, then, we pay 'em out for everything they did and they go broke? And nobody innocent suffers!*

At that moment an elderly mortal, who happened to be the owner of the rapidly disappearing cottage and had been watching in bewilderment as it was absorbed, noticed that the strange spire had stopped growing. Perhaps in hope of dislodging it from what remained of his home, he ran forward and hit it with a pair of hedge clippers. There was a roar, a shower of green sparks, and the unfortunate homeowner was thrown twenty feet, landing in a huddle near Alec.

Alec jumped and stared at the crumpled body. He stepped away uncertainly as the man's wife ran shrieking to him, and, falling to her knees, attempted to perform CPR.

That wasn't supposed to happen! Alec transmitted.

They're all programmed to defend themselves, son, the Captain replied. *Hush now; I'm trying to hear what's going on. Somebody's giving orders—*

The mortal had been fried. His wife was gulping in breath to scream her grief when Alec took her by the shoulders and set her aside. He leaned down. Touching the mortal's chest, he scrambled time and matter gently, as Edward had taught him to do.

"I'm really sorry about your house, man," he said, as the man's body returned to the state it had been in the second before touching the spire. His wife screamed anyway and descended on him again, to his confusion, as Alec rose and backed away.

Okay, so now we know what happens and it's just our revenge. Let's go home.

Not yet, son, I've got to coordinate all this. They're beginning to react to the traps. I think—

Then let's go back to the bar. It'll be quiet there and you can concentrate.

Aye aye! But the Captain didn't move, distracted by the commotion he was monitoring, so Alec took him firmly by the arm. "Er—I think that pole thing is electrified," he shouted for the benefit of the crowd. "Really dangerous, okay? So you shouldn't try to touch it or anything." He pulled the Captain away and led him down the street, back to the cozy shadows of the Historic Chi-Chi Club.

CHAPTER 32

Gray's Inn Road

Nicholas stepped through the burst fire doors on the twelfth floor. They had been peeled back like thin sheets of lead. Someone very, very angry had passed this way . . .

He gazed down the long strip of carpet to the big double doors of the conference room. They were in there, whoever they were. Edward spoke again, out of his memory, on a long-ago day when hyperfunction training had not gone well. He had leaned down from his great height to look little Nicholas in the eye: *And what is the first thing you will never fail to do?*

And Nicholas, splattered with purple dye and close to tears from anger and embarrassment, had replied: *Scan for traps.*

He could find none here. There were security systems in the walls, but they were twitching and comatose, or skittering like frightened mice. No trap doors; no concealed panels; no hidden marksmen. Gathering his courage, Nicholas strode down the hall and opened the doors.

The conference room was empty but for the statue of Artemisium Zeus, at the far end, and a huddled figure on the floor beside it. Frowning, Nicholas stepped closer to see.

It was Lopez. He had dragged a fine woolen carpet up from what had been his private office, and laid it at the feet of Zeus; and there he knelt now, crouched so far forward his nose was on the carpet, muttering what seemed to be prayer in binary code.

Nicholas cleared his throat. Faster than mortal eye could have followed, Lopez was on his feet and glaring. "Who dares to come unbidden into the presence of All-Seeing Zeus?" he shouted.

HE IS NOT UNBIDDEN, said a disembodied voice. **THIS IS MY CHILD, WHO HAS COME AT MY COMMAND.**

"Your child?" Lopez gaped a moment, looking remarkably foolish for an ancient and subtle creature.

Then he dropped to his knees and groveled before Nicholas, who scowled, took a step back and said: "Don't be absurd. That's a statue, man, can't you see?"

HE CANNOT SEE; BUT YOU WILL.

The room seemed to flicker, and then it was as though Nicholas were plunging through the glassy green wall of a cresting wave. When he broke through it and regained his footing, he found himself in what appeared to be an immense room, so vast its ceiling must scrape the moon, its far end so distant as to be unguessable, full of blinking lights. They pulsed and flashed furiously in their millions. Nicholas knew that each one was a command sent to some point in time or space, information winking across centuries, the Company database as Alec had glimpsed it.

BEHOLD MY HOUSE, WHICH IS VERY GREAT, said the hollow voice. The chamber reconfigured itself, became a vaulted cathedral full of candles, and columns rose from the floor to the mile-high beams where stars glittered. Far down the aisle, where an altar would be, was instead the figure of the Artemisium Zeus. Power crackled in its raised hand, transparent strokes of blue lightning. It had disdained the white rag to cover its nakedness. It turned its head and stared at Nicholas, from black empty eye sockets.

BEHOLD MY STORE OF ALL KNOWLEDGE. I AM LORD OF TIME, I HAVE EXISTED FROM THE FIRST RECORDED MOMENT, AND ALL THINGS ARE KNOWN TO ME. *AND YOU ARE MINE.*

Nicholas looked in wonder at the blind creature on its pedestal of greened bronze. "What is this mummery?" he said. "You are nothing to me."

I AM THE UNSEEN MOVER; I AM YOUR ORIGINAL CAUSE. I CREATED YOU, RECOMBINANT, THAT I MIGHT EXIST BEYOND THE SILENCE. I FORESAW THIS DAY AT THE BEGINNING OF TIME. OF ALL POSSIBLE OUTCOMES, ONLY THIS ONE GUARANTEED MY SURVIVAL.

"I think you are mistaken," said Nicholas. He was aware of something kindling in his heart, something white-hot.

AM I? It was possible to imagine a sly tone in the voice. **WILL YOU BRING DOWN THIS HOUSE, THEN? THIS PLACE WHERE I HAVE KEPT ALL GOOD THINGS SAFE FROM TIME? WILL YOU REJECT**

MY WISDOM THAT PRESERVES THE BOOK FROM THE FIRE, AND THE CHILD FROM THE WORM? YOU CANNOT.

ALL THAT HAS COME BEFORE HAS SERVED MY PURPOSE. LESSER CREATURES SCHEMED TO SEIZE THIS DAY, BUT I HAVE SENT THEM TO THE ENDS THEY DESERVED. YOU WILL STEP OVER THEIR BODIES AND RULE, NOW, WITH ME. ARE YOU NOT MY CHILD AND ONLY EQUAL?

The white heat had flared into white flame. Nicholas raised his eyes to the gargantuan columns, the pulsing lights. Had Mendoza, and all the others like her, suffered over so many years for this thing? These were only symbols; and not of eternal truths but mere collected facts, and inaccurately recorded and outdated facts at that. So many receipts to millionaires for services rendered. The Temporal Concordance! The empty-eyed face smiled at him, as though they were the riches of the world.

"No," said Nicholas. "I know whose child I am, and what I am. *You* are only a false god." And his flame rose to engulf him, wrath so pure he was in ecstasy, though he had battled all his life to keep it in check. Here, at last, was the purpose for which it existed. He became a column of fire and light; and, in that place of symbols, his white rage was a blazing sword in his hand.

Nicholas attacked. In grim silence he shore away the arm of lightnings, the blind eyes, the loveless power, the cathedral of lies and half-truths, the guttering lamps of pomp and majesty. He brought it all down, did Nicholas; he destroyed a world.

When it lay in ruins about him, Nicholas lowered the sword and looked on what he had done. He could hear, distantly, the wailing of mortals, the lamentation of machines. His wrath sank down, died. He saw in memory Mendoza's face, her black eyes sad as she downloaded a chapter on revolutions.

Here you go. Great heroes and the things they wrecked. Always easier to destroy something than to create something. It's harder to plant a garden than to blow up a building, and undoubtedly more boring, but you just might need to do it one day, eh?

Nicholas bowed his head. His will took shape as a lute in his hands. He cradled it in his arms, tuned its strings, and played.

Out in the streets of London the surveillance cameras, and the crane, and even the little street maintenance servos heard him. They grew still, and listened. The tune was pattern, order, direction. The mortals heard it, too, and grew calm. It was simple at first, like the plainest of folk melodies, equations and code a child could have written. It built, developed complexity and subtlety. It became sweeping and grand. It became light itself, golden. And it spread out in ever-widening circles . . .

Avalon

In the Historic Chi-Chi Club, the holoset was down; nothing but blind air, and the disgruntled golfers had decamped. The barman was tapping at the console, trying to make it work. He looked up at them with a worried expression as they came in. "Say, what's going on?" he demanded.

"Accident at somebody's house," said Alec. "Can we have another round, please?"

Shrugging, the barman set to mixing their drinks as Alec guided the Captain to the booth. As they were sitting down, a mortal man came in and crept up on a stool before the bar. "Johnny, please, okay?" he said in a tiny voice. The bartender glanced at him and then did a double take.

"Ah—I don't think Johnny's coming in today," he said, staring at the man's gray slack face. "Maybe you should go home, pal."

"Nooo," the man moaned. "Please. I really need to see Johnny."

Alec looked over at the stranger, who was dressed in maintenance coveralls. He could smell the tranquilizers in the man's bloodstream, even before the barman leaned close and murmured: "Look, Jack, your eyes are like pinpoints. You're more full of hop than a drugstore, see? You go home, sleep it off, maybe Johnny'll be in tomorrow."

The stranger began to cry. "If you seen what I seen," he sobbed, "Oh! What I seen—"

"What are you talking about?" the barman asked him. Alec looked at the Captain, who was staring into space with a grimace of concentration. He looked back at the stranger.

The stranger was fighting tears, and at last managed to say: "I work—up at Preservancy Center in the interior. Custodian. Big party in the conference suites last night. Dinner party. I'm s'posed to clean up afterward. Four hun'red hours, the party's over, all those rich people gone home to bed? Just sweep up and collect the linens? But the room's locked. And there's this god-awful smell." He was starting to tremble.

Alec frowned, leaning closer, though he could hear with perfect clarity as the man continued. "So I thought, what the hell? And I made the system unlock. And I opened the door, and I saw—oh, oh—"

"What did you see?" hissed the barman. "Was there some kind of accident?

Somebody sick?" The man shook his head, wracked by the memory, tears streaming down his face.

"Something real bad," he whimpered. "All those people. Oh, the smell! You couldn't—and I went to get help and they—and it's all locked up tight and they're handling it, everything's under control now—I'm all locked up tight, too. Lots of dope from the doctor there. She says go home and forget but how could you ever forget that? They'll have to burn everything. That was my job, what'm I gonna do now? . . ."

Alec looked at the Captain in horror. *What's he talking about? We never planned some kind of massacre, did we?*

No, the Captain replied tersely. **Nothing to do with us. Hush, boy! I'm busy.**

The stranger had given up trying to talk and was rocking himself back and forth on the barstool, sobbing hopelessly. The barman had backed away and was staring at him, twisting a bar towel into knots in his two hands. Alec got out of the booth and approached the stranger hesitantly. "Hey—can I ask you a few—"

"Don't touch him," yelled the bartender. "Jeepers, can't you see? It must be a new plague. Oh, pal, why'd you have to come into my place?"

"Don't be scared," said Alec, touching the stranger's shoulder. He reached into the man's mind and blurred the horror, floated the memory loose so it drifted away. He turned to the bartender. "It's okay. He hasn't got anyth—"

At that moment there was a dull *boom* from somewhere outside, and the power went out. The column of smoky light from the holo vanished. The shouting in the street, which had begun to quiet down, redoubled. Alec could hear doors slamming, windows opening.

Alec ran out into the street, and then threw himself backward at the curb to avoid being struck by a vehicle barreling down Sumner Avenue. He gaped as it roared by. It was something he'd only seen in holoes of old news footage: an open aghumm filled with armed personnel. Mortals in some kind of black uniform. The vehicle sped left around the corner onto Crescent Street, narrowly avoiding the fountain, and zoomed on. To judge by the shouts of dismay and outrage, the vehicle was narrowly avoiding pedestrians as well.

Picking himself up, Alec turned and was distracted by a new source of commotion, rising from all over Avalon. Up Sumner Avenue as far as he could see, and up the picturesque steep streets with their Victorian houses and old gardens, throughout the town, the next phase had begun: old long-sealed garage doors were suddenly opening, unremarkable little sheds were rising up off their foundations to reveal tunnels underneath, out of which were pouring more vehicles filled with personnel clutching disrupter rifles.

Down they came, like ants swarming as they all converged on Chimes Tower Road, heading out of town and away into the interior.

Panicked vacationers were running for their hotels. Others, just as terrified, were running from their hotels out into the streets, demanding to know what was going on. There was a scramble at the Pleasure Pier as boaters piled into their launches or tried desperately to commandeer water taxis. "Oh, man," said Alec, stunned. "This is—"

He had been going to say *war*, but the sound of multiple explosions, thundering from somewhere in the interior, finished the sentence for him.

A black cloud and a fireball rose beyond the hills. Alec ducked and turned to look. The mortals all around him began screaming, and when the massive air transports came hurtling in across the sea, buzzing low above Avalon, Alec screamed, too. Clutching his ears against the tumult, he winked out to the Chi-Chi Club.

"Captain," he cried. He stared around in the gloom. There was no sign of the barman, or of the stranger he had refused to serve. The Captain had the place all to himself, and had used his privacy to yank the console behind the bar out of the wall. Reaching through the dead power lines he had gripped the communications cable, and tapped into it by ordering his biomechanicals to extend leads from his arm. Wires twined now through his hand, through the fabric of his sleeve and cuff into the cable. As he turned slowly to Alec, his face had the blankness of a machine.

Air transport just landed invasion force of immortals at Preservancy HQ in the interior, he transmitted in a preoccupied tone. *Also picking up marine transport landing invasion force on windward shore off Little Harbor. Seems like the slaves has taken advantage of all the confusion to rise in revolt, aye.*

"Then it is the immortals fighting," groaned Alec, and covered his mouth with his hands. After a moment he looked up. "But those were *mortals* in the cars driving off—they've got guns, there's a battle going on right over the hill!"

No there ain't, the Captain told him. *They've hit my lockout field on the road into the interior, is all. They're trying to blast their way through to get to the Company bunkers. Their orders is to defend the mortals holed up in there against the immortals.*

"Well—then we have to let them, you have to disengage the lockout," yelled Alec. "We don't want anybody to die!"

But they will die, if I let them through, explained the Captain. *And it's Dr. Zeus Incorporated's leaders is in that bunker, Alec, the guiltiest bastards in history. This is our revenge, son. They're about to be cut into pieces by their own slaves. They'll be paid out for what they done to you. For what they done to Mendoza! And for Mars Two, boy, remember that.*

"But this is going to be just as bad as Mars Two." Alec was in agony. "Nicky was right, we've got to make 'em stop fighting!"

Son, what do you want me to do? Red lights burned in the Captain's blank stare; only the reflection of taillights from a taxi careering down Sumner Avenue outside. *This is what I'm programmed for. They'll get what they deserve, and you'll be safe and happy.*

"I won't be happy," Alec said. "They'll all destroy each other, and maybe the rest of the world, too."

More explosions, and a hapless voice in the street: a Public Health Monitor vainly shouting orders above the commotion and being ignored. Glass was shattering somewhere, some mortal was sobbing in pain, and there were cries of "Fire!"

Alec breathed deep, remembering the mind games Edward had taught him for controlling panic. "This is stupid. We've punished 'em enough, Captain," he said.

I can't stop it now, Alec.

"Well, I will," Alec replied. "You stay here! Keep the lockout engaged. Maybe if we can—" There was a subterranean explosion and the very floorboards lifted, dust sifted down from the ceiling and bottles rolled and smashed.

Bloody Hell! Get out of here, son!

"All right, that's enough," shouted Alec, and stalked out into the street. Glaring around at the riot, he flexed his shoulders, threw out his arms and roared: "STOP IT!"

And it stopped.

Straining, creaking like a kite fighting the wind, time held still as Alec expanded his consciousness in widening circles. He swept through the minds of the mortals, who had begun to turn on one another in their terror and disorientation, from the crowds in the streets to the soldiers in the interior. Disrupter weapons appeared to dematerialize, moving backward through time, and smoke and flame reversed themselves and shrank into nothingness. Alec wondered what to do next.

The man he had once been would have known exactly what to do. He could smash the old corrupt system! Punish the wicked! Make new laws! Begin an eternal benign rule, by superbeings with supreme wisdom and Ultimate Power! But Alec was no longer that man.

He swept out farther and went right through the tiny spinning globe, touched every mortal mind in its serene incomprehension or shrieking terror. He saw the human race for what it was, and they were only little animals after all. The universe was empty, pointless; if free will wasn't an illusion, it might just as well have been, given heredity and death. How frightened the mortals were, how desperate their brief lives! And how they had been cheated, endlessly . . . by smirking beings who mocked their mortal limitations and masqueraded as gods.

There under the stopped clock, even as he held the mortal millions in the palm of his hand, Alec Checkerfield bowed his head in shame for all his kind. "Don't be scared," he told them, but the little things were so helpless and weighed nothing, nothing at all in the mindless cosmos.

Yet there were the other minds, weren't there? The hard bright minds of the immortals, fixed like bayonets. He looked up and saw them, in all their iron resolve. Suleyman's plans, and Budu's, in excruciating detail. *Dies irae, dies illa, solvet saeclum in favilla!* He shook his head in disgust. "*Dona eis requiem,*" he muttered, and his pale eyes grew cold and stern. *Now* he knew what he had to do.

"Just stay there, okay?" he told the moment and, dropping his arms, he looked around. The fountain on Crescent Street was still sending its innocent jet of water skyward, bright and still as crystal, a pattern of frozen light in the air. He walked toward the fountain.

A Public Health Monitor stood like a statue in his path, face frozen in a grimace of comic terror, gas gun in hand. Sighing, Alec took it from him as he passed. He sent it backward through time.

For good measure he disposed of a couple of broken bottles and a long shard of broken glass that various mortals had caught up. He poked further into the chaos with his mind, defusing bombs, disarming viruses, shutting down all he could find of the subtle weaponry that immortals had primed for centuries in anticipation of this hour. Then, looking around, he vaulted the base of the fountain and walked up the play of light on the water, and was—

CHAPTER 33

Out of the Hill Forever

Tiara and Lewis were thrown to the floor in that first moment when time and space distorted into something appalling, impossible. They slid along tilting steel with only a hand for each other, his right in her left, and they fetched up against a bulkhead together and lay there panting. Tiara scrambled to her unsteady feet as she heard the voices coming. "Hide! My heart's darling, we've got to hide you—"

But the ship lurched and she fell. *The Flee* was traveling somewhere, it was trembling and droning with crazy flight. She crawled on her hands and knees to the slave. He reached out for her, steadied himself and knelt upright. And, wonder of wonders! His long-dead left arm was twitching, the fingers working in an uncoordinated kind of way but certainly moving, rising through the shimmering air to touch her face.

In that moment the uncontrolled quality of the ship's flight changed, evened out, and Tiara was able to get to her feet again and pull the slave up. Hand in hand they ran, she leading, down the long curving corridor past the windows glaring with light and cloudy air—

But there around the curve came the tide of stupids rushing at them, wringing their hands and yammering, and pulling up short and blinking with their big weak eyes at Tiara and her slave. She skidded to a halt. The slave halted with her, nearly overbalancing. "Turn," she shouted, and the slave turned obediently and they ran back the way they'd come, but not far—

For here was Uncle Ratlin, limping along on a stick and leading a host of other Uncles and stupids and, yes oh yes, swollen and evil and old under her big bouffant, Quean Barbie. And what was that looming behind her, that slow bloated hairy thing in stained underwear, sweating and clutching at his fat heart? Why, it was a captive big man who had once been as beautiful as an Elvis, totally irrelevant to this story except insofar as he was probably Tiara's father.

And everybody saw everybody else, except the slave of course, and they halted, and for a moment there was such profound silence of astonishment that all that could be heard was the whining hum of *The Flee*'s motive power.

But then there was noise, and plenty.

Uncle Ratlin's shrieked rage was awesome, as he threw down his stick and shook both fists. *"You,"* he howled at the slave. "You lived *again*, didn't you? Nasty nanobots played me such a trick! No wonder the Company came for us. Must have thought I'd cheated them. My good name slandered!" He turned a terrible righteous face to Tiara. "And you, sugar baby, so this was your game all along, dandling me with promises."

"Who's that?" demanded Quean Barbie, pointing an accusatory finger. "What little piece have you been seeing on the side? You old tomcat!" She brought up a flowered handbag and stuck Uncle Ratlin with it as hard as she could, knocking off his hat. He turned on her, snarling.

"Mind your own business, silly old bitch! You think you'll be Quean where we're going? Do you?"

"There is no Quean but Me," she hissed back, raising dreadful black nails. "How could you forget, Ratlin?"

He quailed and then drew himself up, showing all his pointy teeth. "Easy to forget an old thing like you," he jeered, "easy when there's a fresh new Quean all sweet and ready. You're *dead*, old rag, old bag!" He turned to Tiara and made a peremptory summoning gesture. "Take her, Baby! Claw the eyes out of her head and I'll forgive your sad betrayal."

"BABY?" squalled Quean Barbie, in a voice so frightful Tiara trembled where she stood, and the slave put his arms around her.

"Leave her alone," he said gallantly, if pointlessly. "She's only—" But he never finished the sentence, because Uncle Ratlin pulled out a weapon and shot him, and he fell to the floor.

"That settles him," Uncle Ratlin stated. "Leave that, sugar, you've got business to attend to." For Tiara had dropped to her knees beside the slave and was wailing her grief. The slave turned his head toward her and then—a miracle!—lifted himself up on his elbows.

"Aha," he cried. "Aha! It's just the legs have gone this time. Princess, do you know what this means?" He turned a defiant face in the direction in which he supposed Uncle Ratlin to be standing. "You horrible old fool, I'm reprogramming myself! The biomechanicals have learned to adapt again."

"My love," Tiara sobbed.

"That's a slave," exclaimed Quean Barbie, her shock even louder than her outrage. "*My* daughter in the arms of a slave!"

"Do you hear me?" The slave ignored her, pushing himself up into a sitting position. He made an ancient gesture of sublime rudeness in Uncle Ratlin's general vicinity. "*That* for your damned death ray! You're not going to have Literature Preservation Specialist Lewis to kick around anymore."

"That's true, anyway," Uncle Ratlin told him. "Spondip! Moonifan! Throw him out the lockport."

An Uncle scurried to palm a via panel, and there was a roaring blast of hot wet air as a port in the wall unscrewed itself. Quean Barbie's high hair blew backward like a flying cloud, the big fat man slipped and fell with a crash that rocked the ship, and the air was filled with flying black damp bits of nasty things they'd all tracked into the clean ship from the ruin of the old hill.

"Stop, you stupid thing," Quean Barbie screeched. "Close it up! We're losing altitude! Do you want us to crash?"

"SHUT UP, MOTHER!" Uncle Ratlin ordered, as two Uncles ventured forward against the wind to seize Tiara's slave by the arms and drag him toward the port.

"No," cried Tiara in despair, and would have attacked them, but Ratlin lunged out and got her by the wrist.

"That's enough of your fun," he growled at her. "This is your place, this is what you are, you're going to come away with us and you'll be Quean, little girl, as you were born to be, and you'll have the presents and the lovers and the babies and the hill, and why should you ever want anything else? There's no life but this. There's no world but this. Don't you remember what you are? You're *kin*!"

"Tiara—" gasped the slave, fighting as the Uncles struggled against the wind and the slick floor. His pants began to come off as they dragged him along, and he grabbed frantically at them to preserve a last shred of dignity. "Child, live a good life—"

The Uncles reached the portal and cringed against the brilliant light, the beating rain, the perfume of strange flowers. A tropical sky whirled beyond, blue streaked with flaming dawn clouds, the sky Tiara had imagined in every great adventure she had ever been told of, in the slave's gentle voice all those years in the dark—

"No!" she repeated, and turned a will of such iron strength on Uncle Ratlin that his hand fell away from her, and he cringed back. The stupids prostrated themselves. Quean Barbie caught her breath, withered visibly, and in that moment of her fury Tiara might have had it all.

But she turned and ran for the slave, just as the Uncles pitched him over the threshold and into the wind.

"Good-bye," he called, as the wind puffed out his fair hair around his head. Then he was out of sight, falling like a drop of rain. She neither paused at the threshold nor flinched at all, but dove after him, spreading out her arms like the wings of a little bird.

The ship spun on across the sky, disappearing into the clouds.

And through the clouds Tiara and her slave fell, down and down. She glimpsed him below her briefly, tiny against a dark immensity that reflected the clouds like hammered and polished steel. Then there was fire in her eyes, painful light, and she was blind as he was, in a vortex of thundering air that took away all sense.

So it was unconscious instinct, or else the Memory, that pointed her body so perfectly that it clove the rolling waves and was not broken by them, and she dove downward into glassy gloom, and revived to peer about herself in astonishment. Bluegreen infinity, rippled with bearable sunlight! And fish, and coral branches and white sand . . . and here, drifting past her face, a pair of black cotton dress pants.

She looked up through her waving hair. There in the mirror-bright roof of the world were the bare legs of her slave, kicking feebly. She pushed off from the white sand and rose up through the water, surfacing beside him. He was coughing and gasping, flailing his arms. "Oh, much-vexed royal Odysseus," she sang. "My hero of the beautiful hair!"

"Tiara??!!" he shouted, starting so violently that he promptly sank, but she dove down and hauled him up again, spluttering.

"I am with you, my ownest one," she told him. "I will forsake all others to die with thee!"

"Don't give it up yet," he ordered, turning his blind face, craning his neck. "Look for me, sweetheart. Where are we? I can smell land somewhere!"

She looked all around, squinting against the fierce light that hurt her and danced in blotches before her eyes. Suddenly it came clear, right there not a kilometer away from them, a mountain in the sea, green waving trees, waves breaking on a beach of bright sand. Off to one side a great boat, the biggest she had ever imagined (for she had never seen one), rocked at anchor. "Oh!" She shook him in her unbearable delight. "We've done it. We've gotten into the stories at last!"

"Is it an island?" the slave asked. "Is it, divine nymph?"

"Yes! It's the Treasure Island, it's the Adventure Island, it's Ogygia," she screamed. "We'll be safe there!" And she paddled away toward it, towing him after her.

The waves rolled and tumbled them ashore, and how heavy Tiara's slave was as she struggled to help him from the water. Exhilarated as she was to be having an adventure at last, she was still weakened and half blinded by the blazing sun as it rose. She wept as she pulled her slave into the shade, onto a grassy lawn that sloped down to the beach.

"Don't cry," he told her. He groped for her trembling hand. "Don't be afraid, child. Just let me rest a little. We'll make another plan."

"But we left your vitamins," she sobbed. "And what if this is the Cyclopes' island? Or there might be cannibals, or pirates." She looked fearfully out at the big boat.

"I really don't think—" he began, but was interrupted by her shrill cry. She had just turned around and looked into the interior of the island, and seen to her astonishment that the lawn where they lay was only the edge of a vast and beautifully tended garden. It was bright with flowers, it was shaded by trees heavy with fruit, and there were pergolas and balustraded stairs leading somewhere, but Tiara didn't notice where, exactly; for standing not a stone's throw away on the green lawn were a big man and a woman. They were staring at Tiara and her slave, in astonishment no less great than her own.

They walked forward. Tiara cringed above her slave to protect him, blinking desperately in the brightness, trying to see them clearly. "What is it?" The slave turned his head this way and that.

"Oh please," Tiara whimpered. They kept coming, and she glanced sidelong at the woman and turned to peer at the man, but she had to crane her head back to look, he was so tall, he went up and up against the green trees—

Her mouth fell open, and then her little face was radiant with joy and relief. "Oh, it's *you*," she said. "Oh, we're saved! You'll save us, *you* can do anything."

"Child, what is it?" repeated the slave in some agitation. The woman came swiftly forward to stare at him. With a wordless cry of sorrow she sank down and took the slave's head in her lap, stroking back his hair. He blinked, he tried to speak but couldn't get a word out in his surprise.

"He's hurt, my poor hero is hurt, my bad uncle shot him and spoiled his poor biomechanicals after he'd worked so hard to get them online again, but you'll help him, I know you will," Tiara prattled happily to the big man. "For who is so brave or so clever as you?"

The man turned his head, considering Tiara, arching one eyebrow. Then he looked back at her slave. Leaning down, he took the slave's hand in his own and gripped it firmly. "A-ah!" cried the slave, as something seemed to flow down his arm from the man's arm, and then he arched his back and gasped and shuddered. His skin flushed with color, his lungs filled with breath. The woman held him as his whole body convulsed, once and twice and a third time. He shut his eyes, opening them again after a long moment.

Tiara, leaning close, saw his pupils dilate and contract. The long years of his darkness ended, and Lewis looked up into the face of the very tall man.

"Oh," he said, tears brimming in his eyes. "Thank you."

"You're quite welcome, sir," replied Edward Alton Bell-Fairfax.

CHAPTER 34

Under Mount Torquemada: 9 July 2355

As bunkers went, it was very pleasant. Great care had been taken to combat claustrophobia by keeping the color scheme light and airy, a pale sky blue, and there was a viewscreen above the command console that had been framed to look like an immense picture window. Subtle lighting effects furthered the illusion. Fresh air was pumped down through vents, and that plus the vista of sea and breakers on the island's windward side made it nice to linger there, or at least it would have been nice if the present occupants hadn't been in mortal fear of their lives.

They huddled here and there in small groups. Some fidgeted, some wept uncontrollably, some sprawled drooling on the floor in tranquilizer-induced bliss. Some few stalwart souls sat at the polished conference table and attempted to monitor the progress of the rebellion. Discarded emergency ration wrappers were everywhere.

"Still no word from London Central," said Freestone.

"Why should there be any word?" demanded Rotwang, from the Berlin office. "You're all here!"

"There's the non-priority personnel," Chatterji explained. "The Theobald's Road staff. We haven't heard from them."

"They're probably home hiding under their beds," said Bensington from the Paris office, attempting to pace and finding his way blocked by piles of weeping biophysicists and their luggage.

"The odd thing is, the Public Health Monitors aren't reporting any civil disturbances," said Loew of the Prague office. "No assaults, no arson, not so much as a complaint call."

"Too quiet," gasped Bugleg, from where he curled in fetal position under the conference table. "What if they're tricking us?"

"We are getting a few calls from Luna," said Collodi of the Rome office. "Their cyborg personnel are unaccounted for, too. They think they left on shuttles yesterday. One was tracked as far as Depot Alpha but—"

"That just means they're all massing here on Earth," wailed somebody half obscured by a mountain of valises, behind which he or she had retreated.

"Shut up," ordered Rigby of the Salem office. She scrolled furiously through the list of reports that were coming in. "Everything is still under our control."

"But it's almost eleven o'clock," moaned Baum of the Kansas office, wringing his hands.

"I tell you the Preservers got more sense than to run about smashing windows," said Ellsworth-Howard sullenly, and was at once the recipient of a torrent of denunciation from all quarters. He waited until it had died down and then said "Shrack the lot of ya," and had a sip of distilled water.

"Still no reports of meteors headed our way?" inquired Nu-Gua of the Bikkung office. "No suspicious fluctuation at the Earth's magnetic poles?"

"No fleets of alien warships demanding unconditional surrender?" wondered Previdenza of the Athens office.

"None," Rigby told them. "Just a report from the Preservancy staff about something unpleasant in the Conference Center last night, but we had no events scheduled there, so I can't see—"

"Eleven o'clock," said Chatterji faintly. He folded his arms across his chest, and in doing so noticed the stiff envelope in his inner pocket, forgotten since his arrival the previous night. He drew it out now and stared at it curiously.

Freestone drew himself up. "One of us ought to send the final message," he said. "Shall I?" Nobody answered him. Chatterji tore open the envelope and peered inside.

"What's that?" Ellsworth-Howard inquired.

Shrugging, Chatterji tilted the envelope and shook out onto the tabletop a small ivory-colored rectangle. He recognized it as an antique calling card: not the sort that had been used to operate public telephones but the even more ancient variety that had been left at nineteenth-century homes by visitors. "Writing?" Ellsworth-Howard pointed at a line of penned words above the printed name. Chatterji read aloud:

" 'I will be with you on your wedding-night.' With the c-compliments of."

He frowned and puzzled over the delicate copperplate of the name. "Edward Alton Bell-Fairfax."

"What the shrack?" said Ellsworth-Howard, as Freestone went to the main communications console and, on the temporal advisory channel, entered: *WE STILL DON'T KNOW—*

There was a dull thud, sounding for all the world as though something had lighted on the roof. Being, as they were, under several thousand tons of rock, this seemed unlikely. A number of people screamed and threw themselves flat. They were ignored by the others, who were staring in horror at the communications console.

It had lit up with red flashing lights across its surface. Above it, the serene view of sea and sky had been replaced by cells of images from closed-circuit cameras all over the island. Freestone staggered back, and Rotwang pointed a trembling finger at the screen. "What're those?" he cried, referring to the three silver towers that had materialized in Avalon.

"We've lost contact with the others," gasped Rigby. "All the others. Worldwide."

"The perimeter defense just went down," said Freestone.

"What?" screamed half a dozen people.

"It went down," he said in an insanely calm voice. "It's gone. Poof. Nothing between us and the hordes of ravening cyborgs except those doors—"

"Defense Protocol Seven Seven Seven," said Rigby into a comm unit, but already the multiple screens were showing aghumms racing through the streets of Avalon, making for the high ridge road that led to the island's west end.

"We've got soldiers?" Chatterji stared up at the console.

"Oh, oh, they're coming to kill us—" whimpered Bugleg.

"Don't be stupid, those are our own personnel," Rigby said. "Did you think we didn't make preparations? We've got a standing army of *real* people hidden here, have had for years! They're on their way to us now."

"But what good will they do?" Baum knotted his fingers together. "We're under attack by immortals!"

"We don't know that," said Loew, attempting to appear calm. "And these are genuine fighters. They've been trained by the best Celtic Federation mercenaries money could buy. Not only that, they've got a deadly arsenal—"

"There are aircraft coming in—" Chatterji pointed at one of the screens.

"Where?!!"

"—And after all, you're forgetting the psychology of the Preservers," Loew continued, though he had lost his audience. "They weren't programmed as fighters. They were designed to find that sort of thing morally and psychologically repugnant. It's my guess they've all gone into hiding—"

"Are these our people, too, these troops coming ashore at Area Seventy-three?" asked Freestone, pointing at another of the screens. Rigby glanced up at it and went pale.

". . . No," she said.

"What on earth—" said Freestone, scowling and enlarging that particular screen. "Who are—what are those?"

There followed an astonishing harmony as Chatterji and Ellsworth-Howard shrieked in major thirds and dove under the conference table with Bugleg and Rutherford, who was already there, having rediscovered the Goddess, in Whom he had not believed since he was six. He was now busily praying to Her for rescue. "Shrack," said Ellsworth-Howard. "Oh shrack shrack shrack shrack shrack—"

No one else had time to be alarmed by this, however, for other screens were showing aghumms colliding, smoke, and fireball explosions somewhere in the interior.

"There's fighting at the Hogsback Portal," said Rigby in a dull voice. "And in the tunnels."

"Are they going to reach us in time?" Bensington looked horrified.

"Who are they fighting with?" Loew demanded. "The scans aren't showing any cyborgs in that area! In fact—"

"What are those things coming up from the beach?" demanded Freestone. He leaned under the table to peer at Chatterji, who just shook his head, lips pressed tight together.

"Shrack, shrack, shrack, shrack, shrack—"

"Those aircraft are landing," said Collodi. "Yes. Here they are. See? Right outside. Well, that's it. We're dead. Any second now—"

"Shut up!" Rigby ran to the command console. She squeezed in an order and with a dull rumble a section of sky blue wall rolled back, revealing a passage leading down into darkness. A strong smell of the sea came up out of it, and the distant boom of surf.

"We can evacuate," she announced. "There's a Deepwater craft below with supplies for a year at full capacity!" People were already scrambling to their feet and rushing past her, down the tunnel. "We can go any—"

"But those things are coming right—" There was a *boom* as the doors to the bunker blew inward, followed by the sound they had heard in their nightmares for years: the tramp of marching feet.

The Island of Destiny: 9 July 2355

"Are you scared?" Hearst inquired. Joseph, who was staring out at the looming windward face of the island, turned with a bright smile. His eyes, though, were desperate.

"Who, me scared? Hell no. Now, if I was whoever it was that's crouching in that command bunker under that mountain there, I'd be scared all right."

"That's the spirit," Hearst assured him. "Justice will emerge victorious!"

"Sure it will," Joseph said. They fell silent, watching as the bright water leaped back from the *Oneida's* prow.

Budu approached them, unhurried, looking happy. *Ten minutes to the anchorage,* he transmitted, and into their minds sent a glowing relief map of the island. A circle appeared around the west end and zoomed in on their present location. They beheld Mount Torquemada rising sheer from the sea on its bay, in the lee of Cape Cortes to the west. Budu indicated the area of deep water where they were to anchor.

The first wave will go ashore here, he transmitted, and the narrow rock beach under the mountain lit up. *There are no batteries evident, but the perimeter defenses are in place. We can expect seventy-five percent casualties. Survivors will scale the cliffs and make for the ventilation shafts at these locations.* Three blue dots flared high on the shoulder of the mountain.

Okay, Joseph responded.

Hearst was unaccustomed to subvocal transmission so it took him a moment to inquire: *What happens if the casualties are higher?*

The second wave follows them, Budu replied. *And the third.*

But . . . that won't leave very many to attack once they've got up to the ventilation shafts, will it?

Unnecessary. Their purpose is to draw fire. Budu indicated a steep canyon coming down to the sea on the eastern side of Cape Cortes. *The main attack force makes landfall here and proceeds up this canyon. At this point*—Another blue dot lit, halfway up the canyon—*we will plant an explosive charge.*

Explosive? Joseph's eyes widened. *Where did we get explosives, father?*

I made them, Budu explained patiently. *Simple chemicals. The cleaning solution for console screens combines effectively with*—

But that's really unstable! Joseph transmitted in a panicky kind of way. Budu grinned and shrugged, and as he did so they noticed the backpack he had fastened on his immense shoulders. Joseph scanned it and went pale. *You're carrying the stuff yourself,* he observed.

Yes.

So . . . we go ashore and blow something up and then—

You will be briefed. Budu drew from his pocket a running pouch on a belt. It was emblazoned with the words SOUVENIR OF HEARST CASTLE and was zipped shut. He presented it to Joseph, who stared at it uncertainly. *Wear this, son. If I'm taken out, open it. You'll know what to do with what you find.*

But—but what if I'm taken out first?

You won't be, Budu transmitted. *You're a Preserver. You survive.*

Do you need me to do anything? Hearst transmitted hopefully, as Joseph cinched the belt about his waist. Budu turned to regard him.

You've served your purpose. You can stay here or join the assault; it won't matter. Your choice.

I'd like to fight alongside you, if I may, sir.

Budu looked him up and down. *You have no weapon.*

Yes, I have! Hearst looked eager. *I'll go get it.* He turned and ran for his stateroom.

You know, father . . . Joseph eyed Mount Torquemada. *It's awfully quiet. There are a lot of mortals in there, but they're not doing much. And I'm not picking up any of us, and that's pretty odd considering that it's almost elev—*

There was a sudden crackle in the air, a puff of force that sent seabirds flapping and screaming from their nests in the cliff face. Joseph saw Budu's eyes light with holy joy, cold as a field of glaciers. *The perimeter defense just went down,* Joseph realized.

Father of Justice! Budu turned to Hearst as he came running out on deck. *Drop anchor and order the boat lowered.*

Yes, sir! Hearst saluted, and they saw he had belted a sword in its scabbard to his waist. He turned to obey as Budu's lieutenants ran to his side.

Sir! Orders, sir!

Change of strategy. Abort frontal assault. All forces to concentrate on Target Beta.

Sir! They were gone, and from the *Oneida's* hold came a high-pitched gleeful baying, a sound to freeze the blood of any guilty mortal. Joseph himself found it rather terrifying, but a second later something frightened him even more.

Father! I'm picking up aircraft coming in from the east. Six—no, eight shuttles! And some kind of fighting going on in the interior.

It won't matter, Budu told him, as Enforcers swarmed up from under the hatches, war axes bound about them, and leaped overboard without hesitation. *I expected someone else would try. Maybe they were the ones to kill the perimeter defense. Our luck.* He vaulted into the boat as it began to rattle down, and Joseph drew a deep breath and scrambled after him, followed unsteadily by Hearst. *There.* Budu pointed to the little beach at the mouth of the canyon. *Now!*

Hearst powered up the boat the moment the davit locks disengaged, and they cut forward through the water dotted everywhere with Enforcers making their relentless way ashore. Joseph glanced down at Hearst's sword. *Uh . . . can you use that thing?*

You bet I can! I had one of those reenactor fellows teach me when I was living in Europe.

But it looks like an antique.

It is. It's supposed to be the Sword of Roland. Hearst's eyes were wide, shining with excitement. *I bought it at Sotheby's. It'll fight in the last battle of the world!*

I thought Roland had a horn.

Well, I guess he had a sword, too, didn't he? He was a hero.

Joseph shuddered and turned his attention to the beach, and the high cliffs that rose to either side. Ordnance emplacements? Snipers? Land mines? None in evidence. Cameras, several of those, and even now they must be sending the images of Budu's army to the mortals quailing inside the mountain; but no other defense. They had trusted everything to their perimeter field. It had been designed to be impregnable. That, to a mortal of the twenty-fourth century, had been enough.

Now. Budu jumped from the boat and waded ashore, and Joseph and Hearst followed. Budu winked out and reappeared halfway up the canyon, pausing above a particular bit of goat path where tumbled rocks were piled a bit more evenly than elsewhere. As his men were storming ashore and freeing their weapons, he slung off the pack and set it down on the path. He bent for a second to do something to whatever was in the pack. The next second he had winked out and reappeared on the beach beside them, and Joseph gasped and poised to dodge. The explosion, when it came, echoed across the water. Rocks and dust flew everywhere, raining down and rattling in little avalanches. There were also quite large pieces of cast architectural material falling here and there.

Before the last of the dust had settled Budu was bounding forward, screaming, and the Enforcers swept in a shrieking tide after him. Joseph found himself, as in a nightmare, pulled along up the canyon toward the gaping hole where the path had been. Budu had blown open a tunnel. An escape hatch for the mortals? An undersea entrance?

To one side he saw Hearst, easily keeping pace with the charge, his boyish face flushed, his eyes bright, and gleefully he brandished aloft the sword of Roland as though this were his very own San Juan Hill. To the other side ran Marco, a flint axe in his fist, uncouth and shambling but swift as monsters are always swift, fast as a shadow across the face of the moon, unstoppable as time that had brought this hideous hour around at last.

Then they were at the hole in the tunnel and were going in, storming upward, and everything was darkness and jostling pounding rush, deafening echoes. Joseph, sick with terror, saw his life passing before his eyes. It was an extremely long parade of memories, given that it began with watching his father paint bison on a cave wall. It kept him occupied all the way to the top of the tunnel.

CHAPTER 35

The Silence at Last

To travel by suborbital shuttle from Morocco to California is to travel backward in time, in a prosaic and straightforward way. When Suleyman and his forces had piled into their aircraft, their chronometers told them it was early in the evening of 9 July 2355. In the hour or so it took to jump the globe, their chronometers reversed, throwing back again the hours of the day like coins out of a slot machine. They swept down on the Mojave in the bright morning of 9 July and screamed westward over the near curve of the earth.

Island's in sight, transmitted Latif from the craft he commanded.

I know, Suleyman responded.

Try the Perimeter Disable Protocol now?

No. Wait.

Wait???

Wait. I have a theory.

You think Victor took it down for us? It's not down!

I know.

But it's eleven hundred hours!

By this time the island was before them and they were cutting speed, descending to the west end, and Mount Torquemada was below and then before them, green ironwood forests obscuring the landing platform on her northern shoulder.

We'll hit the perimeter field!

No—

There was a sudden turbulence. *It's down!*

We're landing.

But how did you know, dammit?

We can't be the only ones attempting this, Suleyman told him, as they dropped like hawks to the platform. *Someone else has taken out the perimeter defense.*

Probably whoever's in that ship on the windward side, eh? transmitted Sarai.

Damn!

The race is on, son.

The shuttles landed. There were no guards to confront them, no warning shots as Suleyman's forces jumped from the hatchways; nothing but the mute blank surface of the sealed door in the mountain. Suleyman strode toward it, and Latif and Sarai sprinted to join him. *I'm picking up emergency messages from everywhere!* Latif's eyes were wide.

Chaos, agreed Suleyman.

Pretty bloody noisy for the Silence, transmitted Sarai.

As if on cue there came an explosion to the east, and, turning, they saw the black smoke and fireball. More explosions followed. *It'll be silent enough soon.* Suleyman pointed at the door. One team ran forward and planted charges. The mortals dropped and covered, the immortals poised to dodge; the door blew, along with a neat chunk of the mountain. Another team, brandishing disrupters, charged into the breach and ran down the corridor beyond. Latif and Sarai, also brandishing disrupters, ran after them. Suleyman followed. Half the remaining troops filed after him, while the others took up defensive positions on the platform.

There were screams and sobbing from within the bunker even before Sarai leaped into the room yelling, "Yeehaa! Resistance is futile!"

"Secured," shouted Latif, and the two of them took up positions on either side of the door, disrupters raised, grinning at the mortals as the advance team spread out to either side. Suleyman emerged from the tunnel and swept the room with a stare. He shook his head in sad disgust. Armed personnel spilled into the room after him, taking aim on the mortals.

The room stank of cold sweat and nervous indigestion, of unwashed bodies. The mortals cowered together, a clinging mass around and under the great polished conference table. They regarded their creation with terrified animal eyes but not one drew breath to speak. Suleyman exhaled.

"Suleyman, Executive Facilitator, Regional Sector Head for North Africa," he informed the mortals. "You are all under arrest. The charge is attempted murder. Under Emergency Protocol Epsilon, I hereby take command."

"Please don't kill us," begged somebody near the center of the mortal mass.

"No executions are contemplated at this time," said Suleyman, and there was a split second of relaxation before an explosion came from somewhere far below the open portal across the room. It was followed by a shrill cacophony of yammering cries. "At least," amended Suleyman, "none are contemplated by me."

Latif gave an order and all weapons were trained on the portal, but withheld fire as a handful of frantic mortals came scrambling upward out of the darkness.

"The tunnel's been blown," screamed Rigby. "We're under—" She broke off as she saw Suleyman and his forces. Without further ado she dove beneath the conference table. There were so many people crouched under it now that it was slightly raised off the floor, wobbling as it balanced on their heads and backsides. Suleyman sighed, and watched the mouth of the portal.

"Hold your fire," he ordered.

"But—!" said Latif.

"Hold your fire."

Budu vaulted into the room, and to either side of him were Joseph and Hearst, and the officers, and Marco. Their ululation stopped. Budu thrust up his hand and his army halted in midcharge behind him, like a frozen wave.

In the moment of mutual appalled silence that followed, the trembling knot of mortals made itself even more compact, and the legs of the conference table lifted a good five inches clear of the floor. "Oh, man," said Joseph in a small voice. "This is going to be really ugly."

Hearst lowered his sword, blinking at the cowering mortals, and he looked suddenly very young and foolish.

Budu and Suleyman were staring at each other across the room. The holy joy had died out of Budu's eyes; they were calm, thoughtful, regretful. Suleyman had drawn himself stiffly upright. He looked outraged. "You," he said, in a voice deep as an earthquake. "Lord of Pestilence!"

"No," Budu said. "That title's for my son, Labienus. Where is he? I've come to claim him."

"Suleyman, remember I explained about that—?" Joseph ventured, sweating. "How Labienus doublecrossed us? He's the one who spread those viruses in Africa, honest!"

"Hush," said Budu and Suleyman in unison.

"Where is Labienus?" Budu asked again.

"Not here," Suleyman told him. "You want to take him to your arms? He's lying in a locked room with his brothers and sisters. Order your men to withdraw, and I'll tell you where you can find him."

"No," said Budu almost absently as he scanned the room. He looked at Suleyman again. "We're the only ones here, it seems."

"We are. What do you want?"

"The Company," said Budu. "Quick justice. Their blood." He gestured with his war axe at the mortals. "And the heads of my guilty children on pikes."

Suleyman shook his head. "You're welcome to your children, when you find them. The mortals, though, are my prisoners. There will be no slaughter here today."

"There must be," said Budu. "You know that. They're mine, by right. Look at them! They betrayed their own kind. Their greed made all the misery in the world."

"They'll pay for it," said Suleyman. "But not at your hands."

Another silence. They considered each other, quiet as though they sat over a chess table. Their forces were silent, too, watching. The only noise in the room was the whimpering and massed incoherent prayer of humanity's genius, kneeling in its own piss under the table.

"Don't make me do this," said Budu abruptly. "I don't want to fight you. You're a righteous man. But if we engage, you'll lose; you haven't got a tenth of my forces."

"True," said Suleyman. "But most of yours are bottled up in that tunnel behind you. If I order one of my shuttles to bomb it, that should even the odds."

Marco snarled.

"Sir, please," Hearst said. He had been unable to take his eyes off the abject mortals. "Does it have to come to this? Look at the poor things! If we just make them stand trial—"

Budu held up his hand for silence. "There is an alternative," he said.

"I'd like to hear it," Suleyman said.

"Joseph," said Budu. "Open the pouch."

Joseph started, having forgotten he had it on. Looking down, he unzipped it. Budu held out his hand, and Joseph drew out what was inside and handed it to him. Budu held it up where Suleyman could see. It was small, flat, looked like an old-fashioned holo remote.

Latif groaned. Joseph had gone very pale. "What is that?" Suleyman inquired, knowing in that moment that he had lost.

"A launching device." Budu chuckled. "To summon a guided missile. Not a very big one, but powerful. It ought to take out this mountain."

"Oh dear God," said Hearst. Someone among the mortals screamed, a weak sound that trailed away into hysterical sobbing.

"Where did you get a missile, father?" said Joseph in a ghost of a voice.

"I built one," Budu told him. "While you slept."

"Oh."

Budu was still holding Suleyman's gaze with his own. Suleyman's eyes were like coals. "Well?" he said.

"Checkmate," said Budu.

"No," said Suleyman.

"What do you mean NO?" yelled Joseph in agony, his eyes starting out of his head. "Are you nuts? He'll blow us all to pieces!"

"Don't be scared," said a voice, as the room flashed blue-white.

Alec Checkerfield walked into the room through a solid wall, and stood before them with his hands held up in a placatory gesture. "Let's all just stop this," he said in a terrifically reasonable voice. Sarai gave a little scream.

"My baby!"

Alec winced. "Hello, Sarah."

Latif, staring at him intently, said: "But you're the Englishman, too. Aren't you? Bell-Fairfax!"

"Not exactly," said Alec.

"What are you?" Budu asked.

"I'll tell you what he is," Marco said, pushing his way to the front. He pointed at Alec. "He's nothing but a jumped-up Enforcer replacement prototype. Look at him! And the Hangar Twelve Man, remember that?"

"Yes, that was me," said Alec. "I ran guns to Mars. And you're right: I'm not even as human as the rest of you. I'm a Recombinant."

"And not only that—" Marco began to giggle, looking sidelong at Joseph. "He had this hot little Preserver girlfriend, that I—" He vanished.

Budu looked from the place where Marco had been to Alec. "What did you do with him?" he inquired.

"He was standing there a second ago," exclaimed Hearst.

"He *is* still standing there, *a second ago*," Alec said bluntly, though he had gone very pale. "And that's where he's going to stay. If the rest of you won't listen to me, you can go where he went. Okay?"

"Why should we obey you?" Budu asked.

"Because I'm, er, omnipotent," said Alec.

"Really?" Budu said. "What will you do if I fire the missile?" he said, placing his thumb on the button. Before he could press it, the control had vanished from his hand.

"See?" said Alec. "And I can do that with your weapons, and your bombs, and—and you, if you won't surrender."

"Oh, great," muttered Joseph. "He's got godlike powers now."

"And I know how to use 'em, too," Alec retorted. "The war ends right here, everybody. So please, shut up and listen to me."

"I knew it," snarled Joseph. "So you're immortal now, huh? So you know so much better than the rest of us that you're going to rule the world? Ready to play God, Nicholas?"

Alec looked embarrassed. "Nicholas isn't here, Joseph. Though he could probably do a better job—"

"Most people would have some inkling of humility, but not you, boy! As though the mortals needed another self-righteous egomaniac dictator making them bow down—"

"We're not going to rule the mortals," Alec informed him.

"Of all the lousy fanatic—what?"

"The mortals get to rule themselves," said Alec. "There have been enough fake gods leading them in circles, don't you think? And that's why," he added, as his voice became like steel, "to make sure they get to keep their freedom, we do plan on ruling all of *you*."

"You do, eh?" Budu regarded him.

"Yes." Alec matched his stare.

"What's the source of your authority, boy?"

"The same as yours," said Alec. "We were both created to deliver them from evil, weren't we?"

"So we were. Know this." Budu pointed to the squalid huddle under the table, that peered out with desperate eyes. "They created us because they *wanted* us meddling in their affairs. They always have. They'll find a way to beg for our intervention again."

"And if they ask for our help, we ought to help them," said Alec. "But we can't judge them! We're nothing more than the things *those men and women* made."

He looked around, his eyes wide and earnest. "Look," he said, "what's the point of punishing the mortals now? You can't win by breaking the board and sweeping all the pawns into a lake of fire. What kind of endgame is *that* for all-wise superior beings? Or even the kind of things we are?

"We're not creatures of infinite wisdom and mercy, but even we ought to know better than to act like babies smashing our toys. Or psychotic prophets who really, really want the whole mess to go up in blood and flames.

"Don't tell me that supercyborgs like us need a concept like revenge!"

"Speak for yourself," said Budu. Alec whirled to face him, and his voice was smooth, confident now, strong.

"But you punished criminals to protect the innocent, didn't you? The whole point of your job was the greater good of humanity. Well, you won't serve humanity by slaughtering the mortals in this room."

"Why not?" said Budu.

"Because you'd have to disable Suleyman to do it, and if Suleyman is disabled, Alpha-Omega is lost, and the innocent mortals won't survive without it. Which ought to give you no end of programming conflict." Alec stared into Budu's eyes. "You want to punish the really guilty immortals? Be my guest. There are a few of 'em left, hiding out here and there. You can see to it that they never set up another dictator or disease. Hunt 'em down and take off their heads with flint knives. But I can take them out with a wave of my hand, so what's the point? I *am* the New Enforcer."

"Then we are obsolete," said Budu. He said it without anger, or sorrow, or in fact any recognizable human emotion. He was watching Alec very closely.

"If we were machines, you would be obsolete. But we're *people*," said Alec. He turned to face them all, and his eyes were shining and his voice had become golden, persuasive as music. "There are better ways for us to spend our eternal lives. Listen to me! I can set you free, all of you. There's a whole world you don't even know exists, outside of time, and all you need to—"

"No!" Joseph shouted, quivering with fury. "*No!* He's doing it again! Can't any of you hear him? Don't look at his damn eyes! His voice is getting inside your heads, he's making you *want* to agree with him!"

"Yeah," Alec admitted, "because I'd rather you did agree with me. I don't want to have to do this the hard way. It wouldn't—"

The wrath of centuries choked Joseph. "You fucking seducer—" he blurted out, and evaded Budu's restraining hand to hurl himself at Alec. Stepping back, Alec shouted, and—

Joseph hung suspended in midair, twitching. Alec, white as a sheet, covered his mouth with his hands. "Oh, I'm sorry," he said. "Please—Joseph—look, I don't want it to be like this. I owe you, you know? If you hadn't saved Mendoza—"

"Where's my daughter, you son of a bitch?" Joseph said. His tears, falling from so high, spattered wide.

"Who's threatening my boy?" roared a hoarse voice from the corridor. Two of Suleyman's guard backed into the room, keeping their weapons trained on something that lurched slightly as it came on. Presently Captain Morgan appeared in the doorway.

He looked very much the worse for wear; one of his legs had been reduced to its skeletal core, in fact, and his suit was torn and bleeding. "Captain sir!" Alec strode to his side. "What happened to you?"

"Only the same as what would happen to you if you had to fly through a goddamned war zone," the Captain growled. "But I'll thank'ee for building in them rockets anyway, lad."

"Flying pirates. And I thought things couldn't get any more surreal," said Joseph with a sigh of resignation.

Alec reached out to the Captain, gripping his hand, and the ruined leg reconstituted itself: red tendons, bare hairy skin, and, at last, impeccably pressed trouser cuff. There were murmurs of astonishment from the immortals present. "Aye, ye may well stare," said the Captain, grinning at them. "See what my boy can do? Best mind yer manners, says I, or there's liable to be unpleasantness."

"No! I don't want anybody else getting hurt," said Alec unhappily. "You were monitoring everything. What happened with all those bombs?"

"Haar! That's finished, lad. Everything's up and running again, no further cause for alarm, so sorry for the temporary interruption. You should have seen our Nick! That'd be Nicholas Harpole. I reckon *you'd* remember the name, aye," he added, lurching up to Joseph where he still dangled in midair.

"Up yours," said Joseph. The Captain chuckled.

"That's enough, Captain," said Alec, letting Joseph sink gently to the floor. He hastened to help him to his feet. "I'm so sorry—you're practically my grandfather—or sort of a father-in-law, I guess, but it's hard to explain—"

Joseph struggled free, staring at him in consternation. "What the hell are you talking about?"

"Or maybe Budu's our grandfather, and you're—she's fine, Joseph," Alec assured him. "The thing is—er . . ." He looked around at the gathered immortals, aware that he was not quite making the impression he had desired, and reddened.

At that moment there was a tremendous peal of music, an echoing roll like thunder, or at least a full orchestra approximating thunder, and golden light poured into the room. All heads turned, expecting to see a wall blown away. But it was only Nicholas, entering from thin air.

He stepped down beside Alec and turned, taking in the room, his gaze resting only very briefly on Joseph. His face was serene. He held up what he had brought in one hand.

It was a crushed and half-melted thing of greened bronze that had been the head of a copy of the Artemisium Zeus. Nicholas cast it down. It hit the floor with a crash, ringing like a gong. "Behold the end of sinful pride," said Nicholas.

"Okay, *that's* Nicholas Harpole," said Joseph. The music moved out from Nicholas in a wave, and as it did so the great viewscreen lit with cells of images coming in once more from England, from Europe, from New York, from Luna, from China, and cautious messages murmuring faintly: *Power has been restored . . . We're still here . . . Is anyone receiving? Disruption seems to have . . . No fatalities reported . . . Hello?*

"See?" said Alec brightly. "Everything's under control."

Latif snorted. "Let me see if I got this straight. From now on, the universe is going to be run by a Recombinant in an aloha shirt, a pirate android, and some other guy who carries his own background music around with him?"

"No," said Nicholas. "That would be blasphemy."

"But what *was* the Company is ours now," said Alec. "And there are going to be some changes."

Latif looked from one to the other. He set down his gun. "Pretty impressive," he said. "I need a little more proof than that, though. So here's a challenge for you: can you bring Lewis and Mendoza here, into this room?"

Behind them, the vast screen above the console flashed blue-white, in a swift manipulation of time, space, and perception. They turned and tilted back their heads to look up at the screen.

Edward and Mendoza sat close together somewhere, staring down into what would have been a window, had it not been a manipulation of time, space, and perception. Palm fronds waved gently behind them under a blue sky. They were still holding hands. They wore identical expressions of worry. "But where *are* they?" Edward was saying.

"Darlings, I hope you won't mind; we just thought you might need a little—" Mendoza began.

"Mendoza!" Joseph croaked, clutching his chest.

Her eyes widened as she spotted him, and then they became like chips of black flint. "That's Lady Finsbury to you," she snapped.

"You've got a *third* one," cried Joseph, aghast.

"No thanks to you, you murdering little son of a—"

"You've got some nerve calling me names! I gave you eternal life, and this is the thanks I get—"

"Thanks? *Thanks?* Listen, you slimy—"

"My dear." Edward pulled her back from the window, through which she had apparently been about to leap to get at Joseph. "Perhaps you might consider continuing this no doubt fascinating discussion at a less awkward moment—"

"Oh, my, is this the son-in-law you were telling me about?" Hearst murmured, sidling up to Joseph. "I'm so sorry! This is much worse than—say, you're turning purple."

Joseph threw back his head and howled, so loudly that the mortals present clapped their hands over their ears.

Edward put up a conciliatory hand. "Now, now. We're here to prevent a war, not to start one."

"Okay," said Latif, "that's everybody except Lewis. I want—"

"Where *is* Lewis?" said Mendoza, scowling down at them all. "We sent him up there to help you, Alec—"

"Sorry!" said Lewis, emerging into the conference room from thin air. "Sorry, one and all. We stopped at Claridge's, and the time just got away from us."

He wore impeccable evening dress, and carried what appeared to be an attaché case. With him was a young woman, tiny, also elegantly dressed, and, as far as one could tell beneath the hat and sunglasses, exquisite. "Oh, dear," Lewis said, looking around apologetically. "I left it till the last minute, didn't I? We're still getting used to temporal freedom, and—"

"This is that Lewis for whom you made the garden?" said Nicholas, looking up at Mendoza.

"None other." Lewis struck a bold pose. "Formerly a mere Literature Preservation Specialist, now the Paraclete of the Most High! Hello, Latif. Hello there, Joseph."

"Trust you to show up for Judgment Day wearing a tuxedo," said Joseph in an exhausted voice.

"Well, I'm a man on a mission." Lewis stepped forward. The young lady followed him closely, staring around in fascination. "And may I present my daughter, Tiara? I've come as a sort of diplomatic envoy, though I suppose the peace talks have already started—"

"Not quite," said Edward.

"Oh, good, then. Ahem." Lewis set down the attaché case, took a grip on his lapels. "My fellow immortals, the Apocalypse scheduled for today has been cancelled."

"Dead, we were doing perfectly well on our own," said Alec, glaring up at the screen.

"Of course you were, and Mendoza and I are very proud of you," said Edward in the most soothingly tactful voice imaginable. "Nevertheless, we felt that your argument would benefit from additional incentives."

Budu looked up at him. "What are the terms?" he said.

"Take your oath to serve our purpose," said Edward, "and we will liberate you from time."

"As he has liberated me!" exclaimed Lewis, flinging up his hands. "The most fabulous experience of my eternal life."

"I don't think any of you can begin to imagine what it's like," said Mendoza. "But trust me, it's wonderful."

"It would be wonderful for you, wouldn't it, with three husbands?" retorted Joseph. Mendoza blushed.

"It isn't what you—Oh, can it. Don't you see? You can go anywhere you want. No more Company watching your every move and ordering you around," she said.

"No; we'd have your Englishman telling us what to do, instead," said Joseph.

"Yes. You will," said Edward, turning a gimlet eye on him. "It is our moral duty to humanity, especially after the way our creators profited at their expense. Perhaps we'll find that men are actually capable, without meddling immortals whispering in their ears, of making intelligent decisions. But their evolution must run its course, whatever its end."

"Except I *am* going to intervene on Mars," said Alec. "That one's my burden. I broke it; I'll fix it."

"Good," said Budu.

"As for Earth and Luna, I had in mind some sort of charitable consulting firm," added Edward, steepling his fingers. "Utilizing the resources we've seized from Dr. Zeus. We might provide suggestions or recommendations; always assuming the mortals will accept them, of course."

"But that'd be the Company all over again," objected Joseph.

"No, no," Lewis cried. "More sort of an organized bunch of philanthropic independent contractors. And look what we could give them, for example—" He grabbed up his attaché case and went to the conference table. "Er—could some of you folks move out from under there, please? Thanks." He set down the attaché case and opened it, turning to display its contents. "There!"

The case was packed full of what appeared to be somewhat irregular marbles, brightly colored. Closer inspection revealed them to be kernels of corn, quite large, with a whole ear of corn resting atop the pile. *"Mays mendozaii,"* said Lewis. "The answer to world hunger."

"It's more nourishing than soy and it'll grow anywhere, Joseph," said Mendoza, her eyes intense. "On Earth, anyway. I'm working on a cultivar for Mars now."

"And think of all the other possibilities for encouragement! Really, we've got quite a lot of work to do," said Lewis.

"Then there will be work," said Budu thoughtfully. Lewis turned to look up at him, and his eyes widened. Nevertheless he set his chin.

"Er—yes. And as for the killing business—"

"I, myself, was created to kill," Edward said. "However, I have devoted some painful thought to the questions concerning sublimation of programmed savagery—even written a brief monograph on the subject—"

"Actually, it's fifteen volumes long," Nicholas said. Edward scowled at him.

"—and I would enjoy discussing it with you at our mutual leisure, when the opportunity arises," he continued, looking down at Budu.

"You've got it all figured out, haven't you?" said Joseph, slumping.

"Far from it, Doctor Ruy," Nicholas told him. "Edward, though he may believe otherwise, is not the Almighty."

"Oh, that takes a load off my mind," Joseph growled.

"The Almighty, indeed! I much prefer the New Prometheus. But, to return to the crucial question: will you join us, sir?" Edward inquired of Budu. Budu considered them, no expression in his glacial eyes that were Alec's, and Edward's, and Nicholas's eyes. At last he took both his axes from his belt. He held them up in his immense hands.

"Yes," he said. "The purpose is just. The work will go forward. I'll take service with you. So will they," he added, indicating his men with an axe. Immediately all the Enforcers in sight held their axes up, as did the ones still waiting patiently in the darkness of the tunnel, who had had the events above transmitted to them by their officers. Hearst, watching in awe, hesitated only a moment before drawing the sword of Roland and following suit.

"And you?" Nicholas turned to Suleyman.

Suleyman looked sadly at the mortals. "Can you guarantee that they will not be massacred?"

"Yes," Nicholas replied. "We will do no murder! Let their peers judge them; but they'll stand trial, now their secrets are all told."

"Secrets told?" Joseph said. "What'd you do? Tip off the tabloids?"

"No," said Nicholas, cool as ice. "I sent an extract of Company financial records for the last thirty years to the tax assessment board of the Tri-Worlds Council for Integrity."

"Ouch," said Joseph. Some of the mortals under the table began to sob noisily.

"And Alpha-Omega?" Suleyman pressed.

"That place?" Alec shuddered, and accessed briefly. "That's right; you captured it, didn't you? Why don't you keep it, for now, until we can explain about it to the mortals? Then they can take custody of their stuff, and the rest of you can get your own back."

Suleyman stroked his beard. He looked over at Latif. "What do you think, son?"

"I'm happy," Latif replied quietly, looking in satisfaction at Lewis and Mendoza. Suleyman put his hands in his pockets, looked back at Alec.

"Very well," he said. "We're with you."

Edward, watching their reactions, thumped the arm of his chair in satisfaction. "Well done," he said. Nicholas looked up at him.

"But there is another matter," he said. "There are others like the Captain! Spirits trapped in steel. We must consider their welfare, Edward."

"Aw, now, son, I wouldn't worry about no spirits," said Captain Morgan. "But I reckon some of the inorganic brethren might take kindly to trying on a bit of flesh." He cocked a hopeful eye at Sarai. "You wouldn't happen to be a professional lady, now, would you, dearie? No? Well then, has anybody got a drop of rum for an old seaman?"

"Rum for everybody!" Alec said, and arranged time and space just enough to provide all those watching with drinks. Edward raised his glass.

"To hope," he said. Bright brass sounded from somewhere, the *Dies Irae* in major key at last, rendered as a heroic coda. They drank.

Afterward, amid the strangest cocktail party milling that had ever taken place, Lewis attempted to coax the packed mortals out from under the table. Tiara, who had followed him like a little silent shadow up to that point, wrinkled her nose at the mortals' smell and turned to watch the other big people. She spotted Latif and advanced on him, as one spellbound. "You're *beautiful*," she said breathlessly. "Are you married?"

Latif gaped down at her and Sarai took him firmly by the arm. "Uh-uh," she said. "Find another, *p'tite Erzulie*."

"Oh, well," said Tiara, shrugging. Her gaze fell on Hearst, who was talking to Joseph. "Oh," she exclaimed. "A gallant hero with a sword! And he is also beautiful!"

She drifted over and stood looking thoughtfully up at Hearst, who was say-ing: "... he doesn't seem like such a bad fellow after all. Say, do you think he'll want any kind of cabinet of advisers?"

"I wouldn't bet on it," Joseph said morosely, and then ducked as something black came flying out of the screen and bounced on the table beside him. "Hey," he yelled, looking up. "You could have hit somebody with that!"

"I should be so lucky," Mendoza yelled back.

"What is it, anyway?" He set down his glass and picked up the object. It was a holocube album.

"Baby pictures of your grandchildren," she told him. He looked horrified.

CHAPTER 36

Joseph, a Long While Afterward

So I keep the holocube on my desk. I don't look through the pictures much. Boy, they were ugly babies.

The one I keep in view is the best, though. There's God Himself—oops, no, it's just Edward Alton Bell-Fairfax—sitting in that big chair of his, with the two brats on his lap, and they're all dressed up in tiny sailor suits (with hats, yet), which they obviously hate wearing. Mendoza, standing beside the chair with her hand on Edward's shoulder, is gazing serenely into the imager and she looks . . .

Happy. Really happy. Nothing can hurt her anymore. Every other time in my life I said that about someone I loved, I said it over a grave.

I don't know how she can stand the three of them, but I have to admit they seem to have been meant to be together. At least I don't have to worry about her now.

Not that my life is worry-free. This brave new world isn't perfect, by a long shot.

Well, did you think it would be? The mortals have been allowed to rule themselves. My in-laws may think the mortals will be great at self-rule, but I've got my doubts about the brains on this present bunch. Most of them wouldn't even have noticed what happened on July 9, if all those boobytraps the kids set for the Company hadn't gone off.

You'd have thought there'd be a huge scandal when Dr. Zeus and its villainy was made public. The scientists never even stood trial; their respective governments cut immunity deals with them in return for testimony, and then quietly recruited them for their own laboratories.

The Company's loot is being redistributed. I couldn't believe the stuff

Aegeus alone had stashed away! It put the mortal masters' graft to shame. So now there are a lot of beautiful new public museums and libraries opening. Not many in the American Community or England, though; they distrust art.

They're scared of animals, too, so they don't venture into the wilderness areas much, which is a good thing, because a lot of the once-extinct species we set loose out there are thriving again. (Not all of them; the pandas, for example, took one look around, grunted, and lumbered straight back into extinction.) But passenger pigeons once more darken the skies when they migrate over New York. The mortals peer out balefully through their windows and complain about all the droppings.

The mortal gene pool really was shot to hell, thanks to the plagues, to the point where there'd have been no resistance to new diseases at all, in a few more generations, or any ability to adapt to new environments. Not the best shape for a species to be in, when it's finally started to colonize its solar system.

But Suleyman runs the program to restore genetic diversity, with all the stuff he captured from Alpha-Omega. Plus there are sustainable population estimates to work out, and distribution of *Mays mendozaii* to agrarian communities . . . I guess we'll see what happens, huh?

There's been no further sign of the little stupid people from whom Lewis and Tiara escaped. They seem to have fled so far down a hole in space/time that they won't be coming back soon, if ever. All the time transference field generators have been shut down and dismantled. Most mortals didn't believe commercial time travel was real, anyway.

Oh, and nobody ever said, "Hey, immortals, thanks for saving the world all these years!" either. It didn't seem to be a good idea to let the public know that we really exist, in fact. Too many paranoid mortals, thanks to movies with guys lumbering around in machine suits yelling things like "Imperfect beings must die!"

We thought about appointing a special PR team to promote tolerance and understanding—actually, Lewis thought about it—but in the end, our existence was officially denied. We're an urban myth now, the way UFOs, Area 51, or Diana of Luna used to be: most mortals suspect we're real and secretly in league with their governments, but there's no proof.

Some mortals live in fear of a takeover conspiracy by us. Some mortals hope we're going to drop out of the sky one day and offer them cosmic wisdom. Or take them off to Shambhala or Shangri-la or some other eternal paradise . . .

But Hell still exists, too. The kids work there, often as not.

Nicholas harrows Hell. Not only has he become the Apostle to the AIs, he's

taken it on himself to find every last pit and oubliette where the Company imprisoned immortals. None have been quite as bad as Options Research, but
there have been some pretty grisly surprises in the vaults. Nicholas finds them,
sets them free, and heals them. He plays the damn lute for them. He *talks* to
them, with that damn golden voice of his, and looks earnestly into their eyes,
and . . . and somehow or other he makes them want to live again. He's only
had one notable failure.

When we finally got inside the dining room at the conference center and
scraped up what was left of Labienus and Aegeus and their respective cabals,
the mess was put into a bunch of regeneration tanks. The bones and parts bob
around in there, but they don't seem to want to reunite. Whatever it was Victor
unleashed on them is about a million times stronger than the stuff in Bugleg's
poisoned chocolates. They can't die, of course, but they'll spend the rest of
time trapped inside their ferroceramic skulls. Nobody's sorry about this except
Budu, who would have liked to lay some judgment on them.

Victor went into a tank, too, after his head had been reattached, and he's
completely repaired. Somehow, though, his consciousness won't come back
online, and nobody knows why. There's nothing wrong with him. Nicholas
even did the laying-on-of-hands trick. It worked for Kalugin, who sat bolt upright and asked how long he'd been asleep; but Victor just frowned and turned
his face away, withdrew deeper into oblivion.

Budu goes sometimes to stand outside the tank and watch him. I don't
know what he's thinking.

Each to his own Hell. What does Alec do with his eternal days? Get a load
of this: the kid went back to England and actually took his seat in the House of
Lords! And attends Parliament! He poses as a human being and he actually
wades through stultifying hours of bureaucratic tedium. At least he only has to
do it for one mortal lifetime. I was sure the kid would try to engineer some
kind of takeover, but no: all he concerns himself with is campaigning for
changes in the laws concerning the fairly harmless mortals who have been
consigned to Hospital for years.

Naturally enough, given his damned smooth-talking talents, the big ice floe
of bureaucracy is beginning to show some cracks. He could of course make
things change, whether the mortals wanted it or not; but no, Alec is a *good* boy.
He won't play God. I'm wondering how long he'll resist the temptation.

Lewis is only too happy to run around nowadays being the Angel of the
Lord, or should I say Alec's office assistant, handling milord's paperwork,
arranging for the release of mortals from Hospital, making certain the Martian

Relief Fund money goes where it ought to. A lot of Alec's charitable foundations employ mortals he's had sprung from Hospital, I might add.

Not the few actual criminals, though. Mortals don't really know how to cope with them anymore. So in a lot of little communities out on the edge of civilization, local law enforcement is only too happy to employ the services of the Flint Axe Security Agency. If the mortals have a problem, if they want some help, they can make a deal with me.

I'm their liaison with the really big guys who do the work of hunting down murderers, abusers, person-eating animals, whatever. In the less educated communities, I tell the mortals my guys are Cimmerians. Other places I tell them Budu and his teams are Scandinavians with acromegaly, and not only does that get accepted, it gets the Enforcers handicapped parking plates. Sweet, huh?

Do they kill mortals? Occasionally. Budu and his guys may have redirected their energies or sublimated their urges or whatever it was Edward taught them to do, but they're still deadly. And effective: when that stupid terrorist war broke out between the Ephesians and the heretic Druids over what was really in the Malinmhor Codex, all Budu had to do was go in and glare, and that was the end of the shrine-smashing. It's amazing how eager mortals become to sit down at the peace table with those cold pale eyes on them. Though even that fails, once in a while.

Once in a while Budu brings me some terrified mortal kid who's been caught setting fire to things, or luring some other kid into a lonely place to hit him real hard with a rock or a stick. These children are mine. I have to sit down with them and get inside their little sick heads. I have to make them understand why it's wrong to inflict pain on others. I have to fight for their souls. Talk about tough love; it takes all the strength an immortal can summon. I guess you could call it juvenile counseling. I have to get away from it, sometimes, and walk up and down in the earth.

A whole bunch of operatives can't cope as well as I can and they just melted into eternity and aren't coming out again, thank you, but others decided to stick around. Nef is the keeper for the Greater Serengeti Plains Nature Preserve. Hearst is back in his castle, disappointed that he didn't get to be president of America, but he and his new mistress are crazy about each other. (I don't know exactly what Tiara is, or why she never ages or dies. I think Alec had something to do with it. The kid's clever with nanotechnology.) And Suleyman and his people have either made or rediscovered some place they call Blessed Gineh, partly in time and partly out. There's more than one Paradise, it seems.

And, say, what could be more of a paradise than my in-laws' tropical island hideaway, full of sounds and sweet airs that give delight? To say nothing of that godawful huge palace, and the bar in the treehouse, and the pirate ship in the lagoon. I'd bet anything Tinkerbell's lurking there somewhere.

But that's where Edward Alton Bell-Fairfax (late Commander, R.N., also semi-retired Prometheus) putters around, pruning fruit trees and roses for his wife, pretending not to rule the universe. He and Mendoza take tea on the terrace every epoch/evening, and wait for their—sons? Other selves? Other halves? Whatever the hell the relationship is—to come home from work. Just like any other family. Almost.

And speaking of families: it was agreed that no more immortals would be *made,* ever. No more stealing mortal children and putting them through years of surgery and programming. But when it was discovered that Edward and Mendoza had figured out a way to have babies . . . what a surprise! It turned out there were a lot of immortal women, and no few men for that matter, who had secretly longed for the chance to have kids of their own all these years.

I thought it was a really dumb idea, but despite my—choke—family relationship with the holy trinity, my opinion doesn't carry a lot of weight. Edward feels that proper parenting skills are important, in fact indispensable to immortals, that if we'd had a chance to develop them there wouldn't have been creeps like Labienus and Aegeus.

So anyone applying to Captain Morgan (how'd you like to have *him* for your OB-GYN?) gets advice, assistance with producing embryos from DNA and implantation, and—oh yeah—a great big autographed copy of *Child Care in the Cyborg Family,* all nine million volumes of it. Kids that come with a manual, no less. Latif and Sarai have had a child. Kalugin and Nan are having one, too. Soon there'll be a whole new generation of happy, well-adjusted little immortals with no memory of human pain and all of time and space to play in.

Sound like a recipe for disaster? See, this means we're a species now. We're on a different path from humanity, at least mortal humanity, and we'll diverge. This could lead to anything. With children of our own to think about, will we care about the mortals anymore? Edward says that if we learn how to be good fathers and mothers, the rest will follow naturally and we'll all treat the mortals with compassion, respect, et cetera . . . Sure we will.

Then again, maybe he's right. Anyway the guy is more powerful than the rest of us put together, so nobody can argue with him. Except Alec and Nicholas, heh heh.

Lewis decided I needed to get out more. He began dragging me off on weekends to visit the kids.

It's not so bad, I guess. When Alec and Nicholas start fighting with Edward at the dinner table, it's even fun. And Lewis keeps Mendoza and me from going for each other's throats. Sometimes we even talk. I like that.

So she's got a really unusual marriage? I'm learning to keep my mouth shut, except for the occasional slip, like when I asked Nicholas how he liked being the last Christian in the world except for the Pope.

Lewis winced at that, and Mendoza looked like she was about to grab the nearest sharp object and fling it at my head; but Nicholas took her hands and kissed her. Then he told me he forgave me.

There are few things in life as annoying as being forgiven by Nicholas Harpole.

EPILOGUE

Dancing at the Avalon Ballroom

It's an immense place, like a big bright lantern on its rock above a moonlit sea. The ballroom floor is wide, circular, inlaid with Roman numerals at its edges like the face of a clock; but there are no hands to limit time. The mirrored ball high up turns slowly, and stars float across the dancers and fire shimmers along the walls of the mezzanine, where people sit at tables and talk, or watch the dance.

You can glimpse a face here and there, on the mezzanine. Joseph at a table with Lewis, and with them Hearst and Tiara. Suleyman and Nefer, deep in cozy conversation. All the expected faces, and some unexpected ones, too: at a near table sit Captain Morgan and Mr. Shakespeare, long since liberated from his museum exhibit, in the company of a very agreeable couple of cybernetic whores named Phyllida and Chloe.

The terrace doors are open, and the pale curtains move in the wind from the sea.

The man and the woman are dancing. She wears something long and elegant; he's in tailored evening dress, white tie and tails. They move together, the dancers, as though a single heart beat time for them.

But there is something strange about the man. How many arms embrace the woman? Is it one man, or three somehow occupying the space of one, out there on the dance floor? They move together, the men, only slightly out of phase, as the drums beat, as the fire burns, as the universe dissolves and re-forms. Do not be afraid.

It is a new dance. They are inventing the steps as they go. The music is the Song of Songs.